PATRICK O'HARA

During his childhood, Patrick O'Hara was brought up by various people and in various establishments until he was old enough to run away to sea. At fourteen his first ship was a passenger-cargo liner out of London on the Latin-America run, on board which he washed crockery and polished silverware. Later he served as Quartermaster, Seaman and Fireman with Dutch, German and Danish ships – mostly in Far Eastern and Pacific waters – an area of the world with which he has formed a romantic and lasting attachment. He was introduced to books and writing by an East End priest whose father was a director of a well-known London publishing company.
Patrick O'Hara's previous novels are: *The Wake of the Gertrude Luth; I Got No Brother; God came on Friday; The Red Sailor;* and *The Yangtze Run*. He now lives in Aberdeen, Scotland.

Also by Patrick O'Hara

THE YANGTZE RUN

and published by Corgi Books

The Wohldorf Shipment

Patrick O'Hara

CORGI BOOKS
A DIVISION OF TRANSWORLD PUBLISHERS LTD

THE WOHLDORF SHIPMENT

A CORGI BOOK 0 552 11061 2

Originally published in Great Britain by Arlington Books (Publishers) Ltd

PRINTING HISTORY

Arlington edition published 1978
Corgi edition published 1979

Corgi Books are published by Transworld Publishers Ltd., Century House, 61–63 Uxbridge Road, Ealing, London W5 5SA

Made and printed in Great Britain by
C. Nicholls & Company Ltd, The Philips Park Press, Manchester

CONTENTS

	Prologue	7
BOOK ONE	Anatomy of Shipment No. 11372	25
BOOK TWO	Flight of the *Golden Pheasant*	111
BOOK THREE	Decision at Cabo Verde	211
BOOK FOUR	Twilight of the Gods	265
	Epilogue	291

All things will pass away,
nothing will remain but death and the glory of deeds.

Edda

PROLOGUE

Carmen de Patagones is situated on the north bank of the Rio Negro, across the river from the larger township of Viedma, on the southerly end of the Pan-American Highway north of the city of Bahia Blanca, in the province of Buenos Aires. On the morning of February 10, 1955, a tall distinguished-looking man with greying hair loaded several pieces of luggage into the trunk of a tan and black Buick parked in the driveway of the Villa Corcovado. At forty-eight years old, Rudolf Brunner was a director of New World Development Inc., with registered offices on Rio de Janeiro's Avenida Atlantica at Copacabana. While the two manservants returned inside the villa, Rudolf Brunner took a last look around the spacious grounds before he allowed his gaze to dwell on the emerald green expanse of the South Atlantic out beyond Punta Rasa to north-westward. It was an impressive view, and in certain respects he envied his brother-in-law his early retirement, although not the reason that lay behind it.

Minutes later the sound of voices drew his attention to the villa where he saw his wife, Myra, and his brother-in-law emerge into the sunlight, his wife guiding her brother's wheelchair. Rudolf and Myra Brunner had just completed a three week vacation with Wilhelm von Geyr, and from his wife's expression he saw that she was by no means enthralled at the prospect of their return to the bustle of Rio de Janeiro.

Wilhelm von Geyr's angular frame was wrapped in a blue silk dressing-gown, and after he considered his young sister reflectively, he turned his attention to his brother-in-law. 'Well, Rudolf, it's been most pleasant – but it's a pity you couldn't see your way to stay over for a few more days.'

Rudolf Brunner moved his head in solemn agreement. 'True, Wilhelm. But you know how unsettled the situation is here in this country at the moment. I can't see how Peron can survive much longer, and without his governing hand anything might happen to people in my position. You're lucky enough to be an Argentine national, but those bloodhounds of the Coordinacion Federal didn't miss our arrival at Ezeiza. Besides, we have our flight arranged from Buenos Aires tomorrow evening.'

Wilhelm von Geyr was more than familiar with the existing political situation in the Argentine. While the Peron regime had continued to meet with increasing opposition, the anti-Peron faction, headed by the Generals Eduardo Lonardi and Pedro Eugenio Aramburu, had conspired to apply pressure to the Argentine intelligence service, the Coordinacion Federal and its departments which governed civil affairs and aliens, the Policia Federal and the Division de Asuntos Extranjeros, to institute an intensive investigation of all aliens who had taken up residence in the Argentine since 1945, a tactic designed to provoke and intimidate especially those who enjoyed the personal favours of President Juan Domingo Peron, and a calculated attempt to undermine the President's power over those same government agencies. Ultimately it had proved a highly successful manoeuvre on the part of Lonardi and Aramburu, and consequently many prominent aliens had not only been forced to seek sanctuary in neighbouring Latin American countries, but had also been forced to remove their funds to quarters where they would be safe from investigation and possible confiscation if Peron fell from power.

Yet Wilhelm von Geyr answered with complacency, 'Yes, I know. But things will change again. You'll see. Everything will be as it was before.'

Although Rudolf Brunner did not share his brother-in-law's faith in Argentinian politics, he declined to argue the matter. Instead he said, 'I sincerely hope so, Wilhelm.' Then he shook hands warmly with his brother-in-law before he climbed into the Buick which he had rented three weeks earlier in Buenos Aires.

Myra Brunner kissed her brother on both cheeks. 'Take care, Wilhelm.' Wilhelm von Geyr smiled and raised a hand to touch away the tears on her cheek. 'Don't worry about me, *liebchen*. But remember and call me the moment you arrive home.' Then while he watched her climb into the Buick, he added by way of an afterthought, 'Do you really intend to stay over tonight in Bahia Blanca?'

'Either there or at Olavarria. But it doesn't much matter so long as we're in Buenos Aires in time to catch our flight tomorrow evening.'

'Then if you take the coast road instead of the Pan-Am Highway you'll have the ocean for company most of the way. When you turn west again you can cross the Colorado at Pedro Luro. I assure you it's a much more pleasant drive.'

While his wife waved farewell Rudolf Brunner started the motor, put it in gear, swung the Buick around down the driveway, and headed it north. At his side his wife sat with her eyes fixed on the highway which stretched out before them in a monotonous long flat asphalt ribbon. He remarked comfortingly, 'Wilhelm looked fine – better than when we saw him last year.'

Myra Brunner felt only half-inclined to agreement. 'Perhaps,' she conceded. 'Yet he isn't as I remember him.'

'But as he said himself, he will be all right,' Rudolf Brunner insisted. 'After all, he's among friends here – trusted friends. That's the reason he decided to settle here in the first place. There isn't a day goes by without either the Grothmanns or the Hofbackers calling on him.'

Myra Brunner drifted into contemplative silence and her husband decided to leave her with her thoughts. He adjusted the sun vizor and rummaged through his pockets for a cigarette. He felt sympathy and understanding for his wife. Of the von Geyr family only the one son and daughter remained, and Wilhelm had been confined to a wheelchair since August 1950 as the result of an automobile accident from which he had been lucky to escape with his life. Their father, Hermann von Geyr, founder member of the family publishing house, had died of cancer seven months earlier, two years after his Argentinian wife had died on the operating-table while undergoing surgery for a cerebral haemorrhage.

The von Geyr family had always been ardent Nazis, the father a leading figure in the Ausland-SD – SS Intelligence Abroad – for the Argentine, while the eldest son, Wilhelm, had been a journalist with the Agencia Noticioca Transocean – the Argentine branch of the official German News Agency.

Myra von Geyr had graduated to Nazism in even more spectacular fashion. Educated in Germany, she had made the acquaintance of Reinhard Heydrich and his wife Lina Mathilde in early 1939, some months prior to her intended return to the

Argentine. At once impressed both by her background and her intelligence, Heydrich had persuaded her to join Ausland-SD in whose service he convinced her that she would prove of inestimable value to the security of the Third Reich. Then, instead of returning home as planned, she had arrived in America in early 1940 to assume the post of personal secretary to Dr Herbert Fenzel at the German Embassy in Washington, where she remained until March 1941 when she returned to the Argentine, where her experience in espionage work was requested by the local chief of Ausland-SD, Reichsleiter Bormann's personal agent in Latin America, Dr Alfred Matzhold, also a close friend and business associate of her father, Hermann von Geyr.

In Rudolf Brunner's own case he had first set foot in the von Geyr household in Tigre, the fashionable northern suburb of Buenos Aires, on November 28, 1944, only hours after his arrival off Cabo San Antonio by U-boat. A former employee of the Reichsbank in Berlin, a protégé of Friedrich Schwend, mastermind behind Operation Bernhardt, he had been recommended to Bormann by Schwend as the ideal choice of custodian for Shipment No. 11368 to the Argentine.

Dr Alfred Matzhold, a close, personal acquaintance of Vice-President Juan Domingo Peron, destined to succeed to the Presidency within months of his marriage to Maria Eva Durate Iburguren, had called at the von Geyr house shortly afterwards to extend his personal congratulations on the safe delivery of the shipment, and impressed both by Brunner and his connections with the Party hierarchy, had found a job for him with one of his Nazi-financed property companies with offices on the Santiago del Estero. Over the following months Brunner had become a constant visitor to the von Geyr house, although by then he rented an apartment on the Avenida Santa Fe. During this period he and Myra von Geyr began to find more than casual interest in each other's company, and on April 14, 1946, they were married.

Also around that time the first of many prominent Nazis fleeing from retribution in Allied-occupied Germany began to arrive in Latin America, several of them high-ranking officials of the Parteikanzlei, and on the military side, men such as Kriminaloberkommissar Christian Wirth, and Walter Rauff, men whose nefarious activities were still to shock the world when revealed.

But the one arrival in particular which gave cause to be remembered more than any other was that of the former Reichsleiter, Martin Bormann, in early 1948. Among the guests invited to the gala reception arranged in his honour at a secluded residence in the suburb of Almirante Brown, many of them reputed to have perished during the last days of the war, were such old friends and personalities as Dr Rudolf Schreyer, Friedrich Schwend, Dr Josef Mengele – Doctor Death – chief physician of Auschwitz, an exceptionally handsome man whose family had amassed a vast private fortune from world-wide business interests; SS-Obergruppenführer Heinrich Muller, Head of the Geheime Staatspolizei, SS-Obersturmbannführer Karl Adolf Eichmann, Head of sub-section IVA-4b responsible for Jewish affairs at 116 Kurfurstenstrasse, Berlin, his deputy SS-Sturmbannfuhrer Anton Brunner, his aides SS-Hauptsturmfuhrer Theodor Dannacker, French representative, SS-Hauptsturmfuhrer Heinz Rothke, who engineered the mass arrest of French Jews in Paris in July 1942 and the subsequent deportation of five thousand children to Auschwitz, and SS-Hauptsturmfuhrer Rolf Gunther. Also on hand to extend congratulations were SS-Obergruppenführer Richard Glucks, Head of Amtsgruppe D, Inspector of Concentration Camps, SS-Obersturmbannführer Otto Skorzeny, the originator of Operation Panzerfaust which brought about the suppression of the Hungarian revolt staged by Head of State Admiral Nikolaus Horthy, two former officers of the Kriegsmarine, Fregattenkapitan Werner Penns, Senior Operations Officer U-boats West, and Fregattenkapitan Karl Pfaff of Naval Intelligence at Lager Koralle; and the Italian contingent headed by the Duce's son, Vittorio Mussolini.

Some months later Brunner learned from Dr Matzhold that Bormann had decided on a programme of investment for all Nazi funds which he presided over in Latin America, and that he, Brunner, had been selected on Dr Matzhold's recommendation to become a member of the investment group. Owing to this appointment Brunner had subsequently spent much of the next five years travelling extensively throughout Latin America on behalf of the former Reichsleiter investing and re-investing funds in various legitimate business enterprises and real estate.

Then in April 1954 Brunner had been summoned to a meeting with the former Reichsleiter and Dr Matzhold at the latter's apartment out at Palermo Wood when Bormann explained to him that it was his opinion that if the Peron regime continued to meet with increasing opposition, then the safety of all prominent Nazis residing in the Argentine would become imperilled if he were dispossessed of the Presidency. Therefore the solution, as Bormann saw it, was that everyone should secure a haven for himself elsewhere until such time as the situation was resolved. Bormann had then informed Brunner that, with the aid of Dr Matzhold, he had acquired the papers necessary for Brazilian nationality which would enable Brunner to take up residence in Rio de Janeiro where it was intended to move the cover company of his investment operations, New World Development Inc., in order that it should avoid possible investigation by Peron's successors if he were forced to flee the country.

It had proved a profitable move for Brunner in many ways. He was safe, had accumulated considerable wealth both through his own business efforts and as a result of his father-in-law's death, was in love with his wife, and had set foot in the Argentine twice since without having been in any danger of arrest. But he didn't believe that Peron could last much longer. As Bormann had earlier predicted, Peron's future had continued to become increasingly precarious with the passing of each day. However, Brunner felt that there was no immediate cause for concern. Their return flight from Ezeiza was scheduled for ten o'clock the following evening, and with a glance at his wife's sombre face he remembered what his brother-in-law had said about the coast road. He said, 'What do you say we take Wilhelm's advice?'

From gazing distractedly out across the countryside, Myra Brunner turned at the sound of her husband's voice. A frown puckered her brow. 'I'm sorry,' she said.

'The coast road,' Rudolf Brunner explained. 'Shall we take it?'

Myra Brunner answered with a frail smile. 'What do you think?'

Rudolf Brunner returned her smile, delighted that his suggestion had diverted her thoughts from her brother, even if only briefly. 'Why not?' he said. 'We can quite easily stop over tonight in Bahia Blanca as planned earlier. We have plenty of time to spare. And I know a splendid hotel there.'

An hour later Rudolf Brunner had the Buick headed north on the road which ran parallel with the wide sweep of the shore. The view was superb, breathtaking. Far out the emerald green ocean shimmered under a burnished sky while the long swell rolled itself up the vast expanse of pale sand to foam dazzling white in the sunlight. Although it was a poor secondary road, rough and dirt-packed, both the view and the invigorating, salt-laden air more than compensated for any discomfort. And smiling, Myra Brunner sat close to her husband and pointed out occasional sights that appealed to her in a world that was blue, green, and gold, and in which the sunburned grass moved in the breeze among virgin sand-dunes.

At the end of another hour Myra Brunner remembered the luncheon box which her brother had ordered to have packed for them before they left. She laid a hand on her husband's arm. 'Shall we stop and picnic?' And pointing ahead, she said, 'There – up ahead – where the road runs between those sand-dunes.'

Rudolf Brunner drew the Buick off the road into the shelter of the sand-dunes in accordance with his wife's wishes and stopped, then carried the small wicker hamper down to where the sand-dunes met the shore. In the hamper they found portions of cold chicken, assorted fruit, cheese, biscuits, and a bottle of wine. The breeze was cool and smelled of the ocean, and only the foaming of the breakers on the shore disturbed them while they ate.

Afterwards Rudolf Brunner lay back on the warm sand to light a cigarette while his wife removed her shoes and strolled down towards the ocean. She had left her coat in the Buick and wore only the brown skirt and simple cream blouse. Rudolf Brunner decided that she made an enchanting picture, framed against the emerald green ocean, and he believed that Fate had been especially kind to him. In a country where there was no lack of beauty among its women, Myra Brunner outshone the majority of them. Possessed of a fine figure, beautifully sculptured, long elegant legs, smooth olive skin, dark eyes, she wore her gleaming black hair carelessly wrapped in a large coffee-coloured bandana. She also carried herself well, with a poise and confidence which drew attention to the fact that she was obviously well-bred. And looking at her, his only regret was that he had not met her while still a young man.

He had just extinguished his cigarette when he heard her call to him. He raised a hand to shield his eyes from the glitter of sunlight on the ocean and saw her standing on the shore pointing northward. He climbed to his feet and walked down to join her, and found that it was a crude wooden cross planted high among the sand-dunes which had claimed her attention.

Expressing mild perplexity, she said, 'Do you suppose that could possibly be a grave up there?'

Rudolf Brunner glanced around him at the desolate shore, then with a tolerant smile, he said, 'Out here?'

'Perhaps it was a fisherman – washed up drowned.'

Rudolf Brunner chuckled at the suggestion. 'Isn't that being unduly romantic?'

Myra Brunner gazed around her at the broad sweep of a deserted shore haunted over by the occasional cry of a wheeling sea-bird. 'I must confess that I can't think of a lonelier place in which to be buried.'

Rudolf Brunner said with scant interest, 'It's certainly a long way from the noise and bustle of passing traffic.'

Myra Brunner looked up at her husband from under her lashes. 'You think I'm being foolish,' she accused.

Rudolf Brunner countered with a smile, 'Not really. It's just that I think you're allowing your imagination to run away with you.'

'Then can we take a closer look?' Myra Brunner persisted.

Rudolf Brunner shrugged indifference. 'If you wish.'

They started back hand in hand across the shore.

The cross was fashioned from sun-bleached driftwood, deeply embedded in the sand, tilted at an angle.

'Look – there's a name cut into it!' Myra Brunner observed with excitement.

Rudolf Brunner started up the steep slope only to come to an abrupt halt as he neared his objective.

'*Rudolf*!' There was a sharp note of alarm in Myra Brunner's voice when she witnessed the strange, drawn expression cloud her husband's face.

Rudolf Brunner murmured, 'I don't believe it!' His face ashen beneath its sun-tan, he continued in an astonished voice as he stared at the cross, 'The name – the name is *Wohldorf*!'

At mention of the name Myra Brunner's eyes grew wide and her heart missed a beat. She raised a hand to her breast involuntarily. 'The man who Heinrich went to meet along with the *Santa Elvira* that day?' Her voice was an incredulous whisper as the memories of a June morning ten years earlier crowded her mind mistily. Then to answer her own question, afraid to allow herself any shred of hope, she disputed herself. 'But it can't be the same man – it can't possibly be *him*!'

Rudolf Brunner answered from a great distance, 'It's too much of a coincidence for it *not* to be him.'

'But out *here*?'

Rudolf Brunner's distracted gaze suddenly registered the fact that another piece of driftwood, a solitary piece which protruded from the sand like some half-buried spar, was situated some thirty metres further northward. For several seconds he hesitated as if he was afraid of what he might find, then he stumbled towards it through the shifting sand.

The missing piece of the second cross lay partly buried nearby, and he slowly reached it out of the sand and peered at the partially obliterated name. He could make it out only faintly: *K Dornberger – August* 1945. In an emotionally constricted voice he called back along the shore. 'Read me the date on that other cross.'

Myra Brunner rubbed the film of sand from the cross-piece of weathered driftwood with trembling fingers. 'September – September 1945.'

Rudolf Brunner hurried back along the shore calling out, 'Then it *must* be them! It *has* to be them! Surely there can be no other explanation! The other name is Dornberger!'

Myra Brunner's mind was in a daze. She glanced up and down the shore agitatedly. 'Then poor Heinrich may be buried somewhere out here too!' she cried out in an anguished voice. 'Whatever happened to them, Rudolf?'

Rudolf Brunner slipped a comforting arm around his wife's shoulders and stared out at the shimmering ocean through creased eyes. 'It may be that we will never know. It was a long time ago.' Then he snapped back to the present, took his wife's hand. 'We must get back to the car. Our first duty is to inform Dr Matzhold about our find. He's going to find it very difficult to accept.'

Four kilometres further north the Brunners saw a collection of adobe dwellings and the bell-tower of a chapel up ahead, dirty white, framed against the skyline above a curve in the shore. Approaching the outskirts of the village, a peeling white sign read: San Martes.

As a village it scarcely deserved such recognition. The inevitable Plaza was fronted by a dingy hotel with closed shutters, the Hotel Negro, and on the opposing side was situated the chapel. On the shore below several small fishing-boats lay high on the sand, deserted.

Myra Brunner reached out a hand to her husband's arm. 'Why don't we stop and take a look at the local cemetery?'

Rudolf Brunner saw the logic of his wife's suggestion, eased his foot on the accelerator, and drew the Buick to a crisp halt outside the chapel gate where a faded sign read: The Sacred Chapel of the Sea.

As Myra Brunner alighted she glanced towards the hotel where two half-naked children sat on the front step watching the dust settle over the Plaza with sad, incurious faces. She said, 'This place looks almost as if it has been forgotten by the world.'

The cemetery was laid out on three sides of the chapel, overgrown with weeds and scattered with rubble from the crumbling adobe wall which surrounded it.

'*There*!' Myra Brunner was first to see them, seven identical wooden crosses situated against the wall where it overlooked the ocean.

On closer investigation they found that only three of the crosses bore names, cut roughly into the wood. Two of the names were Latin: Ramon Gutierrez and Manuel Cuartero. The third read: F O Rothfels. All three bore the date September 1945.

A voice behind them said in Spanish, 'They are of interest to you?'

The Brunners turned to find themselves confronted by a young priest dressed in a threadbare brown habit.

'Father Vasquez Barcelo,' the priest politely informed them.

'We were merely curious, Father,' Rudolf Brunner explained. 'You see, we stumbled on two graves back there along the shore while picnicking.'

'Yes, I know of them,' Father Barcelo affirmed. 'They are situated just north of Bahia Anegada.'

Rudolf Brunner indicated the grave which bore the name Rothfels. 'We also saw that they both bore European names like this one here – perhaps German in origin.'

Father Barcelo evinced closer interest in the Brunners. 'You are German?'

'My father was,' Myra Brunner answered. 'And when we saw those graves back there we immediately thought about someone – a friend of ours – who disappeared at sea just prior to the dates inscribed on the crosses.'

'Indeed.' Father Barcelo's brows rose upward a fraction. 'And he disappeared in the vicinity of San Martes?'

'We don't know that,' Rudolf Brunner intervened. 'Perhaps.'

'May I ask your friend's name?'

'Von Geyr – Heinrich von Geyr.'

Father Barcelo moved his head negatively. 'No,' he said, 'I don't recall ever having heard mention of such a name. But then I'm afraid there is little I can tell you about these graves. It happened in Father Barea's time, before I arrived here. However, I know that the bodies were cast up on the shore nearby. Those buried here in the cemetery were found in the vicinity of the village, while the two you came on back there on the shore were buried where they were found on account of the fact they were too badly decomposed to be brought here for internment.' Father Barcelo lifted sombre eyes to the shimmering ocean. 'I believe they were officially thought to have drowned when a freighter of mixed crew foundered somewhere out there, although I'm not acquainted with the facts. What I do remember is Father Barea saying certain of the bodies possessed some sort of discs which revealed their names, while others still retained scraps of letters or documents in the remnants of their clothing not washed from them by the sea.' His sombre gaze returned to dwell on the row of crosses, and he continued quietly, 'And as you can see, the nameless did not possess anything.'

Rudolf Brunner found it difficult to restrain his impatience. 'You say they were *officially* thought to have drowned when a freighter of mixed crew foundered somewhere out there?'

'Yes. When Father Barea informed the Ministerio de Marina about the finding of the bodies they sent an officer from Bahia Blanca to interview him on the matter. From what I remember of our conversation on the subject, I believe he said that the officer in question also took possession of the deceaseds' effects at the same time.'

'And do you know if the Ministerio de Marina were ever able to establish the name of the vessel which foundered?'

Father Barcelo shook his head. 'That I'm afraid I don't know. As I have already said, it happened before I arrived in San Martes.'

Rudolf Brunner began to feel uneasy with the intensity of the priest's gaze, and he decided that he had pursued the subject as far as it was safe to do so without incurring too much curiosity. With his thoughts masked, he again glanced at the graves. 'But no Heinrich von Geyr, eh, Father?'

'No, it would seem not. However, this stretch of shore is so vast and desolate that there may well have been other bodies washed up unnoticed on it and buried in the sands by Nature herself.'

Rudolf Brunner shrugged his resignation. He said, 'Yes, that may well be so. Anyway, thank you for your time, Father. We only stopped out of curiosity.'

Father Barcelo answered courteously, 'I quite understand.'

As the Brunners returned down the path in the blazing heat, they were conscious of Father Barcelo's gaze following them. In low, worried tones, Myra Brunner said, 'Don't you think he became rather too curious?'

'I don't think so,' Rudolf Brunner stated confidently. 'Not when you consider it can't be every day of the week that someone calls to look at the graves of people washed up on the shore ten years ago.'

Myra Brunner's thoughts were already elsewhere. With deep concern she said, 'I just can't bear to think about the possibility that Heinrich may have been lying out here all those years unknown to us.'

'Don't,' Rudolf Brunner said. 'You mustn't torture yourself with any such thoughts till we learn more about all this. And those sort of inquiries are better left in the hands of Dr Matzhold. I intend to put a call through to him as soon as we reach Pedro Luro.'

'I agree,' Myra Brunner quietly conceded. 'But I find it strange that all his previous inquiries around the time of the *Santa Elvira*'s disappearance didn't yield anything about these graves out here.'

Rudolf Brunner was silent in his agreement as he began to realise the enormous importance of their chance discovery, and the colossal repercussions it was certain to create.

*

Rudolf Brunner and his wife arrived at the Hotel Castilla in Pedro Luro at 6.35 pm, booked an early dinner at reception, and stopped at one of the pay-phones in the lobby to place a call to Buenos Aires.

'Ah, Rudolf!' Dr Matzhold's answering voice expressed genuine delight on receipt of the call. 'This is indeed an unexpected pleasure. Tell me – how was the vacation?'

In a state of agitation Rudolf Brunner impressed sternly, 'Dr Matzhold – you must listen very carefully to what I have to say. I'm calling from Pedro Luro. Myra and I have just seen the graves of Wohldorf and several others. Do you understand what I'm saying?'

A shocked, disconcerted silence met his words.

He said impatiently, 'Hello? Are you still with me?'

'Yes – yes, I'm still with you,' Dr Matzhold's stunned voice acknowledged. Then after an interval of several moments, as if he found the news too incredulous to believe, he said in a more firm tone, 'You're certain that you're not dreaming this?'

'Absolutely not!' Rudolf Brunner impressed. 'Myra and I left Carmen de Patagones this morning, and on Wilhelm's advice took the coast road instead of the Pan-Am Highway. On the way we stopped to picnic and came across two graves on the shore. The names on them read Wohldorf and Dornberger.'

Dr Matzhold was again silent for several moments before he spoke further, then moved by Brunner's infectious excitement, he said, 'If what you say is true – then this is truly astonishing news. But can you provide me with more details, the exact location of the graves?'

Rudolf Brunner answered unhesitatingly, 'They're situated on the shore some four kilometres south of the village of San Martes, north of Bahia Anegada, on the road south from Pedro Luro to Carmen de Patagones. Also in the cemetery of the Sacred Chapel of the Sea in the village itself are another seven graves. But only three of them bear names: Gutierrez, Cuartero, and Rothfels. The date of internment is recorded as September 1945. The two on the shore bear the dates August and September of the same year. According to the local priest all the bodies were cast up on the shore nearby and identified either by identity discs or from scraps of letters or documents found in their clothing. He said his predecessor Father Barea passed these effects to an officer of the Ministerio de Marina from Bahia Blanca. I felt that was as far as I dare safely pursue the matter.'

Dr Matzhold expressed approval, 'A wise decision. And when's your flight out to Rio?'

'Tomorrow evening at ten. But we can be in Buenos Aires later tonight, or rather early tomorrow morning.'

'Then call on me the moment you arrive,' Dr Matzhold instructed. 'I will be at home waiting.'

*

In a luxury apartment block out at Palermo Wood in the Federal Capital of Buenos Aires, Dr Alfred Matzhold, an Argentine national and a man of middle age with crew-cut iron-grey hair, sat in his suite eleven floors above the Avenida Libertador General San Martin and stared deep in thought at the phone before him on the vast leather-bound desk. He had never known SS-Hauptsturmführer Ernst Wohldorf personally, but he had every cause to remember the disappearance of the *Santa Elvira*. And if what Rudolf Brunner had just told him was true, then his discovery was indeed something quite extraordinary.

Rising from the desk, he crossed the room to a combination wall-safe and removed a small indexed notebook. At the long picture window which gave a panoramic view of the Zoological and Botanical Gardens, the polo complex, and the rococo race-track, Hipodromo Argentino, he scanned a page of coded numbers before he returned across the room to place a call to Arequipa in southern Peru. He was connected with the number seven minutes later. 'This is Dr Alfred Matzhold speaking,' he explained in Spanish to the answering voice. 'I request that you refer me to Señor Martin. I have a matter of the utmost gravity to discuss with him.'

'One moment,' the voice informed.

Two minutes later a harsh and clipped voice said in English, 'Hello?'

Dr Matzhold at once lapsed into German. 'Matzhold here, Herr Martin. I have just received a call from Rudolf Brunner in Pedro Luro. He informed me that he and his wife today stumbled across the man Wohldorf's grave on the shore between Carmen de Patagones and Pedro Luro, some four kilometres south of the village called San Martes. I hardly dared allow myself to believe him, but he sounded profoundly

BOOK FOUR

Twilight of the Gods

THE crew of *U501* had sighted only one vessel, a shabby Spanish freighter, her flag of neutrality still displayed on her scarred hull amidships. They had met with her one evening in the late dusk, plodding across their bows, all lights ablaze, headed north-west, probably out from Cape Town and bound either for Rio de Janeiro or Santos.

Then on the morning of June 17, thirty-nine days after their encounter with the *Cassiopeia*, the duty bridge watch saw their first cumuliform clouds of any dimension since leaving the African coast behind, clouds painted delicate shades of rose and amber, clouds which were piled high and which appeared to extend a welcome to the continent of Latin America.

An electrically charged air of excitement ran through the boat; the end of the voyage was in sight and the long days of monotony were suddenly forgotten. The men crowded the *wintergarten* and catwalks, eager for a first glimpse of the New World which held so much promise for them, where life was to begin anew, where dark memories of war and defeat, parted families and friends, would fade against its carefree background. It was now a dream on the verge of reality, and the men feasted hungry eyes on every detail of the new morning, the sun to eastward, the pale azure sky, the pastel-tinted mass of cloud, and the emerald green ocean which washed southward under a freshening breeze.

Rink glanced at the bearded faces crowded around him in the horseshoe, Kernbach, Erlanger, Berger, Wohldorf, Schramm, and Kordt, each of them with his gaze fixed intently on the western horizon, each of them engrossed in his own thoughts.

Unable to contain his excitement, Wohldorf said, 'How soon do you expect to sight land?'

'If the morning fix can be relied on, then we ought to be within sight of Punta Mogotes some time around noon.'

'Then we're here – really *here*!' Wohldorf enthused.

Rink searched the crowded faces on the *wintergarten*, saw Bergold, and instructed him to man the radio which he had ordered shut down on the evening of the third day after the incident with the *Cassiopeia*, in a bid to keep the crew from brooding over the constant stream of bulletins, announcements, and proclamations which had filled the ether when the Allies began to wallow in the after-effects of victory. Instead he had decided it was better to remain ignorant of events, and consequently *U501* had become a world on its own, plowing through the vast wastes of the South Atlantic, its existence unknown to anyone outside the hull. At first the men had found it a difficult decision to accept, but as the days had lengthened into weeks, their minds had gradually turned from the past to the future and all it appeared to hold for them.

Over breakfast Rink re-acquainted himself with the procedure for communicating word of their arrival to their anonymous hosts waiting on shore. The instructions were simple. They were to transmit the cryptic signal: ERWACHE – ERWACHE – ERWACHE every fifteen minutes on a given frequency when within fifty miles of Punta Mogotes, a signal which it was hoped would be heard by a clandestine radio station somewhere in the vicinity of General Alvarado. Yet Rink was not wholly certain about what they might expect in the way of a reception. After the incident with the *Cassiopeia* he had decided not to transmit the codeword WESTWARD to signify that *U501* had successfully refuelled and was proceeding on her voyage in the event that it would serve to betray their position, and as a result it was possible that they had been given up for lost.

Bergold and Vogel were at the radio when Rink called at the W/T office, eager to renew contact with the outside world. After issuing them with the necessary instructions for the attempt to make contact with the shore, Rink made his way up to the bridge and found the upperdeck a hive of activity, with men airing their Number One blues while others were bathing from buckets thrown over the side. Also outside ERA Hossbach had set up a barber shop on the *wintergarten* and a line of men were waiting impatiently for the scissors and mirror. Rink offered no comment, although he regarded the shore preparations as being somewhat premature. Even if contact was successfully made with shore he doubted if they would be extended an invitation to enter the harbour at Mar del Plata with the crew lining the catwalks and the War Flag fluttering in the breeze. But in order that he should not be the odd man out he retrieved his own uniform blues from his locker, put them to air on the *wintergarten* and went below to bathe on the after catwalk. Later, when he had shaved and had his hair cut by Hossbach he dressed in his uniform and pulled on a pair of leather seaboots.

The time was 10.18 when Leutnant Berger reported to the bridge. 'Signal, sir. Just this moment received.'

Rink took it from him and read: DELAYED GLAD TIDINGS. RENDEZVOUS WITH SANTA ELVIRA 100 MILES DUE SOUTH PUNTA MOGOTES 18.00 HOURS – MATZHOLD.

He found Wohldorf and Schramm in the wardroom, immaculate in dress uniform, and handed the former the signal. 'We just made contact with the shore. It would appear they intend to effect the transfer of cargo at sea. We're to meet with a vessel named the *Santa Elvira* 100 miles due South of Punta Mogotes, at approximately the same distance south-east of Necochea. My guess is she's probably been lying in Necochea harbour for some time ready to put to sea on our arrival.'

Wohldorf found it impossible to contain his excitement. 'Excellent news!' he jubilantly exclaimed. 'I must confess there were times when I thought I'd never see this moment. How about you?'

Rink's thoughts were elsewhere. 'My concern now is centred on what's to become of my command and her crew.'

'Ach, no doubt the future of both has already been decided.'

From Wohldorf's flippant reply it was obvious to Rink that he no longer cared about either of them, and when he returned to the bridge it was to hear the first sighting of a vessel in the process of being reported. Once again they were in dangerous waters, among the shipping lanes which terminated at such ports as Uruguay's Montevideo, and the Argentine's La Plata, Buenos Aires, and Rosario. It was not the time to cast discretion to the winds. He bent his head to the voice-tube. 'Left rudder. Come to course 190 degrees. Clear the upperdeck of all spare hands.'

U501 swung around on to her new course to southward while the spare hands on deck reluctantly made their way below with a last lingering look at the western horizon.

By noon the breeze had freshened considerably to set up a choppy sea which broke across the catwalks, and by mid-afternoon a haze had formed to eastward and a ghostly sun assumed an ugly opalescent light.

'Fine,' Rink remarked to Erlanger in a caustic voice. 'We come all this way and now the weather deteriorates.'

*

It was 17.42 when Leutnant Berger sighted a vessel making a course of south-south-east towards them. Rink immediately joined him on the bridge and all eyes watched in anticipation as she approached, *U501* rolling in the stiff seas. A motorship of around 2,000 GRT, she was of sleek new design, bridge and superstructure situated aft, painted brilliant white, her funnel a contrasting light blue, the hull dove grey. Driving resolutely to south-eastward on an interceptory course, her bows sent curtains of spray back across her forepeak and well-deck.

When at a distance of nine hundred metres, a signal-lamp winked out from the port wing of her bridge. It read simply: SANTA ELVIRA.

'Small ahead both,' ordered Rink. While *U501* lost headway, the bridge watch waited for the vessel to cross their bows, several figures on her bridge waving enthusiastically. 'Half ahead both.'

The diesels hammered and Rink swung *U501* around the *Santa Elvira*'s stern, the port of registery on her counter reading *Comodoro Rivadavia*, in order to pull in under her lee side sixty metres distant, where at once the War Flag broke from her jackstaff and the emotive strains of *Deutschland uber Alles* boomed out from her upperdeck broadcast system, and in that moment of drama every man snapped to attention.

'Permission to break out the War Flag, sir?'

Rink glanced to see Signalman Meyer stationed beside the jackstaff, and signified approval; and, with a snap of the halyards, Meyer sent *U501*'s War Flag streaming into the breeze in reply.

When the music ceased one of the figures on the *Santa Elvira*'s bridge raised a loud hailer to his mouth. 'Congratulations, Herr Kommandant,' the voice echoed metallically. 'Glad to see you finally made it. We had actually given you up for lost.'

'We had our troubles,' Rink called back in reply.

The metallic voice answered in sympathy, 'So we imagine.

Sorry about the weather. However, the met report indicates that this breeze should blow itself out during the night. Can you keep us company till morning?'

Rink waved acknowledgement, and saw the *Santa Elvira* turn on to a course of west-south-west at slow speed.

With the onset of darkness Rink dropped *U501* further astern to take up station off the freighter's starboard quarter as they stood into the waters of Bahia Blanca, watching her lights pitch in the choppy seas.

Supper that evening was ignored by most of the hands who were impatient and restless now that the voyage was at an end. And for'ard in their own quarters, Wohldorf and Schramm held themselves apart as if, now that their journey was drawing to a close, they were preparing to return to a way of life and matter of interests far removed from that of their late comrades.

*

At around 02.00 on the morning of June 18, the wind dropped and the short, foam-streaked seas began to subside, and then only occasionally did spray drench the watch on the bridge of *U501*, their gaze scarcely leaving the *Santa Elvira*'s lights.

Daylight brought an overcast sky and a choppy green sea which ran in towards the stretch of shoreline between Punta Rasa and Bahia Blanca. Then at 06.20 the *Santa Elvira* eased speed and *U501* drew slowly abeam on her starboard side to see the three figures of the previous evening re-appear on her bridge.

On board *U501* Rink pushed into the starboard sector of the horseshoe in anticipation of receiving orders, and reduced speed to that of the freighter.

'I'm afraid there will have to be an alteration to our plans, Herr Kommandant,' the man with the hailer explained. 'Our original plan was to effect the transfer of your cargo further south in the Golfo de San Matias, but according to the latest met report there promises to be another sharp deterioration in the weather soon. Therefore we now propose to effect the transfer without further delay. I'm sorry.'

'Then it will require the use of every fender you possess,' Rink informed him. 'And if you stand your port side to seaward I will attempt to come alongside in your lee.'

By way of reply the *Santa Elvira* immediately began to turn to port, to leave *U501* wallowing astern.

Rink called below, 'Berthing-party on deck. Standby port side.'

The berthing-party were ready lining the catwalks when Rink saw the *Santa Elvira* lose way and her crew begin to drop fenders across her starboard wall. 'Stop engines. Clutches out. Switches on. Group down. Small ahead both.'

Now on electric drive, *U501* moved cautiously up along the dove grey hull starboard side until level with the well-deck, the hulls of both vessels rising and falling ten metres apart. 'Stop both!' shouted Rink, and watched heaving lines snake down from above before the mooring wires were quickly hauled on board to be secured under the watchful eye of the CGM. Then with All Secure, the *Santa Elvira*'s electric winches took the strain and drew *U501* gently in under her lee side, fenders effectively cushioning the jolt when the hulls impacted.

On the *Santa Elvira*'s bridge tense faces had watched every move. 'Is everything well with you, Herr Kommandant?' the man with the hailer wanted to know.

Rink watched the rise and fall of the cushioned hulls. Conditions for effecting a transfer of cargo were far from ideal but with the *Santa Elvira*'s hull acting as a breakwater the independent movement of the vessels was not sufficient to endanger their safety, although the creaking and groaning of fenders sounded ominous. 'I think we can go ahead and risk it.'

'You don't mind if I take my leave of you now?'

Rink turned to see Wohldorf standing on the bridge behind him, brief-case in hand, muffled in his elegant greatcoat, the War Flag streaming in the breeze from the jackstaff above him on the *wintergarten*. 'As you wish.'

'Then please see to it that my personal luggage is first to be transferred. Schramm will remain with you till that's been accomplished.'

Erlanger watched Wohldorf turn aft to the *wintergarten*, climb below to the after catwalk, then start up the ladder which dangled against the *Santa Elvira*'s hull. 'The SS don't believe in wasting time, do they, sir?'

Rink shrugged indifference, watching the *Santa Elvira*'s derricks swing out overhead. 'Break open the fore and after hatches,' he called below to Kordt on the for'ard catwalk.

From the bridge hatchway Coxswain Lamm said, 'Leutnant Berger reports that he's ready to commence with off-loading, sir.'

'Then inform him to carry on.'

Wohldorf and Schramm's personal luggage, including the two oblong metal boxes, was first out through the for'ard hatchway accompanied by Schramm, who watched Berger and Kordt supervise its loading into a cargo net. Then the first two cases from the after torpedo-room were manhandled out on to the catwalk as the whirr of machinery overhead preceded the first load being lifted inboard from the for'ard catwalk.

Shortly after Schramm had transferred to the *Santa Elvira*, a voice called down, 'Care to crack open that celebration bottle now, Herr Kapitanleutnant?'

Rink found a dark, handsome face smiling down from the bulwarks above, one of the men whom he had previously seen on the bridge. He hesitated, glanced to seaward.

'I assure you that it's quite safe, Herr Kapitanleutnant,' the man confidently announced. 'We're well off the beaten track out here and we have plenty of lookouts stationed to warn us against surprise.'

Rink motioned to Erlanger. 'Take charge till I get back. And keep those cases moving. Begin on those canisters located in the outside torpedo stowage immediately we rid ourselves of the cases.'

The man was waiting for Rink when he climbed in across the *Santa Elvira*'s bulwarks. Snapping stiffly erect, he clicked his heels and flung up his right arm. '*Heil Hitler!*' Then with a smile, offered the same hand and said, 'Welcome on board, Herr Kapitanleutnant. You can't imagine how much pleasure this moment gives me. My name's Heinrich von Geyr, representative of Dr Alfred Matzhold, official agent of Reichsleiter Martin Bormann. May I extend my sincere congratulations on your belated but safe arrival. Actually we had prepared ourselves for the worst. Now if you would care to accompany me.'

Von Geyr led the way aft, climbed to the accommodation deck, and ushered Rink through an inboard companionway to a stateroom below the bridge. After the austere conditions on board *U501* Rink was ill-prepared for the luxury of the *Santa Elvira*. Pannelled with rich mahogany and black leather, the deck lushly carpeted, it belonged to another world along with the concealed lighting and the aroma of cigar smoke.

A punctilious man, von Geyr again stood stiffly to attention, and in a sombre voice announced, 'Gentlemen. Kapitanleutnant Wolfgang Rink.'

Rink saw that apart from Wohldorf and Schramm, there were two other men present, the two men whom he had previously seen on the *Santa Elvira*'s bridge along with von Geyr.

Von Geyr indicated the slightly smaller figure in a tan lounge suit. 'Herr Dassel. Carl Heinrich Dassel. Senior representative of your host Dr Alfred Matzhold.'

A sour-faced and pedantic-looking man, Dassel acknowledged the introduction with an almost imperceptible, but condescending movement of his bald head. 'Delighted, Herr Kapitanleutnant,' he said formally.

'And our Kapitan for the trip,' von Geyr continued in formal explanation. 'Herr Soltmann. Hans-Bernd Soltmann. Formerly of the *Admiral Graf Spee*,' he added with a secretive smirk.

A tall burly man with close-cropped iron-grey hair and a severe manner, Soltmann slicked his heels and stiffly inclined his head. 'Pleased to finally have you with us, Herr Kapitanleutnant.'

Rink studied the ex-Kriegsmarine officer with interest. 'Thank you, Herr Soltmann.'

Von Geyr offered a humidor of cigars while Soltmann cracked open a bottle of champagne at the table and filled six glasses, passed them around, then proposed his own toast. 'To your safe arrival, Herr Kapitanleutnant. The Third Reich salutes you. *Heil Hitler!*'

The gathering drank in sombre and respectful silence.

Then while von Geyr replenished the glasses and offered his gold cigarette lighter, Dassel said, 'We were extremely concerned for you, Herr Kapitanleutnant. We were quite certain you'd met with misfortune. First we heard from home about the unfortunate incident with Norwegian partisans in Hardangerfjord, then later we were informed that U-Bestelmeyer had failed to answer his call-sign and in the circumstances had to be presumed lost. Frankly we didn't know what to think when it was learned that Schemmel had surrendered to the Allies, and from there on the situation became totally confused, so much so that it was generally feared you had also been lost.' Dassel paused to sip at his champagne, then with calculated off-handedness said, 'However, Hauptsturmführer Wohldorf has been recounting some of your adventures to us. And may I say that stopping the British tanker *Cassiopeia* as you did might be considered a stroke of genius. If it's of interest to you, she earned herself the unenviable distinction of being the first peacetime loss of a British ship at sea.'

Rink was disconcerted by Dassel's statement. With a frown darkening his brow, he said, 'I'm afraid you have me at a disadvantage, Herr Dassel.'

'Indeed?' There was a patronising, amused tone in Dassel's voice.

Rink was instantly suspicious of the entire gathering, instinctively sensed that they shared a joke among themselves and that he was the only person in ignorance of it. And busy with his thoughts, he sent a searching glance at Wohldorf who in turn regarded him with the incurious stare of a disinterested stranger.

Dassel thrust a newspaper across the table. 'I wondered about the article at the time, had some sixth sense about it. That was the reason why I retained the newspaper. I think the front page will interest you.'

Rink reached for the newspaper from the table. It was the *Buenos Aires Herald* and carried the date May 14, 1945. In English it read:

SOUTH ATLANTIC CLAIMS FIRST PEACETIME VICTIM

It was established yesterday that the wreckage first observed by an aircraft of British Coastal Command on the morning of May 12, 55 miles south of the Cape Verde Islands has been identified as belonging to the British motor-tanker CASSIOPEIA *registered at Milford Haven. Bound for St Helena and Ascension Island with a cargo of fuel oils, it is believed that she sank a few hours after leaving the fuelling station at Porto Grande on the island of St Vincent. Owing to the fact that no distress signal was reported, it is assumed by the British Admiralty that she was the victim of a drifting mine, although there was no report of an explosion or fire in the area in which she was lost. The* CASSIOPEIA *is believed to have carried a crew of thirty-eight. A concentrated search of the area had revealed no traces of survivors.*

Rink felt the blood drain from his face, felt himself go cold with rage long before he concluded reading the article. Suddenly he knew the reason behind Wohldorf's delay in leaving the *Cassiopeia* after they had refueled, suddenly realised why there had been no hue and cry about the incident, why there had been no large scale sea and air search mounted in an attempt to hunt them down. And experiencing immense difficulty in restraining his anger, he looked up at Wohldorf where he stood with Schramm on the far side of the stateroom. Wohldorf in turn met his gaze with silent defiance, as if assured of Dassel's approval and support. But while Soltmann offered no comment, von Geyr sensed the awkwardness of the moment, and said hurriedly, 'Is it all really so important?'

Dassel ignored him, and instead addressed himself to Rink. 'Ach, what are a few Britishers more or less? No one will ever guess at the truth, nor even suspect it. Hauptsturmführer Wohldorf merely sought to make certain of survival, like I myself would have done. Your conscience is clear, Herr Kapitanleutnant. Forget about it, as everyone else will.'

Embarrassed by the strained atmosphere which enshrouded the scene, von Geyr sought to change the subject, and said with the polished formality of a diplomat while he sipped at his champagne delicately, 'You know, of course, Herr Kapitanleutnant, that the Führer is dead – died on the barricades fighting to his last breath?'

Rink answered without enthusiasm, 'We heard word to that effect, yes. Although the situation regarding any news we received was somewhat confusing.'

Von Geyr proclaimed in a stoic voice, 'Nonetheless it's a tragedy from which we shall recover. Like Barbarossa – the Reich will rise again from the ashes of yesterday.'

Rink murmured, 'Of course.' And found that the atmosphere had turned even more oppressive with von Geyr's impassioned display of patriotism.

In turn von Geyr saw that his patriotic intrusion did not have the desired result. With an embarrassed cough, he drained his glass and set it on the table. 'Well now, Herr Kapitanleutnant,' he declared in more congenial tones. 'No doubt you're anxious to learn what's to become of *U501* and her crew.' Sweeping a chart around on the table, he placed a manicured finger on the Golfo de San Matias, to the north of the Peninsula Valdes. 'Orders are you scuttle your boat here.

We propose to accompany you south immediately the transfer of cargo has been completed. After your charges are set you and your crew will then join us. Arrangements have been made for us to dock at Avellaneda tomorrow morning during darkness. From there you'll be taken to an *estancia* near Olavarria where senior members of our Organisation will be waiting to extend their congratulations to you on behalf of the New Reich.'

The New Reich; Rink listened to von Geyr in amazement.

'I assume the charges necessary for the destruction of *U501* will be in place ready for detonation by the time we arrive in the Golfo de San Matias, Herr Kapitanleutnant?' von Geyr was saying. 'We have no wish to waste precious time.'

'Naturally,' said Rink.

Von Geyr said, 'Then do you have any questions, Herr Kapitanleutnant?'

Rink returned his attention to the chart. 'Wouldn't it have been easier for all concerned to have effected the transfer of cargo in the Golfo de San Matias as originally planned rather than out here?'

Von Geyr looked to Dassel for aid in answering the question.

Dassel said easily, 'I already explained the situation, Herr Kapitanleutnant. According to the Ministerio de Marina's latest meteorological report another sharp deterioration is expected in the weather soon and this influenced the decision of myself and my associates here to make the transfer at the earliest possible moment rather than proceed south to the Golfo de San Matias, primarily for the reason that we have no wish to be forced through adverse weather conditions to have both vessels loitering indefinitely in the vicinity in which *U501* is to be scuttled. That's a risk we don't wish to take. No, it's simply a question of time and opportunity, Herr Kapitanleutnant.'

Rink could find no argument with Dassel's explanation, yet for some unaccountable reason he felt disquieted.

'Now I assume that you wish to return to *U501* in order to inform your officers and crew of our arrangements, Herr Kapitanleutnant,' said von Geyr.

Before Rink turned to follow von Geyr, he flung a challenging glance in direction of Wohldorf and Schramm, but found that neither of them offered the merest flicker of recognition, while Dassel and Soltmann pointedly devoted themselves to lighting fresh cigars. Evidently everyone was eager to have the meeting concluded.

On the way for'ard he made a guarded appraisal of the crew working on deck. Most of them were obviously Latins except for two or three Europeans who might have been German. Yet strangely, they all seemed to studiously avoid acknowledging his presence.

When they reached the ladder von Geyr again snapped to attention, clicked his heels and extended his right arm. 'Long live the Fatherland. *Heil Hitler!*'

Rink in reply touched a hand to his cap in military salute. And dispirited both with his hosts and their reception, he climbed out on to the ladder and dropped down on to *U501*'s after catwalk. When he arrived on the bridge he received a progress report from Erlanger, tossed the stub of his cigar across the side, then climbed into the tower.

Kernbach and Ingersoll were below in the control-room. 'How was the champagne?' Kernbach inquired with bright enthusiasm, then hesitated when he saw the serious cast of Rink's face. 'Something must be wrong,' he accused.

'Perhaps. I don't know,' Rink replied falteringly. 'But there's something about the demeanour of those people that disturbs me.' Then he went on to explain about Dassel, his associates, Soltmann and von Geyr, and the absent Dr Matzhold.

'Who's this Dr Matzhold?' questioned Kernbach.

'According to von Geyr he's the Reichsleiter's official agent.'

'So?' said Kernbach. 'And did you hear any news of the Reichsleiter?'

'There was no reference made to him.'

'Perhaps he went the same way as the Führer.'

'I very much doubt it,' said Rink with a wan smile. 'Certainly not intentionally, not after he arranged for a cargo such as ours to be shipped halfway around the world. A man with such foresight and ability doesn't make mistakes where his own well-being is concerned.'

Kernbach mused thoughtfully, 'Then perhaps he's already here.'

'That may well be so,' Rink conceded. 'But at this moment there are problems which are of more concern to me than the Reichsleiter's whereabouts.'

Ingersoll broke in impatiently, 'What about us, sir?'

Rink said, 'We're to head south for the Golfo de San Matias

when the transfer of cargo is completed. There the boat is to be scuttled. The *Santa Elvira* will then put us ashore at Avellaneda tomorrow morning. From there we're apparently to be taken to a place called Olavarria to meet the senior members of what I assume to be the local Party Organisation – presumably our senior host Dr Matzhold and his associates.'

Kernbach commented with heavy sarcasm, 'What do you know – now we really are travelling in style.'

Rink was silent, wrapt in uneasy thought.

Kernbach's gaze narrowed. 'There's something more, isn't there?'

Rink said quietly, 'The *Cassiopeia* went down with all hands.'

Both engineers were stunned by the disclosure.

'I read a brief account of her loss in an Argentine newspaper dated May 14th,' Rink explained. 'Apparently the British Admiralty attribute her loss to a drifting mine. There were no survivors.'

Ingersoll exclaimed in solemn reflection, 'Ach, so that was why there was never any fuss raised.'

Kernbach was instinctively suspicious. 'That seems one hell of a coincidence, don't you think?'

'It *wasn't* a coincidence,' stated Rink, his face set in a grim scowl. 'And it's a matter which I intend to take up with Berger the moment we clear the *Santa Elvira*. Along with Wohldorf and Schramm, he, Rothfels and Guntel were last to leave the *Cassiopeia*. My guess is they opened the sea-cocks before they left.'

The two engineers stared back at him, incredulous.

Rink said, 'I wondered why Berger became increasingly withdrawn and morose. I was inclined to attribute it to the incident with the Liberator when he panicked, but now I believe that his knowledge of what happened that night on board the *Cassiopeia* had been weighing on his conscience. However, Wohldorf was the brain behind her sinking. Dassel admitted as much.'

At that juncture Coxswain Lamm put his head through the circular opening in the for'ard watertight bulkhead. 'Excuse me, Herr Kommandant. The last canisters are now being removed from the outside torpedo stowage.'

'You had better standby main engines,' Rink told Kernbach and Ingersoll as he climbed into the tower. Two minutes after he arrived on the bridge the last grey metal canisters were being winched inboard across the *Santa Elvira*'s bulwarks.

Shortly afterwards Soltmann leaned from a window in the starboard wing of the *Santa Elvira*'s bridge. 'All accounted for and ready to let go whenever you are, Herr Kommandant.'

Rink looked below to where Berger and Kordt were waiting on the for'ard catwalk. 'Standby to let go fore and aft. Ring on main motors.'

From overhead came the whirr and clatter of machinery and suddenly the mooring wires fell slack.

Rink glanced the length of the upperdeck. 'Let go fore and aft.'

Below on the catwalks the berthing-party dumped the wires over the side and saw them winched inboard across the *Santa Elvira*'s bulwarks.

'All clear fore and aft, sir,' Kordt reported to the bridge, while around him a jubilant cheer went up from the crowded catwalks when the hulls began to edge apart.

With Rink in the horseshoe and Erlanger stationed on the *wintergarten*, both men watched intently while the hulls began to drift apart, rising and falling in the swirl of green water. 'Secure upperdeck. Small ahead both.'

Astern the diesels coughed into a rhythmic roar.

With his attention still focused on the widening expanse of water between the two hulls, Rink did not see the three concentrated charges of grenades lobbed out from behind the *Santa Elvira*'s bulwarks to drop in a lazy arc towards the crowded catwalks. Nor did he see the tarpaulins stripped from the twin 20 mm cannon on her forepeak and from the multiple Bofor gun on the fantail. The first he knew that anything was wrong was when he was dealt a tremendous blow in the back and enveloped in a vivid flash of orange flame, the blast of the explosion flinging him violently against the casing in the forepart of the bridge. Stunned, the breath driven from him, he lay sprawled on the duckboards, his mind only vaguely registering the other shuddering explosions and the bewildered and panic-stricken screams which followed on them. He shook his head in an effort to clear his senses and attempted to claw himself upright only to fall back to the duckboards amid the deafening hammer of guns firing at point-blank range, drowning the sound of the diesels. Then he became aware of a high-pitched scream of agony which seemed to trail on forever, and he twisted his head around to see Erlanger lying beside the periscope standards, his boyish face contorted with shock and pain, threshing about in a widening pool of blood, his left arm blown off at the shoulder. And further aft, sprawled in a crumpled heap of twisted limbs, he saw the blast-mutilated bodies of PO Seaman Hoven, Signalmen Meyer and Hagen, and one of the AA gunners. As for the other three gunners, who seconds earlier had been standing on the *wintergarten* beside Erlanger idly watching the two vessels drift apart, there was no sign.

Then summoning all his strength, he hauled himself slowly upright, the air thick with the stench of burnt cordite, mutilated flesh, and scorched paintwork. Below him the for'ard catwalk was a scene of carnage, with bodies strewn everywhere while a hail of cannon shell scythed along the length of the upperdeck and churned the surrounding water into a white curtain. The few men still on their feet were running desperately for cover on the starboard side of the tower, some to be cut down screaming and disappear outboard across the casing. It was the sheer calculated cold-blooded butchery of defenceless men caught packed together on the upperdeck in party mood and gunned down like unsuspecting bystanders on a crowded pavement.

In the control-room Kernbach and Ingersoll had been slammed to the deck-plates by the combined blast of the three exploding charges, the one on the bridge having occurred a split-second before the other two in the region of the open fore and after hatches, and now Ingersoll scrambled to his feet, conscious of the sound of shooting and the screams of the dying on the upperdeck, and out of instinct threw the engineroom telegraph over to Full Ahead. When nothing happened and the diesels failed to answer, Kernbach pushed past him and started aft, trampling over the torn and blood-stained bodies in the devastated central gangway beneath the open after hatch, vaguely aware that among them lay Kolb and Leading Machinist Guntel. Then a bewildered Dornberger came out of the engineroom and ran straight into him. The young ERA gaped uncomprehendingly at the carnage strewn around him, and said inanely, 'What is it, Chief? What's happening?'

Kernbach did not bother to attempt to answer him, merely yelled at him, '*Give me full ahead!*' Then he returned for'ard to scramble into the tower, thrust aside the sprawled body of Coxswain Lamm, and slid into the helmsman's seat to give the boat full right rudder, the fact having registered automatically with him that by doing so he was pulling *U501* away from the *Santa Elvira*'s hull, and like the few men below deck, all was ignorance and confusion to him regarding what was happening above.

On the bridge Rink had recovered from the initial shock of the attack to realise that it had obviously been cold-bloodedly intended all along to send *U501* and her entire crew to the bottom in order to secure their lasting silence after they had served their purpose. Evidently the mouths of so many men represented too great a risk to take with the blanket of secrecy which surrounded Shipment No. 11372 and its delivery. He also realised that if the other two concentrated charges of grenades had found their intended targets like the one which had dropped cleanly through the after hatch to explode within the hull, then *U501*'s pressure hull would have been ripped apart and she would have sank like a stone. Instead someone had delayed the order to lob the charges for too long, and two of them had missed the open bridge hatch and for'ard hatch, one to explode on the after end of the horseshoe, the other to explode on the for'ard catwalk.

In the grip of overwhelming anger, he stumbled aft to the *wintergarten*, blood streaming down his face from a scalp lacerated by shrapnel splinters, aware that the men still crowding up through the for'ard and after hatches in bewilderment and panic were being shot down before they reached the catwalks, and he swung the port twin 20 mm cannon around to sweep the *Santa Elvira*'s decks with a thunderous burst of fire, spent brass hulls showering the gratings beneath his feet.

Meanwhile in the tower Kernbach was still ignorant of the situation on deck except for the fact that someone on the *wintergarten* was at last returning the fire which had punched gaping holes in the tower casing around him. Then the startled face of Control-room PO Morgen appeared at his side. '*Here – take the helm!*' he ordered, and clambered up the ladder to the bridge where he stumbled across the sprawled bodies of Erlanger, Hoven, Meyer, Hagen, and one of the AA gunners. Blood was spattered everywhere and the reek of the explosion which had shattered the after end of the horseshoe hung about it in an acrid cloud. Then his gaze fell on Rink who, covered with blood, pushed aside the port twin 20 mm cannon and started towards the front of the bridge only for his left leg to collapse beneath him.

Kernbach reached out to help him to his feet. 'What happened?' he shouted into the bloodied face above the noise and confusion.

Rink straightened up and drew a sleeve across his face to wipe the blood from his eyes. 'They tried to sink us as we pulled away!'

Kernbach was incredulous. 'The bastards! The murdering bastards!' Then: 'And you – are you badly hurt?'

'Never mind me – just tell me the situation below.'

'I'm not sure, apart from the fact that there's been an explosion just inside the after hatch and that we're taking water somewhere. Lamm's among the dead and Morgen has the helm. Also the telegraph isn't working. I had to go aft and have Dornberger give me Full Ahead.'

Rink steadied himself against the bridge casing. 'Then get someone in the after hatch to relay engine orders. Hurry!'

As Kernbach disappeared back into the tower, Rink again turned his attention to the upperdeck. Bodies still littered the catwalks, although many had been washed clear by the seas breaking across the casing. Ironically, he saw that among the bodies still lying on the for'ard catwalk below the tower were those of Berger and Rothfels. Yet *U501* herself had suffered serious damage, her bridge and tower riddled by shells, while the piercing shriek of high-pressure air was a certain indication that the ballast tanks were badly punctured. Then he saw Kordt who was covered with blood from shrapnel wounds sustained when the concentrated charge of grenades aimed for the open for'ard hatch had missed to explode on the crowded catwalk. Holding himself steady with the aid of the jumping-wire, the CGM was yelling at the hands who had taken shelter on the starboard side of the tower.

With *U501* still turning to starboard, Rink again wiped blood from his face and looked aft to see the *Santa Elvira* on the port quarter. Had *U501* not been so severely damaged, and had there been sufficient torpedo mixers to muster on Battle Stations, then at such range a single torpedo would have blown her apart. 'Midships!' he called into the tower with ice-cold deliberation, then aft he saw Dornberger thrust his white face cautiously out through the after hatch. 'Slow ahead, Dornberger!'

Dornberger promptly withdrew his head and *U501*'s speed fell away.

On the for'ard catwalk Kordt looked expectantly to the bridge, the hands who earlier had been sheltering on the starboard side of the tower gathered around him, clearly awaiting order to man the 88 mm cannon.

Rink gritted his teeth against the searing pain which burned up through his left leg, then yelled, 'All right, Kordt! Prepare to open fire whenever I put us about!'

The order galvanised Kordt and his men into action and they swarmed around the mounting as Rink turned to the bridge hatch. 'Hard left rudder, Morgen.'

U501's bow swung around to port until she had doubled back on to her previous course, and at Slow Ahead she headed towards the *Santa Elvira*.

Rink had already decided on the course of action to adopt, one which would allow Kordt and his gunners a clear, close-range opportunity to pound their target at will. He called calmly down into the tower, 'Midships. Right rudder. Steady at that.'

U501 slowly angled out on an opposing course, headed back towards the still stationary *Santa Elvira*, committed to a run which would take her down along the freighter's starboard side. And now, unable to bring her Bofor gun to bear owing to the acute angle of *U501*'s approach, only the twin 20 mm cannon on her forepeak renewed fire.

Then a sudden thud and jolt passed through *U501* and cordite fumes gusted back across the bridge as Kordt sent the first round of high-explosive on its way. Rink instantly saw a direct hit register on the *Santa Elvira*'s deck below the drop from the forepeak, then watched the foremast fold crazily on itself amid the orange flash and cloud of smoke.

As yet apparently undecided about what course of action to pursue, the *Santa Elvira* continued to remain stationary, then prompted by the accuracy of Kordt's shooting, the water boiled around her counter and she swung her bows towards *U501* in order to present as small a target as possible while she gathered speed for an attempt to ram.

Then Kordt's third round found its mark high on the starboard bow, and when the smoke and debris cleared, the twin 20 mm cannon was silent.

Rink cupped his hands to his mouth. 'Go for the bridge!' he directed.

*

the evening and that the howling wind now driving vast black seas before it provided another factor in favour of their continuing to make good their escape, for it almost certainly meant that the convoy's escorts would have been unable to call up the assistance of aircraft when they realised that their quarry had eluded them.

'All clear all round, sir,' von Heydekampf reported.

There was no time to waste; they had to clear the area before there was any improvement in the weather.

Rink called below, 'Switch to main engines. Obey bridge orders and ventilate boat. Give me all the speed you can muster, Chief.'

He had already decided not to renew his direct run northward, knowing that it would be exactly what the Allies would expect of him. Instead he would make his run to north-westward, out into the North Atlantic, before he made the wide detour around the Shetland Islands, nursing *U207* along as best he could, then turn for home, an exact course which he would decide on later. 'Come to 315 degrees. Bridge watch maintain an extra sharp lookout.'

With *U207* limping through the darkness, she gradually began to leave the distant coast of Southern Ireland on the starboard quarter while an exhausted crew attempted to restore some semblance of order within the battered hull.

'Excuse me, sir,' von Heydekampf said out of the darkness. 'But do you propose to comply with routine procedure and inform Headquarters about our successes?'

'To hell with Headquarters and operational procedure. To send out a signal now would only serve to bring every Brit for miles around down on our heads.'

Twenty minutes later Rink left the bridge and went below where he found Kernbach and Second Engineer Erich Hunsdorfer directing the machinists and technicians who were attending to the most urgent items of damage. 'Everything under control, Chief?'

Kernbach shook his head wearily. 'We're doing everything possible, but we're in a bad way all round. Unfortunately the motors and diesels have taken a severe pounding, the diesel foundations in particular. Also both shafts have been badly shaken, so badly that I won't be able to give you anything like top speed again on this trip. The port diesel is going to give us a great deal of trouble before long. PO Electrician Vollmer's also back there with his crew working on the batteries. Everyone has a job on their hands, and that's without this mess,' he announced with a gesture at the tangle of cables and smashed fittings that littered the deck-plates.

'Well, I appreciate that you can only do your best, Otto. But if you can give me two hours at your maximum speed, then we can take it more easily from there on. We have a long way to go, so let's be satisfied to get home in one piece.'

Rink next made his way for'ard to the W/T office where Chief Telegraphist Bergold and PO Telegraphist Henneger had a vast array of instruments and components arranged on the radio bench in front of them.

Bergold said in apology, 'I'm afraid that it's going to be some hours before we can send anything, Herr Kommandant.'

'Don't worry about sending anything just yet,' Rink informed him. 'Once we clear the Kattegat will be time enough to think about that.'

When he returned to the control-room he found Leutnant Kappler engaged in sorting through the debris around the chart-table. 'Leave that to me, Kappler. I can attend to it once I enter up the War Diary. But if you go to my quarters there are three bottles of brandy in my locker. See to it that every man gets a measure.'

After entering up the War Diary, Rink applied himself to a study of the charts and plotted what he hoped would prove to be the safest course to set for home.

Home, he thought; and wondered if *U207* was destined to ever again set her bows into the waters of the Kieler Bucht.

*

On the morning of March 29, two sets of dimmed headlights blurred the darkness as they drove north towards Berlin. Hard on the rear lights of the unmarked Mercedes limousine was an Opel truck which displayed the insignia of the Wehrmacht. Both vehicles were dusty and mud-spattered, and there was no slackening of pace while they pushed on through the darkness.

In the Mercedes, the driver, forty-two year old SS-Unterscharführer Heinrich Winckler, a member of the Reichskanzlei Transport Compound, maintained a constant watch on the headlights of the Opel truck that remained focused in his rear-view mirror. At the same time, huddled in his greatcoat in the deep upholstery in the rear, thirty-four year old SS-Standartenführer Otto Langbein stirred himself and rubbed a gloved hand across the misted window. The first grey light of dawn had begun to filter across the sky from eastward and he could just discern the jagged silhouette of pine forest on either side of the highway where it stood etched against a sky whose stars were beginning to lose their former brilliance.

Suddenly he caught a glimpse of a narrow cutting on the edge of the forest on the right of the highway, the only indication of the closely guarded road which lay hidden from the air by overhanging pines, the road which led to the headquarters of Oberkommando des Heeres, the Army High Command, and Oberkommando der Wehrmacht, the Armed Forces High Command; the headquarters of the Supreme Command – Hitler. They were now at a point less than six kilometres south of Zossen, thirty-eight kilometres south of Berlin. And beneath the wheels of the speeding Mercedes lay the broad stretch of asphalt which drove south from the capital through a vast spread of pine forest and prime agricultural countryside parallel to the Berlin-Dresden railroad – Reichsstrasse 96.

By the time they reached Zossen dawn had stained the morning sky oyster pink, creating a conflicting sense of tranquillity when one took into account the town itself, for although the highway had quickly been repaired after the heavy bombing-raid of March 15, gaunt facades and pulverised mounds of rubble interspersed the old-world buildings either side of the highway. And then they were out into the countryside again where the wayside vegetation was crisp and white with overnight frost.

Langbein watched abstractedly while the countryside sped past. At any other time it might have been an invigorating drive, but on this occasion it did nothing to lift the cloud of gloom and despondency which had first settled over him months earlier. It was heart-rending, and it grieved him terribly, but no matter how he viewed the situation, the end was clearly in sight. In the east the Russians had gathered into a formidable wall which stretched southward all the way along the Oder from Stettin on the Baltic coast. And in the west the Allied attack had gathered momentum on a wide front, a powerful, coordinated attack which they were convinced would bring them final victory within the space of a few weeks. He found it a depressing fact with which to live.

Then when they came suddenly on a stretch of open countryside, Langbein saw how the eastern horizon lay blanketed beneath a bank of ominous black cloud, out where the Oder and the Neisse lay, and the cities of Kustrin and Frankfurt an der Oder, where Generaloberst Theodor Busse and the 9th Army were about to become engaged in what promised to be a ferocious battle with Marshal Georgi Zhukov's 1st Belorussian Front, in a bid to contain the Russians in their three bridgeheads on the western shore driven in wedges to the north of Kustrin, and to the south between Kustrin and Frankfurt an der Oder, and the third below the latter, in places only some forty kilometres from Berlin.

As Langbein stared at the eastern horizon he experienced a bitter sense of frustration. He would willingly have changed places with any one of the 9th Army's Officers for another chance to serve the Führer and the Third Reich on the battlefield. Instead he was sitting in the luxurious comfort of a Mercedes limousine, the custodian of a dozen packing cases headed north to Berlin, packing cases that bore the squat, pheasant-like insignia of the Nazi Party along with a stencilled serial number and the words – *Most Secret*.

Langbein leaned back into a corner of the upholstery, his face lost in shadow beneath his black and silver cap. The path which led to his presence on Reichsstrasse 96 that morning had begun at a point on the Caen-Falaise road in Normandy the previous year when serving with remnants of the 12th SS Panzer Division *Hitler Jugend*, under command of SS-Brigadeführer Kurt Meyer, he had been critically wounded in a tank action with units of the Polish and Canadian armoured divisons while directing cover for retreating troops of the shattered 89th Infantry Division.

Three months later, while undergoing a period of convalescence at an SS officer's clinic at Neustrelitz, he had been ordered to attend a special ceremony at the Reichskanzlei to receive a decoration for bravery from the Führer. After the ceremony, he and three other officers had been introduced to the Reichsleiter, Martin Bormann, a short, thickset man with powerful shoulders and an aggressive manner, a man whom Langbein had found difficult to associate with a senior post in the Nazi Party – the Führer's Secretary.

Then as the weeks dragged slowly into months, reports of one catastrophe following on another had filtered back from the various fronts, and Langbein, unable to contain his frustration at being posted to the Reserve List, had begun a campaign of harassment in order to have himself reinstated to the Active List. That a man of his military experience could afford to be ignored was beyond his comprehension. Yet nothing occurred to indicate that his impassioned requests were even being considered in a favourable light, until on the morning of November 19, 1944, he received a phone call at his apartment in Wilmersdorf, a summons for him to appear at the Reichskanzlei Re-Appointments Office next day.

When he duly arrived at the Reichskanzlei next afternoon the reception which awaited him was totally unexpected. The officer in charge of the RAO received him with such cordiality that it almost bordered on obsequiousness, had lifted the phone, mumbled a few words into it, then had shown him into an anteroom off the corridor outside. Ten minutes later Langbein was even more disconcerted when the Reichsleiter had entered the room. Automatically he had leapt from his chair and slammed to attention. Then to his amazement Bormann had spoken to him almost as if they had been old friends, had inquired of his health and explained how he had always taken a personal interest in the Reich's heroes. Also he was acquainted with the fact that not only had Langbein's wife and daughter perished along with his parents in the bombing-raid on Hannover of February 13, 1944, but that both his brothers had fallen with the remnants of Generalfeldmarschall von Paulus's 6th Army at Stalingrad. Next he explained how well he understood Langbein's determination to return to Active Service, but expressed the fact that he personally considered that he had already made sufficient sacrifice. Besides, he informed Langbein, there was more than one way in which to aid and ensure the future of the Third Reich. He had then continued to reveal how at that very moment he was gathering around him a few select officers such as Langbein, men of unquestionable loyalty, men who could expect to take their orders only from the Highest Authority, and who in turn would be restrained in all matters relating to their official activities.

Impressed, Langbein had been provided with a special pass which bore the Reichsleiter's signature, and was first contacted on the evening of November 25, 1944, when he was instructed by phone to call at the Reichskanzlei without delay. Later that evening, on Bormann's personal instructions, he had been driven by SS-Unterscharfuhrer Winckler to the Wehrmacht's Halder Block Supply Depot in the Mitte district where a truck and four Wehrmacht soldiers were awaiting his arrival. Immediately they had set out for Halberstadt, collected nine packing cases from a bombed factory, and delivered them to a basement storeroom in the Halder Block Supply Depot before reporting back to Bormann at the Reichskanzlei.

Over the period from November 25, 1944, to January 26, 1945, he had collected close to one hundred cases from places as far afield as Wittenberge, Gardelegen, and Plauen. He had been naturally curious about the cases, most of them identical, as if made to specification, solid pine cases secured by steel bolts and straining-plates, and for a time suspected them to be the property of the Geheime Staatspolizei, possibly containing records relating to the Jewish Question, collected from various concentration camps situated throughout Germany and the adjoining countries and smuggled to their final points of collection in the fear that they might one day fall into the wrong hands.

Then during the nights of January 28, 29, and 30, he had been provided with cause to review his opinion when he collected a total of forty grey metal canisters of a cylindrical design, and twenty cases from Berlin's Kaiser-Friedrich-Museum, and, considering the building from which they were removed, he had been left in little doubt as to the nature of their contents. And now in the Opel truck following hard in the rear were twelve more cases which they had uplifted the previous night from the derelict Plaas family mansion north-east of Weimar, which he knew to be within close proximity to Buchenwald concentration camp.

Meanwhile up front SS-Unterscharfuhrer Winckler held easily to the wheel of the Mercedes while it sped on through the morning light. He had maintained a steady pace during the hours of darkness, the Opel truck growling hard on their tail. As on all previous occasions he had not known of the assignment until the last moment, when instructed by the Transport Office to collect Langbein at his apartment in Wilmersdorf. They had left Berlin with darkness on March 28, had collected the usual mysterious cases from a big derelict mansion outside Weimar, had then stopped over at Naumburg during the hours of daylight, when the roads were unsafe because of marauding Allied aircraft, and now were on their way home again. Yet he was not happy about it. He had not cared for these mysterious assignments from the start, these runs to obscure parts of the country to collect a few packing cases in the company of an officer, whose bleak silence sent shivers up his back every time they met. But it was better than being shot at. That was one way to look at it.

Yet Heinrich Winkler's run of good fortune bordered on the miraculous. Prior to the outbreak of war he had been chauffeur to a director of an engineering plant in Tegel, and because of his experience had found himself conscripted into the ranks of the SS and assigned to the Reichskanzlei Transport Compound. In the time which had elapsed since, the longest he had ever been away from Berlin was for two weeks in the summer of 1942 when he had driven two members of the Gestapo Economic Delegation to Paris. However, he had never harboured the desire to become a hero. He and his wife Gerda rented a comfortable apartment in the Charlottenburg district, and he could still enjoy the luxury of an occasional roll between her ample hips while his old friends were either dead, or else shivering in their fox-holes on the Eastern Front. Also he had plenty of opportunities to dabble in the blackmarket, so that with a Reichskanzlei posting and a trusted friend in the kitchen, he and his wife had never been forced to go hungry. Now all he wanted was to see the war out and survive. He nodded to himself satisfactorily.

Then when they cleared a dense stretch of pine forest he saw the huge pall of smoke which darkened the morning sky above Berlin, and he forgot himself momentarily. 'Seems we've had another bombing-raid last night, Herr Standartenfuhrer.'

Langbein's reply was an uncommunicative grunt.

Winckler shot a glance at his passenger in the rearview mirror. The gaunt, disfigured face beneath the gleaming vizor of the high-peaked cap stared straight ahead, as if icily condemning everything it saw in the rosy dawn. With his awesome features and empty left sleeve, the man more than amply portrayed the living part of the heroic Teuton Knight returned from the battlefield. And Winckler had driven them all at one time or another while serving at the Reichskanzlei; Goring, Raeder, Keitel, von Rundstedt, List, von Leeb, Rommel, Student – it disappointed him now to realise that he had not kept an autograph book. He ought to have possessed the foresight to have thought of that. When the end arrived there was no guessing at the sort of market there would be for such rare mementoes.

When they approached Berlin from southward, Winckler found himself confronted by one impassive street after another. Fallen masonry, bomb craters, ruptured gas and water mains stopped him at every turn. Then with the truck lurching along in rear, he was flagged down by two elderly members of the Volkssturm, their clothes dusty, faces stained with weariness and grime.

Langbein wound down the window impatiently. 'Is it like this all the way?' he demanded.

Both men nodded. 'It was a big one last night, Herr Standartenführer,' the taller of the two said ingratiatingly. 'A bad night in this sector. If you're headed into town I suggest you try and make it through Friedenau and Schmargendorf.'

Langbein sent a cold, inquiring glance at Winckler. 'Know your way?'

'Of course, Herr Standartenführer.'

Winckler reversed the Mercedes out of the street and turned it westward, and behind him the driver of the truck wrenched the wheel around to follow lurching in rear.

It took ninety minutes to reach the Halder Block Supply Depot, and a further forty minutes to unload and manhandle the twelve cases down into the basement of the old brewery with its worn stone stairs, gloomy corridors, and tiny barred windows. When alone in the huge storeroom, he made a count of the cases and metal canisters and found there to be a total of one hundred and seventy-two. Then, relocking the door, he returned upstairs, crossed the cobbles of the enclosed courtyard to the main gate, and handed the keys to the Duty Guard Officer. Next he dispatched the Wehrmacht soldiers with their truck to the Maikafer Barracks then climbed into the waiting Mercedes and ordered Winckler to proceed to the Reichskanzlei.

On the way across town Langbein decided that after making his report to Bormann his first priority would be a hot bath, something to eat, then a few hours of undisturbed sleep. Afterwards he looked forward to spending the rest of the day alone in the solitude of his Wilmersdorf apartment, something which he regarded as one of his few remaining luxuries. Sitting back, he noted that Winckler also appeared anxious to complete the assignment. Turning on to Unter den Linden, the limousine swept westward without easing speed, with Winckler deftly avoiding bomb-craters and fallen masonry, swung around south on to Wilhelmstrasse, and finally came to a crisp halt outside the entrance to the Reichskanzlei.

Langbein gathered his brief case in his right hand, alighted with a curt nod to Winckler who held the door open, and turned to ascend the flight of steps which lay ahead, black-uniformed SS sentries snapping rigidly to attention. Inside the entrance hall he was instantly confronted by the Reception Guard which maintained a strict check and close surveillance on everyone who entered and left the building.

A tall SS-Sturmbannführer of the *Leibstandarte Adolf Hitler*, wearing an immaculate white tunic, black jodhpurs, and gleaming cavalry boots, politely barred the way. He said curtly, 'Yes, Herr Standartenführer – your business?'

Langbein extracted his special pass from an inner pocket and passed it to the officer along with his identification papers.

The officer scanned the documents and regarded Langbein with a questioning stare.

'To see the Reichsleiter,' Langbein informed him.

The officer returned the documents. 'One moment, please.' Next he retired to a glass-partitioned cubicle, spoke a few words into a phone, then returned to beckon across one of the duty guards. 'Standartenführer Langbein to see the Reichsleiter. Show him to the Führerhauptquartier.'

Langbein was surprised at the instructions. In the months that he had worked for Bormann it was the first departure from what had become a matter of routine procedure. In the past any time they had met had been in the usual upstairs anteroom. Now curious, he followed the SS guard downstairs to the basement of the Reichskanzlei and out into the garden. At the entrance to the bunker his papers were subjected to even closer scrutiny by the outside guards, then again by two officers of the *Liebstandarte Adolf Hitler* once he had gained admittance. Only then, after being subjected to a thorough body search, was he shown to the Entrance Lounge where a number of Wehrmacht and Luftwaffe officers were present.

There he found a seat on an uninhabited chaise-lounge and sat back to await developments. The room was warm and comfortably furnished, the lights shaded, the gathered voices subdued. He glanced about him and saw that the walls were adorned by oil-paintings, mostly landscapes, with an odd seascape intervening. The particular painting by his right shoulder bore the title *Atlantic Morning*, and through the inhospitable clouds of what appeared to be an October dawn, the pale light of the sun probed cold lemon fingers across a turbulent mass of upflung water.

He smoothed down his hair and ignored the self-conscious stares which his disfigured looks drew from two Luftwaffe officers across the room. Next two senior Wehrmacht officers entered from outside. Langbein recognised them as General Wilhelm Burgdorf, Chief of Army Personnel, Hitler's adjudant, and OKH Chief of Staff, General Hans Krebs. He watched them pass hurriedly through the room and disappear beyond.

'Langbein.' Bormann was standing by the inner door, dressed in the inevitable brown uniform devoid of decoration and insignia.

Langbein rose, and with his cap tucked beneath his right arm, crossed the room to follow Bormann who led the way back through the bunker.

On reaching his temporary quarters on the first floor, Bormann halted in the small outer office to dismiss one of his aides, SS-Standartenführer Gustav Zimmer, who was seated before a formidable pile of paperwork on his desk. 'Ten minutes, Zimmer,' Bormann directed. 'Tell Schellenberg I will see him in ten minutes.'

As Zimmer made ready to leave the room Langbein stared pointedly at the opposite wall in an effort to express the fact that he had no interest in hearing anything which did not directly concern him. Yet he was intrigued. The Schellenberg in question was almost certainly SS-Brigadeführer Walter Schellenberg, Himmler's Chief of Espionage. And he recalled hearing vague rumours of how Schellenberg was supposed to have made tentative approaches to Allied representatives in Switzerland with a view to securing terms for peace with Himmler's full blessings. But whether there was any truth in the matter or not, Langbein did not know, although those same vague rumours now served to trigger off his thoughts in another direction, and he wondered if it was possible that Bormann himself was in any way connected with those negotiations.

Bormann closed the metal door to the outside corridor

behind Zimmer and turned his attention to Langbein. 'I trust you didn't encounter any difficulties?' he queried.

Langbein followed Bormann through the inner door which he again closed behind them. 'No, Herr Reichsleiter. None.'

'Good.' Bormann made his way around behind a grey metal desk and slumped into a straight-back leather chair where he rubbed a hand across his jaw and studied Langbein candidly. Then in a conversational tone, he said, 'Well that appears to be it. For the time being we've each served our purpose. You'll long be able to draw a measure of personal satisfaction in the years ahead when you eventually come to realise the extent to which you've helped to ensure the continuing future of the Third Reich. And you won't be forgotten. But unfortunately, I can't go beyond that at present.' Bormann paused, spread his hands wide. 'However, the time has now arrived when we must devote our thoughts and efforts to our own well-being. We owe that not only to ourselves, but to the Fatherland.' He then fell silent, face dark, brooding. 'Those of us who aren't afraid to face reality have reconciled ourselves to witnessing the arrival of Russian troops in the capital within a very short time. The exact day merely depends on the calibre of our opposition.'

Again Bormann lapsed into silence; and on the other side of the desk Langbein was becoming increasingly concerned by the Machiavellian transformations which he had seen take place in Bormann's character, and he found himself waiting in anticipation of the next change, unable to even hazard a guess at its probable nature.

'However, we mustn't allow ourselves to dwell on the dark side of these events. We must accept this setback as merely temporary, and hold ourselves in readiness for the day when our services will again be required.' Bormann had risen from behind the desk, had emerged with a beaming smile to place a comradely hand on an even more greatly astonished Langbein's shoulder. 'Yes, I'm thinking about you in particular now, Langbein,' he stated almost jovially. 'You appear to be in need of a long rest. What do you say to that?'

A rawly astonished Langbein was overwhelmed by the suggestion, and wondered if, now that he had completed his work to Bormann's satisfaction, he was not being shuttled out of the way as a preventive measure against his perhaps being foolish enough to mention something of his activities in the wrong quarter.

Bormann remarked almost absently, 'Don't you have relatives somewhere around Immenstadt?'

It again added to Langbein's astonishment that Bormann should be so well acquainted with his personal life. 'Yes, Herr Reichsleiter,' he confirmed. 'My parents-in-law have a farm close by Immenstadt.'

Bormann's smile was knowledgeable. He said expansively, 'Then why don't you go and visit them? The air will do you good. You'll feel a new man in next to no time.'

Langbein murmured vacantly, 'Do you really think so, Herr Reichsleiter?'

Bormann replied heartily, 'Of course! And don't just think about it – get away tonight. If you go upstairs to the Re-Appointments Office they will make ready the necessary documents.'

In a trance-like state, Langbein found that Bormann had meanwhile walked him to the Entrance Lounge without his being aware of it. There Bormann once again became visibly serious. In a low voice he said with gravity, 'And remember, hold yourself in readiness. You'll be contacted. And should things become too difficult, as they undoubtedly shall for most of us, then take heed of the fact that it's only a short walk from Immenstadt to Switzerland.'

It was only when the chill wind sloughing along Wilhelmstrasse bit through the folds of his greatcoat that Langbein realised his meeting with Bormann had not been a bizarre dream.

*

Bormann's consultation with SS-Brigadeführer Walter Schellenberg lasted fifteen minutes. However, it was not as Langbein had half-suspected, a conspiratorial meeting, but one concerned with the handing over of certain documents of a highly confidential nature relating to the future of Admiral Wilhelm Canaris, at that time held in custody at Flossenburg concentration camp awaiting execution for his part in the conspiracy to assassinate the Führer.

Then with the meeting concluded, he was on his way back to his quarters when he met SS-Oberstgruppenführer Josef

'Sepp' Dietrich, former Commander of Hitler's bodyguard, the elite *Leibstandarte Adolf Hitler*, now Commander-in-Chief of the 6th Panzer Army. Dietrich had paid a hurried visit to Berlin from Vienna in order to seek reinforcements for his Command which was retiring in the face of formidable Russian troop concentrations advancing westward. Bormann spoke with him for several minutes, offered his sympathies and good wishes, then continued on to his own quarters. Although there was no outward indication that he was anything but his usual self, he had been trying to restrain a growing impatience ever since he had received a phone call on the morning of March 28 from SS-Obergruppenführer Oswald Pohl, Head of the WVHA - the Economic Administration Main Office - to inform him that, 'owing to circumstances without our control no more deliveries can henceforth be arranged. However, a final consignment of twelve cases has been placed ready for collection from the basement of the derelict Plaas family mansion five kilometres north-east of Weimar.'

At 4.10 pm Bormann was ready to put his final plans into operation. After locking the door of his office he extracted a thick diary from the Manzler safe, then returned to his desk and riffled through the pages. Next he placed a call to a house in the Schoneberg district, to the home of Korvettenkapitan Gerhard Lamprecht.

Lamprecht had arrived in Berlin only that morning from the Mecklenburg Compound on the Baltic coast, and he answered the call with rank and name.

Without reference to his own identity, Bormann said, 'You had a safe journey?'

Lamprecht answered in a stolid tone, 'No difficulties whatever.'

'Then you know the time and place.' Bormann did not allow for any answer, and without putting down the phone he made further reference to the diary, then put through another call. This time the number was that of a house in Spandau.

Again the call was answered promptly. A voice stated simply, 'Heinrich von Geyr.'

In reply Bormann said, 'Arrange to be at the Lehrter Station this evening at eight.'

The voice in Spandau answered, 'Of course.' And rang off.

Bormann's next call was to the Officers' Quarters at Maikafer Barracks, north of the Stettiner Terminus.

The answering voice reported briskly, 'SS-Hauptsturmführer Wohldorf.'

Bormann replied, 'You know who this is speaking. Be in Vosstrasse at 6.45 pm and bring your aide with you.'

'I understand,' Wohldorf briefly acknowledged.

Bormann's final call was to the offices of the Reichsbank, to the Department of Foreign Affairs, to a man called Paul August Hoffmeister. On this occasion he referred to himself with rank and name.

Hoffmeister's secretary took the call. 'I'm sorry, Herr Reichsleiter. I'm afraid it's impossible for me to contact Herr Hoffmeister. He left for home some minutes ago.'

Bormann replaced the phone, consulted his wrist watch, returned the diary to the safe, then devoted himself to clearing up the remaining business of the day. An hour later he rang Hoffmeister's private address in the south-western suburb of Zehlendorf and again stated his identity.

This time Hoffmeister's manservant answered, 'Herr Hoffmeister hasn't yet arrived home, Herr Reichsleiter.'

Bormann countered impatiently, 'I was informed that he left his office for home over an hour ago.'

'But there's a bombing-raid in progress, Herr Reichsleiter,' the manservant pointed out in a subservient tone. 'No doubt he will have been forced to take shelter somewhere en route.'

Bormann said brusquely, 'I see. I wasn't aware we were in the process of being bombed at this moment. In that case have him call me when he does arrive home.' Bormann replaced the phone and called across the office, 'Zimmer!'

SS-Standartenführer Zimmer presented himself in the doorway within the space of seconds. 'Yes, Herr Reichsleiter?'

'I'm expecting a call from Hoffmeister of the Reichsbank. But first I must go out. If he calls during that time tell him I will be in touch when I return.'

*

When Bormann left the Reichskanzlei building at 6.35 pm he was dressed in civilian clothes. A drab grey raglan-style raincoat covered a clerical grey suit which he wore with a grey shirt and dark blue neck-tie. When he descended the entrance steps where the ever-alert SS sentries rapped to attention, he turned the collar of his raincoat up against the icy drizzle gusting the length of Wilhelmstrasse in the chill wind, paused to glance about him, then walked briskly south towards Vosstrasse where an unmarked limousine was parked on the south side of the street. As always when engaged in his own personal affairs, he had deliberately ignored any of the official vehicles housed in the underground culvert within the Reichskanzlei grounds, and instead had borrowed General Wilhelm Burgdorf's Wanderer. When settled behind the wheel, he adjusted the weight of the Steyr pistol which he carried in his raincoat pocket on such occasions, and sat back to wait.

Less than five minutes had elapsed when he saw the Citroen turn out of Leipzigstrasse and pull to a halt on the opposite side of the street. When its door opened a tall, slim figure alighted and started across the street. Shrouded in black and silver, the man was wrapped in an elegant ankle-length great-coat.

Bormann leaned across and opened the door.

SS-Hauptsturmführer Ernst Wohldorf raised a black-gloved hand to the gleaming vizor of his cap. 'Good evening, Herr Reichsleiter,' he reported, and slid into the front seat.

Bormann studied the handsome, shadowed face. 'You brought Schramm?'

'Those were your orders, Herr Reichsleiter.' Wohldorf's words were taut with respect, his voice quiet, well modulated.

Bormann's gaze did not leave the shadowed face, its clean-cut features only vaguely discernible. The smell of cologne had already pervaded the interior of the limousine. Bormann commenced without preamble. 'An SS officer named Langbein lives in the Weddel Apartments in Wilmersdorf. He will be leaving some time this evening for Immenstadt, from the Anhalter Terminus. The train is scheduled to depart some time around midnight. You know what to do.'

'Yes, Herr Reichsleiter.'

'And that Reichskanzlei chauffeur – Winckler.'

'Of course, Herr Reichsleiter,' Wohldorf assured.

'Then I leave it in your capable hands.'

When Wohldorf alighted, Bormann started the motor. The time was 6.45 pm when he crossed the junction with Hermann Goringstrasse.

Korvettenkapitan Gerhard Lamprecht was a tall, angular man with a narrow pinched face and faded blue eyes. Also dressed in civilian clothes, the wide brim of his dark hat was turned down all round. Huddled in an entrance of the deserted Beethoven Hall on Kothenerstrasse, his eyes searched the dark street alertly. But even there the icy drizzle still sought him out, and with his hands thrust deep in the pockets of his leather greatcoat he stamped his feet frequently in an effort to maintain circulation. He was already so chilled that his pinched features appeared even more hawkish than usual.

At one time a senior cadet in the Kriegsmarine, Lamprecht had served on the flag-deck of the old battleship *Schlesien* under the command of Wilhelm Franz Canaris, later destined to succeed to Chief of the Abwehr Department in the Reichswehr Ministry. However, due to the onset of ill-health, Lamprecht had not been to sea in an active capacity since November 1942, when he was appointed to head the department responsible for the refitting of all craft under command of Senior Officer U-boats West at the Admiralty.

Having seen all opportunity for continuing his career at sea vanish with a doctor's report, he had come ashore an embittered and disillusioned man to assume his appointment at the Admiralty with the only prospect facing him being that of lasting out his remaining service years behind a desk. To add to his bitterness was the fact that there would be little or no real opportunity for further advancement, and he had applied himself to his humdrum task without enthusiasm until overtaken by an unexpected change in events in the Spring of 1944, when as a result of a chance encounter with Bormann at a cocktail party in the War Office, he had found himself being questioned about various aspects of the War at sea on which he had long given up hope of ever being able to express an opinion to anyone, least of all such a distinguished member of the Parteikanzlei as Bormann.

But an even greater surprise came his way a week later when Bormann visited the Admiralty with Luftwaffe General Erwin Dohndorf, and afterwards had sought him out in order to extend his personal sympathies for the ill-luck which had necessitated his premature transfer to a shore post. Lamprecht had been astonished that Bormann even remembered him, let alone the fact that he had obviously taken trouble to acquaint himself with his personal life. A month later he was even more bewildered when he found himself elevated to the rank of Korvettenkapitan and decorated for distinguished services to the Third Reich. Although he had given his unexpected good fortune considerable thought, he had been unable to make anything out of it. Yet he found it odd that his life should suddenly take on new meaning after his meeting with Bormann.

It was not until late September that Lamprecht again met Bormann at a reception party at the Admiralty, when the Reichsleiter had not only been quick to congratulate him on his change of fortune, but had appeared to genuinely share his pleasure. With this in mind, Lamprecht again found himself wondering about Bormann's abiding interest in him, and was further puzzled when unexpectedly summoned to the Reichskanzlei for another meeting with Bormann in mid-November.

Nervous and ill at ease, Lamprecht had listened that afternoon with mounting apprehension when a grave and thoughtful Bormann informed him that he had been selected to undertake responsibility for a task of the greatest magnitude which, due to the unfortunate turn in events that had overtaken the Fatherland, would be demanded of him in the near future.

Bormann had turned eyes on him that reflected a mood of fatalistic resignation. 'Lamprecht,' he had informed in sombre tones. 'It isn't easy for me of all people to admit this – but I fear the time quickly approaches when we shall have to accept the inevitable. Although every true German is committed to fight to the bitter end, we must look to ways to ensure the continuing future of the Third Reich.' Bormann had assumed a dramatic stance in the middle of the room, head bowed, face a mask of gloom. 'It's therefore been decided that in two days time you're to assume temporary command of the Mecklenburg Compound in North Germany where your first task is to find a U-boat, have her refitted to plans already at hand, stored, fuelled, and held in readiness to undertake a long voyage. We shall work on this together, you and I. And any queries we may receive from Headquarters regarding our vessel are to be directly referred to me. Nothing must be overlooked.'

Now huddled in an entrance of the Beethoven Hall, Lamprecht's wrist watch showed the time to be 7.10 pm when he saw the familiar unmarked Wanderer pull to a halt on the opposite side of the street, and head drawn down against the drizzle, he started hurriedly towards it.

Bormann studied Lamprecht's pinched face with concern when he sat in the passenger seat. He had met secretly with him three times in the previous seven weeks on Kothenerstrasse in order to receive progress reports on the work being carried out on *U501*, and it had become obvious that the man was suffering from increasing strain. 'Has something gone wrong? Are you having problems?'

Lamprecht ceased wringing his hands in an attempt to restore circulation and turned nervously in his seat. 'Not exactly, Herr Reichsleiter. However, I received yet another written directive from Headquarters yesterday morning to remind me that all remaining U-boats in training compounds are to be dispatched for Kristiansand at once, and it worries me that it may be only a matter of time before someone discovers the true state of *U501*'s readiness.'

Bormann stared out at the rain-swept street, eyes hooded. 'Then there's no longer any cause for you to worry. When can you have her ready to put to sea?'

Bormann's question took Lamprecht unprepared. He bent his head to peer more closely at him as if he could not believe his ears. 'The time has actually arrived for her to move out, Herr Reichsleiter?'

'That was the intended meaning of the question,' Bormann affirmed.

Lamprecht's whole manner brightened. He sat up as though an invisible burden had been lifted from his shoulders. 'Then she can be at sea within twenty-four hours, Herr Reichsleiter.'

'And what's the exact situation as it concerns her at this moment?'

'I still have her in that secluded creek a kilometre and a half west of the compound, a precaution against further air-attack. But all that remains is for her to be provisioned, and these I'm presently holding in readiness in the old Coastguard Barracks in Greifswald.'

'Then you must get back to the compound at once, tonight, and have her ready to sail by 18.00 hours on April 2nd. A crew will be on their way east tonight from Lubeck-Travemunde. Make certain they meet with no last minute problems. All necessary arrangements have been made and she has been officially cleared to sail for Kristiansand in compliance with Headquarters' directive of March 25th. I saw to it personally.'

Lamprecht was totally ignorant of who else was involved in the conspiracy, and lacked any desire to know; he was simply relieved to be finished with the whole nerve-wracking business. And now he responded with enthusiasm. 'You can depend on me, Herr Reichsleiter.'

'Good. The Kommandant will be an officer named Brandt, Kapitanleutnant Oskar Brandt. Before you leave Berlin you must collect his orders relating to the voyage from Fregattenkapitan Karl Pfaff of Naval Intelligence at Lager Koralle. Then make yourself fully conversant with those orders in the event that Brandt should raise any question regarding them. Pfaff is expecting you. Also a consignment of one hundred and seventy-two packing cases and metal canisters will leave Berlin some time tomorrow for the Mecklenburg Compound and *U501* – Shipment No. 11372. Their safety will be your personal responsibility till *U501* has put to sea, when it will then become that of Brandt and their official custodian, a certain Paul August Hoffmeister, whose arrival you can expect at the compound within the next forty-eight hours. Have I made myself clear on all points?'

'Yes, Herr Reichsleiter.'

'Any questions?'

'I don't see any at this moment, Herr Reichsleiter.'

'Good. Do you have transport with you?'

'My car's parked close by the Tiergarten Station, Herr Reichsleiter.'

Bormann candidly studied the hawked, nervous face for a long moment, then started the motor and headed the limousine down the rain-swept street. 'Should you meet with any unexpected problems I want to hear about them without delay. Understand?'

'Absolutely, Herr Reichsleiter.'

Bormann left Lamprecht on the rubble-littered street outside the Tiergarten Station, headed east along Charlottenburger Chausee, then turned north across the black stretch of the Spree on to Invalidenstrasse, and continued east again until he arrived at the Lehrter Station.

Rain was falling heavily when he wound down the window and peered out at the crowd of people gathered for shelter in the station's drab entrance hall. Then he saw a lone figure in a belted raincoat and dark hat detach itself from the crowd and start across the pavement, and he ran the window back up and opened the door.

Heinrich von Geyr halted at the kerb, glanced both ways along the street, then climbed hurriedly into the limousine.

Bormann's alert gaze swept the pavement and the station

entrance hall before he turned his attention to von Geyr. 'How long have you been waiting?'

'No more than ten minutes, Herr Reichsleiter.'

'Good. How's your father and the rest of the family?'

A flashing smile lighted von Geyr's Latin good-looks. 'Everyone's exceptionally well and send you their best wishes, Herr Reichsleiter.'

'And Dr Matzhold?'

'In excellent health, Herr Reichsleiter. He said I was to assure you that everything is in order – *everything*.'

Bormann evidenced his satisfaction with a curt nod, then extracted a bulky linen envelope whose sewn ends bore his personal seal. 'Then deliver him this. It contains an itemised list of the contents of Shipment No. 11372, together with instructions as to where those items are to be deposited for further safekeeping.'

Von Geyr put the envelope away in an inner pocket. 'Dr Matzhold will have it before the week's out, Herr Reichsleiter. All being well I will be back in Geneva tomorrow evening, and in Lisbon the day after.'

'Then take care,' Bormann impressed. 'And I hope you have an uneventful journey. Doubtless we will meet again one day.'

'I look forward to the day in question, Herr Reichsleiter,' said von Geyr, and alighted into the rain.

Bormann watched the handsome figure disappear into the darkness, then again headed the Wanderer east on Invalidenstrasse where a few blocks further on he slowed and turned south past the Charite Hospital towards Unter den Linden and the Reichskanzlei.

*

At the same time as Bormann was driving south through the Mitte district, SS-Standartenführer Otto Langbein was strapping up his suitcase where it lay on the bed in his Wilmersdorf apartment. Having been informed by the RAO in the Reichskanzlei that a train would travel south that evening some time around midnight, he had decided to make an early departure for the Anhalter Terminus in order that he might find accommodation on it.

With a final glance around the room, he wrapped himself into his greatcoat, the left sleeve of which was pinned by the cuff to the arm-pit, pulled his cap down over his head, then gathered up the suitcase and briefcase in his right hand and started downstairs.

Frau Weltlinger, the matronly wife of the caretaker, was on her hands and knees polishing the hall with homemade wax when she saw him descend the stairs. She straightened up at once, a soft smile lighting her face. She had quickly become fond of Langbein after he had come to live in the Weddel Apartments. He had obviously been such a handsome boy until decimated by his terrible injuries, and many times in the night she had lain awake thinking about him in the silent loneliness of his third floor apartment. And often in the evenings she had waited, listening for him to arrive home, so that she could invite him to eat supper with herself and her husband. It had always seemed so little a kindness, so inadequate a thought, to be able to extend to someone who had sacrificed so much. Now she waited for him to descend the final few steps. 'You're leaving now, Herr Langbein?'

'I'm afraid so.'

'Then I hope you will enjoy your leave.'

'I'm sure I shall.'

She walked with him along the hall and switched off the light before she opened the outside door to the street. 'I wish you a safe journey, Herr Langbein.'

He paused on the top step. 'Thank you, Frau Weltlinger. For everything. And take care of yourselves.'

She watched his heroic shadow descend the steps to the pavement and start down the street in the cold wet darkness, convinced that the war had brought nothing but hurt and grief to everyone.

Langbein had scarcely walked fifty metres when a black Citroen drew smoothly into the kerb at his side. A cold, impersonal voice called out sharply, 'You – come here!'

Langbein stopped, saw that the rear nearside window of the car was open and that a uniformed SS man was looking out at him. He walked across to the car and glanced down at the uniformed head. 'Yes?'

'Your papers!'

Langbein set his cases on the ground and extracted the wallet which contained his identification papers and travel documents from his tunic pocket, and had them snatched impatiently into the rear of the car where they were scrutinised in the glow of a hooded flashlight.

'Where are you going?'

'The Anhalter Terminus. I'm going on leave.'

'I see.' The SS man closed the wallet and handed it back out through the open window. 'You understand that we must check on everyone in times like these.' Something of an apologetic note had appeared in the man's voice.

Langbein returned the wallet to his tunic pocket, then stooped to retrieve his cases.

'You say you're going to the Anhalter Terminus?'

Langbein moved his head affirmatively. 'Yes.'

The SS man nodded, appeared to reach a decision. 'Then perhaps we can give you a lift. We're on our way to Leipzigerstrasse.'

Langbein hesitated. 'If you're certain that it won't inconvenience you in any way.'

The SS man opened the rear nearside door. 'It isn't any trouble. Pass me those cases.'

Langbein passed the cases in through the open door where the solitary figure sat in the rear, then climbed in to join him.

The SS man leaned forward and touched the driver on the shoulder. 'The Anhalter Terminus,' he instructed, then sat back to offer his cigarettes. 'So you're going on leave, eh?'

'Yes.'

The SS man said enviously, 'I wish to hell *I* was going on leave. I've seen enough of Berlin to last me a lifetime.' Then he added as an afterthought, 'Where are you going?'

'Immenstadt.'

'Immenstadt, eh?'

Langbein was suddenly aware that the car had begun to behave awkwardly, he felt it slow, then pull over to the kerb.

The SS man swore irritably. 'Not again! We've been having trouble all evening.' Then when the driver prepared to alight, he leaned forward and laid a restraining hand on his shoulder. 'No, I want to take a look at it myself this time.'

Langbein remained in his seat and saw the man go round to the front of the car and raise up the bonnet. A few moments later he returned with the flashlight in his hand. 'I'm sorry, but I don't suppose you happen to know anything about motors?' he inquired politely.

'A little,' Langbein affirmed. 'What seems to be the trouble?'

'I'm not at all certain,' the SS man confessed with a smile.

Langbein alighted to find that they were somewhere on the fringe of the Schwarze Grund Park. Several bomb craters showed in the close vicinity, and mounds of rubble were scattered along the edge of the park where it had been dumped after being cleared from the battered streets of the city.

The SS man directed the flashlight under the upraised bonnet. 'What do you think?'

Langbein leaned his right arm on top of the radiator and bent his face for a closer examination.

In the same instant SS-Hauptsturmführer Wohldorf fired from the right hip, the bullet from the Luger passing from right to left across the abdomen to take Langbein below the right ear. Langbein was clubbed off his feet by the force of the bullet and came to rest on his back where he emitted a low groan. Wohldorf stepped forward and in the glow of the flashlight retrieved the wallet from Langbein's tunic pocket, then moved back a pace and put a second bullet in his left temple.

SS-Unterscharführer Schramm glanced about him at the darkness as he alighted from the car, keenly alert, and stepped to his superior's side before he had replaced the Luger in his holster. 'Is he dead?'

Wohldorf shrugged his greatcoat aside. 'He's dead,' he affirmed, and, with Schramm's help, dragged Langbein's body into the park where they bundled it into a water-filled crater and covered it with slabs of masonry from a nearby mound of rubble.

While Schramm dusted himself down he looked back in the direction of the car. 'What about his luggage – those cases?'

Wohldorf started back towards the roadway, 'We can attend to it later when we get back to Maikafer Barracks. You can burn it in the boiler room.'

*

Twenty-five minutes later Schramm pulled the Citroen into the kerb outside a rambling apartment block in the Charlottenburg district where the street lay in close proximity to the Spree, and directed his flashlight at the entrance. 'This is it,' he muttered across his shoulder.

From in the rear Wohldorf said, 'Are you sure you know what to say?'

'By heart,' Schramm confidently affirmed as he alighted on to the pavement. Then flashlight in hand he entered the downstairs hall and climbed a wide spiral stairway, booted feet ringing on the slate steps, echoing hollowly all the way to the top of the building. He found the Winckler apartment on the second floor, and rapped on the door.

It was opened by a plump blond woman who wore carpet slippers and a shapeless pinafore over a green woollen sweater. Surprise registered on her face when she saw Schramm framed in the drab glow of light which escaped into the hall.

Schramm gave her a disarming grin. 'I'm sorry if I startled you. Is Heinrich at home?'

The woman backed away a step, glanced across her shoulder. 'Heinrich,' she called inside. 'There's someone here to see you – a friend.' When she returned her attention to Schramm it was to regard him more favourably. She touched a hand to her thin blond hair, primped coquettishly. 'Would you care to come inside and wait?'

'At any other time, but I'm afraid I'm in a hurry.' Schramm made it sound an invitation which duty alone forced him to decline. 'I have a car waiting downstairs.'

Heinrich Winckler appeared to his wife's side in shirt-sleeves and braces. He squinted out into the hall, frowning. 'You want me?'

'It would seem something important has come up,' explained Schramm. 'I was sent to fetch you.'

Winckler scowled, clearly displeased with the summons. 'I was supposed to be off-duty till ten o'clock tomorrow morning,' he grumbled.

Schramm lifted his shoulders in a gesture of sympathetic helplessness, and grinned. 'Perhaps they can't do without you.'

Winckler heaved a sigh of resignation. 'All right. Give me a minute.' He started to turn away, then stopped, struck by a passing thought. 'Are you from the Reichskanzlei?'

'No,' said Schramm. 'They just called and sent me to fetch you.'

Winckler started to say something else, then shrugged it aside.

Schramm said casually, 'You'll find me downstairs in the car waiting.'

Despite Winckler's lack of enthusiasm it took him only a few minutes to ready himself and appear outside. He approached the Citroen, settling his cap on his head. Schramm opened the door for him.

'Where are we going?'

Schramm swung the Citroen around in the roadway and remarked off-handedly, 'No one said anything to me about where you're going. I was just ordered to deliver you to where there's a car parked waiting a little way across town.'

Winckler groaned inwardly at the prospect of yet another junket with his gruesome Teutonic Knight.

When Schramm headed the Citroen east on Alt Moabit the glimmer of a moon showed itself through the thin layer of cloud which lay across the broken city.

Winckler glanced sideways at Schramm, remarked conversationally, 'Do you suppose we're in for another bombing-raid tonight?'

Schramm answered indifferently, 'It would be unusual if we weren't.'

Winckler showed new interest in the hulking SS man as they crossed on to Invalidenstrasse and turned south towards the Spree again, saw in him a sympathetic comrade despite his forbidding bulk and gross appearance. 'I just hope that I'm able to get my wife out of town before the Russians arrive. How long do you think we have?'

From in the rear of the car a well modulated voice answered, 'Oh, perhaps something like six to eight weeks.'

Winckler jerked upright, unaware until that moment of another person's presence in the vehicle. His face paled and he turned his head and felt his heart drop away when he saw the glitter of officer's silver in a corner of the rear seat. His mouth came open and he searched frantically in his numbed mind for some possible way out of his thoughtless indiscretion.

Wohldorf said smiling, 'Relax, Winckler. It so happens that I'm in much the same mind. Only an imbecile would want to be anywhere near Berlin when the Russians arrive.'

The facsimile of a smile touched Winckler's shaken face, although the feeling of nausea in the pit of his stomach remained obstinately with him. 'Yes, sir,' he answered in a weak voice, and turned back to stare out through the windshield.

When the pale glitter of the Spree again appeared ahead, Schramm turned east on the north bank and eased speed. Then in the rearview mirror he saw Wohldorf make a gesture with his right hand, and he slowed the car further, pulled it over on to the cobbled shoulder of the river, and stopped.

Winckler wound down the window and peered out at the dark bank of warehouses to northward. 'Where's this car supposed to be waiting?'

Schramm leaned past him to the open window. 'Across there.'

Winckler alighted with a vexatious frown. 'Where? I can't see it.'

Schramm opened his door and climbed out. 'Over there between those two buildings – see?'

Winckler followed the direction of Schramm's outflung arm. It was cold and he wished he had remembered his greatcoat in his hurry to get downstairs.

Schramm said, 'There's someone waiting with it. You'll see them.'

'Tonight of all nights,' groaned Winckler, and started across the cobbled roadway muttering to himself.

Standing beside the bonnet of the Citroen, Schramm unbuttoned his holster, withdrew his Luger, and shot Winckler through the back of the head at a range of less than five metres.

Wohldorf alighted to join Schramm before Winckler's body came to rest on the wet cobbles. When they approached they found him lying on his back, arms flung wide, eyes open, a gaping hole in his forehead above and directly between the eyes where the bullet had exited. Schramm glanced about him, found Winckler's cap, and spun it out into the darkness above the Spree. Then between them they dragged the body to the edge of the quayside and toppled it over into the black water below.

Wohldorf watched dispassionately as it splashed in the darkness. Then with a glance at Schramm, he said pensively, 'Two in one night. Strange – most strange.'

*

When Bormann returned to the Führerhauptquartier in the grounds of the Reichskanzlei at 8.35 pm he found SS-Standartenführer Zimmer waiting in the outer office. He saw at once from the expression of gravity on the man's face that something was very much amiss. 'Yes, Zimmer?'

'It's Herr Hoffmeister, Herr Reichsleiter. He's dead.'

Bormann was unable to conceal the sense of shock which he experienced at the news. His face immediately lost all colour and it took him a lengthy moment to recover his voice. 'What happened?'

'He was caught in that bombing-raid late this afternoon while on his way home to Zehlendorf. His car was crushed beneath falling masonry when a building collapsed. I was given the news only twenty minutes ago, just after he died from his injuries in the Potsdamer Officers' Clinic. His secretary at the Reichsbank called.'

Bormann knew he now required time to think, alone. He said tonelessly, 'Very well, Zimmer. You can go.'

Zimmer stiffened to attention, clicked his heels. 'Yes, Herr Reichsleiter. I will be available in the Staff Mess if required.'

When Zimmer withdrew Bormann continued into his own office where he sat down at his desk, his gaze distant, veiled. It was a catastrophic blow to receive so late in the day. His association with Hoffmeister went back many years, and like Burghardt, Olbertz, and Brunner, custodians of Shipment Nos. 11359, 11365 and 11368, all of whom had held a senior post with the Parteikanzlei Section II and attached either to the Reichsbank or the RSHA, he had possessed the highest credentials and close affiliations with the Party. And Hoffmeister was the last man he had expected to get himself killed, and it had happened at the most crucial moment, with intricate and unalterable arrangements made for final plans to be put into operation.

His face darkly thoughtful, Bormann finally rose and extracted his diary from the safe, returned to his desk, and commenced a patient scrutiny of its pages. Bucheim was dead. Gorlitz was dead. Herzog was a victim of tuberculosis. Klietmann was still recuperating after losing his right leg in Prague. Bormann's gaze travelled slowly down the pages. Thamm, Weichs, Wendt; he discounted them all for one reason or another. In frustration he rose from the desk and with slow, ponderous strides began to pace the floor of the office. An acceptable substitute for Hoffmeister had to be found somewhere, and there was little time left in which to find him.

Some minutes later he was startled by the shrilling of the phone. He snatched it up irritably. 'Bormann.'

'I thought to inform you that the Wilmersdorf apartment in question was vacated earlier this evening,' the voice on the other end of the line reported in a guarded tone. 'The former tenant has obtained permanent accommodation elsewhere. His associate also decided to accompany him.'

'I trust there were no unforeseen difficulties?'

'None whatever,' the voice assured.

'Good.' Bormann replaced the phone and sat in the chair behind the desk. He was relieved to learn that Wohldorf and Schramm had accounted for Langbein and Winckler, but they were not his immediate problem. For a time he gazed into space, then again consulted the diary, and again met with the same lack of success as before. Men such as Hoffmeister, Burghardt, Olbertz, and Brunner were not to be found lounging on street corners. Then he realised that if men of such calibre were unavailable, he must direct his thoughts elsewhere. It was then that he remembered his conversation of a few minutes earlier with SS-Hauptsturmführer Wohldorf.

He could vividly recall the events that had led to his association with Wohldorf and Schramm. Although he could not dispute the loyalty of either man, nor their unquestioning enthusiasm for executing his orders, he knew very little about their respective backgrounds. And reaching for the phone, he directed a call to be put through to Prinz Albrecht Strasse.

The Service Records of SS-Hauptsturmführer Ernst Wohldorf and SS-Unterscharführer Helmuth Schramm arrived by courier from the SS Personnel Officer fifty minutes later.

Bormann opened Wohldorf's file on to the desk. The man's place and date of birth were given as Regensburg, Bavaria, January 3, 1911. His father, Konrad Wohldorf, had worked as a chemist in the police laboratory in Augsburg from 1932 to 1940, when his services were recruited by the SS and he transferred to Berlin where he was employed at the Kriminaltechnisches Institut. Taken ill in 1941, he had died of kidney failure the following year.

Ernst Wohldorf had found his first job as a clerk with the Bavarian Ministry of the Interior. Two years later he transferred to a civil post with the Bavarian Political Police, which later, in 1933, had come under the command of Himmler. During that period he also attended the Police College, and in 1934 joined the Protection Police. Later that year he had also joined the National Socialist Party, and in 1935 had successfully applied for entry to the Bad Tolz SS Cadet School.

His first posting in the SS was to Dachau, where as a camp guard he served under the command of SS-Brigadeführer Theodor Eicke, the officer directly responsible for the murder of Sturmabteilung Ernst Rohm in Cell 474 at Stadelheim Prison, Munchen on July 1, 1934, following his arrest during the *putsch* of the Night of the Long Knives, and who later as Inspector of Concentration Camps and Commander of SS Guard formations had formed the Waffen-SS *Totenkopf Division.*

On Eicke's personal recommendation, Wohldorf had encountered no difficulty when he submitted an application for transfer to the Sicherheitspolizei, where he was subsequently attached to the Morality Desk at the Alexanderplatz office in Berlin where his previous experience of police work allowed few problems to trouble him. Responsible for the suppression of crime of a moral nature amongst the civilian population, he had swiftly brought about a creditable list of arrests and convictions to impress his worth on superiors, and was regarded as a zealous and conscientious upholder of Law and Order.

Helmuth Schramm was an entirely different specimen. Two years Wohldorf's junior, his parents had owned a dockside cafe in Bremen, and he had left school to work as a labourer in a bakery before embarking on a long succession of menial jobs until landing one in the paint-spraying shop of a Hannover garage. There he had joined the National Socialist Party, and shortly afterwards had successfully applied for enlistment in the ranks of the SS. For three years he had served as a guard in Buchenwald where his dedication to the task had earned him promotion to the rank of SS-Sturmann. In 1938 he had been transferred to Dachau, a posting which indicated his first having met with Wohldorf. And although there was no direct reference made to it, Bormann saw from the dates given for the transfer of both men to the Sicherheitspolizei from the Dachau Guard Unit that it was fairly obvious that Schramm had somehow gained his due to Wohldorf's influence with their superiors.

The events responsible for both men having attracted Bormann's attention occurred during November 1943 when they had almost completed a three-year term at the Morality Desk. Although there was no mention of the incident on either man's file, Bormann's recall of the events that surrounded the Duhring Murder was graphic, a scandal which had been uncovered as a result of a preliminary report of a missing person made to the Criminal Police Office in Niederschonhausen in the Pankow district of Berlin by a distraught woman whose brother had disappeared.

Initial inquiries ascertained the fact that fifty-four year old Hermann Duhring had been a man of considerable wealth, owner of two popular restaurants in Greater Berlin, while he possessed other financial interests in several nightclubs. At the time his sister had reported his disappearance, Duhring had been missing for forty-eight hours, having failed to return to the house which he shared with his sister in Niederschonhausen after he had dined at one of his own restaurants.

Over the next two days police inquiries made no significant headway until on the afternoon of the third day when the duty desk officer in the Niederschonhausen Police Office received routine notification that the body of an unidentified man had been recovered from the waters of The Havel at Pichelsdorf, in that area south-west of the Reichssportfeld Stadium.

Some hours later an hysterical Fraulein Duhring was led away from the Berlin Police Mortuary after she had identified the body as being that of her brother. The first peculiar aspect of the case came to light when the autopsy report was received from the Examining Surgeon. It indicated that Hermann Duhring, far from being an innocent victim of drowning, had been brutally tortured to death. At that juncture in the investigation the case was referred to the Geheime Staatspolizei, whose inquiries soon revealed the fact that Duhring was a noted homosexual. Subsequently, their next action was to round up all known male sex offenders whom they were able to trace, and subject them to interrogation. It was during the course of these events that the first word of blackmail by unknown officers of the Sicherheitspolizei was heard.

In rapid succession statements were pressured from three men, one an elderly dentist from the Friedanau district, the second a lawyer attached to the Propaganda Ministry, and the third a popular radio personality with Deutscher Rundfunk. All three men revealed intimate details of their blackmail after they had been caught *flagrante delicto*. Two of them had been seized in the Tiergarten, and the third apprehended on the service stairway of an apartment building after he had left one of Duhring's restaurants in the early hours of the morning with a member of the Hitlerjugend.

The story had been the same in each case. Beaten and threatened with arrest, all three men had complied with the demands of the arresting officers rather than face certain deportation to a concentration camp, and although none of the men knew the officers by name, they had furnished their description to such good account that the investigating officials had experienced no difficulty in identifying the officers in question.

That same day SS-Haupsturmführer Ernst Wohldorf and his aide SS-Unterscharführer Helmuth Schramm were apprehended and taken to Prinz Albrecht Strasse for interrogation. Despite strenuous denials of any knowledge of the Duhring Murder, or the blackmail of practising homosexuals, their case was referred to the office of the Examining Magistrate, Berlin Police Court, with a view to their arraignment on indictment before a Criminal Court.

Although the evidence at that particular stage had amounted to nothing more than circumstantial, events had taken an even more bleak turn for Wohldorf and Schramm when it was discovered that Duhring had rented a chalet on the east bank of The Havel the previous summer under an assumed name. During the inquiries made among his immediate neighbours, two of them had readily identified the arrested officers as having been among the many regular male visitors to the Duhring chalet, a damning revelation where Wohldorf and Schramm were concerned.

Convinced there was sufficient evidence to secure him a conviction, SS-Sturmbannführer Arnold Brecht, senior officer in charge of the investigation, had considered it to be only a matter of time and routine procedure before the two men were brought to justice. Chief Examining Officer Oskar Leibel of the Reich Coordinating Office for the Suppression of Homosexuality had also shared Brecht's opinion. But what Brecht, Leibel, and Examining Magistrate Walter Ulisch had not known was that news of the pending trial had circulated in Berlin to such good account that it had reached the attention of the Reichsleiter.

Ever inquisitive about matters which through chance might enable him to exercise influence and dominance over an individual, who perhaps would one day prove of personal benefit to him, Bormann's first step had been to direct the Berlin Police Court to provide him with a typescript of the prosecution's evidence. Two days later it had been returned to the Berlin Police Court in the care of an austere senior officer of the *Leibstandarte Adolf Hitler* with the words *Not Conclusive* written across the first page in red pencil, and accompanied by a note which stated tersely: *Case to be suspended indefinitely*.

Ulisch's reaction had been to send a vigorous protest on behalf of himself, Brecht, and Leibel, and to request a private meeting with the Reichsleiter which, if denied, would leave him with no other alternative but to approach a Higher Authority with a view to pursuing the matter further in a bid to achieve justice. In reply Bormann had made a demanding phone call to SS-Oberstgruppenführer Dr Ernst Kaltenbrunner, Himmler's deputy and Chief of the Reichssicherheitshauptamt – Reich Security Main Office – and had heard nothing further until a week later when Kaltenbrunner had phoned him to explain that owing to the fact that the two officers in question, Wohldorf and Schramm, had by their actions become an embarrassment in their present post, and would become an even greater all-round embarrassment if brought before a Criminal Court, he offered the solution that it could be to everyone's benefit if they were quietly transferred away from the capital.

Two days later a surprised and relieved Wohldorf and Schramm had found themselves posted to the SS Guard at Zossen, to Mayback II, the headquarters of OKW where for almost a year they had stood guard over the domain of Chief of Staff, Generalfeldmarschall Wilhelm Keitel, and Chief of Operations, Generaloberst Alfred Jodl, until Bormann had arranged their return to Berlin, to Maikafer Barracks, where they had remained at his permanent call since early December 1944.

Bormann reached a decision at a few minutes before 10 pm and made a phone call to Maikafer Barracks, to the personal quarters of SS-Haupsturmführer Wohldorf. In a strained voice he said, 'Something has just occurred that demands your immediate presence at the Reichskanzlei. You are to bring your aide with you. Am I clear?'

Wohldorf answered, 'I understand. We will be there with the minimum of delay.' The line at once went dead and he was left staring at the receiver, puzzled at what could have happened to cause so much activity on Bormann's part in a single day.

While he dressed he pulled back the blackout curtain and was confronted by total darkness and great blobs of rain streaming jerkily down the outside of the window panes. Within minutes he was on his way across the parade ground to the NCO's quarters where he went to the partitioned cubicles at the rear of the building overlooking the mess hall.

When Wohldorf entered, Schramm was sitting on his bunk in his undershirt, pulling off his boots. He looked up in surprise.

Wohldorf said, 'Come on. We're on the move again, wanted at the Reichskanzlei.'

Two minutes later both men returned across the parade ground to where the Citroen was parked outside the transport compound. Schramm took the wheel and moments afterwards had the car headed south through the rain towards Unter den Linden.

In the front passenger seat Wohldorf sat in silence, puzzled and uneasy. Bormann had sounded unduly anxious on the phone, and he did not like it. It was odd, disconcerting.

As if able to read his superior's thoughts, Schramm said, 'What can he want with us again tonight?'

Wohldorf said uneasily, 'I don't know. But I can tell you this – he didn't sound his usual self.'

On arrival at the Reichskanzlei they found the entrance hall seething with activity. A detachment of Wehrmacht officers led by a Colonel were gathered in a glum huddle, each clutching a bulging briefcase.

Schramm eyed them sourly. 'It looks as if we've just suffered another defeat somewhere.'

Wohldorf strode to reception and, along with Schramm, presented his identification papers, was informed they were expected, and after the customary body search, were escorted to the usual anteroom on the first floor of the building.

Surprisingly, they found Bormann impatiently awaiting their arrival. Slamming to attention, both executed parade ground salutes. In return Bormann made a dismissive gesture with his right hand, and, face grave, shoulders hunched, hands clasped behind his back, he surveyed them with a brooding gaze like a man with a sense of dejection he found difficult to bear. 'Gentlemen,' he announced at length. 'The war is lost.'

Wohldorf and Schramm stiffened involuntarily under the drama of the moment.

'Yes,' Bormann repeated as if his doom-laden words required further confirmation. 'The end is near. Further, we are in possession of certain documents and maps which show that the Allies intend to divide the Fatherland after defeat into separate zones of occupation.'

Wohldorf and Schramm exchanged a shocked glance. Even in defeat it had not occurred to them that the Fatherland would cease to exist, that this should be the price exacted in defeat.

Bormann regarded the two men steadily. 'Yes, I well understand your shock and disbelief. And I've lived with that secret for some time. Yet we aren't without a solution, a solution which will not only ensure the survival of the Third Reich, but will see it flourish in another day when it will grow from strength to strength. And with that day we will arise from the ashes and the world will witness the fact that our defeat was only a temporary setback, and that out of defeat we will have achieved even greater determination to secure lasting dominance over the Powers who would have seen us crushed and deprived of our beloved Fatherland.'

Wohldorf and Schramm listened with increasing bewilderment. That the Reichsleiter should confide such secrets in two lowly members of the SS was beyond comprehension. Urged to express himself, Wohldorf self-consciously cleared his throat. 'I'm afraid I don't understand, Herr Reichsleiter.'

Bormann's smile was almost illusitory. 'Tell me – how long is it since that unfortunate incident with Sturmbannführer Brecht and Chief Examining Officer Leibel?'

Wohldorf stiffened perceptibly with embarrassment of the memory. He answered quietly, 'Some fifteen months, Herr Reichsleiter.'

With the same almost illusitory smile, Bormann said, 'And since then we've come to discover several of each other's secrets, yes?'

Wohldorf's embarrassment and uneasiness suddenly intensified.

However, Bormann did not appear to expect an answer to such a forthright question. Instead his voice dropped to a conspiratorial key and he continued quietly, 'I want you both to listen very carefully to what I'm about to say – nor is it an honour I bestow without considerable forethought.'

*

When Wohldorf and Schramm left the Reichskanzlei shortly after midnight on March 30, they were in jubilant mood. A problem with which they had long been concerned had just been solved by an incomprehensible quirk of Fate; they had just been provided with a guaranteed means of escape from the inevitable holocaust certain to overtake the Fatherland in its final hours. And while they walked to where the Citroen was parked on nearby Hermann Goringstrasse, Schramm exclaimed buoyantly, 'I can't believe it – that this should actually happen to *us*!'

Wohldorf stepped around the bonnet of the Citroen, deposited the brief-case which he had received from Bormann on the rear seat, and slid behind the wheel. His handsome face set in a bleak frown, he said, 'I will believe it only when we put to sea, and not one moment before. A very great deal can happen to upset the most carefully laid plans in a few minutes, never mind days. Something you ought to remember from past experience,' he added significantly.

The sobriety of Wohldorf's words did not fail to transmit itself to Schramm. 'Yes, true. True,' he admitted on reflection. Wohldorf turned the car around and headed north on to Unter den Linden, then swung east towards Friedrichstrasse on the way back to Maikafer Barracks. 'We require three supply trucks, drivers, and escorts. The Reichsleiter will have everything arranged before we arrive. So as soon as you're ready to move, get them across to the Halder Block Supply Depot. You can expect me to join you there in an hour or so. And don't waste time. I want to be well clear of Berlin before daylight.'

After dropping Schramm at the transport compound in Maikafer Barracks, Wohldorf went directly to his own quarters, hurriedly collected his personal belongings together, packed them into two suitcases, returned to the Citroen, and started across town to an address in the Charlottenburg district, the home of an ex-Dachau guard who had been invalided out of the SS after losing his left arm in an automobile accident. There he collected two padlocked metal boxes from an improvised strongroom in the basement of the house, secured them in the trunk of the Citroen, and minutes afterwards was driving east again towards the Mitte district.

Later, at 4.10 am in the enclosed courtyard of the Wehrmacht's Halder Block Supply Depot, Wohldorf looked out impatiently as the last of the one hundred and seventy-two cases and metal canisters were manhandled in across the tail-board of the third truck. While checking off the serial number on the list which he had earlier received from Bormann, he heard Schramm bring the drivers and escorts to attention. He turned a critical eye on them, found them an uninspiring collection, and remarked caustically, 'They can hardly be classed as the backbone of the Wehrmacht, can they?'

Schramm sniggered aloud. 'You ought to have seen the ones I turned down.'

Wohldorf indicated one of the drivers, a tall, gaunt youth with the mournful air of an Einsatzgruppen burial orderly surveying the scene on the Russian steppes after the execution squads had stopped work for dinner. 'You,' he said. 'You'll head the convoy. Keep closed up on my car at all times. I want a good fast pace with no loitering from any of you others. If we run into trouble from the air with daylight you keep going irrespective of what happens till you gain shelter of the nearest woods. So keep your foot down and don't dawdle. And your escorts, one to each cab along with the driver. Now get on board.'

*

They had been on the road since 22.00 the previous evening, and now with the early dawn casting a sullen grey pall across the eastern horizon, the two covered trucks with the insignia of the Kriegsmarine stencilled on the doors of their cabs slowed to a growling whine as they approached the western suburbs of Gustrow. In the second truck, jolted into wakefulness by the changing noise and motion, the crowded mass of navymen stirred themselves. One man near the tailboard squinted out from beneath the canvas hood.

A vexatious voice from the darkness said, 'Where are we?'

From the tailboard came the reply, 'I don't know. It isn't yet light enough to see anything I can judge by.'

In the interior of the truck another man peered at the luminous dial of his wrist watch. 'We slowed like this two hours ago but we didn't stop.'

The man at the tailboard leaned his head out into the cutting chill of the slipstream. In the grey half-light patches of frost gleamed white on the countryside adjoining the roadway, and up ahead the silhouettes of several scattered buildings and a clock-tower showed sharply defined against the eastern horizon like black pasteboard cut-outs. 'We appear to be coming into a fair-sized town,' he observed.

Inside, a man called back to him, 'Can you see the ocean?'

The man at the tailboard withdrew his head and replied with contempt, 'I can't even smell the damned ocean!'

Soon the trucks further decreased speed and the men inside reluctantly began to ease themselves upright in the stuffy darkness from their resting places among the sea-kits on the floor in preparation to face the chill dawn.

In the leading truck, wrapped in his greatcoat, Kapitanleutnant Oskar Brandt peered out at the cold grey light of dawn beginning to filter through the deserted streets of the former Capital of the Duchy of Mecklenburg-Gustrow. 'Keep going,' he instructed the driver, PO Seaman Dehn. 'We can look for somewhere to stop on the other side of town.'

Brandt's *U433* had returned to Eckernforde from her last war cruise in the early morning of February 14. Two days later he had seen her safely on to a dockyard slipway to undergo refit where the following night she had sustained a direct hit from a 500 lb bomb during an Allied bombing-raid. Left without a boat, he and his crew had been transferred to the Reserve Pool at Lubeck-Travemunde on March 3 to await fresh appointments. Resigned to the fact that, should he be lucky enough to be appointed a new command, it would only be when his experienced crew had been transferred to other boats seeking replacements, Brandt had become puzzled and curious when they had unaccountably remained together. Then when he had half convinced himself that through some peculiar oversight on the part of Headquarters, both himself and his crew had been forgotten, he had received a letter from an uncle with a request that he spend a few days leave with him in Berlin.

And so Brandt had duly arrived in Berlin on the morning of March 13 where he was met by his uncle and driven to his house out at Schlachtensee. Dr Rudolf Schreyer was a former leading member of the RKF Office, Reichskommissar fur die Festigung Deutschen Volkstums, where he had served as senior planner responsible for the seizure of all Polish-Jewish property in Poland, a post from which he had been forced to retire on the grounds of ill-health. A close friend of Bormann from early Nazi days, they had served together for a period under Rudolf Hess at his bureau headquarters in Obersalzberg before

Schreyer transferred his talents to the RKF Office. Bormann had never forgotten him, but of greater importance was the fact that his nephew, Oskar Brandt, whom Bormann had first met as a naval cadet in 1935, had attained the rank of Kapitanleutnant with the U-boat Force. Further, Brandt was one of the few still surviving U-boat officers who had previously made the voyage to Latin America.

In January 1944 Brandt had been serving as Executive Officer on board *U353* under command of Kapitanleutnant Wolfram Eckardt. Based at Lorient and officially cleared for a war cruise in the area off Cape Hatteras, *U353* had on secret orders put into a deserted stretch of coast between Cabo Carvoeiro and Cabo da Roca, north-west of Lisbon, and embarked forty-three packing cases and strong-boxes from a fishing schooner, and had later delivered the consignment to a tender in the vicinity of Comodoro Rivadavia, the Argentine.

That first night in Berlin, Dr Rudolf Schreyer and his nephew had been joined after dinner by Bormann who had arrived alone dressed in civilian clothes. As always, Bormann had not wasted time with preliminaries once he had arrived at a decision, and forty minutes later Brandt had been overwhelmed by the honour of finding himself unexpectedly entrusted with the responsibility for the delivery of Shipment No. 11372 to the Argentine. But Bormann did not believe in assigning the entire responsibility for so important a delivery to a mere U-boat Kommandant, even though he was the nephew of a trusted friend. Unknown to Brandt, the real custodian of Shipment No. 11372 was to be a certain Paul August Hoffmeister, by reason that Bormann had long since found it to be at all times advantageous to have someone in overall charge of a situation who was known to be intimately associated with at least one member of the Nazi hierarchy.

On his return to Lubeck-Travemunde, Brandt had held himself and his crew in a state of readiness, prepared to move out at a moment's notice for whichever destination he was ordered. Those orders had finally arrived the previous evening at 21.00 when the Duty Officer had reported to Brandt's quarters with a teletype message instructing him to leave at once with his crew for the Mecklenburg Compound. They had pulled out from the local compound in two allocated trucks at 22.00, leaving behind a thinly clouded sky lit by the glow of Hamburg blazing in the distance under an avalanche of Allied bombs.

Now, two kilometres beyond Gustrow, PO Seaman Dehn, the driver of the leading truck, slowed and changed down gear to pull over to the side of the road.

At Dehn's side, Brandt stirred and looked at him sharply. 'What is it?'

'There, up ahead, Herr Kommandant.'

In the drab grey light Brandt saw a tank convoy headed towards them out of the east. 'Very well. Get us off the road.'

Both trucks were parked high on the shoulder of the road when the eight camouflaged King Tiger tanks, followed by six large supply trucks, clanked dim, ponderous forms towards them. In the leading tank the commander stood in the open hatch wrapped in a dirty sheepskin coat, a muffler wound around his lower face, goggles pushed up on to a battered cap, and a pair of binoculars draped around his neck. When the tank drew abreast of the two naval trucks it lumbered to a noisy halt and the commander stared at them with open curiosity. Then he pulled aside his muffler and called across to Brandt with a wide grin, 'On your way to Berlin, sailor?'

Brandt stared at him frostily. 'Why do you ask?'

The commander, a Panzer Captain, shrugged indifference and said cheerily, 'I thought perhaps you might be looking for Zhukov.'

Brandt missed the point of the remark entirely. 'We happen to be on our way to Greifswald,' he stated coldly.

'And may I ask if you're in any particular hurry?' the Panzer Captain cheerily inquired.

Irritated by the man's cheerful insolence, Brandt said, 'Why?'

The Panzer Captain thought, where do they find all these aloof shits in fancy greatcoats? Then he glanced overhead at the grey sky and with an even more insolent grin, said, 'If you want some good advice you'd do well to get off the road before it begins to get too light.'

Brandt stared at him with cold eyes. 'So you consider the roads to be a death-trap in daylight?'

The Panzer Captain's grin grew wider, more infuriatingly insolent. 'Listen, those Allied pilots can clip the ears off a rabbit at two thousand metres. I'm headed for some woods the other side of town to deploy till nightfall.'

Brandt sent an uncertain glance at the low clouded sky but remained silent.

'Safe journey to you anyway.' With a casual wave of an arm the Panzer Captain called into the turret, and flames belched from the twin exhausts as the King Tiger revved into motion and lumbered towards Gustrow, leaving the others to take up the rear, treads clanking on the metalled roadway.

Meanwhile Brandt scanned the roadway up ahead, undecided about whether or not to heed the Panzer Captain's advice. Some two kilometres further on a dark stretch of pine forest swept over a hillside to northward. He alighted on to the roadway and walked back to meet his Executive Officer, Leutnant Siegfried Harzer, climbing down from the cab of the second truck. 'You heard the tank commander?' he tersely demanded.

Leutnant Harzer pulled the collar of his greatcoat up around his ears, and glanced around him at the countryside. 'Yes, sir. I heard him.'

Brandt gazed off to eastward uncertainly. The sky had lightened considerably. Heavy cloud lay over the sombre countryside, driven scudding before the wind. He decided that the morning already bore the promise of rain. 'I wouldn't have thought it ideal flying weather but I suggest we find shelter for the time being along the edge of that pine forest up ahead.'

Twenty minutes later the two trucks were concealed beneath the overhang of pines, their fifty-four occupants huddled in groups eating breakfast of tinned salt herring and brown bread.

PO Telegraphist Bernard crammed half a herring into his mouth and scowled around him at the gloomy aisles of the forest. The only sound was that of the wind in the tree-tops. He shook his head in disgust. 'What a hell of a way to begin the day.'

PO Electrician Voss was doubtful. 'I don't know about that. It's better than getting shot up on the road. That Panzer Captain ought to know what he's talking about.'

*

By 8.35 am the small convoy under command of SS-Hauptsturmführer Wohldorf was headed north on the stretch of highway between Neustelitz and Neubrandenburg. The four vehicles maintained close formation under a grey sky from which the promise of further rain had receded with the freshening wind.

In the front passenger seat of the Citroen, Wohldorf stared fixedly ahead at the long ribbon of asphalt which unfolded before them when they emerged from beneath a roadside copse of spruce trees. The layer of cloud was still breaking up, driven south by the wind, and now cold fingers of golden sunlight speared across the sombre North German countryside. Not another vehicle showed anywhere in sight, and it had been the same ever since they had left the northern suburbs of Berlin behind. Only once, three kilometres south of Neustrelitz, they had overtaken a farmer leading two horses yoked to muddied carts, but, apart from that isolated incident, nothing.

Once out on the open highway, Wohldorf sat forward and made a careful search of the sky through the mud-spattered windshield. Nothing showed, and in the distance, lying beyond the swathe of evergreen forest which spread itself either side of the highway ahead, was the picturesque town of Neubrandenburg. 'Put your foot down a little further.'

Schramm caught the note of uneasiness in Wohldorf's voice, glanced in the rearview mirror, and eased his foot down on the accelerator.

When the Citroen surged forward Wohldorf turned to look back through the rear window and saw the gap widen between them and the leading truck. Noting that its driver was unable to wrest anything further from his already overstrained motor, he growled, 'Slow it again. We aren't going to get anything more out of those scrap-heaps.' Then he sat back into his seat to light a cigarette.

At his superior's side Schramm glanced out at the deserted landscape with undisguised curiosity. 'It's almost as if everyone's disappeared off the face of the earth. What do you suppose they're all afraid of?'

Wohldorf might not have heard him. His attention was elsewhere. The sky was now uncomfortably clear. Cloud was being driven by the wind in ragged snatches across an increasing expanse of icy blue sky. But they were swiftly approaching the forest now, and then a shadow cast itself overhead when the Citroen entered the cavern of evergreen foliage which overhung the highway. 'Pull over,' he directed.

Schramm slowed and eased the Citroen to a halt on the thick

wayside carpet of pine needles, and while the trucks growled to a halt one after the other in rear, both men alighted and walked back to meet them.

'There's no point in us taking unnecessary risks,' Wohldorf informed the drivers. 'We stay here till dusk.'

*

The time was 14.50 and Kapitanleutnant Brandt was fuming with impatience. He and his men had idled away the day sitting around like idiots under cover of the forest, and now the men had become ill-tempered and morose, the only meal which they had brought with them consumed at daylight. More irritating, no-one had as much as glimpsed an aircraft, friendly or otherwise, throughout the day. He slapped his gloved hands together in frustration and cursed having met the Panzer convoy earlier in the day, knowing that had he proceeded as originally intended they would have been well on their way towards the Mecklenburg Compound.

With a contemptuous snort he walked out into the roadway and scanned the expanse of clear blue sky which was marred only by snatches of fleecy white cloud. There was no sign of an aircraft anywhere in sight, not even a vapour trail. He arrived at a decision and returned to where his Executive Officer and Chief Engineer were waiting beneath the pines. 'That Panzer Captain was obviously talking nonsense. We've wasted enough time sitting around here. Let's get on our way.'

By the time they had covered five kilometres Brandt was convinced that he had made the correct decision; he had not even been able to detect the passage of a bird against the flawless afternoon sky. Trees and hedgerows were in bud and to eastward he caught a glimpse of a greystone farmhouse on the far side of a meadow, its windows reflecting squares of golden sunlight. And then he was suddenly startled by the urgent blast of a motor horn in the rear and glanced into the wing mirror to see the other truck closing fast, its driver, PO Electrician Voss, gesturing at them frantically while Harzer had his head outside the other window gazing back along the roadway. He switched his attention to Dehn. 'What's going on back there?'

Dehn was too engrossed in his own mirror to answer, saw Harzer suddenly withdraw his head while Voss hunched himself over at the wheel, and he instinctively put his own foot to the floor as the quickly growing roar reached an ear-splitting crescendo. Then the shadow swept overhead in a power-pulling scream and the ground either side of the roadway erupted in a flash of orange and red flame, heaving boulders and clods of dirt out of the ground.

Caught in the blast of the exploding rockets, the truck lurched and swayed, threatened to twist out of Dehn's control, then righted itself with him clinging desperately to the wheel.

Meanwhile Brandt's shocked mind dully registered the fact that the aircraft was a Typhoon, the black and white markings and RAF rondels on its wings clearly visible as it climbed steeply upward away from the roadway. And then the air was filled with the hammering of cannon when another aircraft swept down in rear. Again clods of dirt hurtled through the air and shells tore a staggering path around the two vehicles.

In the second truck Leutnant Harzer turned screaming, panic-stricken on Voss. *'Get us off the road! Get the truck off the road!'* Then he felt the jolting shudder of shells hammer through the truck, and amid the confusion and the screams of the dying he saw Brandt's truck disintegrate in a brilliant orange flash. And suddenly a blast of heat, so fierce that it seared his lungs and shrivelled his flesh, enveloped the cab and he struggled to cry out, but with the shattering explosion came merciful darkness.

*

The first thing that PO Telegraphist Bernard became aware of when he regained consciousness was the sound of a voice calling soothingly to him from a very great distance. As the sound gradually drew nearer he groaned aloud and his eyelids fluttered spasmodically. When the voice was so close that it sounded like a whisper in his ear he stirred and tried to raise himself up, but was met by a jolt of pain which knifed through his body.

'No. Lie still like a good fellow. You'll be fine – just fine,' the soothing voice assured him.

He turned his face and felt the touch of dew-wet grass against his cheek. When the feeling of nausea receded he opened his eys and found himself staring up at a sky that glowed the colour of blood.

'You see, you're going to be fine – just fine,' the soothing voice intruded.

He turned his head and saw the tear-stained face of an elderly woman whose white hair was tied under a blue woollen scarf. She knelt on the ground beside him, and beyond he could see a greystone farmhouse on the far side of a meadow, windows glittering as if on fire. Then he felt suddenly cold and began to shiver, and he closed his eyes while the soothing voice drifted far into the distance.

When PO Telegraphist Bernard next opened his eyes he was suffering from a thirst so violent his swollen tongue seemed to fill his mouth.

'Ah, so you're finally with us.'

Bernard turned his head and found himself looking up at a matronly figure in white.

She smiled into his face. 'You're in hospital – in Gustrow.'

Bernard tried to run his swollen tongue around inside his mouth, over his parched lips. 'Give me a drink,' he croaked.

The nurse put the stem of a porcelain cup to his mouth and he sucked on it greedily. When finished, he glanced down at himself, at his plaster-encased left arm, and at his left leg suspended on a sling which hung from a pulley in the ceiling.

'We set your arm for you, and your leg,' the nurse cheerfully informed him. 'You'll be up and around in next to no time.'

For Bernard the blurred events of the afternoon suddenly found pattern; the gloomy forest, the roar of diving aircraft, the thunder of cannon shell, and the blinding flash of exploding rockets. He also remembered the touch of dew-wet grass on his cheek, the soothing voice which had called to him, and the tear-stained face under the blue woollen scarf. Then panic arose in him when he remembered his friends in the second truck: Voss, Bruckhardt, and Horkenbach. He glanced around the small room with its shaded light and green screens around the bottom of the bed as if searching for some clue to them.

The nurse leaned over him attentively. 'What is it?'

'Voss,' said Bernard, a shrill note of alarm in his voice. 'Where's Voss and the others?'

'Please,' the nurse told him. 'You mustn't concern yourself. Someone will be in to see you soon.'

Within a few moments of the nurse leaving, Bernard saw a man in his late forties enter the room. Tall and thin, he was dressed in a dark suit, white shirt, and blue neck-tie. His face was gaunt, his black hair plastered close to his skull, and when he looked down at the bed it was with a dark, penetrating gaze. 'Petty Officer Bernard?' The voice, like the face, strangely lacked emotion.

Bernard felt instinctively apprehensive in his presence. 'Yes, sir.'

The man stood close to the bed. 'How do you feel?'

'Not too badly, sir.'

The man said matter-of-factly, 'Do you remember what happened?'

Bernard raised his head from the pillow in an effort to assure his visitor that his memory for past events was unimpaired. 'Yes, sir. We were strafed, sir.'

Bernard said anxiously, 'The others, sir. What about the others? Are they all right?'

'Perfectly,' the man assured him.

Bernard's relief at the news was evident. He rested his head back on the pillow. 'I can't seem to remember seeing anyone else about except for an old woman.'

'Yes,' the man said; then asked, 'What's your Commanding Officer's name?'

Bernard answered with a perplexed frown, 'Brandt – Kapitanleutnant Brandt, sir.'

'And what were you doing on the road today?'

Bernard answered with increasing perplexity, 'We were on our way to the Mecklenburg Compound from Lubeck-Travemunde, sir. Haven't you spoken with Kapitanleutant Brandt?'

'Don't worry about it,' the man informed him. 'I was merely asking a question or two in order to satisfy my own curiosity.'

'What are you – a doctor, sir?'

The man smiled at some private thought. 'Yes – something like that.'

Bernard was undecided, stared after the man as he prepared to leave. 'Is that all?' he asked.

'Yes,' the man said from the doorway. 'Get a good night's rest.'

*

The time was 11.40 pm when the convoy of three heavy supply trucks preceded by the Citroen swung over the approach road on the hill south of the Mecklenburg Compound and dropped down towards the main gate. Schramm drew the car to a halt in front of the gate where Wohldorf wound down his window and awaited the approach of the guard.

The Duty Guard Petty Officer bent his head to the window, flicked on his hooded flashlight, and stiffened instinctively at sight of the black and silver uniform.

Wohldorf informed him curtly, 'Korvettenkapitan Lamprecht is expecting us.'

The Petty Officer sprang to attention. 'Yes, Herr Hauptsturmführer!' With an impatient snap of his fingers to the two guards waiting nearby, he gestured at the gate. 'Get it open – quickly!'

In reply the two guards hurriedly slung their machine-pistols and shouldered the gate open.

As the Citroen prepared to move off the Petty Officer called into the open window, 'Just follow the road, Herr Hauptsturmführer.' And when the third truck whined past him he turned back to the guardroom and snatched up the phone to ring the Kommandant's Office in the compound below.

The voice on the other end of the line said, 'Korvettenkapitan Lamprecht speaking.'

'This is the guardroom at the main gate, Herr Kommandant. Three supply trucks accompanied by a Citroen car have just entered the compound. The senior SS officer said you were expecting him, sir.'

'Thank you.' Lamprecht put the phone down, collected his greatcoat, and emerged from the Administration building on the south side of the small parade ground in time to see the dimmed headlights of the convoy appear out of the darkness from the direction of the main gate.

When the Citroen pulled to a halt, Wohldorf alighted to confront Lamprecht while the three trucks growled to a halt in the rear. 'Korvettenkapitan Lamprecht?'

Lamprecht affirmed the fact with a polite inclination of his head.

Wohldorf clicked his heels. 'SS-Hauptsturmführer Ernst Wohldorf.'

Lamprecht studied the man uneasily. He had always experienced a vague sense of discomfort in the presence of those beings to whom superiority and confidence seemed a natural endowment, especially so when they belonged to the ranks of the SS. And this one, immaculate and polished, looked as if he had stepped straight out from an early photograph in the *Volkischer Beobachter* when invincible Teutonic legions had first set out across the mighty plains of Europe in a bid to conquer the world. Indeed, all that the night appeared to lack was the tragic and climatic strains of *Die Gotterdammerung*. 'Yes, I received a call from the Reichsleiter this morning to explain the situation. I had, however, half expected you earlier in the evening.'

Wohldorf replied with a coolness which verged on rudeness, 'I decided not to take any risks on the road during daylight, and we stopped in a forest south of Neubrandenburg till light began to fade. Only then did I think it wise to continue.'

Despite a natural dislike for the man, Lamprecht knew he had to tread with extreme care, and above all he could not afford to be indiscreet. The SS man had taken the place of the mysterious Paul August Hoffmeister, and he was totally ignorant of his relationship with the Reichsleiter. He said placidly, 'Well you're here now. That's the important thing.'

'And the contents of the trucks?' Wohldorf curtly demanded.

'Arrangements for their unloading have already been made,' answered Lamprecht. 'My adjutant, Leutnant Berger, and a work-party will be here in a few minutes. I alerted him to your arrival. In the meantime I suggest that your drivers and escorts retire to the galley till they are further required. The less they see the better. Their trucks will be ready to move out again before daylight.' Lamprecht indicated a shadowy cluster of bomb-damaged buildings on the eastern side of the parade ground. 'They will find the galley across there, or that part of it still in use.'

Wohldorf turned towards the trucks and saw Leutnant Berger arrive with a twenty-six man work-party dressed in green battle fatigues. After halting his men beside the trucks, Berger, a young man full of energy and enthusiasm, strode briskly across to report to Lamprecht, and together the three officers watched the Wehrmacht drivers and escorts cross the parade ground in the direction of the galley. Lamprecht then introduced Wohldorf to Berger, and said, 'Do you have the list of serial numbers?'

Wohldorf brought the list from a pocket of his greatcoat and passed it to Lamprecht. 'There's a total of one hundred and seventy-two items.'

'Yes, so I was informed.' Lamprecht scanned the list with the aid of Berger's flashlight, then handed it to him. 'The canisters are for the outside torpedo stowage. Leave them till last, and be careful with them.'

Berger saluted, returned the flashlight to his pocket, shouted instructions to his work-party, and within two minutes the three trucks were headed back in the direction of the main gate above the compound.

Wohldorf watched the dim glow of their tail-lights become consumed by the darkness. 'How many people know about this?'

Lemprecht replied with cool reassurance, 'No more than necessary. The Reichsleiter is acquainted with the situation. In the next day or so most of these men will be on their way to Berlin to form a Naval Division which will join with Army Group Vistula under the command of Generaloberst Gotthard Heinrici. Although one can't expect complete silence, I assure you that every possible safeguard has been taken against there being too many loose tongues.'

Placated, Wohldorf said, 'I was merely curious.'

Lamprecht cast a critical eye over him, and said stiffly, 'Now if you and your aide care to accompany me I will have a steward show you to some temporary quarters in the east wing of the Administration building here. A meal ought to be ready for you soon.'

An hour later, after they had eaten, Wohldorf and Schramm joined Lamprecht in his office. Lamprecht was vexed by the non-arrival of Brandt and his crew and was in a testy and impatient mood. 'They ought to have been here long before now,' he complained bitterly. 'They left the Lubeck-Travemunde Compound at 22.00 hours on the 29th. It's ludicrous that they should be this length of time overdue. There remains a considerable number of last minute checks to be carried out on board *U501* before she can put to sea. One can't expect a crew to take over a U-boat five minutes before she leaves the pier.'

Before he had finished speaking the phone on his desk began to shrill. He snatched it up impatiently, expected to hear the Duty Guard PO on the main gate inform him of Brandts belated arrival, but instead heard the compound switchboard operator say, 'A call for you from Gustrow, Herr Kommandant.'

Lamprecht frowned, puzzled. 'Where? Did they say who it was?'

'No, sir. They merely requested to talk to the Kommandant.'

Lamprecht grunted irritably, 'Very well. Put them through.'

Next moment a voice said, 'The Kommandant Mecklenburg Compound?'

'Yes, Korvettenkapitan Lamprecht speaking.'

'This is Sturmbannführer Manfred Kleist of Geheime Staatspolizei Headquarters Gustrow. I have reason to believe that you may be in a position to aid my inquiries regarding an incident concerning two truckloads of naval personnel.'

Lamprecht went cold. 'What do you mean?' he interjected.

On the other end of the phone Sturmbannführer Kleist said patiently, 'Are you acquainted with a certain Kapitanleutnant Brandt?'

Lamprecht snapped, 'What about Brandt?'

'He's dead,' Kleist said simply.

Lamprecht was stunned. '*Dead?*' he said in rank disbelief.

'And all his men along with him except one,' Kleist confirmed. 'A Petty Officer Telegraphist named Bernard was the sole survivor.'

Lamprecht quickly recovered from the initial shock of the news and inquired sharply, 'Do you have details of what happened?'

'Their trucks came under Allied air-attack yesterday afternoon. Both received direct hits from rockets. A local farmer and his wife drove Bernard to hospital in Gustrow. The incident occurred nine kilometres east of here. I went out to take a look for myself when I heard the news.'

Lamprecht snapped angrily, 'And I'm being informed about this only *now*?'

In calm, unhurried tones, Kleist answered, 'That's simply because I'd no idea who they were, where they'd come from, or where they were going. I sent a detachment of local Volkssturm out to tidy up the mess and attempt to make some form of identification of the dead, but even so my initial inquiries met with no success. No-one I was able to contact appeared to know anything about the men. I had to wait for Bernard to regain consciousness before I was able to establish any concrete facts. Indeed, I returned from the hospital only a short time ago.'

Lamprecht sighed, and in a hollow voice said, 'Then leave

me to notify the appropriate authority. Be assured they will take it from there.' When he replaced the phone it was to find Wohldorf and Schramm staring at him with questioning faces. 'The Gestapo,' he explained, and went on to relate what Kleist had just told him.

Wohldorf was instantly on his feet. 'Then the Reichsleiter must be informed about this at once!'

Lamprecht regarded him coldly. 'I'm quite well aware of what must be done.' Then he again reached for the phone and gave the switchboard operator a Berlin number to contact via Exchange 500 at Supreme Headquarters Zossen.

After an anxious two minute interval a voice in Berlin answered with brevity, 'Bormann.'

Lamprecht had steeled himself to break the news bluntly, determined to have the unpleasantness dispensed with as quickly as possible. 'Lamprecht here,' he announced stolidly. 'I'm afraid I must inform you that I've just received the most unfortunate news. A certain Sturmbannführer Kleist of Geheime Staatspolizei Headquarters Gustrow informed me that the trucks in which Brandt and his crew were travelling were attacked by Allied aircraft nine kilometres east of there yesterday afternoon. He states there as being only one survivor.'

The news was received with a shocked silence. Then in a strained whisper, Bormann said, 'Repeat that!'

Lamprecht stood looking nervously at Wohldorf as he repeated the information.

In turn Bormann found it incredible, inconceivable that he should again be destined to meet with last minute misfortune. 'Why wasn't I informed about this earlier?' he suddenly raged.

Lamprecht argued meekly, 'But it was only a few minutes ago that I myself received the news.'

In his office in the Führerhauptquartier, Bormann simmered with rage and frustration. The meticulous and intricate arrangements which had required months of concentrated work and preparation did not allow for the departure of *U501* to be delayed indefinitely. An experienced replacement crew had to be found at once, immediately, and Bormann saw that Lamprecht was of no use to him in that particular respect. With considerable effort he brought his emotions under control. 'Then I must come back to you on this matter. But first – has Wohldorf arrived?'

Lamprecht was overwhelmingly relieved not to find himself

subjected to a prolonged and enraged tirade. He said quickly, 'He's here with me now, and the cases are in the process of being transferred from the trucks at this very moment.'

'Then have him remain with you till I call back,' Bormann instructed.

In Berlin, Bormann made two phone calls, the first to SS-Obergruppenführer Heinrich Muller, Chief of Gestapo, at his office on Prinz Albrecht Strasse, who, after contacting Gustrow, called back ten minutes later to confirm that Lamprecht's news regarding Brandt and his crew was correct, and the second to U-boat Headquarters at Lager Koralle on the outskirts of Berlin. The phone was lifted almost before it commenced to ring. 'Penns?' he questioned the answering voice. Then said, 'I've just heard that Brandt and his crew were killed as a result of an Allied air-attack outside Gustrow yesterday afternoon. I assume that you appreciate just what this means? We require another crew without delay.'

The voice out at Lager Koralle was hesitant, but answered with polite formality, 'But I'm afraid that's impossible. To find a replacement crew at a time like this is out of the question – truly impossible. A state of utter chaos exists at the moment as far as U-boat personnel is concerned. Headquarters' directive of the 25th stated that all ratings not required for immediate sea-duty were to be dispatched to Lichterfelde Barracks, Berlin without delay in order to form a Naval Division attached to Army Group Vistula. And hundreds, thousands of men are already on their way from bases all along the North German coast.'

Bormann broke in impatiently, 'But a crew must be found somewhere.'

'I'm sorry, no,' Penns argued delicately. 'And to attempt to put one together is also impossible. Such a crew would require weeks, months of intensive training and exercise before they were ready for active duty as a cohesive unit. It was for this precise reason that Brandt and his crew were kept intact after their transfer to Lubeck-Travemunde.'

Bormann's voice sounded close to hysteria as it thundered down the line, 'But a crew *must* be found! You're more than acquainted with the situation!'

'Very well.' The answering voice was not entirely successful in its attempt to muffle its note of exasperation. 'But I'm afraid all I can do is to check around with the various bases.'

Bormann snapped vehemently, 'Then get on with it! And I want results!'

*

U207 had arrived in the Kattegat at dawn on the morning of March 29. Nursing both diesels, they had surfaced in thick fog, and with the crew closed up at Battle Stations, had begun the long run through that treacherous stretch of water towards Flotilla Headquarters at Kiel. By 23.00 they had safely navigated the narrow strip of water that was the Store Baelt and were limping down between Langeland and Lolland with their bows, pushing through an oily sea almost totally obscured by a dank fog which smeared the lookouts' binoculars and trickled in rivulets from their foul-weather gear. At midnight the town of Nakskov was astern on the port quarter, the southernmost tip of Langeland lost on the starboard beam. Out ahead lay the Kieler Bucht, and Rink gave instructions for an alteration of course which brought *U207*'s bows around south-westerly towards Kiel.

Dropping his binoculars down, the vizor of his cap dripping water, he leaned his head to the bridge voice-tube. 'Sound-room?'

The reply came back promptly, 'Faint impulses for 'ard and after sectors, Herr Kommandant.'

Rink returned his attention to the thick blanket of fog which drifted down off the coast of Sweden. There were times when he would have cursed it, but on this occasion he was thankful for its protective cloak which had done much to shroud them from Allied eyes since they had started their run down out of the Kattegat. But his one wish was that they had been able to make better speed, as, due to the dangerous conditions of the boat, the crew were exhausted and he wanted to get them home without unnecessary delay and further trouble.

Their submerged crawl for home had taken twelve long nerve-wracking days during which time they had been continually harried by Allied hunter-killer groups scouring the waters east between the Shetland Islands and the Norwegian coast. Altogether it had been a war cruise fraught with danger from the moment of sailing, although it had turned out to be a profitable one. Yet he knew that, by having deliberately ignored operational procedure in not reporting their position and successes after their attack on the convoy in the later afternoon of March 18, they would almost certainly have been reported overdue, presumed missing. But he was not unduly concerned about flouting operational procedure. At least he had brought them home alive, and if Headquarters' staff in their cosy little complex at Lager Koralle did not like it, then they could all go and jump in the Spree as far as he was concerned.

U207's list of defects was a formidable one, and from the course which the war had taken it was almost certain she would never put to sea again in an operational capacity. And despite their personal victory in keeping *U207* afloat, it appeared that all they could expect in the way of reward was to be drafted into the infantry if the Armed Forces' communiques picked up en route for home bore any relation to the actual truth of the general situation. More disheartening evidence of the devastating trends which events had taken was the bitter fact that they had heard the last pitiful signals of no less than thirteen U-boats in the past four days.

But Rink did not intend to allow himself to become afflicted with an air of defeatism. 'Exec,' he called into the voice-tube.

'Yes, Herr Kommandant?' von Heydekampf's voice carried back.

'I think we can now let Headquarters know we're still alive. Make: ETA KIEL 05.00. REPORT DELAYED DUE TO HAZARDOUS CONDITION OF BOAT. AWAIT INSTRUCTIONS. And add a few choice items from our list of damages. That ought to give them something to speculate about.'

*

U207's signal was received in the Operational Telecommunications Room at U-boat Headquarters Lager Koralle at 02.25 on the morning of March 30, and immediately forwarded to the office of Senior Operations Officer U-boats West where it arrived on the desk of Leutnant Fischer, assistant Duty Officer. Fischer read the deciphered signal with marked surprise, then rose and hurried across the brightly-lit room to his superior's office.

At Fischer's knock, Fregattenkapitan Werner Penns slammed down the phone and beckoned impatiently for him to enter.

Fischer thrust the signal across the desk. 'It just arrived, sir,' he explained. 'It seems we still have *U207* with us after all. But look at those damages. It sounds as if she's fit for nothing more than scrap-iron.'

Fregattenkapitan Penns was no longer listening to his aide, but was already on his feet gazing pensively at the large wall map on the other side of the room. In an almost abstracted voice, he said, 'Very well, Fischer. Leave this with me.'

When Fischer left, Penns immediately placed a call to Exchange 500 at Zossen, and less than two minutes later was talking with Bormann in the Führerhauptquartier at the Reichskanzlei. 'I may have something worth your consideration,' he explained. 'My other inquiries have so far produced negative results but I'm now informed that we have a boat on her way home from a war cruise and headed for Flotilla Headquarters at Kiel. Furthermore, she's of exactly the same Class as *U501*, another point in our favour where her crew is concerned. I believe it's just conceivable that it could be arranged for her to be diverted to the Mecklenburg Compound – if my meaning is clear.'

Bormann readily understood what was being said. 'Is it possible?'

'I don't see why not. But theoretically it must be arranged through Lamprecht. This signal has been logged and therefore everything will have to be taken from there on an official basis. What I require from Lamprecht is an official report about what happened to Brandt and his crew together with details about whom to contact in Gustrow with a view to having his report corroborated. Then I must have a request for a replacement crew to take *U501* to Kristiansand. And if *U207* is really as extensively damaged as her Kommandant appears to claim in his signal to Headquarters, then it shouldn't arouse official argument if she's diverted to the Mecklenburg Compound in order that her crew take over *U501*, so as to comply with the Grossadmiral's directive of March 25th that all seaworthy U-boats be dispatched to Kristiansand with a view to forming a new operational defence arm. In fact I'm confident that such an arrangement will meet with his full approval.'

Bormann replied with an enthusiasm he found difficult to control, 'Yes, I understand perfectly. And from there I assume that we proceed as previously arranged, just as if Brandt was in command.'

'Exactly.'

Bormann hesitated, overtaken by another thought. 'One thing,' he said cautiously. 'Who is this new Kommandant? What do you personally know about him – anything?'

'His name's Rink,' Fregattenkapitan Penns informed him. 'Kapitanleutnant Wolfgang Rink – one of our few remaining U-boat officers on whom the tribute *ace* can be conferred without allowing patriotism to distort one's sense of judgement.'

Bormann remained hesitant, cautious. 'That may be so. And naturally I've heard of the man. Nonetheless I'd like to know more about him. Can that be arranged?'

'Of course, but it will take a little time. I can call you back when the required information is at hand. Meanwhile I suggest that Lamprecht gets in touch with Headquarters at once. I want everything official.'

*

At the Mecklenburg Compound, Lamprecht was composing his signal to Headquarters on receipt of Bormann's phone call. On the signal tablet before him he wrote: INFORMED BY GESTAPO HEADQUARTERS GUSTROW ONLY ONE SURVIVOR FROM BRANDT'S CREW AFTER ALLIED AIR-ATTACK YESTERDAY PM. REQUEST REPLACEMENT CREW BE MADE AVAILABLE IMMEDIATELY TO TRANSFER U501 TO KRISTIANSAND RE-HEADQUARTERS DIRECTIVE MARCH 25 – LAMPRECHT – KOMMANDANT – MECKLENBURG COMPOUND. When finished he called the Communications Office in the west wing of the building and summoned the duty operator to his office.

'This new Kommandant the Reichsleiter mentioned,' said Wohldorf, lounging in his chair. 'Do you know him?'

Lamprecht looked up from his desk. 'Rink? I met him fleetingly last year at Lager Koralle when he received the Knight's Cross to the Iron Cross from the Grossadmiral.'

Wohldorf glanced smiling at Schramm, and said deprecatingly, 'And *what* does that imply?'

Lamprecht's gaze was long and candid. He said with cool reserve, 'Several facts. The first being that if *I* were sailing with *U501* I'd rather do so with Rink in command than Brandt. Not only has he met with spectacular success in his time, but more important, he's an officer with vast experience and an iron will to survive whatever the odds, truly dependable. I don't remember the exact details of the affair now, but he was something of a national celebrity even before he joined the U-boat Force, when during the early days of the war he was serving as an officer in the Merchantile Marine and successfully brought his ship home from a distant foreign port in the face of the British blockade – no insignificant achievement, I assure you, gentlemen.' And interrupted by a knock on the door, Lamprecht lifted his gaze across the room. 'Enter.'

A PO Telegraphist entered the room, glanced uneasily at the two SS men, then devoted his attention to Lamprecht. 'You sent for me, Herr Kommandant?'

'Yes.' Lamprecht tore the top slip from the signal tablet and pushed it across the desk. 'Get this on to the teletype for Lager Koralle at once,' he instructed.

Wohldorf watched indifferently while the PO turned on his heel and left the room, then said, 'Purely as a matter of personal interest, what are we going to do between now and when this *U207* decides to put in an appearance?'

'Tomorrow morning the Compound Chief Engineer and his team of machinists and technicians will commence a final check of *U501*'s machinery in order to save time when Rink and his crew take over. Leutnant Berger will also see to it that the present guard is doubled once Shipment No. 11372 has been safely stowed on board. And after we have had breakfast I will personally show you over her. I'm sure it will prove an illuminating experience for you both,' Lamprecht concluded with a smile.

*

Bormann's second call from Lager Koralle reached him fifteen minutes after receipt of Lamprecht's signal by Senior Operations Officer U-boats West at Headquarters. And with the same polite formality as before, Fregattenkapitan Penns explained, 'I'm now in a position to officially clear *U207* for diversion to the Mecklenburg Compound if the information now at hand concerning her Kommandant meets with your approval. His service record has just this instant arrived on my desk.'

Bormann said attentively, 'I'm listening.'

'Kapitanleutnant Wolfgang Rink,' Penns read over the line, 'born Cuxhaven February 17th, 1918, only son of Johann Hendrick Rink, Senior Kapitan with the Pacific-Orient Line. Both parents now deceased.

'Joined the Backenkohler Line on March 8th, 1932, and was regarded as a distinguished and enthusiastic officer cadet. His promotion was rapid, and he served his early years in vessels plying the South Atlantic, Pacific, and Far Eastern waters.

'While First Officer of the 5,600 tons tramp freighter *Anneliese Menzel*, and with her Kapitan hospitalised on shore, Rink assumed command of the vessel in Singapore on September 2nd, 1939, and put to sea in order to evade internment by the British on the Declaration of War. Crossing the Pacific and South Atlantic, the *Anneliese Menzel* was one of the few vessels to successfully run the British blockade, and docked at Bremerhaven on February 27th, 1940, with a cargo of wolfram and molybdenum.

'After enlistment in the Kriegsmarine on April 12th, 1940, he transferred to the U-boat Force on October 4th the same year, and while he rose to attain the rank of Oberleutnant he served with the 7th Flotilla at St Nazaire, the 9th Flotilla at Toulon, and the 10th Flotilla at Lorient. On March 22nd, 1942, he was appointed his own command, and on February 10th, 1944, was decorated with the Knight's Cross to the Iron Cross on being accredited with the sinking of 103,258 tons of Allied shipping. On May 3rd, 1944, he was promoted to rank of Kapitanleutnant.

'He is regarded as a first class seaman who possesses exceptional skill and judgement, his many exploits bearing the same hallmark of courage and daring.

'I trust this information meets with your requirements?'

'Decidedly so,' Bormann enthused. 'But you made no mention of Party connections.'

'Simply because there's no note of any on record. However, this isn't unusual in the case of men who spent their youth at sea far from the Fatherland. I know several officers of similar background.'

'Yet he appears to possess all the other requirements.' Bormann had quickly regained his former enthusiasm, and he reached a decision without further deliberation. 'Yes, clear him for the Mecklenburg Compound. I will inform Lamprecht about the matter myself. But get this man Rink north as quickly as possible.'

'It will have my personal attention,' promised Fregattenkapitan Penns.

*

At 03.15 Kapitanleutnant Wolfgang Rink was handed the deciphered reply to the signal which he had earlier ordered to be made to Headquarters. At the chart-table in the control-room he quickly scanned the reply: U207 TO PROCEED MECKLENBURG COMPOUND WITHOUT FURTHER DELAY. ORDERS AWAIT – BdU. Rink shook his head. It was concise, to the point, and in the same vein as most other signals dispatched by Headquarters; it contained the absolute minimum of information. He was disappointed. He had been looking forward to himself and his crew being able to sit down to a large hot breakfast on shore by daylight. But such a diversion was not entirely unexpected if Kiel, along with other main North German ports, was being subjected to continual bombardment by Allied bomber fleets, and if such was the case, then there was every likelihood that the majority of U-boats still in service had been dispersed to less vulnerable bases. He sent a glance across the control-room and saw that his Executive Officer and Chief Engineer were waiting in anticipation of learning the contents of the signal. 'We've just been ordered to proceed to the Mecklenburg Compound,' he explained.

'Never heard of it,' von Heydekampf confessed with a frown.

Rink unfolded a fresh chart on to the chart-table. 'Left rudder,' he ordered, then watched the illuminated numerals of the gyro-repeater strip begin to swing around as the bows responded to the helmsman's alteration of course. 'Set course 095 degrees.'

Slowly *U207* steadied on her new course to run the Fehmarn Strait, to put Kiel astern on the starboard quarter. Once around Gedser on the southern promontory of Falster, the next landfall would be Kap Arkona.

Kernbach leaned over the fresh chart which Rink had unfolded. 'I thought as much,' he mused. 'It's south of Greifswald, the old Navigation School and the Baltic Training Flotilla Repair Compound.'

'Well I suppose that might please the Berliners we have on

board,' was von Heydekampf's wry comment. 'If we're destined to find ourselves with a few days of leave.'

'Perhaps so,' said Rink. 'But I sincerely doubt if they will be able to do very much in the way of making repairs to our old friend here if that's their reason for sending us north. In fact, we may not even yet make it there the way those diesels are behaving.' Then he reached overhead for the microphone of the broadcast system. '*Achtung!* This is the Kommandant speaking. We will not now enter Kiel harbour. Orders have been received to the effect that we proceed to the Mecklenburg Compound south of Griefswald. That is all.'

March 31. The night was cold but clear, the sea comparatively slight. Rink found what he was searching for at 20.40; the twin breakwaters which enclosed the harbour of the Mecklenburg Compound were just discernible against the base of a low hill on the thin dark strip of shore to south-eastward. He studied the area carefully through heavy night binoculars. Pines covered the dark slope right down to the pale gleam of sandy beach which adjoined the breakwaters on their inner ends. And beyond the breakwaters he picked out the dark silhouette of a signal tower where it stood etched against the starless skyline. He turned to the Signalman at his side. 'See the tower, Meyer?'

'Yes, Herr Kommandant.'

'Then let them have our recognition signal.'

Meyer leaned the hand signal-lamp on to the wind-deflector starboard side, sighted it on the jutting tower, and triggered off *U207*'s recognition signal.

Rink maintained a close watch on the shore for any reaction, saw a pin-prick of light wink out against the darkness to signify acknowledgement of the signal, and lowering his binoculars, said, 'Make: REQUEST PERMISSION TO ENTER HARBOUR.'

Again Meyer triggered off the signal; and from shore the light returned: STANDBY FOR ESCORT.

As they waited, the bridge watch huddled in the darkness of the horseshoe while they scanned sea and sky. Ten minutes elapsed before Rink saw the small vessel clear the entrance between the two breakwaters, an ancient coal-burning tug with a flurry of burning soot clearing her funnel. At a distance of two hundred metres she put herself cumbersomely about, her gun crew closed up at the multi-barrelled 20 mm anti-aircraft mounting abaft the funnel staring curiously out into the darkness, where the narrow column of *U207*'s tower showed dimly against the northern skyline, and then with her bows again aligned with the harbour entrance a light winked out from an after window of her wheelhouse: PLEASE FOLLOW.

Rink snapped open the cover of the voice-tube. 'Stop engines. Clutches out. Switches on. Group down. One-third ahead both.'

Now on electric drive, *U207* silently held to the tug's stern, and soon after they passed through the narrow entrance between the breakwaters with their blacked-out beacon standing on their extremities like blind sentinels.

Rink watched the tug draw aside to starboard and pull inside the western breakwater, while on the eastern breakwater a masked light flashed across the intervening expanse of enclosed water, and he saw the dim figures of a berthing-party awaiting them on the wall. 'Berthing-party on station. Small ahead both. Left rudder. Steady.'

When *U207* swung herself parallel with the breakwater her berthing-party was ready lining the for'ard and after catwalks.

'Midships.'

Next heaving-lines snaked out from the figures on the breakwater and were quickly hauled inboard to bring the mooring wires with them.

'Stop both.'

The reports from the catwalks came back swiftly when the boat rubbed her port saddle tanks gently against the bulky rubber fenders lining the breakwater. 'All secure for'ard – all secure aft – all secure fore and aft.'

'Boat secure alongside,' Rink called below. 'Ring off main motors.'

Then in the glow of masked lamps milling around on the wall opposite the tower, he caught a glimpse of gold and silver braid beside the gangway being manhandled on board abaft the *wintergarten* ladder port side.

Von Heydekampf's alert gaze also narrowed. He remarked uneasily, 'What do you suppose the SS are doing in a place like this?'

With a shrug of indifference, Rink answered, 'Perhaps they intend to shoot us because we chose to ignore operational procedure and didn't report to Headquarters earlier.' In the next breath, he added, 'Secure all hands.' Then he pulled off his sheepskin coat and passed it to von Heydekampf along with his binoculars. 'See to these while I go and meet our distinguished deputation. They appear to be somewhat anxious.'

Rink swung down the ladder from the *wintergarten* to the after catwalk, then strode up the gangway. When he stepped ashore it was to be met by a tall, hawk-faced officer. He touched a hand to the vizor of his battered white cap. '*U207* returned from war cruise, Herr Korvettenkapitan,' he intimated officially.

The officer stiffly returned the salute. 'Glad to have you with us, Herr Kapitanleutnant. Allow me to introduce myself. Korvettenkapitan Lamprecht, local Kommandant.'

Rink said, 'I'm afraid that due to our condition it took us rather longer to get here than I originally anticipated, sir.'

Lamprecht flung a glance through the gloom at *U207*'s scarred superstructure. 'Yes, you appear to have experienced a somewhat unpleasant time of it. It seems to be much the same story everywhere these days.' Then he glanced at Wohldorf who stood close by watching attentively. 'This is SS-Hauptsturmführer Wohldorf,' he explained in his brittle, over-anxious voice.

Both men exchanged acknowledgement of the introduction with a curt inclination of the head.

'I'm afraid that your officers and crew will have to remain on board for the time being,' Lamprecht continued, 'the reason being that you'll have to be moved to safer quarters before daylight. But first there's a more important matter which we must discuss with you in private. Now perhaps you'll accompany us to my office in the compound.'

Rink searched the hawked face which was almost lost in darkness beneath the high peaked cap. Like the brittle, over-anxious voice, it failed to conceal a sense of nervousness. He turned to where von Heydekampf stood watching the scene from *U207*'s bridge. 'I will be in the compound if required,' he called across to him. 'We shift berth before daylight. No one ashore till I return.'

The three men started along the breakwater. In the clear starless darkness Rink saw that the two concrete slipways on the south side of the small harbour had been torn apart by heavy bombs, while in the immediate vicinity of the harbour there was not a single craft of any description to be seen anywhere in sight; even the ancient tug had contrived to vanish. And when they neared the end of the breakwater he saw the fire-blackened shells of two fuel tanks among the clutter of store-sheds that also showed considerable signs of bomb-damage. Now, because of this, his curiosity and puzzlement grew when he tried to fathom why Headquarters had decided to divert *U207* to a base which was so extensively damaged.

Lamprecht explained the situation in one word. 'Russians,' he announced. 'We suffered our third heavy bombing-raid three weeks ago. I'm afraid there isn't much of the place that remains inhabitable.'

At the bottom of the roadway which led up to the compound above the harbour, Schramm was waiting with the Citroen. At the approach of the three officers he stood aside and silently opened the rear door.

'My aide,' Wohldorf explained to Rink. 'SS-Unterscharführer Schramm.'

Rink sent an inquisitive glance at the hulking figure when he climbed into the rear seat behind Lamprecht.

Half a kilometre further on, the roadway flattened out on to a small parade ground which was pitted with bomb craters and rubble, and again the nearby buildings showed signs of severe damage. And when Schramm drew the Citroen to a halt on the south side of the parade ground, Rink saw that the building outside which they had stopped showed its eastern gable open to the elements, and two gaping holes in the roof.

As he alighted Lamprecht explained, 'Our Administration building.' He then made a gesture towards a collection of low timbered dwellings on the eastern side of the parade ground, and added, 'The crews' billets, galley, dining room, bath-house, and laundry, or what remains of them.'

They entered the Administration building through a blacked-out screen door and walked to the Kommandant's office which was situated at the far end of the hall. When they entered the room, Schramm remained outside to take up a stance beside the door. While Lamprecht and Wohldorf removed their gloves and greatcoats, the former indicated a chair on one side of the room. 'Please make yourself comfortable, Herr Kapitanleutnant.'

While Rink settled himself he watched Wohldorf take a chair on the opposite side of the room. Resplendent in dress uniform, the gleaming vizor of his cap perched squarely above his eyes, the SS man slouched back into the upholstery, burnished cavalry boots elegantly crossed, exuding supreme confidence. Meanwhile Lamprecht, his hawked face darkly pensive, assumed an uncertain stance in the middle of the room; a man searching for exactly the right choice of words with which to broach a subject of considerable delicacy. He stared at Rink uneasily. Finally he said, 'No doubt you're naturally curious about why Headquarters should have ordered you north to the Mecklenburg Compound. Is that so, Herr Kapitanleutnant?'

Rink answered unhesitatingly, 'Yes, sir. Especially when I saw how extensively damaged the place is. It's hardly the ideal location to attempt to carry out the type of repairs which *U207* will require.'

Lamprecht held Rink's gaze frankly. 'But repairs aren't the reason for your presence here, Herr Kapitanleutnant,' he said mysteriously, then turned to a safe in the corner of the room, opened it, and returned with a slip of signal paper which he handed to Rink without comment.

Rink accepted it and read: ON ARRIVAL MECKLENBURG COMPOUND KAPITANLEUTNANT RINK AND CREW OF U207 TO ASSUME IMMEDIATE COMMAND OF U501 AND SAIL FOR KRISTIANSAND BASE APPROX 18.00 APRIL 2 – BdU. Rink lifted his gaze from the slip of paper, his natural reaction one of surprise, but nothing like astonishment. He knew from past experience that it was exactly how Headquarters always acted, without hint or preliminary warning.

Lamprecht studied him intently. 'You don't appear unduly surprised,' he accused.

Rink smiled. 'No, sir.'

At Rink's reply Lamprecht exchanged a sideways glance with Wohldorf who had remained silent since entering the room, then returned to the safe to produce a bulky linen envelope which bore the heavy crusted seal of the Parteikanzlei at either end. For a brief moment he studied Rink indecisively, as if trying to gauge the sort of reaction which he might expect to his next revelation. 'That signal is merely a covering order, Herr Kapitanleutnant. The real reason for your presence here is because you've been selected to undertake a voyage of a most exceptional nature, a voyage which will take you to the other side of the world, to a sympathetic country far removed from the approaching chaos which threatens to engulf the Fatherland in the days ahead, where on arrival an Organisation composed of our fellow countrymen will by way of reward attend to the rehabilitation of yourself and your crew should the necessity of eventual capitulation deem it necessary before, or by the time the voyage is concluded.'

Lamprecht's dramatic announcement struck Rink to silence. He marvelled both at it and at its unvoiced complications. He also noted that Wohldorf had discarded the role of a disinterested spectator and was sitting upright in his chair.

Lamprecht continued forthrightly, 'I'm talking about a voyage to the *Argentine*, Herr Kapitanleutnant.'

Rink said quietly, 'Yes, sir.'

'Then perhaps you might care to express your views at being honoured with such a rare opportunity to serve not only the Fatherland, but to guarantee your own future.'

Rink deliberated for several moments before answering, faced with widely conflicting thoughts and emotions. But convinced that to prolong the struggle against such overwhelming odds was both futile and insane, he had long since made secret plans of his own to contend with the eventuality of capitulation, and he now felt obliged to speak the truth without regard to the possible consequences. He met Lamprecht's anxious gaze with level grey eyes. 'Allow me to put it this way, sir. If I'd been at sea and my command in condition to reach the shores of Latin America, then I'd unhesitatingly have made every effort to do so on receipt of any order which gave indication that the capitulation of the Fatherland to the Allied Powers was in any way imminent. Naturally I'm aware that by expressing such intention I could justifiably be shot as a traitor, but providing circumstances had allowed me that opportunity, I'm speaking not as a traitor as I see it, but simply as a man attempting to face up to the reality of the demands likely to be exacted by the victors on our defeat. In my opinion I'd be saving at least forty-eight men from revenge, humiliation, and the accompanying ignominy of that same defeat, something which I believe far more important than the possibility of my being branded a traitor. I'm also convinced that to continue to throw away lives in a vain cause is nothing short of an act of lunacy. And frankly, I've never been able to reconcile myself to accept personal defeat.'

Lamprecht nodded in solemn reflection of Rink's unrestrained statement. 'Yes, I think you've adequately expressed your views on the subject, Herr Kapitanleutnant. You've most certainly simplified matters where I'm concerned, and I believe your reply will be received with favourable reaction by those people more intimately involved.'

Rink countered in honesty and sincerity, 'A reply which might also be regarded as being motivated out of self-interest, sir.'

Lamprecht made a dismissive gesture. 'I hardly think we need enter into complex matters of the conscience, do you?' he inquired of Wohldorf.

Wohldorf indicated agreement, then addressed himself to Rink. 'All that concerns *me* is that we reach our destination without trouble or incident, Herr Kapitanleutnant. Apparently you're considered by those acquainted with such matters to possess the necessary qualifications to carry through the voyage in question, and I'm not in the position to even offer an opinion on the subject. However, I'm determined to see to it that the voyage is brought to a satisfactory conclusion. Yes, Herr Kapitanleutnant, my aide and I are to accompany you. Does that surprise you?'

Rink suddenly understood the reason for Wohldorf's presence in the room. 'I've carried passengers on other occasions, Herr Hauptsturmführer.'

Wohldorf relaxed back in his chair with a smile. 'But never the SS.'

'No, never the SS,' Rink admitted.

Lamprecht intervened. 'Before we proceed further, I think you ought to acquaint yourself with the contents of this envelope, Herr Kapitanleutnant.'

Rink accepted the envelope, broke the seals, and inside found four typewritten sheets of foolscap corded together with red silk thread. He saw that the document carried the official Parteikanzlei heading and embossed seal, and contained the itinerary for the proposed voyage designed to take *U501* and her crew to the Argentine. The final sheet bore the personal seal and signature of the Reichsleiter, Martin Bormann. Rink dwelt momentarily over the signature. The Reichsleiter was a figure he knew little about. Apart from the generally known fact that he was the Führer's Secretary, Head of the Parteikanzlei, he was a man shrouded in mystery. And so too his signature posed more than one bizarre question. Was it, he wondered, arranged for the Nazi leaders to desert their people now that the end was approaching? Was the Führer himself involved? And was Shipment No. 11372 and its contents designed to ensure a trouble-free exile for its owners in the years ahead? He knew, however, that they were questions which might remain forever unanswered. Finally he raised his attention to Lamprecht.

'We can go into details of the document more fully tomorrow,' stated Lamprecht. 'My orders were simply to try and ascertain whether or not I considered you the ideal choice of officer to undertake this mission. Personally I'm convinced that you are, but first I must convey my impressions to Berlin before we proceed any further. At this moment our first priority is to have *U207* moved to a safer berth before daylight and have your crew transferred to the compound where they will be able to take advantage of our remaining facilities before they board *U501*.'

Rink said unexpectedly, 'There is one point on which I have reservations, sir.'

A frown darkened Lamprecht's brow. 'Yes?'

'I'd welcome the opportunity to rid my crew of as many married men with families as possible, sir. On a voyage such as this there ought to be as few prospective dissidents as can be afforded, and a married man with a family at home in these times could not only prove difficult, but even a liability to the safety of the boat should his mind not be on his task. And without the full cooperation of every member of the crew this voyage could prove impossible.'

Lamprecht nodded sympathetic understanding. 'True. And do any of your officers belong to this category?'

'Unfortunately, yes. Both my Second Officer and Second Engineer.'

'Then I may be in a position to replace those two. But we must draw up a list of the others as soon as possible, and if they can be classed as unnecessary personnel, then I want them out of the compound at the earliest. They can be transferred to the old Coastguard Barracks at Greifswald where leave can be arranged for them within the next day or two. But first we must arrange for you to shift berth.' Lamprecht reached for the phone and made two brief calls, the first to order the tug to made ready to shift *U207* to another berth, the second to the transport compound to instruct the Duty Petty Officer to have two trucks waiting ready to convey *U207*'s crew to the compound. Next he returned the signal and the envelope to the safe, and relocked it.

Meanwhile Wohldorf had taken the opportunity to make a critical appraisal of Rink. From the information which the Reichsleiter had passed to Lamprecht, the man's service record appeared impeccable. However, Rink wasn't his idea of a U-boat ace. In his opinion the man's personal appearance left much to be desired. Slim, although not exceptionally tall, with direct grey eyes and straight blond hair which was too long and ragged, he was dirty and bearded, his blues slovenly, soiled and creased trousers thrust into heavy leather seaboots ringed with salt rime. However, he wasn't without an imposing array of decorations. Together with the U-boat Insignia was the Iron Cross 2nd Class, the Iron Cross 1st Class, and over the blue and yellow striped silk scarf around his neck and buttoned inside the tight-fitting blue uniform coat was draped the much coveted Knight's Cross on a grimy sash. Overall, Wohldorf decided that he fell far short of the image normally projected by members of the Officer Corps, despite obviously being held in high esteem by Bormann and Lamprecht. But one important point which he failed to take into consideration was the fact that most U-boat Kommandants and their officers were of a different breed from officers of the other Armed Forces, and those of the Kriegsmarine itself. Also the conditions existing in an operational U-boat did not allow for the luxury of indiscriminate bathing and the use of a laundry.

Lamprecht's opinion of Rink was a vastly different one. He had taken to the man instantly, envied him, saw in him something of the same swashbuckling qualities which the older aces, Prien, Kretschmer, and Schepke, had possessed. And now as he rose from his desk, he said, 'Are we ready, gentlemen?'

Wohldorf gathered his gloves and draped his greatcoat around his shoulders. 'If you don't mind I think I shall leave you to your own arrangements meantime. Right now I want to go down and take a look at *U501* in order to satisfy myself that an alert watch is being maintained over her.'

Lamprecht regarded him coolly. 'I'm certain you'll find that *every* precaution has been taken, Herr Hauptsturmführer.'

Wohldorf hesitated by the door, an arrogant smile on his face. 'Thank you, Herr Korvettenkapitan. But I intend to form my *own* conclusions on the matter.'

Lamprecht stared after him with dispassionate eyes, heaved a weary sigh, then donned his greatcoat. 'Shall we go?' he asked Rink.

On the way down to the harbour Rink suppressed a natural curiosity to question Lamprecht in more detail about Shipment No. 11372, decided the time was probably inopportune and that Lamprecht's existing mood was unresponsive to his broaching the subject. Yet he had already formed his own conclusions regarding the contents of Shipment No. 11372; it was highly improbable that *U501* was bound for the Argentine with a cargo of *liverwurst*.

The only figures on *U207*'s upperdeck when they clambered on board were those of the boat guard and the Duty Watch Officer, Quartermaster Erlanger. When they entered the control-room they found von Heydekampf at the chart-stowage locker engrossed in a technical book on yachting, one of the Executive Officer's peacetime pursuits at which he had achieved a measure of international success. 'I'm afraid we must disturb you,' said Rink. 'We require a list of all married men among the crew, and head it with those men who have families. That includes Kappler and Hunsdorfer.'

Although surprised by the request, von Heydekampf made no effort to pass comment, and hurried for'ard to the ward-room. Ten minutes later he was back with the required information.

While von Heydekampf retired to the cramped confines of the W/T office, Rink and Lamprecht studied the list of names and ranks. Out of a complement of forty-eight officers and ratings there were eleven married men with families, and a further sixteen married men without families. Rink marked off seven names in the first category, and added to it those names of two married men, one a steward and the other the second chief, Deutschmann. Along with Second Officer Kappler and Second Engineer Hunsdorfer, other key ratings on the list included PO Telegraphist Henneger, and PO Seaman Orb. Yet like his two experienced officers, Rink was prepared to let them go.

'Are you satisfied you can manage without these men?' Lamprecht queried.

'Replacements for my two senior officers would be appreciated if they were available, sir. You did mention the possibility earlier.'

'That's something else we can go into later. But our first priority is to shift berth.'

Rink directed a glance through the circular opening in the for'ard watertight bulkhead. 'Exec!'

Von Heydekampf made a hurried reappearance from the W/T office. 'Yes, Herr Kommandant?'

'Prepare to shift berth. Duty Watch and berthing-party to their stations. Stand by to receive the tug starboard side. And one thing more – see that everyone's ready to go ashore with their sea-kits the moment we secure at our new berth. Transport will be on hand to convey them to the compound. That includes all officers. A boat guard will be provided from compound personnel.'

'Yes, Herr Kommandant.'

Twenty minutes later, secured to the tug, *U207* slipped from the breakwater and swung out across the harbour, her berthing-party lining the catwalks fore and aft.

BOOK TWO

Flight of the Golden Pheasant

Daylight had broken across the eastern horizon when the tug edged *U207* into the uppermost reaches of the creek on the western side of the harbour, where pines grew thickly on both shores to overhang the flat black water. Standing for'ard on the bridge, Rink saw *U501*'s tower ahead on the eastern shore where she was lying moored to an old jetty, heavily screened with camouflage nets. 'Prepare to secure port side,' he called down to the catwalks.

A compound berthing-party was ready waiting on *U501*'s upperdeck, and within minutes *U207* was safely moored along-side, the crew watching the tug cast off and pull out astern.

Rink's first reaction to a close-up view of his new command was one of disappointment. Like *U207* she was one of the old medium-sized boats, Class IXc, a later improvement of the famous Atlantic Type Class VII boat, but whereas *U207* was as adequately armed against air-attacks as her class allowed, with two twin 20 mm cannon on the *wintergarten* abaft the bridge, and a 37 mm automatic situated on an additional platform abaft and below the *wintergarten*, *U501* carried only the two twin 20 mm cannon on her *wintergarten* and an antiquated 88 mm cannon on her for'ard catwalk below the bridge. He had frankly forgotten when he had last seen a boat so ineffectually armed against air-attack. Over the previous two years every operational boat he had seen had discarded the obsolete 88 mm cannon in favour of the 37 mm automatic, or at the very least were equipped with a quadruple 20 mm mounting in order to add flak power.

Von Heydekampf clambered across the *wintergarten* rails. 'Boat all secure, Herr Kommandant. Are there further orders? The men have made ready their sea-kits.'

'All officers and ratings proceed ashore when ready.'

Von Heydekampf saluted briskly. 'Yes, Herr Kommandant.'

As the crew began to stream up through the for'ard and after hatches, Lamprecht leaned on to the wind-deflector alongside Rink. 'What do you think of her?'

Rink's critical gaze travelled along the length of *U501*'s upperdeck. With both her diesels running at full power, their echo thundered across the creek and drifted muffled through the pines. Obviously Lamprecht had ordered preparations to be made for sailing, normal procedure before a U-boat put to sea, during which time all machinery, and the diesels in particular, was thoroughly tested in order to ascertain that everything was in first-class order, that not even the smallest defect passed rigorous trial and inspection. Finally his gaze came to rest on the 88 mm cannon mounted on the for'ard catwalk below the bridge. 'With all respect, sir. As the biggest threat to us is now from the air, I'd rather she'd been equipped with something more formidable in the way of flak power.'

'I agree,' Lamprecht conceded unreservedly. 'Although I've done everything in my power to have her more adequately armed, anti-aircraft armament is impossible to come by, and unfortunately we don't have the time available to arrange for the necessary structural alterations to be made to allow for the transfer of *U207*'s armament to *U501*. I assure you that if it was at all possible . . .'

'Yes, I understand,' Rink reluctantly agreed.

'However, I'm sure you'll find that she's in excellent condition within the hull. Her refit has been most intensive, nothing overlooked. She has also been subjected to the most intensive trials both in harbour and at sea. And in order to avoid any last minute defects having to be put right before you sail, I had sailing procedure adopted thirty-six hours ago. Taking everything into consideration, it ought merely to be a question of acquainting oneself with a new command. I know time is against us but I propose you sail tomorrow morning and carry out your own trials offshore in the Baltic here preparatory to your departure.'

Rink sincerely hoped that Lamprecht was right. With sailing time scheduled for approximately 18.00 the following evening such a brief period of acquaintance could hardly be considered the ideal preparation for a voyage of something in the region of nine thousand nautical miles.

Von Heydekampf appeared on *U501*'s after catwalk. 'All officers and ratings now mustered ashore, sir.'

'Is transport waiting?'

'Yes, sir.'

'Then carry on to the compound.'

Lamprecht said, 'Perhaps you ought to attend to your own personal effects. My adjutant and a work-party will be here soon and I want them to transfer all remaining effects such as foul-weather gear and watch-clothing to *U501* as soon as possible.'

Rink went below to his quarters for'ard of the control-room, packed his few effects into a small canvas suitcase along with his Walther PPK, bundled his battle fatigues, leather suit and sheepskin coat together, then collected his navigation instruments from the control-room. He then carried everything aft and heaved it out on to the after catwalk. When he clambered out on deck he saw Lamprecht standing beside the tower in discussion with a youthful Leutnant. They walked aft to join him. 'My adjutant,' Lamprecht explained. 'Leutnant Hermann Berger.'

The dark, handsome youth sprang to attention with a crisp, military salute. 'This is an honour, Herr Kapitanleutnant. I've heard so much about you. It must be very difficult at sea in these times.'

Rink said amiably, 'Nothing's easy in these times, Herr Leutnant.'

Ram-rod straight, Berger said, 'Of course, Herr Kapitanleutnant.'

Lamprecht said, 'See that Kapitanleutnant Rink's effects are placed in my car, Berger. We're going across to take a look around *U501*.'

'Yes, sir.'

'And see that your work-party leave nothing behind here when they arrive. The tug will be here in about an hour to take *U207* down to the old breakwater berth on the south side of the harbour.'

Once they boarded *U501* Rink followed Lamprecht through the after hatch to the narrow central gangway beside the galley. Provisions spilled over everywhere. While the galley itself was piled high with hams and sausages, the gangway was stacked with crates of apple-juice, tins of sardines, herrings, butter, and cooking oil. Further for'ard Rink found the Petty Officers' mess equally crowded. So too was the control-room. Crates of vegetables and eggs, sides of beef and mutton, hampers, boxes, tins of coffee, tea, and more bulging sacks were piled everywhere. He wondered from where such highly prized items had appeared. Although the U-boat Force had always been more thoughtfully provided for than the other Armed Forces, both quality and quantity had understandably deteriorated over the past two years. But now it appeared that whoever was responsible for the provisioning of *U501* was something of a magician.

Lamprecht saw Rink's surprise. 'I did say that *nothing* had been overlooked. I had her provisioned yesterday. However, I thought it advisable to leave your own crew to attend to their stowage in order that they know where everything is.'

For'ard were still more provisions, boxes of powdered egg, sacks of potatoes, tins of meat, rice, and waxed cartons of cigarettes. In his own quarters Rink found several crates of beer and boxes of chocolate stowed beneath his bunk which was covered with a mass of paperwork.

He followed Lamprecht past the soundroom and W/T office opposite his own quarters and along the cluttered gangway on through the Wardroom where he stopped beside a photograph taken at *U501*'s launching. Underneath was written: DESCHIMAG SHIPYARD – BREMEN – OCTOBER 5, 1941.

'She must have been around in her time.'

Lamprecht was in agreement. 'Certainly so. When we found her last November she was laid up at the AA Training School at Swinemunde after being rammed astern by a freighter off Danzig. I assure you her refit presented us with more than one major problem. Luckily the main work had been completed and she was safely off the slipway when we received our first visit from Russian bombers. She'd been moved from the harbour just the previous afternoon.'

Rink refrained from further comment, although he realised that if Lamprecht had been looking for a U-boat as far back as November of the previous year it was clear indication that the venture had not been hastily conceived. Nor was there any apparent lack of expert planning, even down to the provisions, which in itself served as corroboration of what had first occurred to him when reading through the itinerary for the proposed voyage; only the best minds were involved.

In the locker space in the dispensary flat between the Wardroom and the Warrant Officer's mess, Rink saw the first pine cases secured by wire stays to eye-bolts specially welded to the hull, each of them bearing the stencilled insignia of the Nazi Party, a serial number, and the words: *Most Secret*.

Lamprecht stood watching him, hawked face impassive. 'Shipment No. 11372,' he said simply.

Rink's only acknowledgement of the fact was a curt nod.

'A total of one hundred and seventy-two cases and metal canisters,' explained Lamprecht. 'The canisters are hermetically sealed and have been stowed in the outside torpedo stowage on the upperdeck casing.'

They passed for'ard to the bow compartments, the fore-ends, the junior ratings quarters. Again provisions were stacked everywhere, on the deck-plates, in folded down bunks, and in hammocks slung from the deckhead. Rink had never seen a U-boat so crowded to capacity.

Lamprecht gestured at the wooden gratings which functioned as an adjustable deck over the torpedo-stowage space. 'Most of the cases are stowed below here, hence the reason you're only armed with three torpedoes which are loaded in tubes One and Two and the stern tube, and only to be used in self-defence.'

Rink foresaw possible problems. 'May I ask if any test dives have been made since the shipment was embarked?'

Lamprecht smiled. 'No, but please don't allow it to worry you. Full tests were successfully carried out with a substitute cargo of much the same approximate weight distributed through the hull as these cases are at present. Everything has been most carefully taken into consideration. Nothing, absolutely *nothing*, has been overlooked. Personally I'm satisfied there will be no problems whatever concerning *U501*'s manoeuvrability and seaworthiness.'

When they started aft again, Lamprecht continued, 'She has also been provided with a great many accessories designed to combat possible damage sustained during the voyage, as the last thing anyone would wish is for you to founder on the way.'

Despite certain reservations, Rink was impressed by what he had seen. *U501* was an old, out-dated vessel, but there was no question that her refit had not only been thorough, but meticulous attention had obviously been paid to the smallest details. Machinery glinted under the bright lighting, the air was clean and smelled of ozone, fresh paint, the clutter of provisions, and the usual overbearing smell of oil and diesel fuel encountered on board most U-boats was scarcely discernible.

Then approaching the engine room he saw five Schmeissers racked and chained on either side of the narrow central gangway.

Lamprecht glanced at them with a wintry smile. 'Let's hope you don't find cause to use them.'

When they passed through the circular bulkhead into the engine room they were instantly met with the thunderous roar of the two huge six cylinder MAN diesels running at full power. On the after watch-keeper's platform three green overalled figures were engaged in a full-throated conversation, oblivious to the arrival of Lamprecht and Rink. Then one of the men caught a glimpse of them, hurriedly wiped his oily hands on a wad of cotton waste, adjusted his cap, and started smartly along the narrow gangway between the two huge hammering diesels.

'Our compound Chief Engineer,' Lamprecht explained above the pulsating roar. 'Oberleutnant Ingersoll.'

Ingersoll snapped to attention.

Rink judged the man to be in his late twenties. Small and wiry in stature, he reached to little more than Rink's shoulder. Yet despite the typical U-boat engineer's sallow face he had a cheerful countenance with a grin he obviously found difficult to suppress and which exposed a gap-toothed mouth.

'Ingersoll has been with *U501* ever since we brought her down from Swinemunde,' Lamprecht continued. 'And in charge of her refit throughout.'

Rink nodded, and glanced around the confined space. 'Are those diesels behaving themselves?'

Ingersoll grinned proudly. 'Like a pair of Swiss watches, Herr Kapitanleutnant.'

Lamprecht and Rink left the three engineers taking readings and passed on through the doorway of the next bulkhead aft into the gleaming motor-room, again to be met with more cases. And further aft, in the after torpedo-room were still more cases along with sacks of provisions.

Glancing around him Lamprecht remarked with a humourless smile, 'Whatever else might happen along the way you shouldn't have to go hungry.'

Rink's enthusiasm did not require further kindling. As he had earlier explained to Lamprecht and Wohldorf, he had never accustomed himself to accept the role of loser, and now the challenge of the forthcoming voyage held magnetic appeal for him.

Lamprecht consulted his wrist watch. 'Now I suggest we make our way up to the compound and an early breakfast. Afterwards you must let me have your last war cruise report so it can be forwarded to Headquarters for the records.'

Rink tapped the breast of his uniform coat. 'I have it here. Half an hour will see it completed.'

Together they retraced their steps to the after hatch and climbed out on to the after catwalk into the cold morning air. Lamprecht's car, a much-travelled Mercedes, was parked close by on the jetty, a young Able Seaman chauffeur at the wheel. Also parked nearby was the Citroen in which Wohldorf and Schramm sat watching the four compound sentries patrolling *U501*'s catwalks with machine-pistols slung across their shoulders. Lamprecht walked to the car without passing comment on Wohldorf's presence, ushered Rink inside, then directed the chauffeur to drive to the compound.

The dirt-packed road led along the shore of the creek southward, then swung east to climb steeply through the pines to where the compound was situated in a fold on the hill above. After weeks spent at sea in the close confinement of a U-boat, Rink found the cold pine-scented air a welcome and stimulating change.

When they reached the brow of the hill they emerged on to the asphalt road below the main gate and turned north down the hill towards the compound. Rink studied his surroundings with interest. To a visitor the place would have appeared deserted, and he also noted that the buildings still standing were even more extensively damaged than they had appeared in the darkness of early morning.

Lamprecht sat staring out at the scene with no outward sign of emotion. 'By the end of the week the Mecklenburg Compound will almost certainly have been evacuated, and within range of advancing Russian artillery. That's how far away they are at present.' He gestured to north-eastward where the dismal grey ocean met with a sullen morning sky in the far distance. He murmured gloomily, 'Out there in those bleak waters we presently have the Panzerschiffes *Lutzow* and *Prinz Eugen* bombarding advancing Russian forces night and day while the mass exodus of refugees and troops continues from

Danzig after our encirclement in East Prussia. The *Admiral Hipper* returned to Kiel only last week with her gun barrels worn out, and the *Admiral Scheer* is also on her way to Kiel suffering from the same defect. Surely it will now be no small miracle to stage anything like a successful withdrawal without their fire-power to aid us.'

When they reached the Administration building the two men went directly to Lamprecht's office, where Lamprecht immediately called the messroom and instructed the duty steward to report to him. Replacing the phone, he turned to Rink. 'He will show you to some temporary quarters which we set up in the east wing after the last bombing-raid. After you bathe, breakfast, and complete your cruise report, perhaps you'll come and see me again and we can discuss details of the forthcoming voyage. Meanwhile leave me to deal with the list of married men for Greifswald. I think it's better you don't become personally involved in any of it at this stage.'

The time was 09.35 when Rink reappeared in Lamprecht's office. Bathed, shaved, his blues sponged and pressed, a clean white cover on his cap, and his leather seaboots polished, he looked a vastly different man. Even the blue and yellow striped silk scarf had been laundered along with the remainder of his sea-kit, and the cleaned and pressed sash of the Knight's Cross gleamed against it.

Lamprecht greeted him with a warm smile. 'Ah, at least our laundry hasn't let us down,' He indicated a chair. 'Please.'

Rink passed his war cruise report across the desk before he accepted the invitation.

Lamprecht read through the report, visibly impressed. 'Headquarters will certainly be delighted with this. It must be a long time since anyone was able to register such a degree of success on a war cruise.'

Rink said self-effacingly, 'Luck was on *our* side for a change, sir.'

Lamprecht was sceptical. 'Everyone must have the Lady smile kindly on him on occasion, but surely Success can't be entirely due to Her alone.' Folding the report aside, he continued, 'However, your officers Kappler and Hunsdorfer, and the other ratings left for Greifswald an hour ago. Naturally they were surprised by the unexpectedness of their transfer, but I explained to them that because *U207* wouldn't put to sea again,

Headquarters had ordered the dispersal of her crew.' While speaking he rose to open the safe and hand Rink the itinerary for *U501*'s voyage. 'Your appointment as Kommandant of *U501* was confirmed by the Reichsleiter a short time ago. He spoke to me by telephone. Now I want you to read through this document very carefully again so I can assure myself that you're fully conversant with the orders contained therein.'

Rink complied. In brief, *U501* would sail from the Mecklenburg Compound ostensibly bound for the U-boat base at Kristiansand in Norway, but divert instead to Hardangerfjord on Norway's west coast to refuel from the oiler *Nordhorn* at the Hordaland Garrison before attempting the breakout into the North Atlantic. A further refuelling was to be effected either in an area south-west of La Palma, or due West of the Cabo Verdes, before continuing to the Argentine. At the end of ten minutes Rink glanced up to find Lamprecht watching him intently from the other side of the desk.

Lamprecht raised his brows quizzically. 'Yes?'

Rink said, 'I don't foresee any great difficulty when topping off our fuel bunkers in Hardangerfjord, but refuelling south-west of La Palma may prove a very different matter. The U-tanker under command of Oberleutnant Bestelmeyer is stated to have been ordered to operate in the refuelling area from April 25th until our date of arrival, but what if during that time she was to meet with difficulty? That's an extremely dangerous area in which to operate, a veritable graveyard, equally as dangerous as that area further north in the vicinity of the Azores.'

'I agree,' replied Lamprecht. 'But you'll note that the U-tanker under command of Kapitanleutnant Schemmel will be waiting in reserve, operating in Grid Square DF, south Mid-Atlantic. If by 06.00 hours on May 5th she hasn't picked up your codeword signal to Headquarters verifying the fact that you've successfully refuelled from U-Bestelmeyer and are continuing towards your destination, or that Bestelmeyer should at any time meet with trouble previous to this date, then Schemmel's orders are that he proceed to the secondary rendezvous position one hundred and fifty miles due West of Santo Antao in the Cabo Verdes at once.'

'But if she were also to meet with difficulty?' Rink doggedly maintained.

'Your orders are quite specific,' stated Lamprecht. 'By topping off your bunkers and filling the bilges with fuel at Hardangerfjord, your destination is still within cruising range. However, I believe you're worrying unnecessarily. Either Bestelmeyer or Schemmel is certain to meet you at one or other of the rendezvous positions. Surely *both* can't meet with difficulty.'

Rink did not press the argument, partly because the anonymous conspirators at Headquarters had produced a miracle in finding not only *one* seaworthy U-tanker but *two* of them, for as far as he was aware all U-tankers in the U-boat Force had been destroyed before the end of 1944.

Lamprecht sensed his line of thought. 'It will interest you to know that both these U-tankers were specially refitted for the occasion, an ample illustration of how *nothing* has been left to chance. Even now few people know of their existence, and officially they are operating in areas designed to aid any U-boat returning home from distant waters, few as they are, should we be forced to concede defeat.'

Rink turned the latter part of Lamprecht's statement carefully over in his mind, seeing the problems and difficulties which it veiled. 'And if the Fatherland *is* forced into the position whereby capitulation becomes inevitable before completion of the voyage?'

Lamprecht answered tersely, 'You ignore all orders not directly addressed to you.'

Rink decided to explore another point which had already provided him with cause for considerable thought and speculation. 'I see it states here that on approaching our destination we're to transmit the codeward ERWACHE on a certain frequency in order to establish contact with a clandestine radio station somewhere in the vicinity of General Alvarado. However, nothing is mentioned to give any indication of what's to become of the boat and her crew, or, indeed, of what's to become of our cargo.'

Lamprecht shrugged. 'I'm afraid only the Reichsleiter and the people awaiting your arrival off Punta Mogotes can provide the answers to those particular questions. I'm sorry.'

As he had already suspected, Rink saw that Lamprecht did not know all the answers either. 'And Kristiansand?'

'Forget Kristiansand,' said Lamprecht. 'Your orders are to maintain strict radio silence from the moment you sail tomorrow at 18.00 hours. On failing to acknowledge your call sign after it has passed beyond your estimated time of arrival at Kristiansand, then Flotilla Headquarters at Kristiansand and the High Command at Lager Koralle will simply post you as missing, presumed lost on voyage. The only occasions on which you're to break radio silence are when you've completed refuelling from the *Nordhorn* in Hardangerfjord, again after you've refuelled from either U-Bestelmeyer or U-Schemmel, and on your arrival off Punta Mogotes, and then it will only be to transmit the specified codewords. Any further questions?'

'Yes, sir. What about the present state of hostilities which exists between the Fatherland and the Argentine?'

Lamprecht spread his hands. 'Forget about it. It's nothing more than a mere technicality as far as we're concerned. Anything else?'

Rink said quietly, 'I'm also curious about what precise part SS-Hauptsturmführer Wohldorf has in this affair.'

Lamprecht weighed his words carefully before answering. 'His task is simply to make certain nothing goes wrong, that at no time should the safety of Shipment No. 11372 be placed in jeopardy by reason that anyone's resolution should weaken. In this respect he has absolute authority to take whatever steps necessary to right the matter. The voyage must be brought to a satisfactory conclusion whatever the personal cost. I trust I've answered your question.'

Rink was under no illusions about the meaning behind Lamprecht's words. 'I understand perfectly, sir.'

'Good, because the measure of responsibility which goes with this undertaking is a large one. However, even though my knowledge of you is confined almost exclusively to your service record, about which the Reichsleiter has fully informed me, I have every faith in you as an officer and man equipped to assume that responsibility.' Then he abruptly changed the subject and reached for a slip of paper on his desk. 'Here are the names of four experienced U-mariners presently on my staff and whom you may wish to consider as replacements for those men who left for Greifswald. None of them is married.'

Rink glanced over the names: Oberleutnant Kurt Ingersoll, Leutnant Hermann Berger, PO Seaman Fritz Otto Rothfels, Leading Machinist Paul Guntel.

'Berger was with the Arctic Flotilla at Hammerfest,' explained Lamprecht, 'and has two war cruises to his credit, sailing as Second Officer. He was on leave in Berlin when he was hospitalised with appendicitis. That was how he eventually came to arrive here. Perhaps you might find him a suitable replacement for Kappler.'

'If he can keep a responsible watch, then I have no objection,' said Rink. 'He certainly didn't appear to lack enthusiasm from what I saw of him. But Ingersoll interests me most.'

'I thought he might,' said Lamprecht. 'And his experience with *U501* alone would be invaluable. Further, he's served with the U-boat Force since 1942. I recruited him from the staff at Flensburg.'

'What about the other men, Rothfels and Guntel?'

'They too have worked on board *U501* from the outset, and both are experienced U-mariners with several war cruises to their credit.'

Rink replied thoughtfully, 'Then all four men must have their own ideas about *U501*'s probable destination.'

'Yes, all must undoubtedly harbour suspicions of some form or another,' Lamprecht admitted. 'They certainly aren't what one would term unenthusiastic volunteers. But none of them can possibly know *U501*'s destination for certain.'

'Then I'm prepared to accept them on your recommendation, sir.'

'In that case arrangements will be made for them to join *U501*'s complement at the earliest. Which reminds me, I intend to inform your officers and crew of their destination before you sail on trials tomorrow morning. Those are my orders.' Lamprecht rose from the desk to collect his greatcoat and cap. Continuing, he said, 'Before you arrived I instructed your Executive Officer to muster your crew in the rear of the building here where I propose to have a few words with them prior to their joining *U501*. And take those orders with you. From now on they are *your* responsibility.'

Outside Rink found his crew looking much improved on their appearance of earlier in the morning. They stood in three ranks, scrubbed and shaven, wearing clean battle fatigues, sea-kits bulging with freshly laundered clothes. A general air of expectancy presided over the scene.

Von Heydekampf called them smartly to attention on the appearance of Lamprecht and Rink, '*Achtung*! *Stillgestanden*!'

Lamprecht began his address in a sombre voice. 'Officers and men of *U207* it is my duty to inform you that because of the unseaworthy condition of your boat, Headquarters has decided that your Kommandant, Kapitanleutnant Rink, will assume immediate command of *U501* along with his present crew.' Faces changed instantly, and Lamprecht raised a hand 'Yes, I well understand your disappointment at such news, but in these dark days everyone must be prepared to make personal sacrifices. Tomorrow morning before you sail on trials in the Baltic I propose to speak to you again on the subject of your destination. That is all. Those two waiting trucks will convey you to the jetty.'

'Carry on to the trucks,' Rink informed von Heydekampf.

As soon as the men were stood down a disgruntled murmur ran among the assembled ranks.

'I go to hell!' Torpedo Gunner's Mate Scheel growled darkly. 'We come all this way only to find ourselves headed back out to sea without being able to spend even *one* night ashore!'

Engineroom Artificer Dornberger, a twenty-six year old former diesel mechanic from Emden, had experienced it all before. 'What I'd like to know is *where* we're going.'

Chief Gunner's Mate Kordt, who at forty-two was the oldest hand among the crew, flashed a grin at Dornberger. Having served with such distinguished Kommandants in the U-boat Force as Schepke, Topp, and Rosenbaum, he was immune to surprise. 'Wherever it is we're going, I just hope we don't meet up with any aircraft on the way, because we'd find it difficult to knock down a schoolboy's kite with that pop-gun I saw on board *U501*.'

PO Seaman Hoven commented thoughtfully, 'What strikes me as being strange is Leutnant Kappler and the others disappearing with their sea-kits the way they did. If they went for good, then I say we can't be going far without a Second Officer and Second Engineer on board. It stands to reason.'

'Perhaps so,' Engineroom Artificer Steiner conceded. 'But one point you seem to overlook about Leutnant Kappler and the others is that they were all married men with families.'

The men within earshot fell silent, suspicious.

PO Electrician Franz Vollmer glowered about him with sullen, envious eyes. 'Deutschmann and that steward Ehlers didn't have families. And I've a son back home in Munchen I've never even seen. There are one or two others like me too.'

Kordt sent a questioning glance at Coxswain Lamm. 'What do you say, Cox'n?'

Of short and portly stature, and possessed of an easy-going nature, all of which belied his authoritative position as Coxswain, Lamm had been a regular navyman who had served on destroyers until February 22, 1941, when his ship Z1 *Leberecht Maas* was blown from under him by an overzealous Heinkel III bomber which had attacked her by mistake. One of the few survivors, he had transferred two weeks later to the U-boat Force, convinced it was far safer going to sea *beneath* the waves rather than *above* them. Lamm now drew dark and shaggy eyebrows together when he glanced about him at the many despondent faces. 'I say we get on board those trucks before they think we're about to stage a mutiny. The speculation can wait till later. If the past is anything to go by, then we're going to find out soon enough where it is we're going.'

*

On arrival at the jetty, Rink again had the crew mustered and they waited until Leutnant Berger and his work-party came ashore before he gave the order to board. Although Wohldorf and Schramm, who stood apart at the far end of the jetty closely watching the proceedings, drew curious glances from the crew, the men kept any comment on the SS men's presence to themselves. But while stowing his effects in his locker, Rink could not help overhearing the surprised remarks of the crew when they streamed on board through the for'ard and after hatches.

Even Chief Engineer Kernbach was taken aback by the mass of provisions cluttering the boat. 'Good Christ! I haven't seen anything like this in years. Where did they find all this stuff?'

Dr Kosney, the boat's medic, was next to express wry comment. 'It looks as if we could be about to embark on a round the world cruise.'

'It puts me in mind of Kernmayr's Delicatessen,' announced PO Seaman Weber. 'And that's the biggest grocer in Dortmund.'

'To me it's like the Golden Days of '40 and '41 when I was with the 10th Flotilla at Lorient,' Kordt declared.

'Christ,' said another voice from somewhere for'ard. 'Look at the size of those hams.'

'Never mind the hams,' spoke someone else. 'Look at those cases. They're stowed everywhere. What do you suppose there is in *them*?'

'Goring's medals,' someone else said irreverently. 'We're

shipping them out to an agent of Ausland-SD in Sweden for safe-keeping.'

The comment was met with a guffaw of laughter which ran through the hull for'ard.

Rink was aware that rumour and speculation were inevitable. However, his prime concern was to have the boat made ready for sea, to have the men familiarise themselves with their new charge. He found von Heydekampf in the wardroom. 'Get Lamm and Kordt and have them put every available man to work on stowing these provisions away, then get the hull squared off so that a general inspection can be made.'

'At once, Herr Kommandant.'

By 12.30 the mountain of provisions had disappeared under the combined supervision of the Coxswain and Chief Gunner's Mate. The foul-weather gear and watch-clothing transferred from *U207* by Leutnant Berger and his work-party had also vanished along with the stream of men moving about the hull, rumour and speculation becoming even more rife while they gossiped among themselves. However, Rink was not surprised by even the most outrageous rumour to reach his ears, for it did not require a genius to realise that *U501* was bound for more distant waters than the Nord-Ostsee Kanal.

Then at 12.45 Rink began a tour of inspection in the company of Coxswain Lamm. A sense of orderliness had quickly been attained in the fore-ends where TGM Scheel and his crew of torpedo mixers were packing the last hard loaves of Kommissbrot into two hammocks slung from the deckhead.

'Any problems?'

'None, Herr Kommandant,' replied Scheel.

'Then see me later. I have some information about the eels we have on board. There are only three.'

Scheel was unable to hide his astonishment. '*Three*, sir?'

'Yes. I have details of them somewhere amongst the mountain of paperwork littering my bunk.'

Rink and Lamm moved aft to where the Warrant Officers' mess was squared off and deserted. In the dispensary flat between it and the wardroom, they found Dr Kosney at his dispensary cabinet.

'Everything to your satisfaction?' Rink inquired.

Dr Harold Kosney, a twenty-three year old Berliner, had joined *U207* the previous Summer after graduation. Quiet and unassuming, an avid Skat fan, he rose with a bashful smile from the cabinet. 'Oh, yes, Herr Kommandant. There's no lack of anything in this department. I seem to be stocked for a cruise of considerable duration.'

Rink concealed a smile. 'Is that so?'

The wardroom, the central gangway, soundroom, and W/T office were also squared off, as was the control-room. In the Petty Officers' mess, further aft, the last boxes were being stowed away, while in the galley PO Chef Kolb was already busy preparing a cold meal. The next oldest member of the crew to Kordt, Kolb had worked in several of Germany's most celebrated hotels prior to the outbreak of war. While a commis chef he had been in the kitchens of the Dreesen Hotel at Bad Godesberg when the Führer had called his meeting of senior Party members there on Friday, June 29, 1934, a meeting which had led to the mass murder of his suspected enemies in the Sturmabeilung during the Night of the Long Knives.

'Any complaints?'

A rotund little man with a balding head, Kolb answered cheerily, 'No, Herr Kommandant. Everything's fine, like the old days, sir.'

'You know, of course, that Deutschmann's no longer with us?'

'Yes, sir.'

'It seems we're also unlikely to be provided with a replacement for him. How do you feel about that?'

'I can manage quite well on my own, sir. You can count on me. There won't be any problems. And the galley will be less crowded too.'

As they proceeded towards the engine room, Rink commented to Lamm, 'Well we appear to have at least one satisfied rating on board.'

'I think the big disappointment is at being ordered to sea again without a break on shore, sir,' observed Lamm. 'Not that it worries me. I don't have anyone waiting for me on shore. And Kolb's one of the best. The general disappointment will soon be forgotten when he gets around to producing one of his specialities.'

Kernbach was checking over the diesels along with Dornberger and Steiner when Rink and Lamm arrived in the engine room. 'Have you seen the compound Chief Engineer, Oberleutnant Ingersoll?' asked Rink.

'I think he went ashore with that work-party under Leutnant Berger,' answered Kernbach. 'You want him?'

'No. But come and see me for'ard when you have a moment

The motor-room and after torpedo-room were also squared off, and PO Electrician Vollmer was supervising the checking out of the starboard switchboard, while Outside Engineroom Artificer Hossbach and two machinists were milling around on the stainless steel deck-plates checking over the compressors responsible for blowing the main ballast tanks.

At 14.10 Rink dismissed Lamm and returned to his own quarters to concentrate on the mass of paperwork still to be gone through. He found that among the recent innovations made to his new command was a new type Schnorchel designed to improve performance. A new radar set had also been installed in an effort to combat the Allies' micro-wave system as well as the metre wavelength. Nonetheless he had reservations regarding the claims to its abilities contained in the accompanying literature.

At that moment Kolb arrived with cold cuts of meat and potato salad, with TGM Scheel close behind him.

Rink sorted through the papers until he found those referring to details of the torpedo armament, then handed them to Scheel. 'As I've already explained we only have the three eels Type V Zaunkonig. According to this information they were overhauled just four days ago.'

Scheel, a former tin-smith from Leverkusen studied the overhaul report with a conscientious frown.

'And only to be used in the event of our being attacked' said Rink.

Scheel's eyebrows rose upward. 'Yes, Herr Kommandant.'

Rink watched him disappear for'ard, shaking his head ruefully to himself, armed with yet another source for further speculation among his torpedo mixers.

Next to appear was CGM Kordt. 'Excuse me, Herr Kommandant. I've just checked the armament and there's enough ammunition on board for us to fight a campaign single-handed compared to what we've had on board at other times.'

Rink feigned surprise. 'You think so?'

'Yes, sir. At least that's my opinion, sir.'

'Well the armament report appears quite in order.'

Kordt was taken off-balance. 'I see, sir,' he murmured.

His face blank, Rink said, 'As a matter of interest, does that pop-gun actually shoot?'

Kordt's weatherbeaten face expressed perplexity. 'Shoot, sir? It ought to. I've just checked it out, sir.'

'And when was the last occasion you fired one?'

Kordt's face puckered with the effort of thought. 'I'm afraid I don't quite remember, sir. But it was a long time ago.'

'Then you had better find a gun crew who know which end to point outboard should an emergency arise. There isn't time for intensive practice, but we may just be able to frighten away a bomber with the bang it gives off.'

Kordt was openly sceptical. 'Yes, Herr Kommandant.'

Chief Engineer Kernbach was next to arrive, overalls open to the waist, face gleaming with sweat. Short, stocky, and broad-shouldered, Kernbach was yet another regular seaman, an engineer of exceptional talent who had risen through the ranks despite a penchant for becoming involved in shoreside brawls.

Rink looked up from the writing-shelf at the ex-*Deutschland* crewman. 'Uncovered a problem?'

'Far from it,' answered Kernbach. 'She's in faultless condition as far as I'm concerned. So much so, that to my mind, this can't be an every day jaunt we're about to embark on.'

Rink met Kernbach's searching gaze levelly. 'I guess not, Otto.'

'You wouldn't believe half the rumours flitting around.'

'It's Lamprecht's intention to put everyone's mind at rest before we sail tomorrow. You know I can't say more at present.'

Kernbach readily understood the situation, and also understood that Rink in his own way had informed him that it certainly was not anything like an everyday jaunt which lay ahead.

'Meanwhile,' Rink continued, 'I've other news to interest you. Oberleutnant Ingersoll, the local compound Chief Engineer will be joining us as Hunsdorfer's replacement. I'm told he's been with *U501* throughout her refit.'

'Excuse me, sir,' von Heydekampf interrupted. 'Four replacements, two officers and two ratings, have just reported on board. I have them waiting in the control-room.'

'This will be Ingersoll now,' Rink informed Kernbach, and rose to step through the circular opening in the for'ard watertight bulkhead into the control-room where Ingersoll, Berger,

Rothfels, and Guntel were waiting with their sea-kits. He accepted a folder from Ingersoll which contained a brief synopsis of each man's record, made out by Lamprecht. He looked at the four men in turn. Ingersoll, the senior officer, was from Neubabelsberg beside Lake Wannsee. Berger was an East Prussian from Konigsberg. Rothfels, blond and impassive, was stated as being from Munster; and Guntel, dark and sour-faced, was a Sudeten German. 'Leutnant Berger will assume the duties of Second Officer and also serve as senior radio officer,' Rink informed von Heydekampf. 'See to it that he meets his watchmen. You yourself can take care of Petty Officer Rothfels here who will take over Orb's duties as Petty Officer of the Second Watch, Leutnant Berger's watch. Leading Machinist Guntel can report to Outside ERA Hossbach. He's already two machinists shorthanded.' Rink next turned to Ingersoll and Kernbach. 'I trust you'll both be able to get along together. You know of course, Ingersoll, that despite your equivalent rank you'll officially act as Second Engineer?'

Ingersoll answered readily, 'I don't mind at all, Herr Kommandant. I was only too delighted to be given the opportunity of a berth on board *U501*.'

Rink and Kernbach exchanged a fleeting glance. 'Indeed,' said Rink; then to Kernbach he said, 'I leave you to see to it that our new Second Engineer finds a berth in the wardroom, Chief.'

Korvettenkapitan Lamprecht was next to board. With him he carried a large, slim metal case which he handed to Rink in the seclusion of his quarters. 'These are charts of the Latin America coast from Porto Alegre south to Cabo Virgines. I thought it better not to have them lying around in the chart-stowage locker for everyone to see. Naturally I hope you don't ever require to consult more than just one of them, although it's always better to be prepared for all eventualities.'

Rink put the case away in his locker.

Lamprecht, clearly nervous, said, 'Have Ingersoll and the others reported on board yet?'

'Ten minutes ago, sir.'

'I hope they prove up to standard. I always found them to be efficient and dependable. I wouldn't have recommended them otherwise. Meanwhile I hope you haven't met with any problems.'

'None have reached my ears, sir.'

With Rink's reply some of the tension seemed to drain out of Lamprecht. 'But plenty of rumour and speculation, eh?'

'I'm afraid so, sir.'

Lamprecht shrugged fatalistic acceptance of the fact. 'Well it was to be expected. However, my sentries on the gangway and the jetty have strict orders not to allow anyone ashore. Now shall we go topside?'

Rink followed Lamprecht through the tower to the bridge. The afternoon had dulled and the sky was heavily overcast with a thin drizzle blowing in off the Baltic in the breeze which bent the tops of the pines overhead.

'Once you complete your manoeuvres off shore tomorrow I will await the signal AM PROCEEDING, before I confirm your sailing to Berlin.'

'Yes, sir.'

Lamprecht caught sight of the Citroen when it drew to a halt on the jetty close by. 'So, it appears that the Black Order is about to embark.'

From Lamprecht's remark it was obvious to Rink that Lamprecht did not hold Wohldorf and Schramm in high esteem.

Both men watched with interest while Wohldorf ordered four of the sentries patrolling the jetty to unload the car. First, three suitcases appeared, followed by two oblong metal boxes, heavily padlocked. Rink saw that it required all the strength of the four sentries to manhandle the boxes over the gangway to the after catwalk. 'They don't believe in travelling light,' he wryly observed.

Lamprecht grimaced a smile. 'Perhaps it's their intention to set up a machine-shop in Buenos Aires. You can never tell what the SS have in mind.'

'Take those along to the for'ard hatch,' Rink called down to the four sentries.

Out on the for'ard catwalk Kordt and his newly formed 88 mm gun crew ceased their practice shoot to allow the men and boxes past without bothering to conceal their curiosity.

Rink waited until Wohldorf and Schramm followed their luggage on board, then went below to meet them, leaving Lamprecht on the bridge. 'This way, gentlemen.' When he dropped down through the for'ard hatch he led them aft to where two bunks were crammed into the narrow locker space on the port side, opposite Dr Kosney's dispensary between the Warrant

Officers' mess and the wardroom. 'I'm afraid it isn't in the same class as the Berlinerhoff,' he quipped with a smile.

Wohldorf evidently found no humour in the remark. Instead he called out in sharp rebuke as his luggage was being lowered through the open hatch, 'Be careful with those boxes!' Then he glanced around him with obvious distaste at his cramped quarters.

In an effort to put him at ease, Rink said, 'If you wish I can arrange for my Executive Officer to show you around.'

Wohldorf quickly spurned the invitation. He said acidly, 'Thank you, but Korvettenkapitan Lamprecht has already conferred that particular *honour* on me.'

Rink smiled good-humouredly. 'Then you must excuse me. There are a number of problems which demand my time and attention.'

When he returned to the bridge Lamprecht looked at him inquiringly. 'Obviously you made them feel at home,' he remarked with a thin smile.

'To tell the truth,' answered Rink. 'I formed the opinion that they expected a berth like they were perhaps travelling with the Hamburg-Amerika Line.'

'Yes, they weren't too enthralled when I showed them around either,' said Lamprecht as he prepared to leave, to return to his car waiting on the jetty. He smiled wearily. 'Now I must go and prepare my farewell speech for you tomorrow morning. Try not to be too surprised at what you might hear. And get a good night's rest. It may well be your last for a long time to come.'

*

The time was 6.20 pm when Lamprecht picked up the phone to talk to Bormann in Berlin via Exchange 500 at Zossen. 'I thought to call and inform you that there have been no last minute problems and our charge will sail tomorrow morning at 06.00 hours to carry out manoeuvres in the Baltic. Should any difficulty arise during these manoeuvres to necessitate a delay in the scheduled sailing time at 18.00 hours, then I will be in touch with you at once. Otherwise my only report to you will be when Rink officially clears himself for Norway.'

'And Rink himself?'

Lamprecht said unhesitatingly, 'I personally harbour every

faith in him. As I reported earlier, I find him supremely enthusiastic and confident.'

In his quarters in the Führerhauptquartier in the Reichskanzlei, Bormann sat back with a relieved smile while Lamprecht concluded his report from the Mecklenburg Compound. After the initial setbacks concerning Hoffmeister and Brandt everything was now proceeding as planned. And fifty minutes earlier he had received word indirectly from an agent of Ausland-SD residing on Lisbon's Calle Estremoz that Dr Alfred Matzhold, Bormann's official agent in the Argentine, had been in contact with him to announce the safe arrival in Buenos Aires of his liaison officer Heinrich von Geyr and that preparations were already being undertaken in anticipation of *U501*'s arrival off Punta Mogotes.

Now Bormann's next move would be made on receipt of Lamprecht's report to confirm the departure of *U501* for Norway with Shipment No. 11372, a shipment believed in official High Command circles to amount to nothing more than a few pouches of secret documents intended for delivery to various garrison commanders in Norway, and was therefore being shipped to Kristiansand with their full knowledge and blessing. Bormann was amused at the thought.

Meanwhile in his office at the Mecklenburg Compound, Lamprecht sat hunched wearily over at his desk, immersed in thought. He was tired, and only with the sailing of *U501* did he expect to regain any peace of mind. He had never possessed the necessary qualities to make a conspirator, and it did not make it any the more bearable to know that he was not the only senior officer involved in the plot to deceive the High Command about *U501*'s *true* destination. Also he had long previously begun to regret ever meeting with Bormann, and nothing would give him greater joy than to see the last of *U501* and the Mecklenburg Compound. Indeed all he looked forward to now was his return to Berlin and his wife, Erna, at their home in Schoneberg. The only remaining problem then would be getting out of Berlin before the Russians arrived, and with that particular problem Bormann had promised him every cooperation in the way of reward for his services and loyalty over the past few months; a safe and unhindered passage to Konstanz within easy access of the Boden See and Switzerland. And he saw no reason why Bormann should not keep his promise. He had served Bormann faithfully in his plans for his own future, a future which would be far removed from that of those unfortunates destined to remain behind in Germany under the Allied yoke.

But the first task at hand was to compose a farewell speech designed to instill faith, courage, and dedication in the crew of *U501*. And how, he wondered, did one begin to compose such a speech when one had long since forgotten what it was to possess those same admirable qualities? A sad, regretful smile passed briefly across his hawked face when he reached for the signal tablet on the desk before him. Had Fate not decreed otherwise it might all have been so much different, so very much different.

*

Next morning, April 2, Rink awakened at 04.30. After an early breakfast he commenced a thorough inspection of the boat in company with von Heydekampf and Kernbach. When satisfied as to her state of seaworthiness he returned to the control-room to finalise preparations for the trials and manoeuvres to be made later in the morning.

Some time later PO Seaman Weber of the watch on deck interrupted. 'Excuse me, Herr Kommandant. Korvettenkapitan Lamprecht has just come on board. He wishes you to join him on the bridge.'

Rink glanced at the chronometer over the flooding panel; the time was 05.40. Next he reached overhead for the broadcast system microphone. '*Achtung*! This is the Kommandant speaking. All hands will clear lower deck in five minutes time. Prepare to slip at 06.00 hours. Secure for sea. That is all.'

When he climbed to the bridge he found Lamprecht waiting for him on the *wintergarten*. Lamprecht leaned gravely up off the rail, his long hawked face bearing evidence of the anxiety he was experiencing that everything should go exactly as arranged. 'No problems?'

'No, sir.'

Lamprecht relaxed visibly. 'You have everything? Clear on all points? No last questions?'

'I have it all, sir,' Rink assured him. '*Everything*.'

Lamprecht nodded gravely. 'Good. Good.'

Below them the first crewmen began to climb out through the after hatch on to the catwalk dressed in full blues, cap ribbons fluttering in the chill morning breeze which rustled the pines overhead

Rink said, 'I gave orders for the crew to clear the lower deck in anticipation of your address, sir.'

Lamprecht sighed, drew himself slowly upright, and braced his shoulders like a man preparing to face a harrowing ordeal. 'Whenever you're ready.'

Rink saw von Heydekampf on the starboard side below the *wintergarten*. 'Muster everyone on the for'ard catwalk, Exec.'

At 05.55, with *U501*'s entire complement mustered on the for'ard catwalk, Lamprecht stepped to the front of the bridge with Rink at his shoulder and looked down at the expectant faces gathered below him. Suddenly a transformation went over him. 'My valiant fellow-combatants,' he began in an impassioned voice. 'You have crushed the enemy in many great sea-battles in the past, an enemy which now through sheer overwhelming numbers threatens the Fatherland with defeat and horror. However much all may seem lost at this moment, and the possibility of German victory on the battlefields of Europe scarcely conceivable – it is not so. As the situation changes, then so also must our methods of battle. Therefore it is with special pride and humility I can inform you that in reward for your past victories you have been awarded the honour of making an historic voyage, a voyage which will ultimately ensure the continuing existence of the Great and Glorious Third Reich despite the tragedy with which we presently find ourselves faced. And of even greater honour to you is the fact that your leaders accept unquestioningly that they can place their undying faith in you to attain your goal whatever obstacles the forces of tyranny may attempt to place in your path. Comrades! Your destination is the *Argentine*! And remember, the Fatherland is unwaveringly behind you. Long live Germany! *Heil the Führer*!'

Rink had listened to Lamprecht with sympathy and understanding, convinced the display of patriotic zeal was foreign to his true character, that he was merely conforming to orders.

Then Lamprecht wheeled quickly about in the for'ard sector of the horseshoe, turned his back on the stunned faces of the men gathered below as if in acute embarrassment of his own words, and extended his right hand to Rink. 'I'm sorry. My apologies,' he offered in a tired, worn voice. 'But may my own personal good wishes for a safe journey go with you, Herr Kapitanleutnant.'

Rink executed a text-book military salute. 'Thank you sir. Permission to sail, sir?'

'Carry on.'

Rink watched him go ashore, an old and weary man, to take up a stance on the jetty opposite the tower, a signal for the compound berthing-party who had been waiting on the roadway out of earshot to fan out along the jetty. Rink then turned back to the for'ard catwalk. 'Hands prepare to leave harbour. Secure all hatches and close all watertight doors. First Watch, sea-dutymen, and gunners to their stations. Ring on main motors.'

For several moments the catwalks were a hive of activity while the men disappeared down through the hatches, then suddenly quieted when reports of readiness began to filter back from within the hull.

Rink glanced at his wrist watch; the time read precisely 06.00. Then when von Heydekampf and the First Watch joined him on the bridge, he turned to Signalman Meyer. 'Break out the War Flag.'

In reply Meyer stepped up to the jackstaff on the *wintergarten* and snapped at the halyards. Instantly the scarlet, white, and black War Flag broke out into the breeze in full glory.

Rink glanced at the berthing-party strung out along the catwalks, then leaned his head to the voice-tube. 'Standby main motors.' And the catwalks below called, 'Let go fore and aft.'

Seconds later CGM Kordt turned smartly to face the bridge. 'All clear fore and aft, sir.'

Again Rink turned his attention to the voice-tube. 'Group down. Small astern both.'

Slowly *U501*, her grey wolf's coat of war paint gleaming like a silken skin, began to glide soundlessly astern as the majestic drum rolls of the *Badenweilermarsch* thundered out across the harbour from the broadcast system.

Meanwhile on the jetty the compound berthing-party and sentries stood rigidly at attention while Lamprecht saluted *U501*'s departure.

In reply Rink raised a hand to his cap as *U501* drew slowly away gliding out from under cover of the pines in the harbour on electric drive. Then suddenly they were out in the harbour to leave the creek lost under its cloak of frowning pines. 'Stop both. Full ahead starboard. Hard left rudder.'

'Fore and after hatches secure, sir' Kordt reported from the for'ard catwalk. 'Upperdeck secure for sea.'

Rink signalled acknowledgement and glanced around the bridge. Closed up with him in the horseshoe was von Heydekampf and the First Watch; PO Seaman Hoven and after lookouts Signalmen Meyer and Hagen their binoculars searching the overcast sky in their own particular sectors. Further aft on the *wintergarten* the 20 mm AA gunners crowded around their mountings while Kordt and his newly recruited 88 mm gun crew stood on Battle Stations on the for'ard catwalk.

'Stop starboard. Midships. Slow ahead both.'

With her bows now aligned with the narrow harbour entrance, *U501* went slowly ahead between the two breakwaters and once outside a choppy sea sent flurries of spray spattering across the for'ard catwalk.

'Steer 040 degrees. Half ahead both.'

U501 silently increased speed to leave the Mecklenburg Compound behind, choppy seas breaking over her bows and gurgling through the gratings on the casing.

At a distance of two miles from shore, Rink again bent his head to the voice-tube. 'Switches off. Clutches in. Half ahead both.'

A shudder ran through the boat and astern the diesels exploded into life. A cloud of acrid fumes belched upwards from the exhausts to momentarily obscure the sea astern before being plucked away by the breeze, and now the jumping-wires and their insulators reverberated in rhythm with the throbbing diesels.

Rink searched the sea and sky to north-eastward. Visibility was moderate although a low dark blur of rain-cloud obscured the northern horizon. 'Two-thirds ahead both,' he ordered.

The boat moved ahead, the bows lashing spray back over the 88 mm gun crew to spatter against the tower.

Rink narrowed his eyes against the icy breeze which blew down from the direction of Bornholm, and astern, the Mecklenburg Compound was now lost in the murk. 'Full ahead both,' he ordered; then, with spray driving across the bridge, ordered, 'Both three times full ahead.' The boat shuddered against the seas, water hissing through the gratings, a creaming wash boiling astern. Then: 'Both emergency ahead.' The bridge watch crammed their binoculars to slitted eyes as *U501* leapt in the water and the breeze sang in the jumping-wires. And astern the diesels roared in unison, the sea a boiling cauldron.

Again Rink bent his head to the voice-tube. 'What speed do we make?'

'Eighteen-and-a-half knots, sir.' There was an unmistakable hint of pride in Ingersoll's voice.

Rink turned to his Executive Officer. 'Better see to it that our guests remain in their quarters when we go under. We don't want them to think we're about to join Old Man Rasmus.'

Von Heydekampf grinned hugely.

Rink held the boat at top speed for a further ten minutes, the War Flag streaming scarlet in the wind against the drab grey sea, the 88 mm gun crew strapped to their mounting, water swirling around them waist-deep. Then he called below to Quartermaster Erlanger, 'Make to Mecklenburg Compound: AM ABOUT TO EXECUTE DIVING MANOEUVRES.' Then with another glance around him at the sea and sky added, 'Hands to diving stations.'

'Hands at diving stations,' the cry from below came seconds later. 'Boat ready to dive, sir.'

Rink made another all round sweep with his binoculars, wind buffeting against the wind-deflectors and singing in the jumping-wires, insulators throbbing. Nothing showed anywhere in sight, not even a wheeling seabird. 'Standby for diving manoeuvres. Clear upperdeck and bridge.'

Instantly Kordt and his 88 mm gun crew on the for'ard catwalk secured their mounting, cleared away ready-use ammunition, scrambled over the *wintergarten*, and plummeted down through the bridge hatch on the heels of the 20 mm gunners and the bridge watch, seabooted feet thudding on the deckplates below.

'Ease to half speed.'

U501's speed fell away abruptly, and another sea and sky sweep revealed nothing.

'Alarm for exercise. Prepare to dive.'

Klaxons screamed throughout the boat.

'Check main vents! De-clutch engines! Switches on! Motors full ahead!' yelled Kernbach.

From fore and aft voices yelled orders and reports while lights flashed and bells jangled.

'Dive — dive — dive!' yelled Rink. 'Boat to 20 metres!'

Amid a rush of orders in the control-room men swung on leverage valves, spun wheels, inclined the hydroplanes, and called out reports while air screamed out from the ballast tanks and the depth-gauges flickered.

On the bridge Rink dropped through the hatch and closed it behind him as seas thudded against the tower and flooded the horseshoe.

On the flooding panel lights flashed and blinked.

'Flood Q!' barked Kernbach.

In the space of seconds *U501* dropped away into a silence disturbed only by the gurgle and swirl of water.

Kernbach's alert gaze swept over the array of coloured dials and gauges, still issuing orders, Ingersoll standing at his side ready to deal with any unforeseen emergency. When the boat levelled out she remained inclined towards the stern. Kernbach countered with another stream of orders and they gradually achieved a level keel. 'Trim dive completed, sir. Boat at 20 metres.'

From where he stood leaning against the chart-stowage locker, Rink's gaze swept the control-room. 'Shut main vents. Check the hull.'

Reports came back within seconds. 'Boat secure for'ard — boat secure aft.'

Rink inclined his head towards Kernbach. 'Boat to 50 metres.'

'Boat to 50 metres, sir.'

U501 dropped deeper into the cold depths of the Baltic, Kernbach's attention focused on the master depth-gauge indicator. When she again levelled off, he called out, 'Boat at 50 metres, sir.'

'Check the hull.'

Again reports of leaks were negative.

Satisfied with the dive, Rink again turned to Kernbach. 'Boat to periscope depth.'

At his station behind the planesmen Kernbach repeated the order and *U501* angled her bows upward while he called out the depth as the depth-gauge indicator receded steadily back around the numerals on the big dial.

Rink next moved to the search periscope.

'Boat at periscope depth, sir,' Kernbach reported.

'Up 'scope,' said Rink. Eyes jammed to the rubber cushion

of the eye-piece, he straightened up as the column of gleaming steel rose out of its housing. A sea broke over the lens, then daylight revealed a lowering grey seascape. 'Down 'scope.'

Rink next climbed to the tower where Coxswain Lamm was seated at the helm, and squeezed himself in at the attack periscope to repeat the test; both periscopes functioned perfectly.

Pleased with *U501*'s performance so far, he called into the control-room, 'Standby to surface. Duty bridge watch to the tower. Surface!'

'Standards awash — bridge clear.'

'Blow main ballast by diesel. Surface two-thirds ahead both.'

Rink flung the hatch open while the port diesel reduced the internal pressure and heaved himself out on to the bridge, water streaming outboard through the scuppers and across the *wintergarten*, both diesels hammering in unison, sky and sea clear. 'Bridge watch up.'

The watch tumbled out on to the duckboards behind Rink with their binoculars, while the ventilators hummed into life to draw cold fresh air down into the hull.

Rink snapped into the voice-tube, 'Hard right rudder!'

U501 responded instantly to her helm and drove around in a tight turn to starboard.

'Steady on 220 degrees.'

U501 settled her bows on the Mecklenburg Compound.

'Standby to test artillery and schnorchel.'

The chronometer in the control-room showed the time to be 17.40 when *U501* gently heaved herself up out of the dark depths of the Baltic Sea, her diving tests and manoeuvres completed, and, satisfied with the overall performance of his new command, Rink turned her around off the Mecklenburg Compound's twin breakwaters. Binoculars focused on the signal tower, he called Signalman Meyer to him with the hand signal-lamp. 'Make: AM PROCEEDING,' he instructed.

Within seconds of Meyer sighting the signal-lamp and triggering off the signal, an answering light winked out acknowledgement, and added: BON VOYAGE.

Rink waited for Meyer to return acknowledgement of the signal, then issued orders to set a fresh course. 'Both two-thirds ahead. Right rudder. Steady on 015 degrees.'

U501's bows quickly settled on a course which left the Mecklenburg Compound and Greifswald astern, and put the north-easterly tip of the deeply indented island of Rugen ahead on the port bow. Visibility had further deteriorated during the afternoon and dark rain-clouds were massed low over a choppy sea. Rink stared impassively astern where a cheerless grey sea and sky merged into one. It was a depressing farewell, empty and forlorn. Behind them they were leaving the charred remains of the Fatherland where the death of many thousands was certain to follow with the terrible last hours still to exact their grim toll in the final humility of defeat. He had seen the end two years earlier, the first unmistakable signs that the war was lost, and victory for the Allies inevitable. Yet he had continued to give every effort in a vain attempt to turn the tide of battle, effort which he had known could only result in further grief, despair, and death. When he finally turned away he was afflicted by a deep feeling of sadness and regret in the knowledge that so much had been sacrificed for the vanity of so few.

*

Reichsleiter Martin Bormann was in the Entrance Lounge of the Führerhauptquartier in the Reichskanzlei, engaged in personal discussion with SS-Brigadeführer Hermann Fegelein, brother-in-law of Eva Braun, and former Reichskommissar for Holland, SS-Obergruppenführer Dr Arthur Seyss-Inquart, when his aide SS-Standartenführer Zimmer interrupted them to inform him of an urgent call awaiting his attention in his quarters at 5.55 pm.

Bormann hurried off at once. The call proved to be from the Mecklenburg Compound. With his voice expressing a sense of overwhelming relief, Lamprecht said, 'I beg to report the departure of our charge fifteen minutes ahead of scheduled sailing time after the successful completion of manoeuvres in the Baltic. A teletype signal has just been dispatched to Headquarters to this effect in order to officially inform of her departure for Kristiansand in compliance with their directive of March 25th. I trust this information meets with your approval.'

'Excellent news,' Bormann enthused. 'And now I assume you're also ready to move out.'

Lamprecht said hurriedly, 'Whenever I'm in receipt of the official signal ordering the evacuation of the compound and the dispersal of all personnel.'

'Then leave it to me. Report to the Reichskanzlei when you arrive in Berlin.'

Bormann's next stop was to place a call to U-boat Headquarters at Lager Koralle, to the office of Fregattenkapital Karl Pfaff. 'You have those orders necessary for the evacuation and dispersal of all personnel at the Mecklenburg Compound?' he questioned Pfaff's answering voice.

'As a matter of fact, I have them lying here ready on my desk. All that remains to be done is to arrange transport.'

'Then activate those orders tonight, at once.'

'I understand.'

Bormann hung up and reached for the internal phone. His call was to the steward's pantry. 'Sponheimer? The Reichsleiter here. I will be working late tonight. Have dinner ready in fifteen minutes.'

*

At 19.00 the bridge watch of *U501* was afforded a glimpse of the great white beaches around the easterly tip of Rugen, a pale blur in the gloom.

'Left rudder,' Rink called below. 'Come to course 345 degrees.'

When *U501* settled on her new course she had the prewar seaside resort of Sassnitz fine on the port bow, the Baltic stretching away to starboard.

'I'm going below for a time,' Rink informed von Heydekampf whose watch was standing the Dog Watches.

In the control-room he entered up the War Diary, brought the chart up to date, then made a general broadcast to the crew. '*Achtung*! This is the Kommandant speaking. We are proceeding to Norway to replenish our fuel bunkers at the Hordaland Garrison in Hardangerfjord where the auxiliary oiler *Nordhorn* will be awaiting our arrival. That is all.' Then he turned to Kernbach who was standing beside the chart-stowage locker in company with Ingersoll and Quartermaster Erlanger. 'Make your own arrangements for refuelling,' he informed Kernbach. 'That includes the bilges as well.' Then relaxing against the chart-table, he studied the three officers contemplatively. 'Now that we're under way perhaps you'd care to let me have your reactions to the fact that our destination should prove to be the Argentine.'

Kernbach said, ' It may be selfish of me, but you don't hear me complaining, sir.'

'Nor me, sir,' stated Ingersoll. 'I'm not leaving anyone behind. I was brought up by my grandmother, and she died the day we marched on Poland. Besides, like Berger, Rothfels, and Guntel, I volunteered to join *U501*. I didn't know her destination would be the Argentine but we all had our own pet theories.'

Rink turned his attention to Erlanger. 'And you?'

'Like the Exec, I have an open mind on the subject, sir.'

'But I wouldn't say it suits everyone,' Kernbach reflected. 'There's more than one glum face around.'

'So I noticed,' said Rink. 'However, circumstances didn't allow me to let everyone go like Kappler and the others. Frankly, I'd have preferred to command a complete volunteer crew, but then I'd no say in the matter. I just hope everyone decides to make the best of it.'

Next Rink went for'ard to his quarters, changed into a freshly laundered set of battle fatigues, then called at the W/T office where Chief Telegraphist Bergold was on watch. 'From now on we maintain a strict radio silence at all times. Any signals addressed directly to us you must refer either to myself or Leutnant Berger without transmitting acknowledgement. Understand? Monitor everything but transmit nothing unless on my specific orders. Impress that on Vogel.'

'Yes, sir.'

'And by the way, I'm sorry we had to lose Henneger but it couldn't be avoided. I hope you and Vogel will be able to cope. There shouldn't be any heavy traffic, just a listening watch to maintain.'

'There will be no difficulties, sir,' Bergold stated confidently.

Rink continued for'ard to the dispensary flat where Wohldorf and Schramm were seated on the lower bunk, both men clearly ill at ease in their claustrophobic surroundings. Although they were still in uniform, Rink saw that they had removed their caps and he was at once struck by Wohldorf's suave good looks. More Gallic-looking than Nordic, he possessed a curious silver streak which grew back through his tightly curled brown hair from a point above his right temple, a startling contrast to the colour of his hair and his tanned complexion. On the other hand Schramm looked even more brutal, a typical physical bully. And to accentuate his brutishness was the fact that his bull-neck tapered to a bullet-shaped head on which his blond hair was shorn close to the scalp. 'I hope the events of today haven't proved too galling an experience for you, gentlemen. I well know how it can be for people when they first put to sea in a U-boat.'

'Yes, it isn't quite as I'd expected,' Wohldorf confessed in honesty. 'Nor is there a great deal of room for one to move around.'

'I know, but I'm sure you'll become accustomed to conditions in a day or two. Also I instructed Cox'n Lamm to find you both a set of battle fatigues. You'll feel more comfortable in them than in uniform. Now perhaps you'd care to join us in the wardroom for supper.'

The two SS men arranged themselves beside Kernbach whose bunk served as the wardroom settee. Across the table they were faced by Dr Kosney and Leutnant Berger, while Rink sat in a corner of von Heydekampf's bunk.

After supper of rice soup and beef, Rink said to Berger, 'I will be on the bridge when you relieve von Heydekampf. We might as well get to know each other on watch.'

On his way aft Rink collected his sheepskin coat and a woollen muffler. When he arrived on the bridge he found von Heydekampf and his watch huddled against the superstructure for what meagre shelter it afforded against a heavy rain-squall.

'All clear all round, sir,' von Heydekampf reported.

Rink drew the collar of his coat up against the rain. 'Let's hope this weather holds till we clear the Store Baelt. It will at least afford us some protection against air-attack, however slight.'

At 19.50 the Second Watch arrived on the bridge. Berger, PO Seaman Rothfels, Able Seaman Bartz, and Ordinary Seaman Zeller had donned oilskins, prepared for the worst.

'Heavy rain-squalls with wind north-north-east,' von Heydekampf informed Berger on handing over the watch. 'Visibility worsening. Course 345 degrees. Speed two-thirds ahead.'

For a time Rink was content to keep a judicious eye on Berger. Although he appeared lacking in neither confidence nor alertness, he obviously lacked the most important requirement of any U-boat officer: experience. 'Something for you to remember,' Rink informed him. 'On receiving any report by radar of air contact we go downstairs at full speed with either hard right or left rudder. But if in visual contact with approaching aircraft, then remain on the surface and take avoiding action. More important, on any report of air or surface contact I'm to be informed without an instant of delay. Those are standing orders with my own crews. They know the routine.'

Berger replied stiffly, 'Yes, sir.'

'Another thing, in your duties as radio officer I want all signals you decipher passed on to me at once, and to me *only*. I've already informed Bergold there's to be no acknowledgement of any signal unless on my specific orders.'

'I understand, sir.'

Rink turned to the open hatch. 'Time?'

'20.40 hours, sir,' was the prompt reply from the helmsman.

Rink stared into the darkness where Sassnitz now lay lost astern on the port quarter. 'Come to course 305 degrees.'

On her new course the wind and sea was on *U501*'s starboard beam and she began to roll uncomfortably in the choppy sea which broke and slapped against her hull.

From the tower the helmsman called out, 'Man on the bridge, sir?'

'Carry on,' said Rink, and saw Wohldorf and Schramm clamber out on to the duckboards wrapped in oilskins, both gratefully breathing down the icy salt-laden air, oblivious to the rain.

'Kernbach suggested we get some fresh air,' Wohldorf explained when he joined Rink in the for'ard sector of the bridge; and peering about him in the darkness added, 'May I ask where we are at present?'

'Headed towards Kap Arkona,' answered Rink. 'We ought to clear it shortly before midnight.'

Wohldorf tugged the collar of his oilskin more closely around his ears. 'Is there any likelihood of our being attacked in this area?' he asked with a glance at the pitch dark sky overhead.

'We're liable to attack in *any* area,' was Rink's uninspiring answer. 'The life expectancy of a U-boat in these times is counted in days, and that's official. I've known at least two comrades lose their lives within an hour of leaving Kiel.'

Wohldorf's disquiet was evident even in the darkness. Changing the subject, he said, 'I noticed that some of your crew are quite young.'

Rink gestured towards the after end of the horseshoe where Schramm stood leaning his head into the wind and rain. 'See those two lookouts? Zeller isn't yet seventeen and he already has a war cruise to his credit. Starboard side is Bartz. He's just turned eighteen and he's been with us for a year. But Zeller is the youngest rating we have on board.'

Wohldorf stared reflectively at the vague silhouettes of the two youths whose eyes never stopped their ceaseless searching of the darkness. None of what he had just heard inspired confidence, and again he decided to change the subject. 'According to Lamprecht, I believe you know the Americas quite well.'

'I've operated off the American seaboard both as First Officer and as Kommandant,' answered Rink. 'From as far north as St John's in Newfoundland, to as far south as Pernambuco in Brazil. And prior to the war I visited most Latin American ports with the Merchantile Marine.'

Wohldorf was silent while he digested the news, pictured in his mind the immense coastline which stretched between the two points. 'That's a long way,' he announced, and allowed the conversation to drop.

A short time later Schramm blundered against the periscope standards when he made his way for'ard. 'It's cold up here,' he growled against the wind.

'Yes, I think we might go below now,' said Wohldorf. 'Thank you for allowing us on deck.'

Rink watched the two muffled figures disappear awkwardly down through the bridge hatch into the tower, as yet uncertain about both men.

By 23.10 the wind had eased and the rain had stopped so that visibility increased considerably. Rink made a slow and methodical search of the darkness to port. The northerly headland of Rugen showed fine off the port beam, just discernible in the darkness. He allowed *U501* to remain steady on course until the thin shadow of coastline fell to two points abaft the port beam, then called in through the open hatch, 'Time?'

'23.35 hours, sir.'

'Left rudder. Steady on course 250 degrees.'

With Kap Arkona astern *U501* was now headed down toward the island of Fehmarn.

'I'm going below now,' he informed Berger. 'Erlanger will be here soon to relieve you.'

In the control-room he shrugged his sheepskin coat aside along with his muffler, and spent the next ten minutes working on the chart and entering the War Diary.

All around him men were making ready to change watches.

While the engineer officers and ratings worked six hour watches, everyone else on board worked the normal three watch system of four hours on watch at any time, and now the hull was congested with men moving for'ard and aft. He saw Erlanger enter the control-room with his watch of PO seaman Weber, Able Seaman Hessler, and Signalman Glaser, all buttoning oilskins and pulling on sou'westers. 'Pass word to the Exec when he takes over the morning watch to have me called at 05.30 hours if I'm not required earlier,' he instructed Erlanger. 'We ought to be within sight of the Falster coast around then, depending on visibility.'

Rink then went straight to his quarters, kicked off his boots, swung himself on to his bunk, and drew the green curtain. And before the watches had completed their change-over, he was asleep, undisturbed by the bodies milling around in the narrow gangway outside.

After they placed their watch-clothing to dry in the after torpedo-room, Able Seaman Gerhard Bartz and Ordinary Seaman Wilhelm Zeller of the Second Watch moved into line for coffee outside the galley wearing only their blue woollen underwear, then carried their steaming mugs for'ard through the dimly-lit hull, where green curtains were drawn across the narrow bunks in the various quarters where men were asleep.

In their own quarters in the fore-ends they sat down at one of the tables and carved themselves bread and sausage. While eating they were joined by Leading Machinist Reinhard Elser, a twenty-one year old from Munchen.

'Want the sausage?' asked Zeller.

Elser shook his head. 'Not me. Pass that tin of sardines instead. By the way, any idea where we are?'

'Headed west,' said Bartz through a mouthful of bread and sausage.

'We cleared Kap Arkona just before we changed watches,' added Zeller.

Elser sandwiched a layer of sardines between two slices of bread. 'Well, how does it feel to be headed for the Argentine?' he asked generally.

Zeller said wistfully, 'I just wish that I'd had the chance to see my mother and sister before we left.'

'Listen to mother's little boy there,' jibed Bartz who came from Heilbronn in Baden-Wurttemberg. 'I haven't seen home since last April, and Christ knows when I'm likely to see it again.'

'I bet those two shipmates of mine from Munchen aren't too happy about things,' Elser announced authoritatively.

'You mean Vollmer and Wassermann?' said Bartz.

'That's right. I went to both their weddings when we got home last April. What a time we had. Still I'm glad I'm not married. I'm going to look for an heiress in Buenos Aires. That's why I've been keeping myself pure.'

Bartz stared at him long and hard. 'Shit,' he said.

Across the table Zeller drained his coffee and climbed into his bunk on the port side, and was followed by Bartz who hoisted himself into the bunk directly above, squirming into the narrow cavity between the mattress and the packing case secured above him. 'They don't leave a man much room, do they?' he complained, trying to settle himself comfortably. 'It's just as well I don't suffer from claustrophobia.' Then gazing contemplatively at the underside of the case above him, he said wonderingly, 'What do you suppose is in there?'

Still seated at the table eating, Elser said, 'How the hell would I know?'

Bartz was struck by a sudden inspiration. In a hushed whisper he said, 'Maybe they contain parts of a secret rocket — like those VI's and VII's we hear about. There's a rocket research station at Peenemunde just along the coast from the Mecklenburg Compound. I've got an uncle in the Luftwaffe who was a guard there.'

'Rockets my arse,' scoffed Elser. 'My bet is they contain the secret files of the Parteikanzlei. Either that or those of the Gestapo. Why else do you think those two SS men are on board?'

Bartz was partially swayed by Elser's argument. Undecided, he said, 'Do you really think so?'

'What does it matter what I think?' muttered Elser, losing interest.

From the for'ard bottom bunk starboard side, Leading Machinist Paul Guntel spoke out angrily, 'Why don't you kids shut your mouths and put your heads down? You're a typical example of the so-called sailors around these days — you've got no consideration for anyone except yourselves.'

Subdued, Elser rose from the table and crawled into the bottom bunk starboard side opposite Zeller and in the dim light looked for a glance of sympathy from either him or Bartz, but found none. Worse, Guntel was not even one of the original crew. And muttering darkly to himself, he turned on his side to face the hull.

Meanwhile Zeller was staring in the gloom at the underside of Bartz's bunk. He had not seen his mother and sister for more than a year, fourteen months to be precise. He had not even been able to pay them a flying visit at Rendsburg on return to Kiel from the Training School at Warnemunde. Apart from a snapshot which he had sent them, his mother and sister had not even seen him in uniform. Even more sad was the fact that his father was not alive to see him. He remembered vividly the day his mother had received official notification that his father, PO Seaman Gunther Zeller had died on board the *Scharnhorst*. That afternoon he had sat alone on the bank of the Nord-Ostsee Kanal in tears and had sworn to follow his father into the Kriegsmarine; and he had not only fulfilled that promise, but he was already a veteran U-mariner. And drifting into sleep, he was filled with a sense of pride.

Sleep did not come so easily to SS-Hauptsturmführer Ernst Wohldorf. The time spent on the bridge had certainly cleared the oppressive headache which had troubled him since shortly after sailing, but he was still unable to bring himself to totally relax amid the strangeness of his surroundings. The movement of the boat itself was discomforting, let alone the disturbing sound of the sea washing along the outside of the hull. And when he had eventually been on the verge of sleep the broadcast system had jerked him back wide awake with the metallic instruction: 'Middle Watchmen on station. Patrol Routine.' Then had come the tramp of feet as bodies passed back and forth on the deck-plates in the dispensary flat outside, the clatter of crockery, the hum of the ventilating system, and the incessant hammering of the huge diesels.

Yet he knew that he could count himself lucky not only to be on board *U501*, but to be alive. For whatever reason Bormann had chosen to favour himself and Schramm with his aid at the time of the Duhring Murder, the support, loyalty, and secrecy which he had demanded of them since was minimal repayment when the outcome of a trial would undoubtedly have been a bullet in the nape of the neck. And not only had Bormann saved their necks, literally, he had also presented them with a means of escape from the final holocaust about to overtake the Fatherland. Again, he had no idea why Bormann should have chosen him as custodian of Shipment No. 11372, but it was an opportunity he could not afford to miss out on, an opportunity not only to further impress Bormann, but to impress the Party Organisation in the Argentine, and more important, an opportunity to assure himself of a bright new future by making certain of the shipment's safe delivery.

Also he was not without personal funds to see him start out on that same bright new future. The two oblong metal boxes which were securely lashed to the hull beneath Schramm's lower bunk contained not only a collection of precious jewellery confiscated from the prisoners at Dachau and smuggled to Berlin, but also a hoard of gold marks and Swiss, Belgian, and French francs which he had acquired by means of blackmail while attached to the Berlin Morality Desk when he had served with the Sicherheitspolizei. They were the boxes which he had collected that morning when he had left Berlin for the last time, and the reward which ex-SS-Hauptscharführer Josef Stuckart had received for guarding the treasure in his house in Charlottenburg had been a bullet through the skull.

But now that his future suddenly promised to be so richly rewarding he was determined that nothing should thwart the safe delivery of Shipment No. 11372, absolutely *nothing*. He swore to it. As for Schramm, he did not enter into his long-term plans. He had used Schramm like he had used countless others to further his own interests. All he envied Schramm was his animal snores, but then the man was completely bereft of imagination. He would not even be able to accept his own end if shot by a bullet with his name, rank, and SS serial number inscribed on it. Yet he was indispensable, for the time being.

And so it was late when Wohldorf fell into a fitful sleep, his mind reluctant to relinquish hold of its wheeling thoughts and stagnant fears.

Rink did not require to be awakened at 05.30 on the morning of April 3; he was on the bridge at 05.20. The overcast was low and heavy, and the choppy sea had settled into a light, irregular swell that ran in directly astern.

'Land shadow right 20 degrees!' the starboard for'ard lookout, PO Seaman Hoven, reported.

Rink put his binoculars on the thin dark shadow which showed against the overcast that crouched low over the horizon; the coastline of Falster.

When at 07.25 the town of Gedser was on the port beam, Rink called below, 'Come to course 270 degrees. Schedule trim dive for 08.30 hours.'

Linked to the island of Falster by two bridges, Lolland's shallow coastline became visible shortly afterwards when Berger and the Second Watch arrived to relieve von Heydekampf.

'Keep a sharp watch for aircraft in this overcast,' Rink warned the new lookouts when they settled on watch. 'Our radar might prove slow to detect them despite its exorbitant claims. The Brits and their friends maintain a regular shuttle service from here on.'

When the time for her trim dive arrived *U501* slipped smoothly below the cast-iron grey surface of the Fehmarn Baelt, then with buoyancy and ballast established, resurfaced at 08.55, and all forenoon maintained her course westward unmolested, although the sky was filled with radar impulses on all sectors.

Weather conditions had again worsened when at 14.00 Rink brought *U501*'s bows around the south-westerly shoulder of Lolland to put the elongated island of Langeland on the port beam and began his run in on the Store Baelt. In continuous rain and with a low cloud ceiling, radar impulses became faint and infrequent as flying conditions deteriorated. Determined to clear the dangerous stretch of water in the shortest time possible, Rink called below, 'Both full ahead.'

The jangle of the telegraph repeater echoed through the tower from below and the diesels immediately gathered in power and rhythm, dirty exhaust fumes clouding the boiling wash astern.

The rain fell straight down to hiss on the dirty flat grey surface, and streamed from the oilskins of the bridge watch. By 15.50 *U501* had the islands of Fyn and Zealand on either beam, with radar impulses continuing to be picked up intermittently, faint and away to westward.

At 18.10 Rink altered course slightly to northward on clearing the promontory north of Kalundborg on the island of Zealand and put Samso on the port beam; and they were into the Kattegat unscathed.

Having been on the bridge almost continually since 05.20, Rink went below at 19.00 soaked through and numb with cold. After checking out the chart and entering the War Diary, he put his clothes to dry and called for the signal log from the

W/T office. The ether had been congested throughout the day with signals, orders, and distress calls. Three U-boats had been sunk since 15.10, two in the English Channel, the other north of the Shetland Islands. Also on record was an official announcement made by Headquarters which related to the bombing in Kiel of the *Admiral Hipper*.

Accompanying copies of Armed Forces communiques showed the situation on land to be even more depressing. The Rhine defences were being methodically pounded into incohesive units incapable of halting any concentrated Allied attack. And General Patton's Third Army which had crossed the Rhine at Oppenheim was powering its way towards Frankfurt, while British Forces under Field Marshal Montgomery had shattered Generaloberst Johannes Blaskowitz's Army Group H in the north. Overall it appeared that the entire Western Front had begun to wilt under the sustained onslaught as the Western Allies hurled themselves towards the waters of the Elbe.

Nor was the news of fighting on the Eastern Front any more heartening. From a general broadcast released by Deutschlandsender it was evident that the main Russian offensive was not expected to be long delayed, with huge concentrations of troops poised ready to drive a massive assault westward all along the River Oder.

Without offering comment, which would only have served to depress Chief Telegraphist Bergold further, Rink went aft to the galley, secured a hot meal from Kolb, and ate it at the chart-table in the control-room while contemplating the safest course to set for Hardangerfjord once they entered the waters of the Skagerrak. Finally he decided their best chance of survival in an area constantly haunted by Allied warships and aircraft would be when clear of The Skaw on the northernmost tip of Jutland, to drive directly out towards the North Sea instead of attempting the normal route towards Norway in line with Kristiansand. Then once out in the mouth of the Skagerrak a more direct run could be made north towards the Norwegian coast between Mandal and Farsund.

When he had finished eating he found himself joined by Kernbach. 'No problems, I trust?'

'No, no problems. I just came to inform you my arrangements have been made for refuelling from the *Nordhorn*. My only hope is it's going to be carried out during darkness, or else those Norwegians will have the Brits alerted to what's going on before we show our nose back outside the fjord.'

'Those are my intentions. We go in tomorrow night if all goes well. The *Nordhorn* berthed at the Hordaland Garrison on the evening of the first and will be standing by ready to refuel us whenever we secure alongside.'

'I'm relieved to hear it,' said Kernbach. 'And we won't loiter around longer then necessary. Frankly, the sooner I see the South Atlantic the easier I'm going to sleep.'

When Rink returned to the bridge the rain had eased to a fine drizzle in which hung patches of fog. Reluctant to decrease speed, he ordered extra lookouts to the bridge, and at 01.00 *U501* had the island of Laeso astern to starboard while ahead on the port bow lay Frederikshaven. And thrusting through patches of fog which at times brought visibility down to as little as one hundred metres, he drove the boat on towards The Skaw, and at 03.20 finally moved out into the Skagerrak.

Yet Rink remained impatient, in a hurry to be clear of the area. 'Come to course 275 degrees.'

U501 came around sharply, leaning the tower to starboard as she fastened on to a new course almost due West. Now headed out towards the North Sea the fog thinned and the first heavy rain-squall lashed across the black waters. Cold, wet, eyes red-rimmed, and weary from long anxious hours of peering into darkness, Rink fervently hoped the existing weather conditions would continue for another twenty-four hours, and so shield them from the air during their crossing of the Skagerrak to the shelter of the Norwegian coast.

But despite adverse weather conditions radar impulses had increased on all sectors by 05.00, and soon afterwards the W/T office received a brief signal flashed from another U-boat in distress: BEING DEPTH-CHARGED BY AIRCRAFT. SINKING 61N 01E —. Thirty-five minutes later a general alert from Headquarters read: ACHTUNG. BRITISH DESTROYERS ACTIVE AREA SOUTH-WEST SKAGERRAK — BdU.

U501's own radar corroborated the information, and indicated the strongest impulses to be in the south-west, in the area of the Jammerbucht, off the north-west coast of Jutland.

Rink decided to hold his original course. Although a steady northerly breeze had dispersed all trace of fog, the rain had begun to fall steadily from a low sullen sky. Then at 08.50 with the trim dive completed, he ordered an alteration of course to

285 degrees and *U501* turned to bear in towards the southerly coast of Norway.

Crossing the Skagerrak proved uneventful although the rain eased until it ceased altogether at midday when the earlier breeze freshened considerably, so that by the time the first snow-peaks of Vestagder were sighted west of Manal the sea had broken and white crests flung spindrift before an icy wind.

'Impulse 220 degrees — increasing sharply!' the voice from the soundroom was inflected with a raucous note of alarm.

Rink and Erlanger had their binoculars focused on the reported bearing before the radar operator's voice died. The thin black silhouette had already dropped down through the cloud base to south-westward, having homed in on radar until its target was within visible range.

'*Gott verdammte noch mal* — that radar of ours!' swore Rink; then, 'Open fire when ready!' he flung across his shoulder to the 20 mm gunners on the *wintergarten*, and with the binoculars still focused on the Mosquito fighter-bomber, he saw its machinegun and cannon flame as *U501*'s gunners opened up with their own reply.

Suddenly the sea around the boat erupted in a ragged curtain of water. Shells and bullets whined, clattered, and ricochetted off the casing and armour plating around the bridge, and through it all Rink saw the two bombs begin their long dropping arc towards their target. 'Hard right rudder!' he shouted in reaction.

U501 swung violently to starboard while Rink followed the flight of the bombs until they hit the water simultaneously and exploded to raise towering columns of dirty water some thirty metres short of the for'ard catwalk port side. Then the aircraft was overhead, motors screaming as it passed on over to disappear into the murk above the cliffs to northward.

Rink did not require time to deliberate his next course of action. With broken water subsiding back across the bridge and *wintergarten*, he yelled, 'Emergency dive! Clear the bridge! Dive — dive — dive! Depth regulator hard down! Hard left rudder!'

Bodies hurled themselves into the tower to the accompaniment of screaming klaxons, and the horseshoe was already awash when Rink snapped the hatch shut behind him.

Kernbach had the boat safely beneath the surface, still turning hard to port, when the next two bombs erupted astern, two ferocious blasts, this time on the starboard quarter well astern.

Rink evinced approval. 'Resume original course - steer 310 degrees. Full ahead both.'

At the end of an hour he ordered the boat to periscope depth, found sea and sky clear, and surfaced again on course north-westward towards Flekkefjord and Egersund, and at 20.40 had Haugesund astern to starboard, so that shortly afterwards they came within sight of the entrance to Hardangerfjord at a point 30 miles south-south-east of Bergen.

Having once navigated the fringe of islands, Rink made a critical survey of the scene through binoculars. With the onset of darkness the sky had shed all but a few scattered clouds and the soaring snow-clad peaks glistened with peaceful crystal brilliance under a bright moon and stars, while the sea, cresting white under a stiff northerly breeze, flung itself against the granite shoreline to break in a vivid phosphorescent upsurge, white and sparkling.

'Slow ahead both. Right rudder. Steer 020 degrees.'

U501 moved cautiously into the fjord and crept up towards the soaring expanse of the northern shoreline. The water was now flat calm, black, and mirrored the moonlight which cast its brittle light down across the sheer granite walls of the fjord.

At a point two miles beyond the entrance Rink gave the order, 'Clear the bridge. Prepare to dive.' Then he took a last look all round while the bridge watch and AA gunners disappeared into the tower. 'Dive easy. To periscope depth, Chief,' he ordered, and swung unhurriedly into the tower to clamp the hatch shut behind him as water gurgled into the ballast tanks.

U501 slid so gently beneath the black water that anyone watching from shore might have been convinced she had never actually existed, that she had only been a figment of their imagination.

Rink stepped to the search periscope in the control-room, 'Up 'scope,' he ordered, and rose with it as the tube hummed out of its housing. To all appearances the fjord was deserted, cast in black shadow, its surface unruffled.

'One-third ahead both.'

Rink remained at the ocular while *U501*, holding to the middle of the fjord, eased silently through the black glacial water. Between sheer granite cliffs, pine-clad gullies and ravines stood watch above the placid waters along the shore, snow-caps glittering in the moonlight. With his attention focused on the north shore, Rink waited to catch a first glimpse of the Hordaland Garrison. Then he suddenly froze, and the periscope halted in its search when he saw the faint glow of light in the darkness up ahead. A few minutes later his fears were confirmed when he saw the bright flicker of orange flame beyond a screen of pines close above the north shore. Stepping back from the periscope, he beckoned to von Heydekampf who stood waiting beside the chart-stowage locker in company with Wohldorf and Schramm.

Von Heydekampf put his brow to the rubber eye-cushion and focused the ocular, face impassive. Clear of the screen of pines on the north shore, several low timbered buildings almost gutted by fire passed into view, and below them at the bottom of the clearing, a short wooden jetty which struck out into the fjord stood abandoned in the garish light. He stepped aside with a perplexed frown. 'The Hordaland Garrison?'

Rink inclined his head in the affirmative, and took another long searching look at the scene outside. 'There's no trace of the *Nordhorn*.'

'What do you make of it?'

Rink shrugged. 'Norwegian partisans — perhaps even an Allied commando raid. I don't know.'

Wohldorf stepped forward from the chart-stowage locker, his face expressing anxiety and concern. 'What's happening out there?'

'Nothing,' Rink was still at the periscope. 'The place is already burned out.'

Wohldorf's face registered instant disbelief. 'Impossible!'

Rink stepped back from the periscope with a grim smile. 'Then look for yourself.'

Wohldorf gazed through the ocular for fully a minute, then turned away in panic. 'The oiler — what happened to the oiler?'

Rink said calmly, 'Perhaps I will be better prepared to answer that question once we take a closer look upstairs.' Then: 'Down 'scope. Crew to Battle Stations. Bridge watch, AA gunners and 88 mm gun crew to the tower. Standby to surface on electric drive.'

With compressed air roaring into the tanks, *U501* lifted herself gently up out of the black water, men clambering out behind Rink on to the streaming bridge, Wohldorf and

Schramm among them. For seconds the upperdeck bustled with activity while the gun crews cleared away and made ready their guns on the for'ard catwalk and *wintergarten*, the lookouts focusing their binoculars on various sections of the fjord.

Rink made a meticulous sweep of the garrison compound, satisfied himself that it had clearly been abandoned, and issued a further stream of orders so that *U501* swung silently around and started back towards the entrance with both motors at one-third ahead. 'I want every single metre of these shores covered between here and the open sea,' he instructed the bridge watch. 'That garrison shows all the evidence of having come under a methodical and concentrated attack. As to what happened, I don't profess to know, but I'm extremely doubtful if survivors would retreat deeper into the fjord where they'd stand every chance of being completely trapped. With any sense at all they'd make for the entrance.'

His face set grimly, Wohldorf stepped close to Rink's shoulder. 'This is catastrophic. Berlin must be informed at once about what has happened. Plans will require to be altered. You know the position very well.'

'Then we will have to put into Bergen,' Rink informed him. 'Any such contact will have to be made by phone. My orders state specifically that I'm to observe strict radio silence except as instructed.'

'*Shadow, angle right 5 degrees!*' PO Seaman Hoven's binoculars were focused on a darkly shadowed stretch of shore to north-ward.

Rink quickly discerned the black shadow of a vessel where she lay in under the shore. With a stubby forepeak, low for'ard well-deck, bridge superstructure situated aft above what appeared to be an enclosed companionway around her stern, he was left in little doubt that she was anything other than an oiler. 'Stop both! Meyer — a signal lamp!' Rink searched the vessel from stem to stern; not a glimmer of light showed anywhere. And as she continued to lose way, *U501* eventually glided to a silent halt three hundred metres distant.

Meyer thrust his way to the starboard side of the congested bridge with the signal-lamp.

'Make her our recognition signal,' Rink instructed.

Meyer sighted and triggered the lamp.

The reaction was immediate, and an answering light winked

briefly out across the darkness from the port side of the oiler's bridge superstructure: NORDHORN.

Wohldorf crowded forward and demanded anxiously, 'What did they say in reply?'

'It's the *Nordhorn*,' answered Rink; then called out in a warning voice, 'Gun crews keep your wits about you. We're going in to take a closer look. Half ahead port. Hard right rudder.'

They had drifted seaward with the ebb current to leave the *Nordhorn* astern, and now *U501* swung around under hard right rudder.

'Midships. Stop port. Small ahead both.'

A cupped voice hailed them from the *Nordhorn*'s darkened bridge. 'Ahoy, *U501*! We're prepared for you port side!'

As they crept up on the oiler Rink saw several indistinct figures hurriedly throw fenders across the side while others appeared to stand ready with wires. 'Take her alongside,' he informed von Heydekampf. 'But remain alert till I find out what's been happening.' Then he turned to Wohldorf. 'You had better come along with me so you can have a report of the situation at first-hand. However, I suggest that your aide remains here in case we have to move out in a hurry if everything's not to my satisfaction.'

Both men were waiting ready to step off the for'ard catwalk on to the oiler's low well when von Heydekampf brought *U501* expertly alongside.

A young Leutnant wrapped in a heavy watchcoat was waiting for them. 'This way, Herr Kapitanleutnant.'

Rink and Wohldorf followed him aft on the port side, and in the gloom saw several greatcoated figures huddled in the mouth of the companionway which enclosed the stern.

The *Nordhorn*'s Kommandant, who proved to be an elderly Oberleutnant, was awaiting their arrival on the bridge in company with another greatcoated figure. 'Oberleutnant Fodor,' he explained, and indicated his companion. 'This is Captain Seldte of the Austrian Alpenjagers, adjutant of the Hordaland Garrison.'

Rink made his own introduction, and that of Wohldorf.

'We've been watching for you from here since 17.40 this afternoon, Herr Kapitanleutnant,' Fodor explained. 'I can't understand why my lookouts missed you.'

'We came in submerged,' said Rink. 'But what happened back there?'

Captain Seldte answered, 'We were attacked by a large force of Norwegian partisans shortly after midday, Herr Kapitanleutnant. They cleverly set up a diversion in the early hours of the morning when they blew up the railway track between Granvin and Voss. As a result of this our Kommandant was instructed by Senior Operations Officer Bergen to make an immediate investigation with a view to apprehending the culprits. He left at daybreak and took all but thirty men with him. Subsequently we were ill-prepared when we came under mortar and machinegun attack later in the day. But luckily for us Oberleutnant Fodor was on hand to aid the escape of the survivors. There are seventeen military and civilian personnel on board,' he concluded bitterly. 'And several are seriously wounded.'

'Do you have an experienced medic at your disposal?' asked Rink.

Captain Seldte said, 'Only a young orderly, I'm afraid.'

Rink focused his attention on Fodor. 'Is it at all possible that you may have been followed by those partisans?'

'I posted lookouts on shore the moment we tied up and there's been no report of any movement on shore, Herr Kapitanleutnant.'

'And you're ready to proceed with refuelling?'

'The moment you are, Herr Kapitanleutnant.'

Rink fell silent. He did not care for the situation at all, yet he had been provided with no alternative means of refuelling. 'Very well,' he told Fodor. 'You can start to make ready. But at the first suspicion of trouble — we slip.'

'I understand the situation perfectly, Herr Kapitanleutnant.'

Rink walked to the port wing of the bridge and called out to von Heydekampf on *U501*'s bridge, 'Tell Kernbach to prepare to refuel. We can proceed whenever he's ready. And get Dr Kosney across here with his medical kit. We have several wounded on board.'

Captain Seldte said, 'I'm most grateful to you, Herr Kapitanleutnant.'

'It's the least I can do,' said Rink. 'And the moment we complete refuelling, I advise you to make full speed for Bergen and medical assistance,' he told Fodor.

When Rink and Wohldorf returned on board *U501* Kernbach was already engaged in supervising the refuelling. 'Don't waste time, Otto,' Rink warned. 'Norwegian partisans were active around here earlier.'

Once on the bridge he directed his attention at the shore. A U-boat was vulnerable at any time when refuelling but in the existing circumstances *U501* was virtually helpless. With the *Nordhorn* moored to some pines growing on the lower reaches of the cliffs above a granite ledge which rose to form a buttress forward of her bows, her stern lay at an angle to the shore where it fell away to sweep down into a gully thickly covered with pines. Also with both vessels lying stem to stern, port side on to each other, only the twin machinegun situated abaft the *Nordhorn*'s bridge could be brought to bear on the wooded gully because her bridge superstructure restricted the angle of fire where *U501*'s 88 mm cannon was concerned, while the 20 mm AA mountings on the *wintergarten* were effective only over a field of fire astern and on either beam.

Unhappy with the situation, Rink sent for CGM Kordt. 'Break out those machine-pistols and form a gun-guard on the catwalks.' Then to von Heydekampf, he said, 'Make certain the lookouts maintain a keen watch on the shore. If those partisans saw the *Nordhorn* tie up out here they must realise she's waiting for someone and we could be in for trouble.'

While the refuelling progressed a stiff breeze began to funnel through the fjord, bringing with it an occasional shower of sleet. Overhead the sky shimmered with stars of a cold and detached brilliance, and now with the moon lighting only on the tips of the surrounding peaks, the granite walls of the fjord were lost in steep black shadow.

'That promises to be quite a blow getting up outside,' von Heydekampf remarked, his face lost in the shadow of his watch-coat collar.

Rink grunted in agreement, his binoculars searching the wooded darkness of the shore.

Suddenly Kernbach appeared on the bridge at his side. 'Ten minutes and we can start on the bilges,' he reported.

With Kernbach's words a sharp detonation echoed along the shore and the glaring white light of flare exploded overhead. Upraised faces gazed at it startled, and immediately from shore three dull coughing *thumps* echoed among the pines, beaten back off the soaring cliffs. Then a machinegun hammered out its lethal message from somewhere on the edge of the shore and white tracer shell screamed across the *Nordhorn*'s bridge superstructure. At the same time three crashing explosions occurred simultaneously in close proximity to her stern and sheeted water broke across *U501*'s for'ard catwalk.

'Mortars!' was Kordt's shouted reaction.

'Clear those hoses!' Rink yelled to Kernbach who was already on the after catwalk shouting orders at his refuelling party. 'Standby to slip mooring wires!'

A second flare burst overhead and tracer shell found the *Nordhorn*'s bridge. The crew at her machinegun offered an uncertain reply and their tracer shell drifted erratically into the pines far up the gully.

'Open fire at anything you see!' Rink shouted aft to the *wintergarten*. And into the tower yelled, 'Standby main engines!'

The catwalks were in confusion when the next mortar bombs hit the fjord, two of which exploded under the *Nordhorn*'s stern, while the third landed beyond *U501*'s bows to rain water down on the figures milling around on the for'ard catwalk. Then Rink saw the *Nordhorn*'s machinegun crew leap across the stern when flames belched from her bridge superstructure starboard side. Two further explosions meanwhile occurred on the *Nordhorn*'s forepeak, grating crashes, followed by another on *U501*'s after catwalk, and in the vivid photoflash Rink saw two figures fling up their arms and topple outboard, still clutching their Schmeissers.

Kordt gestured at the ledge of rock above the *Nordhorn*'s fore-peak.

'Someone's lobbing grenades off that ledge!'

As two more flares ignited overhead the AA gunners on the *wintergarten* opened fire on the ledge at point-blank range.

'Hoses clear — diesel loading hatch secure!' Kernbach's voice was only just audible above the raucous bark of the guns.

'Let go all wires!' Rink yelled to the catwalks.

'All clear for and aft, sir!' was the shouted reply from below.

Rink sent a hurried glance fore and aft. 'Small ahead both! Rudder amidships!'

The diesels suddenly added their own thunder to the night and the water boiled astern as *U501* edged ahead.

With a backward glance at the *Nordhorn*, Rink saw a man hacking at the for'ard spring with an axe while the fire on the bridge rapidly gained hold.

By the time *U501*'s bows cleared the *Nordhorn*'s stern CGM Kordt was with the 88 mm gun crew on the for'ard catwalk and caught a glimpse of muzzle flame on the edge of the shore. Issuing rapid orders, he laid the cannon himself. '*Fire!*' The jolt of the recoil sent a shudder through the boat, and in the next instant the shore erupted with the yellow flash of high-explosive, the blast felling pines and sending debris hurtling through the air.

Further up the gully the machinegun switched targets when *U501* surged clear of the *Nordhorn*'s stern to expose herself in full profile, and bullets lashed the water on the port side before they found the casing. Somewhere a man crumpled with an astonished cry, and then the bullets raked the bridge, whined off the armour plating and ricochetted through the *wintergarten* rails. As he gazed anxiously astern, Rink was vaguely aware that more than one figure slumped to the duckboards while he waited for them to pull clear of the *Nordhorn* where she struggled to wrench herself free from the shore, water threshing white under her stern. And then they were clear. 'Full ahead both! Hard right rudder!'

CGM Kordt was aware that only one of the twin 20 mm mountings was still firing when he brought the 88 mm cannon to bear on the edge of the pine-clad slope where the machinegun was sighted, the tracer shell betraying her position. '*Fire!*' he yelled above the din while *U501* rapidly picked up speed, and saw the shell explode among the pines with another blinding flash. This time the machinegun ceased firing abruptly in the midst of the ringing explosion.

Aft on the *wintergarten* both twin 20 mm mountings were firing again, and Rink saw the port mounting now manned by Schramm, an animal snarl twisting his face as he hugged himself to the shoulder-cushions, pumping a vicious stream of shells into the pines along the shore. Further aft Wohldorf hung across the rails with a machine-pistol which someone had dropped, directing his fire out across the swinging stern.

The shooting stopped abruptly when *U501* swung around out in the fjord and every face on deck was directed towards the *Nordhorn*, tragic and silent witness to her struggle to pull herself clear of her moorings, her blazing superstructure lighting the shore.

'Stop both,' ordered Rink.

As the last flares drifted down to extinguish themselves on the surface of the fjord, the *Nordhorn* finally pulled clear of the shore only to instantly lose way and begin to settle by the stern.

Meanwhile a stretcher-party was busily lowering the wounded down through *U501*'s bridge hatch.

'Who have you got there?' Rink called to them.

'The Executive Officer, sir,' PO Seaman Weber answered.

Rink was startled by Weber's announcement. In the confusion he had not noticed von Heydekampf's absence. 'Who else have you wounded?' he asked, recalling the two figures he had seen disappear across the side when the grenade had exploded on the after catwalk.

'Able Seaman Krebitz for one, sir. But I'm not sure who else at the moment.'

'Then do everything you can for them. Kosney is with the *Nordhorn*.'

PO Seaman Hoven interjected loudly, 'They're abandoning ship, sir!'

Rink hurriedly focused his binoculars on the stricken oiler. She was now fiercely alight aft and figures could be seen jumping into the water across the port side to join several swimmers already moving out towards *U501*. 'Standby to receive survivors!' he called to the catwalks.

'Let's hope Dr Kosney is among them,' said PO Seaman Hoven, binoculars gripped to his eyes.

Rink did not hear him. Instead he was engrossed in trying to manoeuvre *U501* in as close as he dared to the blazing oiler. 'Small ahead both. Right rudder — steady.'

U501 crept ahead, angled in towards the *Nordhorn* where she lay down by the stern taking water inboard across her after bulwarks, while several figures still struggled to pull themselves clear of the flooded companionway. Adding to the hazardous conditions, diesel fuel was spewing out across the waters of the fjord from more than one ruptured tank, the smell hanging oppressively in the wind.

'Stop both,' Rink reluctantly called into the tower, knowing if he put them too close inshore there was every chance that when the flames, roaring through the *Nordhorn*'s superstructure, touched the surface of the fjord the spilled fuel would ignite like a giant torch, and having seen more than one tanker fall victim to the same fate, he could not put *U501* further at risk. As a result all the crew could now do was to look grimly on, unable to be of any direct aid.

The first swimmer was less than one hundred metres from *U501* when the fuel covering the surface of the water ignited, flames darting swiftly out to encircle the sinking oiler. Within seconds all but two of the swimmers had disappeared, engulfed in the roaring carpet of flame, and then they too were devoured by hungry tendrils which struck out across the surface.

Rink turned away, face lost in shadow. 'Full ahead both!' he shouted below with unnecessary harshness in order to conceal the emotion which threatened his voice. 'Left rudder! Steady! Steer so!'

U501 quickly pulled abeam of the inferno roaring around the *Nordhorn* where she was settling close to the shore in the throes of a horrifying death, then thrust ahead into the darkness. When at a distance of under six hundred metres, the *Nordhorn* suddenly blasted apart with a detonation which shook the surrounding countryside, and sent a ball of flame skyward to illuminate the cliffs and peaks with a terrifying glow, the searing blast of heat being felt by every man on *U501*'s upperdeck.

Rink stared fixedly ahead. 'Secure for sea. All spare hands below. Berger — check the for'ard hatch and after casing. See if we suffered any damage aft from that grenade. I didn't hear of any being reported from below.'

U501 was in the entrance to the fjord by the time Berger completed his inspection of the upperdeck and climbed to the bridge. 'For'ard hatch and upperdeck secure, sir. The grenade doesn't appear to have caused more than superficial scarring of the casing, although I believe it accounted for one of the ratings.'

'I saw *two* men blown outboard,' said Rink. 'I'm certain of it.'

'I didn't know that, sir. But I heard someone say Torpedo Gunner's Mate Scheel was caught in the blast.'

Rink stared at him in silence. Scheel was another of the old hands from *U207*, a solid, reliable Petty Officer. The law of averages seemed to catch up with everyone in time. 'Take over the watch till I see what's happening below.'

Rink stepped into the control-room and was met by numb, shaken faces.

Kernbach thumbed back his cap and shook his head gravely. 'I'm afraid the Exec's dead,' he announced in a disconsolate voice. 'He died just after they brought him below. He took two bullets through the upper chest.'

Rink accepted the news in grim and bitter silence. Like Kernbach, Scheel, and several others, he had known von Heydekampf since the day he assumed command of *U207*, and not only had he lost a skilled and competent officer, it being only the lack of U-boats that had prevented him obtaining his own command long since, but also a close friend. The son of an eminent Austrian family with an estate near Innsbruck, he had been a sportsman of considerable acclaim before the war, a banker in civilian life. It was not easy to accept his death.

'I believe we also lost Kosney,' Kernbach said in dejection.

'Yes. Like the others on board the *Nordhorn* he never had a chance,' said Rink, and made his way for'ard to the Wardroom. Von Heydekampf's blanket-covered body was laid out on his bunk, and outside the dispensary two more bodies lay side by side on the deck-plates, those of Able Seaman Rolf Krebitz and Joel Sommer, both still in their teens, the former having been one of the 20 mm gunners.

'Sommer was one of the gun-guard on the for'ard catwalk, sir,' Coxswain Lamm quietly informed him. 'We also lost Machinist's Mate Hildebrandt. He was the other one who went over the side along with Scheel when that grenade exploded.'

Rink silently nodded acceptance of the fact. They had paid a heavy toll in order to top off their fuel bunkers. Altogether six men were dead or missing: von Heydekampf, Scheel, Krebitz, Sommer, Hildebrandt, and Dr Kosney. It was a bitter loss to accept. 'There was no one else hurt?' he asked, half afraid of the reply.

'Luckily no, sir,' said Lamm, and paused to clear his throat awkwardly. 'Shall I prepare them for burial, sir?' he wanted to know.

'Yes. We can bury them at first light.'

When Rink returned to the control-room he found Wohldorf waiting for him, trying to restrain his agitation and impatience. 'I'm told we lost six men back there. Is that true?'

'Unfortunately, yes,' Rink affirmed.

'Then I must know if their loss is in any way going to prevent us from continuing the voyage.'

Rink met Wohldorf's challenging gaze with level grey eyes. 'On the contrary. Because of what happened back there I'm all the more determined to continue on our way. I wouldn't like to think that those men sacrificed their lives for nothing. Does that answer your question?'

Wohldorf was visibly embarrassed by Rink's forthrightness.

He said defensively, 'I simply wished to have the situation clarified.'

'Then it's clarified,' Rink stated coolly, then turned to Kernbach. 'What's our position regarding fuel, Chief?'

Kernbach made a moue. 'We didn't get anything into the bilges, but our tanks are as good as topped off.'

Rink made his mental calculations in silence. 'I haven't troubled you with the details yet, but it's arranged for us to take on a further supply of fuel from a U-tanker either at a position south-west of La Palma, or at a secondary position west of the Cabo Verdes. However, what we've just taken on board ought to see us through.'

'So long as we don't meet with further trouble on the way,' Kernbach solemnly reminded him.

Rink knew that Kernbach was right, and he fervently hoped that the incident in Hardanger fjord was not going to be the harbinger of further misfortune. However, he was uncomfortably aware that certain voyages were destined to be troubled from the outset with one problem after another, persistently dogged by misfortune. With fatalistic resignation, he said, 'I'm afraid that's something no one can prophesy.'

'I suppose not,' Kernbach gloomily conceded.

Rink was suddenly aware of Chief Telegraphist Bergold standing uneasily in the background, waiting. 'Yes, Bergold?'

Bergold turned to lead the way for'ard to what privacy the W/T office afforded, and there handed Rink a slip of signal paper. 'A request from Headquarters seeking acknowledgement, our position, and our ETA at Kristiansand, sir.'

Rink had been expecting the signal since early the previous afternoon; Kristiansand had become worried about their non-arrival. 'Forget it. But transmit the one word signal BREAKOUT at fifteen minute intervals for the period of one hour. Someone's waiting for it somewhere. Only don't acknowledge whatever curious mode of reply it may raise in answer. Is that clear?'

'Yes, sir,' answered Bergold whose intense, studious face expressed no trace of surprise at such cryptic instructions. Among the most conscientious men on board, Bergold was an ardent Party member and intensely patriotic, responsible for *U207*'s adoption of the *Badenweilermarsch* as her signature march on the grounds that it was listed high among the Führer's favourites. Yet unlike most Party members, he kept his ideals and views strictly to himself. On his service record his father was entered as being Geheime Staatspolizei Liaison Officer to SS-Oberstgruppenführer Otto Ohlendorf, Reich Security Main Office Amt III. And in such circumstances Rink accounted for the man's presence in the U-boat Force as an indication of his fierce sense of patriotism, and not because of lack of influence in higher circles, something for which he respected him both as a man and a Warrant Officer.

When Rink returned to the control-room the time was 04.10 on the morning of April 5.

*

At 4.20 am that same morning Korvettenkapitan Gerhard Lamprecht was driving south towards Berlin in his Mercedes. After he had attended to the evacuation and dispersal of all personnel to Berlin and Plon, he had left the Mecklenburg Compound late the previous evening and was in good spirits, eager to see his wife and to report his presence in Berlin to Bormann at the Reichskanzlei later in the morning. And with good fortune on his side, he decided there was every likelihood that he and his wife would be on their way to Konstanz before the day was out.

Then where the highway entered a dense stretch of evergreen forest south of Neubrandenburg, the same forest in which Wohldorf had concealed his convoy on the journey north to the Mecklenburg Compound some days earlier, he suddenly and unaccountably found himself flagged down by two men armed with flashlights. Sweeping the Mercedes to a crisp halt on the wayside carpet of pine needles, he wound down the window and peered out at the two men whom he saw were muffled in dark overcoats and hats. 'Yes?' he curtly demanded. 'What's going on here?'

The two men stepped close to the car and looked in at him uncertainly.

'Well?' Lamprecht retorted with mounting impatience at his unexpected delay.

The taller of the two men bent his face close to the open window. 'Korvettenkapitan Gerhard Lamprecht?' he queried as if to establish the fact beyond doubt.

Exasperated, Lamprecht snapped, 'Yes! Now what is it? What's the reason for this delay?'

'Would you kindly mind leaving the car and coming with us, sir?' the man asked with a cordial tone of inquiry.

Lamprecht's temper suddenly erupted. '*Verdammter Scheisz*! What in hell do you want?'

'Please,' the man said with stolid patience. 'We were instructed to intercept you on the way south. I assure you it's important, vital. Now if you would be so kind.'

Seething inwardly, Lamprecht thrust the door open and stepped out into the chill early morning air. 'Where are we going?'

'Please. This way. Follow me.' The taller man started across the highway in the manner of a man confident of the direction in which his objective lay, stopped when he reached the opposite verge, and stepped adroitly to the side.

Held in the dim glow of the flashlight following him, Lamprecht hesitated in consternation, started to turn around, and was immediately dealt two blows of such stunning force in the back that he was clubbed to his knees.

Standing behind his victim, SS-Obersturmführer Arendt of the Geheime Staatspolizei Berlin Office, watched Lamprecht struggle to regain his feet, took deliberate aim with the Walther P38, fired a third time, and saw Lamprecht lurch forward on to his face. Then pocketing the Walther, he grabbed Lamprecht's feet and glanced up at his hesitating companion. 'Come on!' he snapped. 'What are you waiting for? Into the woods with him, hurry!'

The two men between them carried the body a short distance through the pines to the prearranged spot, laid it out in the undergrowth, and with the aid of Arendt's flashlight, his companion removed all identification papers from the body, then together they toppled it down a steep embankment and watched it disappear into a dense clump of gorse.

Switching off his flashlight, Arendt mused, 'I wonder why he had to go — a Korvettenkapitan nonetheless.'

'Who cares?' his companion growled in an undertone. 'We've done our part. Now let's get back to Berlin.'

*

Kapitanleutnant Wolfgang Rink was engrossed in the chart on the table before him. His instructions on leaving Hardanger fjord were that he set a north-westerly course and schnorchel his way out into the North Atlantic between Shetland and the Faroe Islands, the normal passage for U-boats entering and leaving the North Atlantic to or from their bases in North Germany and Norway. But with the events of *U207*'s journey home still fresh in his mind he was far from confident of making a successful break-out. With Allied aircraft and surface vessels prowling every metre of water it was an extremely hazardous undertaking. However, he swung up through the tower to the bridge where Berger had his binoculars on the rugged coast to southward.

Out clear of Hardanger fjord the wind gusted strongly from northward and *U501* yawed and rolled in the seas breaking white across the casing.

'Leave it with me,' Rink informed Berger. 'Right rudder. Come to course 315 degrees.'

Dawn had tinted Norway's peaks to eastward pale green when the canvas-shrouded bodies were brought up on deck and laid out on the after catwalk. Then with the lookouts keeping a sharp all around watch on sea and sky, Rink gave the order to heave-to. Muffled in oilskins, the few bareheaded figures of the burial party allowed on deck heard their Kommandant's words plucked away by the wind as he read the short burial service, and with *U501* heaving restlessly among the white-capped seas, the weighted bodies were committed to the deep. When the last grey shape sank beneath the icy waters Rink ordered both engines two-thirds ahead so that the bows buried into the broken crests, gathering themselves under a cloudless sky whose stars still shimmered in the clear dawn light, to leave the crew not only with memories of departed comrades but also to reflect on the perils they might expect to encounter in the coming days ahead.

Throughout the morning *U501* thrust her way north-westward, the incident in Hardanger fjord a few hours earlier imprinted on everyone's mind, which, coupled with the memory of *U207*'s nerve-wracking homeward journey, cast an air of deep foreboding throughout the hull, leaving the crew grim and silent while they brooded on their chances of making a successful break-out into the North Atlantic.

Yet Rink was aware of one factor in favour of success; the barometer had continued to fall rapidly all forenoon, an indication of a sharp deterioration in the weather. Meanwhile he held to their prescribed course, schnorchel functioning as well as its designers could have hoped, drawing a continuous supply of air down to the diesels while the electric batteries were recharged. But by early afternoon even the improved schnorchel was engaged in a losing battle with the elements, when heavy seas began to break over the float to continually choke off the air supply.

The control-room chronometer showed the time to be 14.25 when Rink issued orders to cease schnorchelling and brought *U501* to the surface with fuming diesels. The scene which met the bridge watch when they hauled themselves out on to the bridge was one of bleak desolation. Long seas reared up, one behind the other, glassy slopes dirty grey, flecked with boiling foam. The boat pitched and rolled wildly. To northward an ugly grey-green curtain of gloom had been drawn across the earlier flawless sky, and the sun, exposed briefly between mounting clouds, lost itself in a gangrenous pall of light.

Rink reached a decision and left Erlanger and his watch on the bridge to return below to the chart-table. Five minutes later he sent Control-room PO Morgen for'ard to inform Wohldorf that his presence was required in the control-room.

Wohldorf arrived some moments later, moving unsteadily on the pitching gangway, clearly puzzled by the summons.

Without preamble Rink indicated their position on the chart west-north-west of Hardanger fjord. 'As you must be aware, the weather has deteriorated greatly since mid-morning and the barometer is still falling, a sign, I'm convinced, that we're in for a storm of exceptional severity which will last for several days.'

Wohldorf stared back at him, uncomprehending. 'I'm sorry,' he said.

Rink said, 'Then let me put it this way. I'm of the opinion that these conditions offer us the ideal opportunity to make a straight dash for the comparative safety of the North Atlantic.'

Wohldorf realised at once the full implication of Rink's statement. 'You mean you intend to disregard your orders.' It was not a question.

'Exactly,' Rink calmly affirmed. 'But I haven't arrived at my decision without considerable forethought. I've taken every conceivable factor into consideration. With conditions deteriorating as they are at present it will make things far more difficult for the Allies than for us. Almost certainly all their aircraft have already been grounded, while their escort vessels will have their speed and manoeuvrability seriously impaired by these ever-mounting seas. I've seen it all before.'

'Perhaps so,' Wohldorf grudgingly conceded. 'But you haven't yet explained just what course of action you intend to pursue.'

'I simply propose to make our run on the surface. However, it isn't as foolish nor as reckless as it may at first sound. Distinctly in our favour is the fact that without air patrols the Allies will be virtually blind. And whether or not you're aware of it, the U-boat is a vastly superior seaboat in the prevailing conditions, conditions which I'm convinced will deteriorate even further, conditions which will enable us to out-run and out-manoeuvre any type of surface vessel not forced to take shelter and prepared to offer a challenge to us.'

Through ignorance of the subject, Wohldorf remained silent, indecisive.

To further his argument, Rink jabbed a pencil at the chart, at a projected line from their present position above the 60 degree Latitude mark down through between the Orkney and Shetland Islands — Fair Isle Passage — to emerge into the North Atlantic north of the islands of Rona and Sula Sgeir. 'What I propose to do is to make a straight run at maximum speed. Once out into the North Atlantic we can then, still taking advantage of the weather if it continues to hold, turn on to a south-westerly course and roughly follow the 100 fathom isobath mark till we meet with the Bathyal Zone beyond Erris Head in Southern Ireland.'

Wohldorf knew that he was not in a position to argue. To him the chart was nothing more than a barely decipherable map, most of it composed of a vast expanse of ocean, seething and foaming in wild tumult if the motion of *U501* was an indication of its present condition.

Rink saw his indecision and pressed his argument home. 'Naturally I'm prepared to accept responsibility for my decision to disregard orders,' he announced, but refrained from mentioning the fact that if he *was* in the act of committing an error of the first magnitude, then there would not be anyone in a position to answer for it, unless Old Rasmus himself decided to adjudicate at his own Board of Inquiry.

Wohldorf was clearly uneasy, worried. 'You're certain about all this?'

'Absolutely,' Rink was emphatic.

'You know, of course,' Wohldorf frankly admitted, 'that I'm not in the position to argue with your decision. I know nothing of these matters. But if you're convinced in your own mind that this is the best course of action to pursue, then I must leave it with you.'

'Thank you,' said Rink. 'However, I felt I must at least inform you of my intentions.'

At 14.40 Rink altered course to west-south-west in the face of a Force 9 gale towards the stretch of water flanked by Sumburgh Head and Fair Isle. With negative buoyancy tank preflooded, *U501*'s decks were awash, the towering seas breaking directly across the bridge from northward, her bridge watch secured by steel safety-belts, fighting to maintain their footing under the torrents of icy water which roared through the horseshoe and cascaded across the *wintergarten*, only periscope standards and twin 20 mm AA mountings visible at times.

When at 20.00 the Dog Watches were relieved, the men struggled below, bodies numbed by cold and wet, pinched faces encrusted with rime: the radar operator reported radar impulses as becoming widely scattered and faint, something which Rink had earlier predicted.

During the late morning they passed Fair Isle to starboard, lost in darkness and roaring seas. Some time later dawn broke fighting against a lowering sky, the ominous mass of black cloud reflecting itself on still mounting seas that now foamed angry white on their crests and filled the air with a blizzard of spindrift.

All morning the storm continued to build, the sky in the north blanketed by an ever darkening overcast, great banks of purple black clouds scudding across lengthening seas gathering in size and momentum while the wind gained steadily in force, conditions which eventually forced Rink to order a further reduction in speed.

At midday the bridge watch were provided with their first of two brief glimpses of the Orkney Islands when the rocky tip of Papa Westray exposed itself through the mountainous seas breaking around it. Some time later came the storm lashed black cliffs of Westray, then emptiness except for a turbulent mass of sea and the sky whipped by a shrieking wind.

During the Afternoon Watch Rink bowed his head against the stinging lash of spindrift and his slitted gaze found PO Seaman Hoven huddled in the starboard for'ard sector of the horseshoe. 'Odin's certainly beating his drum today!' he bellowed against the wind screaming in the jumping-wires and periscope standards.

Hoven's numbed features twisted into a grimace and his reply was lost as an urgent report arrived from below. 'Radar contact on 170 degrees — faint!'

Rink was unworried by the information and called into the voice-tube, 'Keep me informed'.

Twenty minutes later the warning was again issued from below. 'Contact holds position on 170 degrees — making slight headway!'

Rink continued on course knowing *U501* had almost certainly been detected on radar and that somewhere to southward an escort was making an attempt to get within striking distance. Yet he was not unduly concerned, for a surface vessel with an extensive freeboard, labouring through such mountainous seas as they were encountering, scarcely presented a serious threat.

But before fifteen minutes had elapsed, yet another report reached the bridge. 'New radar contact on 310 degrees!' And again later: 'New contact holds steady!'

The contact was to north-westward, and now *U501* was suddenly being converged on from opposite directions, a fact which forced Rink to consider the possibility that yet another escort had decided to make an interceptory dash towards them.

Yet he continued steadfastly on course, and over the next eighty minutes the bearing and range of the new contact continued to close steadily until finally the blurred shadow loomed into view through the ghostly white wall of rain and spume on *U501*'s starboard bow, an enormous freighter of around 16,000 GRT, wallowing alarmingly in the precipitous seas, colossal bows blasting massive cascades of water high into the air back across her forepeak to batter her bridge superstructure amidships. And still closing, she exposed herself in clear detail, the seas on her port quarter lifting her stern high to show racing screws and the American flag streaming from her jackstaff, then marching beneath her hull they dropped her stern back down into the following trough, bows again flinging skyward, her decks awash, derricks and superstructure sheeted in driving clouds of rain and spume.

With her colossal bows buried deep in a trough, Rink swept his binoculars over her as they passed ahead, and when her bows flung clear her name showed plainly to the naked eye: *Oregon Trader*. Then while *U501* battled on westward, her bridge watch locked to the safety-rail, the tower constantly awash, the freighter was gradually left astern headed towards the northerly coast of Scotland to southward. And within an hour darkness had closed down over the raging ocean, both radar contacts slowly fading, before they altogether vanished from the oscillograph in the soundroom to leave the radar screen blank except for misted sea return.

*

SS-Hauptsturmführer Ernst Wohldorf lay in his bunk staring at the swaying, plunging deckhead with frustration and resentment. Only by grasping the safety-rail of his bunk with one hand, and placing the other firmly against the bulkhead, could he keep himself relatively still while the boat performed an extensive and alarming repertoire of acrobatics. He had never experienced anything approaching it, had never imagined anything approaching it. And what made it all even more frustrating was the fact thet he could not see anything, nothing except the gyrating deckhead and the pitching deck-plates of the dispensary flat outside his bunk. The noise was also fearful, like huge chains being dragged rattling along the outside of the hull, accompanied by a great irregular roaring sound as if the plates were being scoured by a coarse grade of emery-cloth. Like most people unacquainted with the ways of a U-boat he had been of the impression that they skulked placidly along far beneath the cantankerous ocean, only surfacing occasionally for air in order to recharge their batteries. Now he knew differently.

But more difficult to accept, especially with so much at stake in the future, was the realisation that he was totally ignorant of what was happening around him. And it was a matter which had to be rectified as quickly as possible. He had already experienced one example of just how easily Rink could decide to ignore orders, to take matters completely into his own hands. He saw the situation as critical.

'Coffee, sir?' a polite voice self-consciously inquired.

Wohldorf turned his head to see Leutnant Berger beside his bunk, a thermos flask and two china mugs balanced to counteract the violent motion of the boat.

'It will probably be the only thing hot to come from the galley for the next few days, sir,' Berger explained.

Wohldorf snapped open the safety-rail, sat upright, swung his legs over the edge of the bunk, and accepted one of the mugs. 'Thank you, Berger.'

Berger poured coffee from the thermos, glancing at Schramm who was lying wedged into the bottom bunk.

Wohldorf followed Berger's glance. 'I don't think we ought to bother him.' Then conversationally, he said, 'You've just come off watch, haven't you, Berger?'

'Yes, sir.'

Wohldorf sipped his coffee and made an aggrieved gesture at the swaying deckhead. 'Tell me, is it always like this?'

'To be honest, sir,' said Berger. 'I've never experienced this sort of weather before. The Kommandant expects it to develop into a storm of hurricane proportions.'

Wohldorf found it difficult to accept such a prediction. He regarded Berger as if he had in some unwitting way offered a personal insult. 'You actually mean that conditions are going to get *worse* than they already are?'

His voice respectfully apologetic, Berger replied, 'It would appear so, sir.'

Wohldorf regarded Berger critically, suddenly seeing in him a possible ally, and the opportunity to rectify the problem of his ignorance of shipboard matters. He said, 'I believe that you volunteered for this voyage, Berger.'

'Yes, sir.'

Wohldorf appeared to reflect on Berger's reply for several moments, then said, 'Why, Berger? Tell me why.'

Berger was disconcerted by the forthrightness of the question, uncertain of his answer.

Wohldorf decided to answer for him instead. 'I don't suppose it was because you suspected that *U501* was bound for the *Argentine*?'

Berger said hurriedly, 'No, sir. I was never at any time aware of her destination.'

'But you suspected she was being made ready for no ordinary war cruise?'

'Yes, sir. I did,' Berger admitted, uncomfortable with his inquisition.

Wohldorf gave an almost imperceptible nod of approval. 'How old are you, Berger?'

'Twenty-three, sir.'

'Twenty-three, eh,' mused Wohldorf as if in private reflection of the fact. 'And do you have any relatives or friends in Latin America, Berger?'

'No, sir. I don't know anyone in Latin America, sir.'

'Mm, pity that, Berger. Tell me, have you considered what you might do should the war be over by the time we reach our destination?'

'No, sir. I haven't given the matter any thought, sir,' Berger said uneasily; then added hurriedly, 'I mean about the war being over, sir.'

'No, perhaps not,' Wohldorf politely conceded. 'That might be unpatriotic. But being at all times a realist, it's a possibility which *I* haven't entirely discounted. Does that surprise you, Berger?'

Berger swallowed awkwardly under Wohldorf's searching gaze. 'I don't know, sir,' he mumbled.

Wohldorf seemed not to have heard him. Sipping at his coffee, he said judiciously, 'You know, Berger, I may be in a position to offer you aid and advice when we reach the Argentine. I'm not without influence. Indeed, I may be in a position whereby I can be of very great aid to you, especially if I'm able to recommend you to our waiting hosts for the cooperation you've given me on the voyage. And I have faith in you, Berger.'

Berger found he was not displeased with the compliment. 'I assure you that you can depend on my cooperation at all times, sir.'

'Good,' Wohldorf announced with a smile.

'If I can be of any assistance whatever –'

Wohldorf cut Berger short. He stated bluntly, 'What I require to know, discreetly, of course, is what's happening on board this vessel at all times, the Kommandant's actions and intentions, our day to day movements, gossip, everything in general. It would be very much to your advantage at a later date if you were able to furnish me with such details. Do you understand my meaning, Berger?'

Berger understood. 'Yes, sir.'

Wohldorf's gaze was both direct and candid. 'Yes, I know what you're thinking, Berger. But forget the Kommandant. He will have no influence whatever once we arrive in the Argentine. His task is merely to get us there. I don't know f whether or not you've given thought to these packing cases and canisters we have on board, but they're my responsibility, not the Kommandant's. *I* am in charge, Berger. Remember that.'

'Yes, sir.'

'It's a matter to which you ought to devote your most careful consideration, Berger,' Wohldorf impressed.

Berger was already swayed by Wohldorf's offer. As the SS man had clearly intimated, he would not always have to serve on board *U501*, his loyalty dedicated solely to Rink. He had to give thought to the future. He was alone. His mother had died while he was still at school, his elder brother had been killed in Normandy the previous year, and his father had perished with the refugee ship, *Wilhelm Gustloff*, when sunk by a Russian submarine in the Baltic earlier in the year. 'You can be assured I will carry out your wishes to the best of my ability, sir.'

'Then you won't find cause to regret your decision, Berger. I promise you,' Wohldorf replied with a meaningful smile. 'Now how well do you know Ingersoll, Rothfels, and Guntel? Do you have their confidence? Can you rely on their discretion? You must have known them at the Mecklenburg Compound.'

Berger cast a wary glance around the dispensary flat as ERA Dornberger passed aft on his way towards the engineroom. He said, 'Yes, sir. I know them better than anyone else on board. Rothfels and Guntel will almost certainly agree to anything I ask of them, but I hesitate to vouch for Ingersoll. First, he's senior to me, second, I know that he respects the Kommandant's confidence, something which I don't believe he'd be prepared to betray.'

Wohldorf raised a hand to cut him short. 'Then leave him out of it. But have a discreet word with Rothfels and Guntel. Explain what's expected of them. Tell them that their loyalty, like your own, won't go unrewarded. They have my word on that.'

'I will speak to them at the first opportunity, sir,' Berger promised.

His mind greatly relieved now that an ally had been acquired, Wohldorf drained his coffee and said expansively, 'Good. Excellent. Thank you for your cooperation, Berger.'

*

The time was 03.35 when Rink awakened to find *U501* still battling through huge seas, torrents of water thundering against the hull and tower. Climbing from his bunk, he pulled on his sheepskin coat and crossed the central gangway to the W/T office where PO Telegraphist Vogel was on watch. 'Have you monitored anything interesting?'

Vogel shook his dark head negatively. 'Only distress signals, sir. The ether's thick with them. Positions range from as far north as Svalbard to as far south as Punta de la Estaca.'

'But nothing else?'

'No, sir.'

Rink struggled aft, face pale and haggard, eyes puffed and red-rimmed. Since assuming the duties of First Officer on von Heydekampf's death he had scarcely left the bridge since they had surfaced, had slept in snatches and had eaten a hurried meal only when time allowed in between attending to his own duties as Kommandant. Now the strain showed in every line of his bearded face while he crammed oilskins on over his sheepskin coat and gulped down a mug of coffee in the control-room.

'Kommandant to the bridge!'

Rink hurled himself on to the bridge, prepared for any emergency.

With both hands to his mouth, Erlanger shouted against the shrieking wind, 'Shadow, left angle 20 degrees, sir!'

Rink focused his binoculars on the bearing indicated. The shadow was faint, seen only intermittently in the phosphorescent glow which surrounded it. 'I think we will find that's the island of Rona,' he predicted.

Rink allowed *U501* to remain on course until the shadow was on the port quarter, then turned her south to put Sula Sgeir to starboard, and with the seas on the port quarter headed south-west by west with the Butt of Lewis on the port bow. Like the *Oregon Trader* which they had earlier seen labouring with the seas astern, *U501* now set herself in motion accordingly. For what seemed an eternity the bows would lie buried under tons of broken water at the bottom of a trough while the stern reared clear above the following crest, screws racing until the crest of the sea passed beyond the point of equilibrium when the bows were flung skyward in a cloud of spindrift, and the screws bit deep into the down-rushing slope of the following sea. And continuing south-west in close proximity to the 100 fathom isobath, there was no determinable horizon anywhere now that the storm had reached hurricane force, just wall upon wall of upflung water lowered over by an angry black sky.

U501 was scarcely making noticeable headway when Rink ordered the daily trim dive to be made south-east of the lonely and desolate island of St Kilda in the Outer Hebrides, forty miles west-north-west of North Uist. When he went below to the control-room preparatory to the dive, he found Kerbach entering up his log at the chart-stowage locker. 'Is everything all right with you?'

'Fine,' Kernbach replied. 'But this is quite a storm we've got ourselves into, one of the worst I can recall. I doubt if many of those big lumbering merchantment will be able to ride it out without encountering extreme difficulty.'

Rink said, 'I just hope it holds, because my aim is to put as much distance as possible between us and the Brits before it blows itself out.'

Kernbach grinned approval. 'I've never heard anyone express a better idea. And my men will give you every effort.'

*

Four nights later *U501* was battering through immense seas one hundred and fifty miles south-south-west of Dunmore Head in Southern Ireland. In the past days progress had been minimal, and every bearded face on board showed signs of strain and weariness from the punishment which the boat was receiving at the hands of the elements. Even more depressing for everyone else were the chaotic conditions being experienced within the hull. With condensation running in streams from deckheads and bulkheads, dry bedding was a luxury of the past, while the nauseating stench of rotting food and the humid smell of oil and diesel fuel was everywhere.

Then during the Dog Watches the hurricane began to show the first signs of beginning to abate when the wind began to fall away perceptibly. Also adding to the general rise in spirits was that fact that they were now headed south on a course of 165 degrees which would take them clear of the Bay of Biscay, Spain's Cabo Finisterre, Portugal's Cabo de Sao Vicente, the Straits of Gibraltar, and on towards the next expected landfall, the Portuguese islands of Madeira four hundered miles west of Morocco. Such was the situation when the Second Watch climbed below from the bridge a few minutes before midnight.

On the way for'ard after putting their watch-clothing to dry in the after torpedo-room, Able Seaman Bartz and Ordinary Seaman Zeller stopped in line for coffee outside the galley, their normal practice when relieved on watch. Ahead of them, Leading Machinist Elser fought to retain his balance while he filled a mug from the urn above the range. 'To hell with this weather!' he grumbled. 'I haven't been able to remain upright for a single minute since we left Hardanger fjord.'

'Well you shouldn't have to put up with it for much longer,' Zeller offered in sympathetic agreement. 'The wind is still easing.'

Elser's bearded face expressed doubt. 'You think so?'

'That's true,' stressed Bartz. 'In another day or two it will all be calm seas and blue skies.'

Elser was sceptical. 'You think I came across the Starnberger Sea in a rowboat?'

Bartz stepped up to the urn before Elser could leave the galley. 'Wait,' he said in a low whisper. 'Can you get me a drilling-bit?'

Elser regarded him with puzzlement. 'What do you want with a drilling-bit?'

Bartz winked. 'Just go and get me one.'

'You mean *now*?'

'*Now*,' Bartz affirmed. 'Leave me to take your coffee for'ard.'

Elser obediently disappeared towards the engineroom as Bartz started the precarious journey for'ard with the coffee, Zeller in rear.

At the instant they stepped into the dimly-lit fore-ends the bows dropped deep into a trough without warning and the sea exploded on the casing overhead with a thunderous roar. Bartz stopped in mid-stride, like a drunken man. '*Himmel herrgotts* – when is this going to end?'

The deck abruptly stopped its downward plunge with a violent shudder which ran aft through the hull, followed by a hollow thud and rumble as the sea avalanched aft along the for'ard catwalk towards the tower. Bartz chose the moment to throw himself down at the table while Zeller hurriedly wedged himself into a corner of his bunk. From lying steeply down by the bows, *U501* struggled upwards again, the sea passing on aft, the for'ard catwalk shedding torrents of water, rearing high in the air, the stern buried deep.

Bartz was holding determinedly to the mugs when he saw Elser come through the doorway. 'Get it?'

Elser nodded, took his mug in one hand and passed the drilling-bit to Bartz with the other.

Bartz peered at it in the dim light, thrust it into his sock, then gulped at his coffee as the huge crew-cut figure of Torpedoman 1st Class Horst Wassermann lumbered through the door to join them at the table.

'What is it, Horst?' asked Elser. 'Is this weather getting you down too?'

Wassermann, who before his entry into the U-boat Force had worked as a labourer in an iron-works, turned a morose face on his fellow townsman, started to pass a remark, then decided against it with a resigned shrug of enormous shoulders, Although normally a talkative, good-natured individual, he had scarcely spoken a word since they had left the Mecklenburg Compound. Instead his thoughts had been constantly with his wife Herta back home in Munchen.

'Know something?' Bartz commented earnestly. 'I wish we were sailing along that Argentine coast right this minute.'

Wassermann studied him with sullen eyes. 'Who the hell wants to go to the Argentine?' he growled belligerently.' I'd rather take a walk through the Englischer Garten with Herta anytime.'

Bartz decided not to argue, but shrugged indifference, then got up and hoisted himself into his bunk above Zeller. Once settled, he retrieved the drilling-bit from his sock, rummaged beneath his pillow for the piece of wood which he had earlier put away, fitted the two together in the fashion of an awl, then with a sly glance around the gloomy compartment, he drove the tip of the drill between the wooden slats of the packing case stowed above him, then exerting pressure, began to drill. He found that the pine gave way without too much effort, then felt the drill meet with more stubborn opposition.

At the table Wassermann sat watching him with a puzzled frown on his sullen face. 'Hey — what's he doing to that case?'

Bartz froze, blinked sweat from his eyes as Wassermann's voice boomed through the fore-ends.

At the table Elser whispered harshly, '*Keep it down*!'

The dawning light of comprehension moved slowly across Wassermann's big face. 'Then why didn't he say what he was going to do?' he remonstrated.

The bows went deep, rose sluggishly, and when no one else in the compartment evinced interest in the matter, Bartz returned his attention to the packing case. After several minutes of concentrated effort he stopped to extend a hand to the light and peered at it closely.

Out of curiosity Elser and Wassermann rose from the table to join him. Elser said, 'What have you got there?'

Bartz shook his head. 'I don't know — metal filings of some sort — see?'

In a low voice Wassermann said, 'Give them here.'

Bartz brushed the filings into Wassermann's huge hand for him to spread out on his palm and make a discriminative appraisal of them in the dim light.

Bartz hissed impatiently, 'Well?'

'There are two different kinds of metal here,' the big ex-ironworker stated with authority.

Bartz and Elser pressed forward for a closer look.

Wassermann rubbed several silvery particles of metal to one side. 'Those are lead. And those others look to me like —' he paused to stare hard at his palm, at the particles which gleamed with a dull golden light. 'Hell, if those *are* what I think they *are*,' he breathed in wonder, as if afraid to believe in his own judgement.

Bartz lost all remaining patience. 'So what are they?'

Wassermann looked slowly from one to the other of the waiting faces. 'I'd say they were gold — bullion.'

Elser said in awe, 'You *mean* that?'

'That's my opinion,' Wassermann stated flatly.

'And the lead?' questioned Bartz. 'Where does the lead come into it?'

'If you were to open those cases,' said Wassermann, 'then you'd almost certainly find that they were lined with lead.'

'Jesus,' breathed Elser. 'Then what's in all those other cases?'

'If I were you I wouldn't even *think* about it,' Wassermann warned in a low growl. 'If Himmler's two friends back there get to know about this there will be hell to pay.'

Bartz panicked. 'Throw those filings in the bilges!'

Wassermann eagerly complied while Bartz snatched the drilling-bit from between the slats of the case and hid it beneath his pillow. Then the three men stared at each other mutely, fellow conspirators pondering their next move. With an edge of fear in his voice, Bartz said, 'We must keep this to ourselves.'

'I don't know *anything*,' a voice weakly impressed.

The three men automatically dropped their attention to the bottom bunk where they saw Zeller staring up at them wide-eyed. In the excitement of their discovery no one had remembered Zeller.

'You're in this whether you like it or not,' threatened Bartz. 'Remember that.'

'True,' Wassermann warned. 'And *I* don't know anything either. You hear?'

'The same goes for me,' stated Elser.

With a racing heart Bartz brushed together the shreds of sawdust and filings on his blanket, wetted them with saliva, then stopped them into the tiny hole between the slats of the case while the sweat of fear and guilt coursed down his body.

Next day, shortly after midday, Leading Machinist Guntel was in the motor-room carrying out a routine inspection of the high-pressure compressors when Leutnant Berger, relieved of the Forenoon Watch, went aft to put his clothing to dry in the after torpedo-room. Guntel flashed a stealthy glance at the duty electricians on the switchboards, then followed. He spoke quickly, in a confidential whisper. 'You asked me to keep my eyes and ears open, sir.'

Berger's gaze narrowed sharply. 'Yes?'

'Some of the crew tampered with one of the packing cases in the fore-ends last night. I didn't see anything myself, but one of them couldn't keep his mouth shut. Now it's being said that the cases contain bullion.'

'Who are the ones involved?'

'Bartz, Elser, Wassermann, and Zeller.'

'You're certain about this?'

'Yes, sir.'

'Who talked?'

'Elser. He told one of the machinists about it. Bartz is supposed to have drilled some sort of hole in the case above his bunk.'

'Then keep this quiet and leave it to me,' Berger informed him.

It was not until mid-afternoon that Berger found the opportunity to broach the subject with Wohldorf, when afternoon coffee arrived in the Wardroom. 'I see the wind is still easing,' he said generally. 'Another forty-eight hours and the storm should blow itself out.'

Wohldorf saw from the cast of Berger's face that his statement was meant to be more than an offer to casual conversation.

Schramm put down his coffee mug, glanced around the deserted Wardroom, then leaned closer across the table. 'Do you have something on your mind, Herr Leutnant?' he asked on his superior's behalf.

Berger dropped his voice low. 'Guntel spoke to me earlier in the day,' he addressed both men. 'He said someone tampered with one of the cases in the fore-ends last night.'

Wohldorf and Schramm exchanged glances. 'Go on,' said Wohldorf.

'Rumour has it the case contains bullion.' Berger allowed a brief moment of silence to add emphasis to his revelation. 'Apparently Bartz drilled some sort of hole in the one stowed above his bunk.'

'*Bartz*?' Wohldorf strove to put a face to the name.

'The port after lookout of my watch.'

Wohldorf nodded. 'Yes, I remember him.'

'Four men were involved,' Berger explained. 'Bartz, Elser, Wassermann, and Zeller.'

'Isn't Zeller also in your watch?'

'Yes, the young blond boy,' Berger confirmed. 'But according to Guntel the ring-leader is Bartz.'

'Then we must make an example of him,' Schramm stated in a menacing growl.

Wohldorf instanced his agreement with a brief nod.

Berger glanced from one to the other of the two SS men, at a loss to understand the implied threat. 'You mean inform the Kommandant?'

'The Kommandant doesn't enter into this,' Wohldorf scorned. 'I told you before — *I* am in charge of those cases, *not* the Kommandant.'

Schramm's face twisted into a brutal grimace. 'Let me walk up there and shoot him right in front of everyone.'

Berger paled, unable to believe his ears. 'You can't possibly mean that!'

Wohldorf laid a hand on Schramm's arm. He said, 'The Leutnant's right. It has to be something with a touch more inventiveness.'

Berger swallowed uncomfortably, moistened a suddenly dry mouth. He said uneasily, 'What do you mean?'

An idea had already occurred to Wohldorf. The shadow of a smile touched his mouth. He said complacently, 'Tell me, when is Bartz next on watch?'

Berger said uneasily, 'At 20.00 hours.'

'And isn't Rothfels also in your watch?'

'Yes. Rothfels, Bartz and Zeller,' answered Berger, uncomprehending.

Wohldorf nodded approvingly. 'Then I would suggest that you keep a conscientious watch, Herr Leutnant. On the *ocean*,' he added cryptically.

'But . . .' Berger's voice trailed, silenced by the cold menace on Schramm's face.

*

Although conditions had continued to improve throughout the afternoon and early evening, seas still ran high from northward to lift *U501*'s stern and drive her bows deep into the preceding troughs, a long ponderous and uncomfortable motion which was even more difficult to endure than the unpredictable motions produced by the storm.

Rink and the First Watch had been relieved ten minutes earlier by Berger and the Second Watch and he was at the chart-table in the control-room with Erlanger, both men engrossed in the problems of blind navigation.

Erlanger, the quiet, soft-spoken ex-student from Oldenburg who had served for a time as Navigator's assistant on board the *Prinz Eugen* before his transfer to the U-boat Force, said on sombre reflection, 'I asked Leutnant Berger to inform me if the overcast shows promise of breaking up, although that's probably being over-optimistic at this moment. Nonetheless a starfix would be useful right now.'

Rink grinned good-humouredly. 'It isn't quite as far out of the question as a sun-shot.'

A boyish smile passed across Erlanger's face. 'I suppose not, sir.'

Rink returned his attention to the chart and *U501*'s estimated position. Since St Kilda they had been without any sort of fix whatever, and although the situation wasn't in any way desperate it was always a good thing to know one's precise whereabouts if an emergency arose. 'This storm has certainly kept the Brits off our necks, but just the same I'm going to feel easier in my mind once we're south of the Straits of Gibraltar.'

'Excuse me, Herr Kommandant,' a voice intervened.

Rink saw Chief Telegraphist Bergold in the central gangway outside the W/T office, and at once made his way for'ard. 'What is it?'

Bergold glanced through the open door of the office to where PO Telegraphist Vogel was seated at the radio bench. 'Vogel just broke in on a Spanish radio broadcast, sir. It contained an announcement that the Western Allies have crossed the Elbe on a wide front and are moving towards Berlin. It was also stated that massive concentrations of Russian troops and armour are poised ready to launch an assault on the capital along the highway from Kustrin.'

For Rink it was grim, forbidding news, but not unexpected. He looked at Vogel where he sat at the cramped radio bench. 'You're certain of this?'

His face pale and strained, Vogel said, 'I heard the announcement quite clearly, sir. They interrupted their programme with a special broadcast.'

Rink nodded. Vogel, whose father had served as a military advisor with General Franco during the Spanish Civil War, spoke the language fluently and was unlikely to have been mistaken. 'Then say nothing of this to anyone. Every man on board has problems enough without being burdened with this sort of news. However, inform me at once if you hear anything from home on the subject. I will be in my quarters if required.'

Minutes after Rink drew the curtain on his bunk, Schramm wandered into the control-room where Erlanger was still working at the chart-table. 'Do you mind if I take a breath of fresh air on the bridge?'

Erlanger regarded the hulking SS man with undisguised surprise. 'You know it's still quite rough up there and that we're taking an occasional heavy sea across the bridge from aft?' he warned. 'However, if you really feel you must go up there, then you had better go into oilskins and take a safety-belt along.'

Schramm said, 'I can take care, but I have to get some fresh air into my lungs before the stench down here drives me crazy.'

'Yes, I know how you feel,' Erlanger sympathised, then started aft to the galley to get himself coffee.

Chief Engineer Kernbach gave Schramm a curious glance when he passed through the control-room on his way for'ard and saw him climbing into a set of oilskins. Then continuing for'ard he stepped through the watertight bulkhead doorway and stopped outside Rink's quarters. 'Are you awake, sir?'

Rink turned in his bunk and thrust the curtain aside. 'Yes. What is it?'

'I've just come from the engineroom,' explained Kernbach. 'There's something I think you ought to hear – we've found ourselves a name.'

Rink frowned.

Kernbach said, 'The *Golden Pheasant*. It may be rather appropriate too. Those cases with the Party insignia stencilled on them – you know how it bears more than a passing resemblance to one of those birds.'

Rink saw at once what Kernbach was driving at, had himself long been aware that the term *Golden Pheasant* was derived from the gilded swastika insignia of the Nazi Party. He said drily, 'Then my only surprise is that some lower-deck genius didn't come up with this before now.'

'But that isn't all. It's also being rumoured that someone tampered with one of those cases and it contained bullion. They then apparently put two and two together and decided that our trip to the Argentine can only mean that the Golden Pheasants of the Party have it arranged to make certain of their own financial future, or at least the elite few have decided to do so.'

Rink remained silent. Privately he had formed the same conclusion at the outset.

Although Kernbach had harboured his own suspicions without giving voice to them, he was now moved to broach the subject directly. 'I don't suppose you also happen to go along with that?'

Apart from von Heydekampf, Kernbach had become one of Rink's closest comrades over the years, an officer whose confidence and trust it was impossible for him to be without, and he had no hesitation in placing his own confidence and trust in the tough navyman from Wilhelmshaven now. 'Perhaps we will never find ourselves in a position to prove the truth of the matter either way, Otto. But frankly, I wouldn't be surprised at *anything* those cases might contain.'

Kernbach said with dark solemnity, 'As you know, I never was a member of the Party, but I'd never have believed that the Führer would run out on his people when things became black, not for all his deficiencies.'

Rink regarded him steadily. 'Our orders were signed by the Reichsleiter – *not* the Führer.'

Kernbach's tough dark face registered instant surprise. 'The Reichsleiter, eh? Well I've heard it quietly opinioned on a number of occasions that he was a man who was always two steps ahead of the standard-bearer. Not that I've ever seen him apart from in photographs looking over the Führer's shoulder.'

'Likewise,' said Rink.

'Then I wonder who else is in this?'

'I don't know. But it's unlikely that Bormann is in it alone when one takes into account the amount of preparation which a voyage like this required.'

Kernbach's curiosity changed direction. 'And Wohldorf and his aide?'

'According to Lamprecht, he's on board in order to make certain that no one should suffer from lack of resolution. And I'm prepared to accept that explanation. I believe him to be a man who would prove both capable and ruthless if put to the test. Whether or not he has plans of his own for the future, I wouldn't know, but he certainly intends to make certain that our voyage meets with a satisfactory conclusion.'

'Then it's for the good of everyone we don't upset him,' Kernbach reflected.

'That's what worries me,' Rink admitted. 'Should he and that friend of his get to hear about a case being tampered with, then we will undoubtedly have trouble on our hands.'

'Well I'm pretty certain it isn't just a false rumour,' stated Kernbach. 'I heard about it from ERA Steiner. I don't pretend to know where he came by it, but he sounded mighty certain of his facts. However, I seriously doubt if you'll get anything out of anyone you might decide to interrogate. No one on board our little steamer is going to open his mouth on his comrades.'

'Yes, something which I can accept,' Rink acknowledged. 'But impress the necessity of silence on Steiner about this. And have him pass the word along, discreetly. The trouble is it's difficult to know just *who* we can depend on.'

'Then don't worry about where Ingersoll's loyalties lie,'

Kernbach stressed. 'We can count on him. He's with us all the way.'

'Good. Add Erlanger to the list too, along with Lamm and Kordt. But I'm afraid it's impossible to visualise how certain others will react in what will certainly prove to be a deteriorating situation as the voyage progresses.'

*

Once on the bridge Schramm stationed himself on the after end of the horseshoe starboard side and clipped his safety-belt to the rail. The murky wall of darkness which lay across the ocean was disturbed only by the phosphorescent gleam of foam-streaked seas where they boiled up to surge on past to southward. For a dullard bereft of imagination. Schramm was surprisingly adept at the art of drawing comparative description. All around him rose waves as he had never dreamed there could be, but monuments to Nature, occasionally one seemingly as tall as the Brandenburg Tor and equally as formidable, troughs as deep and as wide as Unter den Linden, great watery furrows marching resolutely southward. And although naturally apprehensive of such conditions, Schramm did not lack courage and determination. Peering about him as he grasped the safety-rail with both hands, he saw the shadowy figures of Berger and Rothfels in the fore part of the horseshoe steadfastly ignore his presence on the bridge.

Bartz was first to see the dimly growing shape of a particularly heavy sea gather itself up aft to lift the stern before it surged forward along the after catwalk, increasing in momentum as it approached. 'Hold tight everyone!' he hurled across his shoulder.

Dropping their binoculars down around their necks, everyone on the bridge grabbed for the safety-rail with both hands when the sea boiled in across the *wintergarten* from aft, hissing and foaming, to bury everyone in a turbulent swirl while it raced through the horseshoe.

Shocked and gasping, Schramm clung to the rail, amazed by the sheer weight and force of the icy deluge, until the last of it roared outboard. He then edged cautiously aft until he was close to Bartz's shoulder, his gaze fixed astern, waiting.

Several minutes passed before he saw the next huge sea gather itself up out of the darkness to surge along the after catwalk, a great patch of foam lighting its flanks, and he drew a deep breath and steeled himself to meet the icy onslaught.

Bartz grabbed for a handhold. 'Here comes another!'

This time it was a sea of such proportion that it threatened to wash the boat under, and Schramm had to fight to smother his own fear when the towering avalanche of water reared up across the *wintergarten* to bury the twin 20 mm mountings under a cloud of foam; then at the instant it broke into the horseshoe he reached out a hand to where Bartz's safety-belt was clipped to the rail. Buried under tons of water, his own feet threatening to be swept from under him, he then drove his elbow into Bartz's throat, felt him instantly dislodged, and caught a blurred glimpse of the terror-stricken face flash past to disappear into the darkness.

Zeller was the first to note his fellow lookout's disappearance when the water began to subside. '*Man missing*! *Man overboard*!' he screamed at Berger.

Rink was on the bridge within seconds of hearing Berger raise the alarm.

'He's gone! He's nowehere to be seen!' Berger shouted in the confusion.

Rink thrust him aside and began a frantic search of the horseshoe and *wintergarten*. Huge seas bulged and heaved all around in the darkness, constantly changing shape and form, and he knew that any attempt to find a man in such conditions was an impossible task, that dressed in heavy foul-weather gear and seaboots, he had already disappeared forever, dragged down like a stone. Reluctantly he turned back aft to where Zeller still clung to the safety-rail. 'Did you see what happened? Did you see anything at all?'

'No, sir. It was only when the water began to clear that I saw he was gone,' Zeller gasped in a dazed voice.

Rink crossed the bridge to where Schramm stood clutching the periscope standards. 'How long have you been up here?'

Schramm's response was to shake his head like a man in a state of shock. 'Only a few minutes. I asked the Quartermaster if I could get some air.' Shakily he went on, 'I don't remember even seeing him. It was all that water. I lost my balance. It drove my feet from under me. But I think I heard a cry – a shout.'

Rink swore and ran a hand along the rail half-expecting to encounter the broken clip of Bartz's safety-belt, but encountered nothing. Yet it was not the first time that such an incident had occurred in a following sea, and more than one unfortunate sailor had preceded Bartz to a watery grave in an identical manner. 'You had better get below,' he told Schramm, and followed him into the tower.

Erlanger and Kernbach were waiting in the control-room.

'It was Bartz,' explained Rink. 'Swept away by that last big one we took across the bridge. You had better find another lookout, and a relief for Zeller,' he instructed Erlanger. 'That boy's in a state of shock.'

The three officers and the duty control-room crew watched in silence while Schramm discarded his oilskins and pushed his way for'ard.

Rink turned again to Erlanger. 'What was he doing on the bridge?'

'He asked if he could get some air, sir. He couldn't have been up there more than a few minutes.'

'All right. Go and get those lookouts. Use two of the torpedo mixers. I trust we won't require them for anything like their own duties.'

Kernbach looked on, grim-visaged. 'One disaster after another. We've been dogged by ill-luck almost right from the moment we sailed. And now this, just when I thought the general situation was beginning to look more favourable.'

Rink remained silent, non-committal.

Kernbach studied the blond face contemplatively. 'You don't think Schramm had anything to do with this?'

'I don't know *what* to think,' Rink stated bitterly.

'But you know it would be impossible to prove anything,' Kernbach quietly opined.

Rink's bearded face was set in a bleak expression. He fully accepted that what Kernbach said was true. To attempt to prove anything was completely out of the question, whatever his suspicions. In the circumstances all he could hope for was that no further misfortune lay in wait for them. Yet it seemed too much to hope for in the light of past events. He turned to the control-room messenger. 'Tell Chief Gunner's Mate Kordt to report to me in my quarters.'

The big, wide-shouldered CGM arrived from the Warrant Officers' mess a few moments later. 'You sent for me, Herr Kommandant?'

'Draw the curtain.' Rink waited until Kordt drew the outer

curtain which shut off his quarters from the central gangway outside. 'No doubt you've already heard about our latest misfortune.'

'Bartz? Yes, sir. The Quartermaster just ordered Torpedomen Wassermann and Bittrich to the bridge as replacement lookouts.'

'And what do you know about this rumour that someone tampered with one of those packing cases?'

'Nothing, sir. I mean I heard the rumour but that was all.'

'No names?'

'No, sir.'

Rink deliberated the situation. 'Do you think you can make a search of Bartz's bunk and take a look at the cases in its immediate vicinity without creating too much fuss?'

Kordt had already guessed at Rink's thoughts. 'I can try, sir.'

'Then let me know what you find – if *anything*,' Rink instructed.

Close on forty minutes elapsed before Kordt returned. 'Nothing, sir,' he reported. 'Absolutely nothing. I inspected the case directly above his bunk, and two others close by, but I couldn't see any superficial evidence that they'd been tampered with in any way. However, to make absolutely certain, they'd have to be taken down from their lashings and examined more closely.'

'Very well,' Rink said in acceptance of the report. 'But from now on keep your eyes and ears open. Understand?'

'Yes, sir. I understand.'

Next morning a general air of gloom was in evidence throughout the boat, the one bright aspect being the fact that the weather had quickly improved so that by midday the seas had abated noticeably. For supper that evening Kolb produced a huge stew which he served with buttered potatoes and greens, and by the time that Rink was relieved on watch at midnight he was able to sense a perceptible improvement in the general atmosphere of the boat. Faces had brightened and the earlier air of gloom appeared to have lifted at least the edge of its mournful veil. Yet he had scarcely climbed into his bunk and drawn the curtain when he was startled by a raucous shout from the soundroom opposite his quarters. *'Radar contact 050 degrees – approaching fast!'*

In one movement he swept the curtain aside, swung booted feet to the deck-plates, and raced for the control-room.

On the bridge Berger heard the soundroom report only a split-second before the growing roar of aircraft motors above the hammering diesels, and he spun on his wheel, briefly catching sight of the huge black shadow as it dropped out from within the broken layer of cloud on the port quarter. And in instinctive reaction to the approaching danger his mind went numb and panic seized him. '*Achtung! Dive – dive – dive!*' he screamed without hearing his own voice.

Wassermann, Bittrich, and Rothfels hurled themselves in through the hatch at the instant *U501* was suddenly illuminated in the blinding glare of light when the Leigh searchlight snapped on in the belly of the Liberator.

Rink was in the tower when the three bodies hurtled in on him to leave Berger swinging frantically on the bridge hatch locking lever, and he knew instantly that Berger in his panic had dived too late and that he ought to have remained on the surface to take avoiding action in an attempt to out-manoeuvre the first stick of bombs or depth-charges. But now there was no way in which he could counteract the order, for *U501* was already on her way beneath the surface, and he turned to scramble back into the control-room. '*Emergency dive!*' he screamed at Kernbach. '*Depth regulator hard down!*'

Aft in the motor-room the running charge had been broken the instant the klaxons began to emit their first frenetic scream, the grouper switches snatched over to put the batteries in series to give full power for the dive, the diesels lapsing into silence as ballast tank vents swung wide open.

The deck-plates were already inclined for'ard as *U501* drove her bows below the surface in a frenzied dive for what seemed long agonising minutes, an eternity, but what added to no more than the space of twenty seconds, while she laboured to secure downward momentum, all other shipboard sounds drowned in the high-pitched scream of the electric motors on full power.

With Ingersoll roused from his bunk, both he and Kernbach had their eyes riveted anxiously on the master depth-gauge. 'Thirty-five metres, sir!' Kernbach called out penetratingly.

In the same instant the hull was plunged into chaos when two enormous explosions occurred, one to port, the other to starboard. Electric light bulbs, dial-glasses, gauges, and crockery shattered under the terrible impact of the detonations.

'*Schweinhund!*' Rink clung to the chart-table while *U501* cannoned back towards the surface for the stern to fling clear, screws racing, until her bows finally dropped away again at an acute angle, went down steeply, scattering men across the deck-plates and slamming them against bulkheads. Then *U501* gradually slowed in her plunge while the control-room crew fought in the darkness to hold her, to wrest her back on to an even keel. Meanwhile water spurted alarmingly from valves and ducts to the chilling accompaniment of the piercing scream of high-pressure air escaping, the stench of burning rubber, and a brilliant display of multicoloured sparks flowering from the diving-panel. Then a faint light seeped through the battered hull, the eerie blue glow of the few emergency lights still functioning, and ghostly faces peered apprehensively around them, haunted, bearded, wide-eyed, and sweat-streaked.

A stream of damage reports was hastily relayed to the control-room. 'Boat takes water for'ard! For'ard hydroplanes jammed! Telegraph circuit out! Revolution indicator out! Angle-gauge out!'

Kernbach's voice intervened authoritatively, 'Boat holds at 186 metres, sir!'

'Motor-room takes heavy water!' was the next alarming report relayed from aft.

In answer Ingersoll clambered aft, while Kernbach, without the aid of the angle-gauge, struggled to maintain an even keel.

'For'ard hydroplanes still not responding!' Coxswain Lamm reported.

'Check damage reports!' Rink called into the gloom to Erlanger.

While Kernbach and his crew were still struggling to keep them on a level keel and, with the smell of ozone beginning to seep through the hull, several flashlights were flicked on and in their combined glow Rink saw Berger crouching in the for'ard part of the control-room like a hunted animal, his face slack, eyes wide and staring, a man poised on the threshold of the next world, held numb in the grasp of shock and fear. Yet he experienced no ill-will towards him, felt merely sympathy and understanding of his lack of experience, having witnessed older and far more experienced men come apart at the seams in far less demanding circumstances.

Rink ignored him, his gaze fastened on the gyro-repeater strip overhead, aware that they were still on the same course as when the bomber had pounced on them. Whether or not her crew had accepted the brief reappearance of *U501*'s stern as proof of her destruction, or had even witnessed it, it was impossible to guess, but he knew they would have plotted the boat's position and apparent course at the time of bombing, and consequently it was now vital to get away from the point of contact. 'Right rudder. Come to course 240 degrees,' he called to Coxswain Lamm in the tower.

To all-round relief the boat answered her helm without difficulty, creeping her bows around on to her new course.

Meanwhile, further reports of damage were still finding their way to the control room. There were numerous leaks throughout the hull, and it was evident that most of the valves on the outer hull had suffered varying degrees of damage, likewise the air vents. In the engine room ERAs Dornberger and Steiner were hard at work in an effort to stop a fuel-tank relief valve spewing fuel into the bilges, and further aft, Ingersoll had taken charge of operations to wedge and shore a loose plate over the starboard main motor, the deckplates beneath their feet awash with black oily water.

Suddenly four jarring explosions rumbled through the depths from astern on the port quarter, evidence as Rink had envisaged minutes earlier that the bomber had plotted their original course and had decided to make another attack with depth-charges for good measure, her commander obviously not entirely convinced that he had made a certain killing. How long the bomber would continue to hunt around was anyone's guess, but it was fairly certain that she would remain in the vicinity of contact until her reserves of fuel forced her to turn for home. And in order to remain secure, *U501* therefore had to remain deep while she hurried away from the scene with all available speed.

Chlorine fumes were hanging thick in the air when Rink noted that Kernbach was still finding it extremely difficult to maintain an even keel. 'What's the problem, Chief?'

Kernbach shook his head. 'We're still checking out.'

Kordt appeared from for'ard.

Rink said, 'What's the situation with you?'

'There doesn't appear to be any structural damage, although there's a badly weeping seam in the Warrant Officers' mess, sir. The electricians are also working on the for'ard hydroplane motor.'

'And our passengers?'

'Badly shaken, but they appear to have found their way past the worst of it, sir.'

'Then try and assure them everything is well and that I intend to surface once time has forced that bomber to call off the hunt.'

Rink then started aft to the engine room were Dornberger and Steiner had newly completed a successful repair on the fuel-tank relief valve. In the motor-room Ingersoll was still working on the leak over the starboard main motor, but had successfully reduced the flow of water entering the hull. Men were also at work on No. 2 battery which had suffered a number of damaged and broken cells.

When he returned to the control-room he saw that exactly one hour and twelve minutes had elapsed since the time of the attack. 'Soundroom?'

'All clear all round, sir.'

Vogel's report at least appeared to indicate that the bomber had not called up the assistance of any surface craft in the area.

'For'ard hydroplane motor repaired, sir,' PO Electrician Vollmer reported.

Rink nodded acknowledgement, glanced again at the chronometer, then turned looking at Kernbach in the dim glow of the emergency lighting. 'Think our friend upstairs has left for home yet?'

Kernbach armed sweat from his face. 'I sure as Christ hope so.'

'Then standby to surface. Take her up gently. Bridge party on station.' He then stood waiting in readiness while Kernbach and his control-room crew slowly wrestled *U501* to the surface.

'Standards awash – bridge clear,' reported Kernbach.

Rink thrust the bridge hatch upward and jumped out on to the duckboards, the bridge watch right behind him, and was at once met by the stench of diesel fuel. Patches of ragged cloud trailed southerly across the star-lit sky overhead and in the sheen cast on the ocean he saw the long, broad oily wash clearly visible astern.

'All clear all round, sir,' PO Seaman Hoven reported.

'Very well,' said Rink; then called urgently below: 'Boat loses fuel starboard side – check for spillage!'

'Radar impulses negative,' was the following report from below.

Although the bomber had obviously decided to call it a night, she had been doubtful enough of claiming a kill to have dropped a pattern of depth-charges over the initial attack area, and Rink believed there was every likelihood another aircraft would appear with first light, even if only to check the area, when *U501*'s new course would be plainly visible from the fuel spillage left astern. Further, an inspection of the upperdeck revealed that the schnorchel had been irreparably damaged in the bomb blast, its head and float sheared away.

Rink summoned Erlanger to take charge of the bridge and returned below to instruct Kordt to form a work-party to cut away the wreckage of the schnorchel, and also found that an inspection of the starboard ballast and storage tanks undertaken by Kernbach and Ingersoll revealed that the near miss starboard side had cracked the main ballast tank and ruptured the adjacent storage tanks, with the result that they had been losing fuel from the very first moment of the attack.

Kernbach further explained, 'What little fuel we have left in those tanks is too badly contaminated to be of any use to us.'

Rink was shaken by the news, and his face assumed an even more bleak expression. 'You know what this means?'

'Yes,' Kernbach gloomily affirmed. 'If we don't meet up with those U-tankers for any reason, then we won't be going much further. Not even home, not with the fuel we have left.'

Rink saw that the die was cast. 'All right. Get rid of it and wash the tanks thoroughly. We can't afford to leave any trace of fuel to mark our course from here on.'

Rink found Wohldorf and Schramm in the wardroom, faces strained and ashen, cast in sickly pallor in the dim lighting. 'All right, gentlemen?'

Wohldorf was already on his feet. 'What happened out there?' he raged. 'What's going on?'

'Please,' Rink said patiently. 'We were attacked by an aircraft and we've suffered quite severe damage. Right now Kernbach is jettisoning what fuel we have left in the starboard storage tanks.'

Wohldorf's face appeared to visibly shrink with the news. 'What exactly does that mean?'

'It means our voyage is in jeopardy unless we meet with the U-tankers Besltemeyer or Schemmel,' Rink calmly replied.

Wohldorf said uncertainly, 'Then the situation isn't so critical after all?'

Rink was non-committal in his reply. 'Only time will provide us with an answer to that particular question.'

Wohldorf demanded querulously, 'Isn't that as it's arranged?'

Rink said cryptically, 'We will see.'

Wohldorf decided that a scapegoat was required for this new misfortune. 'Why didn't we receive warning of the aircraft's presence in the vicinity before we were attacked? Who was on watch?'

'Our radar isn't all it should be,' Rink answered quietly. 'And Berger was on watch. But I don't hold him entirely responsible for what happened. Quite simply the Allies caught us on the wrong foot. I didn't expect them to resume air operations till weather conditions improved a little more. Obviously I underestimated them. Now I'm afraid there are more pressing problems to which I must give consideration.'

Later, when the ballast tank and adjacent storage tanks were washed clean, Rink turned *U501* south again, and on completion of work on No. 2 battery, they limped slowly on their way to meet with U-Bestelmeyer at the prescribed destination while one diesel put in charge so that they were ready to go deep when the first hint of dawn touched itself to the eastern horizon.

Long days and nights of continuous and exhausting work was required of the crew before *U501* was restored to anything like her former efficient self, then at economical cruising speed she plodded south towards Madeira, grey leaden skies giving way to a cobalt blue vault whose clouds were billowed to immobile mountains of cream and gold, while the ocean shimmered like rippled silk, its horizons sharply defined. Not a single impulse disturbed the ether, nor did any suspicious drift of smoke cast a blemish across the sky. Yet faces became increasingly gloomy when news from home continued to indicate a rapidly deteriorating situation.

One of the controversial items picked up by the W/T office

was heard during the evening of April 29 when a Radio Stockholm broadcast announced that Reichsführer-SS Himmler had commenced tentative negotiations for terms of surrender with the Allied High Command, and reaction to the news ranged through the spectrum of emotion from outright rage to joyous relief. Further argument and speculation flared around the possible future of *U501* in the event of the Fatherland's capitulation, and, privately, Rink was relieved to be approaching the rendezvous position south-west of La Palma where they were to establish contact with Bestelmeyer. Once refuelled, he intended to use trimming tanks and bilges instead of the ruptured storage tanks, he would then push on hurriedly in order that they would be well on their way towards the Brazilian coast before serious trouble could break out among certain members of the crew.

Before he turned in that night, he again acquainted himself with his instructions for establishing contact with Bestelmeyer. Because strict radio silence was to be maintained by both U-boats, each was to cruise for a specified period of time in the rendezvous area during darkness, then submerge to listen on hydrophones for the propeller sounds of the other boat. Rink had experienced more dependable arrangements, but accepted that it was the only safe one if the positions of both U-boats were not to be traced through breaking radio silence, or by emitting a beacon signal to enable the other boat to home on.

Shortly before first light Rink climbed to the bridge where he found that not even the most frail breeze marred the silken sea which sparkled under the serene light of fading stars. To westward the sky was clear where it spanned the vast waters of the South Atlantic, although a massive bulk of darkly billowed cloud lay in a sullen mass across the distant African coast to eastward. It was a strangely emotive and tranquil scene after the long uncomfortable days just over, and Rink found it difficult to associate it with the death and destruction which were being endured by fellow countrymen at home; men, women, and children – thousands of them at that precise moment living out their last hours. And the faces of the men on watch around him did not require lengthy study to define their own personal thoughts. He felt overwhelemed by the silence, a silence everyone appeared reluctant to sully with the sound of a human voice. It was as if they wished the moment to remain with them forever, troubled by a collective premonition that their world was destined never to be the same again.

Gradually the faint light of the false dawn turned the heavy bank of cloud above Africa to shades of purple and grey while the ocean mirrored the translucent sky overhead, and Rink at last added his voice to the morning. 'Standby to dive,' he called below to Ingersoll. 'Take her down gently. Clear the bridge. To 30 metres.'

With a last look around him at the gathering light of dawn and the flawless horizon, he dropped into the tower and secured the hatch. Seconds later the ocean closed over the standards as Ingersoll slipped *U501* beneath the surface to leave scarcely a ripple to betray their disappearance.

For the rest of the day they continued southward, cruising silently at thirty metres, hydrophones manned, making an occasional sweep with the search periscope, but no contact of any form was made and the periscope revealed nothing, except the billowed mass of grey and gold cloud which appeared to be situated permanently above the great land mass of Africa. Then suddenly at supper the distance-muffled rumble of depth-charges carried down through the ocean, caused men to stop eating and conversation to fall away.

Rink raised his head from the chart-table and was met by the anxious faces of Kernbach and Ingersoll. 'Take her to periscope depth.'

Ingersoll turned with a stream of instructions to the control-room crew and *U501* rose in a silent glide towards the surface. 'Periscope depth, sir.'

Rink was already stationed at the search periscope. 'Up 'scope.'

The scene outside was the same as when they had slipped below at first light, and as it had remained throughout the day, one of absolute tranquillity. The sun had set and the sky was filled with its afterglow, golden clouds tinted pink and lemon in their folds, the ocean a delicate shade of mauve dappled with shadows. Further eastward stars winked pale light in open patches of sky, where lowering masses of cloud gathered over the land to assume their night-long vigil.

Then again they heard the distant rumble growl through the depths.

Rink shifted his gaze for'ard. 'Soundroom?'

'Very distant, sir,' was the reply. 'Port for'ard sector.'

'Down 'scope.' Rink turned his attention to the chart-table, made some calculations, and was interrupted by an anxious-looking Wohldorf.

'Is it true?' the SS man demanded accusingly.

Rink regarded him with unworried grey eyes. 'Is *what* true?'

'I heard it said depth-charges were exploding, that Bestelmeyer is under attack.'

Rink leaned across the chart-table. 'It isn't impossible,' he reflected without emotion, mild grey eyes studying the chart meditatively.

Wohldorf's temper surged upward. 'But I thought we were safe now,' he remonstrated.

Rink said placidly, 'I'm afraid no one's ever *safe* – not even on a bicycle.' Then he returned to work unconcernedly on the chart, aware that if Bestelmeyer *was* the victim of the depth-charge attack, then he was a considerable distance from the rendezvous area. However, he was also aware that if Bestelmeyer had been cruising around in the area waiting for *U501* since April 25, then there was every possibility that he had been forced to move further to the south-east in order to evade detection by Allied air or surface craft engaged in regular reconnaissance patrols of the area. Also the possibility could not be ignored that another U-boat had come under attack while passing unsuspectingly through the area on her way home.

'And may I ask how you intend to ascertain whether or not it *is* Bestelmeyer who is under attack?' Wohldorf asked testily.

Rink turned cool grey eyes on him. 'Because I intend to make a search of the area,' he explained, then turned to Kernbach. 'Standby to take her up, Chief. Bridge party and AA gunners on station.'

When Rink and the bridge party spilled out on to the duckboards they found sky and ocean clear on all sectors. A sultry breeze stirred from the African coast and overhead stars shone to etch the superstructure with a soft silver light. It was Rink's intention to make a searching run to south-eastwards, in the general direction of Port Etienne on the border of Spanish Sahara and Mauritania, and he called into the tower, 'Left rudder. Steer 145 degrees. Full ahead both.'

The diesels fumed and gathered rhythm to hammer up a foaming wash which stretched itself out astern, shot through with green and gold flashes of light that flitted through the clear dark depths.

At the end of sixty minutes Rink ordered the boat submerged, continued on the same course listening on hydrophones, then surfaced to repeat the previous procedure at the end of another sixty minutes. Again nothing showed except the distant flicker of an electric storm in the area to northward beside the Canary Islands. Ten minutes later Berger appeared on the bridge. Since the evening of the Liberator attack he had become overly quiet and withdrawn, as if he believed that the majority of *U501*'s officers and crew still held him responsible for the near loss of the boat and despised him for his lack of courage and self-confidence. Now he saw to his duties attentively, yet shunned all off-duty contact with his fellow officers. 'Herr Kommandant,' he reported stiffly. 'We're in receipt of several news items which I think may interest you.'

Rink left Erlanger with the watch and climbed below to the control-room where Berger handed him several slips of signal paper. 'We tuned into these shortly after we surfaced, sir.'

Rink scanned the flimsy slips of paper. The first copy was of a BBC news bulletin which stated that Mussolini and his mistress Claretta Petacci were dead, executed by Italian partisans late the previous afternoon. A further item revealed that Generaloberst Gotthard Heinrici's Army Group Vistula, charged with the task of defending Berlin, was in disarray. Russian tanks and troops were also reported as taking part in bitter hand to hand fighting in the streets of the capital, while General von Manteuffel's Third Panzer Army was heavily engaged with Russian armour in the area of The Havel.

It was disheartening news to receive on top of everything else that had happened, but keeping his thoughts to himself, Rink passed the copies to Kernbach and Ingersoll who read them through in gloomy silence. When finished with them, Rink handed them back to Berger. 'Give these to our passengers. They ought to find them illuminating reading.'

'Things also look bleak for ourselves,' Kernbach grimly observed.

Rink nodded agreement. 'Yes, especially if that *was* Bestelmeyer we heard going down earlier.'

At the end of the prescribed run Rink again ordered the boat submerged, but once more the hydrophones failed to detect even the faintest sound on any sector, and now that the very real possibility that Bestelmeyer had been sunk forced itself among the crew, a blanket of despair and hopelessness spread itself throughout the boat.

U501's final surface run next morning brought her close to first light, as it had done the previous day. The indigo sea gleamed like a mirror, reflecting the stars and scattered cloud, a beautiful morning warmed by the sultry breath of a light breeze off the vast West African deserts, watched over by the inevitable mass of cloud piled high above itself, towering, sullen mountains of purple and black.

'Herr Kommandant!' Berger's voice was hesitant, yet bore a constrained note of excitement. 'That strangely glittering patch of water, sir' His binoculars were focused to southward, at a point just beyond the starboard bow.

Rink's binoculars slowly swept the horizon from east to west. Scattered patches of cloud laid dark shadows on the star-lit ocean so that it was dappled with light and darkness. Then he found it, one particular area of water which reflected the sheen of starlight with a gleam more brittle to the eye than the surrounding area. 'Come to course 195 degrees. Both emergency ahead.'

Excitement swept through the boat when the bows turned southward and the thunder of the diesels gained in intensity as Kernbach piled on the revolutions. Astern, the screws thrashed the ocean into a boiling cauldron and shot incandescent balls of phosphorescent light through the depths to linger far behind, an unwelcome phenomena in the event of an Allied air patrol being active in the vicinity, yet a calculated risk on Rink's part in order to defeat early light.

Approaching the area, the reek of diesel fuel hung far and wide in the sultry air and every member of the bridge watch knew only too well the reason for such a large patch of ocean to be covered with spillage; they were witness to the death scene of a U-tanker Type XIV, her shroud, her cargo consisting of something like 800 tons of diesel fuel.

'Small ahead both.'

U501's diesels lost their urgent clamour and her bows nosed gently through the outlying fingers of oily swill. There was very little debris, a few oil-blackened spars of shattered wood, some panelling, a mattress, some items of clothing, but no bodies in evidence. Now there was no doubt whatever in anyone's mind that they had borne silent witness the previous evening to the destruction of U-Bestelmeyer.

Rink turned his attention to the sky which had lightened considerably, the bank of cloud to eastward assuming its familiar mottling of purple and grey. To linger any longer in the area tempted disaster.

'Standby to dive. Clear the bridge.' He paused for a final look around while the bridge watch and AA gunners crowded below. 'Boat to 30 metres,' he instructed, and dropped into the tower to clamp the hatch shut.

This time the faces awaiting him in the control-room wore an expression of resignation and defeat. He saw no need to explain the grim discovery, news of it had preceded him. He motioned for Wohldorf, Kernbach, and Ingersoll to join him at the chart-table. He said quietly to all three, 'I'm afraid we must now accept the fact that without Schemmel all prospect of our completing this voyage is out of the question. At present he's operating in Grid Square DF –' he paused, to indicate the area on the chart in front of them '– roughly about here, south Mid-Atlantic. His instructions are that if he hasn't intercepted our codeword signal WESTWARD to Headquarters verifying the fact that we've successfully refuelled from Bestelmeyer and are continuing on towards our destination by 06.00 hours, May 5th, then he must make for the secondary rendezvous position 150 miles due West of Santa Antao in the Portuguese islands of Cabo Verde with all speed.'

Wohldorf said disdainfully, 'And in the meantime?'

Rink looked at him levelly. 'In the meantime, one thing I don't intend to do is to cruise around the ocean till Schemmel arrives. One reason is that we'd only be using up precious fuel unnecessarily, and another is that, after the destruction of Bestelmeyer, the Allies will doubtless maintain a close surveillance on this part of the ocean due to the fact that their victim was a U-tanker, which means she must have been on station to meet with other U-boats.'

'Then what do you suggest?' Wohldorf's voice did not conceal his irritation.

Rink returned his attention to the chart. 'What we need is somewhere to lose ourselves till Schemmel arrives at the secondary rendezvous position, and that won't be for several days, perhaps not till the 8th or 9th.'

Even Kernbach was surprised at Rink's casual announcement. 'A place to *lose* ourselves?'

'Yes, explain what you mean,' said Wohldorf.

Rink again indicated the chart. 'The Provincia de Cabo Verde, gentlemen. I know them relatively well, having visited them on two previous occasions when I served as Executive Officer with Oberleutnant Storch while operating off Freetown in early '42. The first time was when we refuelled, the second time when we replenished our stock of torpedoes.'

The men expressed new interest in the chart.

'As you can see,' Rink explained, 'they're Portuguese territory, situated 350 miles west-north-west of Dakar. Ten islands and five islets divided into two groups, Barlavento and Sotavento. It's with the latter group my interest lies, Sao Tiago, Maio, Fogo, and Brava. The last named is where Storch chose to rendezvous with Renner and Schacht. Apart from a few mountain goats, it was uninhabited. We used a remote inlet on the south-west shore of the island which provided an excellent anchorage, entirely concealed from seaward.'

Wohldorf did not hide his surprise. 'Then you've already given this idea serious consideration.'

Rink inclined his head affirmatively. 'It occurred to me last evening after we heard that depth-charge attack, when I saw the possibility that Bestelmeyer had been caught on the surface. Besides, I don't intend to find myself stranded through shortage of fuel on some remote African shore and forced to accept my ill-luck gracefully. Nor do I intend to find myself in the unenviable position whereby there's no way out of our predicament except through the surrender of my command to the Allies or Portuguese.'

Wohldorf was impressed by Rink's determination. 'Then you'll find that both myself and my aide share your sentiments.'

Kernbach added hurriedly, 'Naturally I will go along with whatever course of action you decide on, Herr Kommandant. I don't have any inclination to spend the next two or three years breaking rock in some French West African penal colony – nor in a Portuguese penal colony either for that matter.'

'The same goes for me, Herr Kommandant,' declared Ingersoll.

'May I ask what you intend to tell the crew?' Wohldorf wanted to know.

'Merely that it's my intention to put *U501* ashore on one of the islands of Cabo Verde till Schemmel has time to reach the secondary rendezvous position,' explained Rink.

*

That afternoon PO Electrician Vollmer was at work in the motor-room when Torpedoman 1st Class Wassermann approached him. A tall, angular young man of twenty-five, with sparse black hair and a long sallow face set in a mood of perpetual worry, Vollmer straightened up from the port switchboard when he saw Wassermann at his side. 'Any idea what's happening?'

Wassermann shook his big blond head. 'No, but I bet it's something none of us expects.'

A look of anguish passed across Vollmer's face. 'You know, Horst, I have a premonition we're never going to see home again. I just wish I'd been one of the lucky ones put ashore at the Mecklenburg Compound.'

Wassermann's jaw set in a grim line. 'And *I* just wish to hell there was something we could do about it.'

Vollmer swept a stealthy glance around the motor-room. 'Like what?'

'I don't know,' Wassermann growled in frustration. 'But there must be *something* we can do.'

Vollmer said bitterly, 'I'd willingly have taken my chance on dry land. At least I could have headed for home when I found the opportunity. But it's like being a prisoner on board here, you can't go anywhere.'

Wassermann said, 'I don't know what you're worrying about. Elser and I are the ones who are in real trouble. You must have heard about the packing case.'

Vollmer's eyes grew wide, 'It was *you*?'

'Yes,' Wassermann affirmed. 'Bartz, Elser, Zeller, and I were the ones involved, only I didn't mention it before. But you can take it from me that Bartz didn't *fall* across the side that night. That big SS man was up there when he disappeared. It was too much of a coincidence.'

Vollmer stared at him in disbelief. '*You really mean that*?'

'Yes. But don't ask me how word got around. My guess is either someone saw us, or else someone opened his mouth, perhaps Bartz himself, and he died for it. Anyway, I can tell you that we're sleeping with our eyes open. I feel bad enough, but Elser's nerves are shot to hell. I don't know what I'm going to do, but given half an opportunity I'm going to disappear, and Elser along with me. If anyone else is going to get himself killed on board here, it isn't going to be us.'

'Why don't you go to the Kommandant and tell him everything?' Vollmer offered in feeble sympathy.

Wassermann regarded him with disgust. 'With those two SS bastards on the loose? No, we're going to bide our time. And if we ever find the opportunity to disappear you're welcome to come with us. After all, we're all from Munchen, neighbours as well as comrades, you might say.'

When Wassermann returned for'ard, Vollmer remained deep in thought. Like Wassermann he had been married just over a year and in that time he had spent only five days with his wife Elfride. More heart-breaking was the fact that he had never seen his son Franz Vollmer junior.

*

The relatively short period of twilight had turned into another calm star-strewn night when *U501* surfaced. With one diesel running a charge into the batteries, she drove unhurriedly south at economical cruising speed, the sea foaming along the casing to boil astern in a single furrow of incandescent light. When relieved of his watch, Rink returned below to the control-room where the fans pulled a steady draught of cool air down into the hull, a welcome relief after the humidity and accumulation of stale air during the day.

'Herr Kommandant!'

Rink saw Chief Telegraphist Bergold beckon to him from the W/T office. Hurrying for'ard, he wondered what sort of calamitous news had stirred the usually unflappable Chief Telegraphist, and received the answer the instant he stepped into the W/T office when Bergold thrust a slip of signal paper at him, explaining in a leaden voice, 'I just heard this on a Radio Casablanca news bulletin, sir.'

Rink read: OFFICIAL GERMAN NEWS BROADCASTS INTERCEPTED FROM 21.30 HOURS ONWARD LAST NIGHT DISCLOSED WITH ONE ACCORD THAT THE FÜHRER, ADOLF HITLER MET HIS DEATH SOME TIME YESTERDAY AFTERNOON IN HIS BERLIN OPERATIONAL HEADQUARTERS IN THE REICHSKANZLEI. IT IS BELIEVED THAT

BEFORE HIS DEATH, THE CAUSE OF WHICH IS AS YET UNKNOWN, HE APPOINTED GROSSADMIRAL DONITZ AS HIS SUCCESSOR. Then he read it a second time. Even so, it was several moments before its full impact registered. It was devastating news, and embodied so much that was actually unsaid. 'Keep this to yourself,' he told Bergold.

'Yes, sir.' Bergold had the look of a man who could not reconcile himself to accept what he had just heard with his own ears; he was afraid to accept it.

Wohldorf was asleep when Rink arrived in the for'ard locker space, the curtain drawn across his bunk. Rink thrust it aside and snapped on the light. Wohldorf awakened with a start, peered at Rink in the bright light and immediately sensed that he had awakened him only because he had received news of the utmost gravity. Rink passed him the slip of signal paper without a word. Wohldorf read it slowly, almost laboriously, emotionally shocked. 'Is this a reliable source?' he asked as if afraid to hear his question answered in the affirmative.

'I imagine it is.'

'Do the crew know about this?'

'No, but I intend to inform my senior officers Kernbach and Ingersoll about it.'

'I see,' Wohldorf replied, and added grimly, 'You must keep me informed of any further news when it's received. It's imperative that we keep abreast of the overall situation as it develops.'

On his return to the control-room Rink saw that Ingersoll had been joined on watch by Kernbach. 'You had better have a look at this.'

Kernbach accepted the slip of signal paper, read it, and commented darkly, 'Then Berlin must be in Russian hands.'

Ingersoll said dispiritedly, 'I suppose the end can't be far away now.'

Rink had no wish to become embroiled in a discussion about the past or the future, and tucking the slip of paper away in a pocket of his blouse, he returned to the W/T office. 'From now on you had better maintain a constant watch for short wave transmissions from Headquarters,' he informed Bergold. 'For some reason we appear to be missing out entirely where first-hand news is concerned.'

BOOK THREE

Decision at Cabo Verde

At 14.00 on the afternoon of May 4, Rink ordered the search periscope raised, made an all-round sweep, then allowed the lens to linger on Pico do Cano, the volcanic peak situated on the island of Fogo, where it jutted out of the sparkling blue ocean to lose its sharp definition in the heat haze to south-eastward; *U501* was within sight of the Portuguese islands of Cabo Verde, the first landfall since being afforded a distant glimpse of Madeira's Pico Ruivo with its basalt peaks.

Soon Rink was able to distinguish the rugged volcanic formations of several other islands to seaward, the northernmost Santo Antao, Sao Vicente, Sao Nicolau, and to south-eastward, towered over by the jutting mass of Pico do Cano on nearby Fogo, the islands of Sao Tiago and Brava.

'Down, 'scope. Boat to 30 metres.' Rink next reached for the broadcast system microphone. '*Achtung!*' This is the Kommandant speaking. We are now in a position west-north-west of the Portuguese islands of Cabo Verde. Because of Bestelmeyer's loss it is my intention to lay the boat ashore on the island of Brava in order to conserve fuel while we await the arrival of a U-tanker under command of Kapitanleutnant Schemmel at a secondary rendezvous position 150 miles due West of Santo Antao. That is all.'

An hour later Rink returned to the search periscope. The all round sweep disclosed no sign of either air or surface craft in the vicinity. The ocean sparkled peacefully in the sunlight and the cloudless sky was blurred only by the heat haze. A study of the rugged formation of volcanic rock that was the island of Brava divulged no trace of human habitation. Rising to over three thousand feet, and with only an odd patch of greenery to adorn its rocky slopes, it possessed nothing in the way of spectacular vegetation. It was exactly as Rink remembered it from his last visit with Oberleutnant Storch in early 1942, stark and unattractive.

'Left rudder.' Rink scanned the south-westerly tip of the island while *U501* turned eastward. 'Steady on 090 degrees.' The entrance to the inlet was also as he remembered it, a narrow fissure in the cliffs which backed into what appeared from seaward to be a solid wall of rock, but what in fact was a rocky gully which rose between the jagged cliffs to east and west, and so assured the concealed inlet within from surprise approach if lookouts were posted on the adjoining cliffs.

As *U501* continued eastward, the southern shore remained bleak and uninviting. Several goats scampered among the rocks and the ocean washed a clean white line of foam along the black foreshore between soaring cliffs. Again there was no evidence of human habitation on the eastern side of the island, just a monotony of rock and boulder. He turned his attention eastward to the island of Fogo where Pico do Cano frowned down on the small township of Sao Felipe, a scattering of dwellings on its south-westerly flank. Further eastward was Sao Tiago where the capital Praia was situated. All was quiet, without even the passage of a fishing schooner to disturb the placid waters.

By 16.10 the island had been circumnavigated and Rink called a meeting of all officers and Warrant Officers in the control-room. 'I intend to put the boat ashore at dusk,' he informed them. 'I visualise no great difficulty in manoeuvring her alongside. The inlet is situated in a narrow depression between two cliffs, from which a gully extends northward. You'll find that a ledge of rock will serve as a natural jetty. Once we secure alongside I want a work-party formed to scour the neighbourhood for scrub in order to camouflage the boat. Cox'n, you'll arrange for lookouts to be posted on the cliffs to east and west, dependable men with good eyes. Although we were never troubled in any way on my previous two visits, the situation may well have changed, and the last thing I want is for us to be taken unawares. For tonight, at least, everyone else will remain on board in a state of first-degree readiness. Any questions?'

No one spoke.

'Very well. Stand down.'

With the approach of dusk, Rink ordered the boat to periscope depth and made an all-round sweep with the search periscope. The sun hung suspended on the western horizon, an orange-red ball, a band of pale lemon for a backdrop, the inevitable mound of cloud piled high to eastward, tinted red and gold, its belly a sullen hue of cinerary grey. Around them the mauve and violet ocean was mill-pond flat, a vast sheet of darkening glass. 'Down 'scope. Bridge party and AA gunners on station. Surface on electric drive.'

Seconds later *U501* rose slowly out of the ocean, water streaming from the bridge superstructure, AA gunners and lookouts spilling out on to the bridge and *wintergarten* behind Rink.

'Group down. Small ahead both. Left rudder – midships.' Rink watched the bows steadily close the three hundred metres to the dark fissure of rock which marked the entrance to the inlet, creeping silently through the water, AA gunners and lookouts anxiously scanning sea and sky.

'Berthing-party on deck. Standby wires and fenders port side.'

U501 edged cautiously between the soaring black walls of volcanic rock either side of the entrance, catwalks manned by men with wires and fenders ready, CGM Kordt stationed right for'ard on the shark-nose, one hand resting on the jumping-wire.

Soon the sheer walls fell abruptly away to reveal the inlet backed by the rocky gully to northward, its shore a steeply inclined shingle beach, the long ledge of rock forming the western shore, a natural jetty, its incline boulder-strewn.

Standing right for'ard on the bridge, Rink concentrated his attention on not allowing the saddle tanks and hydroplanes to make contact with the ledge of rock while the bows nosed in towards the shingle beach. 'Stop both!'

At Kordt's signal, men leapt for the shore trailing the mooring wires, leaving the remainder of the berthing-party waiting patiently with fenders ready.

'Small astern both,' ordered Rink. Then with the quiet swirl of water sweeping forward, he shouted, 'Stop both!'

As *U501* held way, mooring wires were quickly hauled ashore and secured to outcrops of rock on the incline at either end of the jetty.

Satisfied with the operation, Rink signalled to the for'ard catwalk.

'Standby with those fenders,' warned Kordt. Then: 'Take up the slack.'

In answer heavy-gloved hands reached out to take the

strain, and the port side edged slowly in towards the ledge of rock, the men with fenders strung out along the catwalks. When *U501* put her side to the shore it was without a perceptible jolt.

'Secure wires,' shouted Kordt, and around him a collective sigh of relief went up on deck and bearded faces split into wide grins.

Kordt made a thorough inspection of the wires, then turned to the bridge. 'Boat secure fore and aft, sir.'

Rink raised a hand in acknowledgement, and called into the tower, 'Secure main motors.'

Coxswain Lamm was on the bridge immediately. 'Permission for the camouflage-party to proceed ashore, sir?'

'Carry on, Cox'n,' said Rink, his gaze sweeping the inlet in the growing darkness, memories of his previous visits flooding back.

After the camouflage-party disappeared across the *wintergarten* to join Kordt on shore, Lamm returned to the bridge with Signalmen Meyer and Hagen, both men carrying watch-clothing and binoculars. 'Lookouts as ordered, sir.'

'One on either cliff,' Rink explained to them. 'No sleeping and no smoking. I don't want any lights shown, not even a cigarette-end. And keep a sharp lookout, especially for small boats and aircraft. If you aren't certain about anything you might sight – shout. Understood?'

Both men nodded in unison. 'Yes, sir.'

'Then carry on. And watch your footing in the darkness. We can't afford any broken limbs. Someone will relieve you in the morning.'

Rink and Lamm watched the two lookouts start ashore as the first of the camouflage-party arrived back on the jetty laden with scrub.

'How do you want this stuff arranged, sir?' asked Kordt.

Rink glanced about him in the gloom. 'I think all we can do tonight is to festoon the jumping-wires and the *wintergarten*. With daylight we can adopt a more professional attitude.'

Suddenly Kolb's sweat-streaked face appeared in the bridge hatchway. 'Permission to open the after hatch, sir?' he pleaded.

Rink glanced at Kordt. 'Can you arrange a screen? I don't want some Allied pilot to pass overhead and see what we're having for supper.'

'Leave it to me, sir.'

As Kordt disappeared over the *wintergarten* to the after catwalk, Lamm pushed his cap back off his brow and armed the sweat from his face. The air was hot and humid, without a breath of movement, the sky overhead lit by humidity-magnified stars. 'I didn't think it would be as hot as *this*, sir.'

'No, it isn't exactly Paradise, Cox'n,' Rink remarked. 'Apart from a scattering of Portuguese troops, these islands are mostly inhabited by coloureds.'

Supper was smoked ham, potatoes, and pickles, followed by stewed prunes. Rink ate his in the control-room while he entered the War Diary. When finished he went for'ard to the W/T office. 'Any news?'

PO Telegraphist Vogel removed the earphones from his head. 'I'm afraid not, sir.'

Anxious to take the opportunity of a night's undisturbed rest, Rink turned to his own quarters, climbed into his bunk, drew the curtain, and was asleep instantly.

May 5. To Rink it seemed he had been asleep only a few minutes when a voice called to him. Blinking sleep from his eyes, he saw Torpedoman 1st Class Wassermann towering over him.

'Leutnant Berger said to inform you that it's close to first light, sir.'

'Thank you, Wassermann.' Rink swung out of his bunk, pulled on his sheepskin coat, then called at the W/T office.

Bergold glanced up from the radio bench the instant he saw Rink appear. 'I'm afraid there's nothing to report, sir.'

'Well, stay with it. There ought to be *something* soon.'

In the galley he poured a mug of coffee and carried it to the bridge.

'All quiet, sir,' Berger informed him.

It was still dark, the air chill. A heavy dew had fallen in the night and it glittered with the needle light of diamonds on the greenery which festooned the jumping-wires fore and aft.

'Quite an impressive sight,' mused Rink. 'I wonder how far we'd get on open water dressed overall like this?'

The bridge watch grinned at the thought.

Rink sipped his coffee and glanced at the cliffs either side of the shadowed inlet, whose flat clear water reflected the cold sheen of the stars overhead. 'Anything at all from above?'

Berger said, 'Not a single report from the lookouts all night, sir.'

Huddled in his sheepskin coat, Rink finished off his coffee and watched dawn creep across the patch of sky overhead as it gradually assumed a pale orange light, while the stars faded into the background.

Shortly afterwards Coxswain Lamm and CGM Kordt appeared on the bridge, grasping mugs of coffee. 'As soon as the hands have breakfasted we can finish camouflaging the boat, sir,' said Kordt.

'Do that,' said Rink.

Lamm gestured along the ledge of rock to which *U501* was moored. 'It wouldn't be a difficult task to construct a lean-to shelter against the slope and roof it over with scrub, sir. It could prove especially useful if anyone was ashore and we were disturbed by a passing aircraft.'

Rink nodded his satisfaction with the suggestion. 'Perhaps you can also construct some sort of shelter on these cliffs for the lookouts, to enable them to keep out of sight. Drill that into them. The same goes for anyone down here in the gully during daylight. And something else,' Rink indicated the cliff to westward. 'Over beyond there, higher up, we had a lookout post which gave an almost unhindered view of the entire area. I intend to take a look at it again. It's just possible we can arrange for a watch to be kept up there.'

Over breakfast in the wardroom, Rink explained his intention of climbing to the old lookout post above the island. 'Perhaps you and your aide might care to accompany me?' he suggested to Wohldorf.

Wohldorf accepted the invitation enthusiastically. 'Nothing would give me greater delight than to get my feet on solid ground again.'

'How about my hands checking out some of those remaining defects in the engineroom and motor-room, sir?' asked Kernbach.

'Very well. But don't impair our readiness for sea,' Rink impressed. 'We may have to pull out of here at an instant's notice.'

When breakfast was over Rink went to his quarters, buckled on his Walther PPK, collected his cap, blouse, and slung his binoculars around his neck. Next he called at the W/T office where Bergold and Vogel were on watch. 'I'm going ashore for a time. If you hear anything, keep it till I get back.'

Out on deck Kordt reported the camouflage work concluded, and walked the length of the jetty with Rink who found the overall effect to be far in advance of anything he had expected. 'Excellent,' he told Kordt. 'Now I think you ought to come with me. I'm taking our two passengers up to see the old lookout post on the knoll which we used when I was last here. It may be useful to organise a watch up there and it's better that you know the place.'

It was an arduous upward slog through scrub-entangled gullies and rain-washed culverts where the rock was polished to a slippery smoothness. Not a breath of air moved across the island, and the sunlight struck up a blinding glare from the ocean below. Sweat coursed down the men's faces to sting their eyes as they fought to suck down lungfuls of the humid air, and formed ever-widening dark patches on their green battle fatigues.

When at last the ground began to level out, Rink saw the old lookout post up ahead on the knoll. The low rubble wall around the shallow depression was matted with coarse brown grass, and although the four weathered logs that had supported the slatted roof still remained in the upright position, the roof had disappeared, swept away during some long past storm.

'We're silhouetted on the skyline up here,' Rink pointed out. 'Better that we keep down.'

The four men climbed into the small depression atop the knoll and surveyed the panoramic vista spread out below them. The haze of the previous afternoon had not reappeared with the morning, and from east around to northward the various islands and islets of the Cabo Verdes spread themselves wide, brooded over by the jutting mass of Pico do Cano on nearby Fogo. Only to the south-east where the island rose to a higher elevation was the superb view in any way restricted.

Rink made a sweep with his binoculars. To eastward a small fishing schooner under a spread of orange sail made her way south beyond the tip of Sao Tiago. Nothing else disturbed the tranquil scene until he caught sight of the plume of brown smoke which cast a blemish on the skyline above Sao Vicente. Moments later he saw the unmistakable silhouette of a tanker edge into view when it cleared the western shore of the island.

He passed the binoculars to Wohldorf and indicated the direction of the tanker. 'Take a look.'

Wohldorf found her where she stood out to sea.

'She's just put out from Sao Vicente, from the fuelling station at Porto Grande,' Rink explained.

Wohldorf continued to hold the tanker in focus. 'Do you have any idea where she might be headed?'

'It's too soon to hazard a guess. First we have to see which way she turns once clear in deep water.'

Schramm crowded forward to peer across the edge of the depression. 'How big is she?' he asked hungrily.

Rink shrugged. 'Around 5,000 Gross Register Tons.'

Schramm's eyes gleamed. 'Could you sink her?'

Rink answered with professional detachment. 'The way she's steaming at the moment she'd present little difficulty. And that plume of smoke will be seen from a long way off.'

Kordt remarked across his shoulder, 'There's another vessel here to southward, sir.'

Wohldorf swivelled the binoculars to the position Kordt indicated.

'This is one of the world's busiest shipping lanes, or was before the war,' Rink went on to explain. 'Vessels from every European port passed here on their way to Latin America and South Africa. That freighter you're now looking at is probably headed north from South Africa. Durban, Port Elizabeth, Cape Town, St Helena, Ascension Island, Lagos, Freetown, are all to southward.' Rink noted that the tanker had also turned southward, 'See, our tanker has also headed south. Had she stood out to sea on a westerly, or south-westerly course, she'd have been bound for Latin America.'

Kordt said, 'Do you want me to arrange for a watch to be kept up here, sir?'

'I think we might as well. Although we haven't seen any sign of an island patrol, the Portuguese must carry out some sort of check on these islands.'

Kordt glanced off to south-eastward, to where the higher elevation of the island obscured part of Fogo and Sao Tiago. 'What about that direction, sir? The view's pretty well restricted.'

'Our lookout on the cliff to eastward will have to take care of the area to the south and south-eastward. But regarding this position you can bring someone up here before it gets dark tonight. It's a long climb so it will require two good pairs of eyes on twelve hour watches. Kolb will have to pack meals and a thermos for them.'

'And if they sight trouble, sir?'

'We can do as Oberleutnant Storch did with his lookouts. If the man in question sights a patrol boat headed toward the island, then he gets back down to the inlet as fast as he can shift himself. If, on the other hand, something goes wrong below that he doesn't know anything about, then we fire two shots and he comes running. That's if there's trouble from the south, or south-east. And if for any other reason we have to pull out before he reaches the inlet, then he will have to try and keep out of sight till we pick him up at the first opportunity.'

Kordt nodded, grinning. 'Even our most dim-witted individual shouldn't get confused with those arrangements.'

'Let's hope not,' Rink drily observed.

They waited on the knoll until the two vessels passed off shore. The tanker was in ballast and her single screw clipped the water up white beneath her rust-streaked counter. Although her name was indecipherable even with the binoculars, she flew a tattered Dutch flag astern. The freighter from southward was British, around 6,000 GRT, her name and port of registry clearly visible: *Mount Eden – Glasgow*. Loaded to the Plimsoll line, she was a neat vessel, well-cared for, her hull carrying a fresh coat of grey paint, her superstructure white. The two vessels passed at a point less than two miles from shore.

When the four men arrived back at the inlet they found all spare hands engaged in erecting three shelters which backed against the slope above the ledge of rock on the western side of the inlet, some twenty metres from where the boat was moored.

'We're just about through, sir,' Lamm reported. 'I also took care of those shelters on the cliffs.'

'Good work, Cox'n,' said Rink, and went on to explain about the old lookout post on the knoll above the cliffs. 'Kordt will arrange the lookouts beginning tonight. However, we will still retain the lookouts on the cliffs above. They're within shouting distance of the inlet, while the one on the knoll isn't. His interest is in what's happening at long-range.'

'*Herr Kommandant?*'

The men saw Leutnant Berger start ashore, and Rink knew

from his manner that it was nothing routine he was on his way to report. He went to meet him in company with Wohldorf and Schramm.

Berger extended a deciphered signal. 'We picked this up an hour ago, sir. Very faint and obviously relayed by one of our boats. I deciphered it as soon as Vogel had it down.'

Rink was stunned by the contents of the brief signal: ACHTUNG. ALL U-BOATS. ACHTUNG. AS OF 0800 HOURS MAY 5 CEASE FIRE. REPEAT CEASE FIRE. SUSPEND ALL HOSTILE ACTION AGAINST ALLIED SHIPPING IMMEDIATELY. AWAIT TO RECEIVE FURTHER INSTRUCTIONS – ORIGINATED BdU 0314 HOURS MAX 4.

Wohldorf reached out a hand. 'May I?'

Rink passed him the signal.

When Wohldorf again raised his eyes his face was ashen. 'But how can this be? That's now – this morning – past!'

'Somehow we've missed out on a great deal of what's been happening, that's obvious,' said Rink. Then struck by another thought, he fixed his attention on Berger. 'Did Vogel say whether or not this signal could possibly have been relayed by Schemmel?'

'He said he thought it highly unlikely it was from a U-boat in our general vicinity, sir. There was no call-sign to distinguish the sender either, sir.'

'Then go back on board and remain with Bergold and Vogel. We must try and learn about what's not only happening around us at this moment, but what's been happening elsewhere in the past few hours. And listen out for Schemmel. If he's in receipt of this signal, then he may attempt to contact us now the overall situation has become this precarious. As a last resort we may even have to try and establish contact with him ourselves. It would be disastrous if he too has fallen victim to the Allies without our knowing.' Then he suddenly became aware of the strained silence which enveloped the inlet, and he turned to find that the men working on the shelters had ceased their tasks and were watching intently as Berger made his way back to the boat. He beckoned Kordt and Lamm to him. 'Keep the men busy. With time on their hands they start thinking, and sometimes thinking can be dangerous. Back there, up the gully, there ought to be a small stream, if it hasn't dried up since I was last here. Get every container you can find and begin replenishing the water tanks. Get them washing clothes, bathing, anything, but don't allow them time to think.'

Wohldorf scowled after the two Warrant Officers when they started back along the gully. 'Do you expect trouble?'

Rink led the way back towards the boat. 'We've more than enough trouble on our hands already without courting any more. But precautionary measures cost nothing.'

They reached the bridge at the same time as a harassed PO Telegraphist Vogel scuttled out through the open hatchway. 'Leutnant Berger sent me to fetch you, sir! There's another signal coming through!'

Rink pushed through the hatch and hurried for'ard to the W/T office where Bergold and Berger were huddled over the radio sharing earphones. Berger at once offered his to Rink. 'Our anonymous friend again, sir,' he explained.

Rink clamped it to his ear and watched Bergold jot down the coded signal on a tablet of flimsy paper. The morse was faint and distorted. Whether it was being interfered with by man or Nature was impossible to say, but portions of it were lost completely. Glancing up, he saw the anxious faces of Wohldorf, Schramm, Kernbach, Ingersoll, and Berger pressed in around the door. Then the signal terminated abruptly, with no call-sign to identify the sender.

Bergold lifted his strained face from the radio bench and shook his head. 'Same as last time, sir.'

Rink tore the top slip of paper from the tablet and thrust it at Berger. 'Get it deciphered – hurry!' Then knowing exactly the risk he was taking with the safety of *U501* and her crew, he snapped at Bergold, 'Ask for a *repeat!*'

The morse key skittered under Bergold's experienced hand. Three times he made the request but was met only with silence.

'*Again!* Rink snapped edgily.

Bergold complied, and again silence.

'*Verdammt!*' swore Rink. 'Call U-Schemmel!'

Bergold never lifted his gaze from the key, earphone clutched to his head in the other hand, and three times in rapid succession sent the brief signal.

Rink waited, sweat streaming down his face.

Wohldorf broke in anxiously. 'Nothing? Nothing at all?'

Rink moved his head negatively. 'No, but if that *was* Schemmel he's a hell of a long way from here. Also he's making no attempt to acknowledge our signal.' He left the earphone with Bergold. 'Stay with it,' he told him.

In the control-room Berger completed his work with the decoding machine and passed the deciphered signal to Rink who was waiting impatiently at his shoulder. 'I'm afraid there are parts of it missing, sir.'

Rink quickly read it through and found that what there was of the signal made sense. Originating from Headquarters, it contained details for the surrender of all U-boats operating at sea. Instructions were to surface on receipt of the signal, radio their position, then set course for the nearest Allied port with a black flag hoisted. Allied ports listed to receive U-boats operating in the vicinity of the eastern seaboard of the South Atlantic were the British Naval Bases at Simonstown in South Africa, Freetown in Sierra Leone, and Gibraltar. The remainder of the signal was directed at U-boats operating in the vicinity of the American seaboard in the North Atlantic, and in home waters.

Wohldorf was impatient to learn the contents of the signal. 'Please?'

Rink passed it to him, and to Berger said, 'You had better get back to the W/T office. If you hear anything further on the subject let me know at once. And keep a sharp ear open for Schemmel. So far he may have deliberately chosen to remain silent despite our attempt to raise him. But again, *anything* may have come of him.'

Wohldorf concluded reading the signal and turned to look at Rink with shock and disbelief. 'Does this mean that *all* hostilities have actually ended?'

'On that point I'm not clear,' said Rink. 'Personally I'd have expected some reference to an official cease-fire deadline concerning all branches of the Armed Forces to be included if that were the case. As it reads, that signal appears to be directed only to operational units of the U-boat Force presently at sea. But as you're well aware, my orders are to ignore all signals not directly addressed to us, and I intend to abide by those orders – *meantime*.'

'And Schemmel?' Wohldorf said in agitation. 'What about Schemmel? He must be under similar orders.'

'Presumably so,' said Rink.

Wohldorf sighed in frustration. 'If only he'd acknowledged our attempt to contact him earlier I'd feel easier in my mind.'

Rink gave a philosophic shrug. 'Perhaps it's his intention only to make contact with us in the manner laid down in his orders, at the secondary rendezvous position. It may even be that he's cruising around out there at this very moment.'

Wohldorf was prepared to argue. 'And if he *isn't* cruising around out there? What course of action do you then propose to adopt?'

'Frankly, I don't know,' Rink confessed. 'But if we've heard nothing from him by midnight it's my intention to sail for the secondary rendezvous position in the hope that we can make contact with him as instructed. Other than that . . .' He turned away, and anxious to be alone with his thoughts, he climbed to the bridge where he saw Kordt and Lamm headed down the gully towards the boat.

At a distance Kordt called out, 'We found that stream, sir.'

'Forget the stream for the meantime,' Rink directed. 'Get everyone back on board except for the lookouts. We broke radio silence a short time ago and it's possible that we may have company at any moment.'

When the men on shore had returned on board Rink began to prowl the cramped confines of the horseshoe, hands clasped behind his back, deep in thought. He was now faced with the most intricate and conscience-weighing problem with which he had ever been confronted; the future of *U501*, her crew, and her cargo, should they for any reason fail to make contact with Schemmel. Somewhere there had to be an alternative to surrender if Schemmel failed to keep their rendezvous, but he was acutely aware that there could be no latitude for mistakes, and if he *did* make a mistake, then it would be the most costly one he would ever make. And so he mentally began to compute the many aspects of the situation with infinite care.

At 21.50 Rink eventually went below, collected supper from Kolb in the galley and carried it for'ard to his own quarters.

'*Herr Kommandant?*'

Passing the W/T office, Berger's voice stopped him in his tracks, and he turned to see the Second Officer rip a slip of signal paper from the tablet on the radio bench.

'Plain morse – on the 600 metre wavelength, sir!'

Rink glanced at the slip of paper which conveyed the fact that the first two U-boats had surrendered to the Allies, and he at once began to realise the full impact of the situation: the decimated, but still fiercely proud U-boat Force which had long been engaged in fighting a losing battle with superior forces, was now having inflicted on it the ultimate in humiliation by its own High Command. With a heavy heart, he returned the slip of paper to Berger. 'Check those positions they give.'

He was sitting at the writing-shelf in his quarters when Berger returned from the control-room. 'Yes?'

'Both positions are in the English Channel, sir. One south of Lizard Point, the other west of Boulogne.' Rink nodded in silent reflection. 'Very good. Now lock that signal away in the confidential cabinet.'

Alone again, Rink pushed his supper away untouched, overpowered by emotion, yet more determined than ever that whatever might happen to *U501*, her crew, and her cargo, they would not fall into Allied hands. But it would not be easy, and there could be no faltering of spirit among the crew.

Without warning, Berger suddenly flung the heavy green curtain aside, his face ashen, and in an oddly distorted voice declared, 'Another signal, sir!'

Rink snatched the slip of paper from the Second Officer's hand and read: C-IN-C BRITISH NAVAL FORCES MEDITERRANEAN TO ANDROMEDA. LATEST REPORTED POSITION U-SCHEMMEL 34/10N 21/150W AT 21.10 HOURS. PROCEED MEET AND ESCORT TO GIBRALTAR. He was stunned. The news was bitter, shattering, totally unexpected. For reasons known only to himself, Schemmel had decided to ignore his own orders and instead comply with the general signal to surrender.

Berger was still incredulous. '*He surrendered, sir?*'

'Yes, Berger. And he was also a long way from here too. This position is somewhere north-west of Madeira.' Rink's mind was already beginning to range over the various problems with which he now saw himself faced. Then as he rose from the writing-shelf his voice reasserted its authority. 'Get all officers and Warrant Officers to the control-room at once. Also our two passengers.'

Three minutes later Rink ordered the for'ard and after watertight doors of the control-room shut and looked at the puzzled and uneasy faces assembled before him. He put the situation to them with brutal frankness. 'I'm afraid we cannot expect to meet with Schemmel – not now or ever. Our W/T office has just intercepted a British naval signal which gives clear indication of Schemmel having surrendered to the Allies some time earlier in the day in accordance with the general signal for surrender from Headquarters. At this moment he's about to be escorted to Gibraltar by the British naval vessel *Andromeda* from a position north-west of Madeira.'

The news was collectively received as if it were a physical blow.

With a plea which was almost that of helplessness, Wohldorf said in a curiously plaintive voice, 'What are we to do now?'

Rink ignored him. His gaze sought out Kernbach. 'Will you explain our position regarding fuel, Chief?'

Kernbach said tersely, 'We possess just about sufficient fuel to enable us to make six hundred miles, and even then it would depend on the sort of weather we encountered along the way.'

While despondent glances were being exchanged, Rink said, 'Gentlemen, I think the overall situation now demands that we give the fullest consideration to the few alternatives available to us.'

Wohldorf's head snapped upward. 'And what might they be?'

Rink said quietly, 'The first must surely be obvious to everyone – surrender as Schemmel did and make for Freetown.'

Wohldorf's face contorted and his eyes blazed. '*Surrender?*' he raged. 'We daren't even consider such action. It would amount to nothing more than the betrayal of trust placed in us by the Higher Authority. Also we would most certainly face some form of retribution if we were to commit such an unthinkable act, if not immediately, then at some time in the future.'

In the same calm and quiet voice as before, Rink said, 'Yes, I agree.'

Wohldorf glanced about him, disconcerted to find Rink in agreement with him. Then in a more composed tone, he said, 'So what's our next alternative?'

'We might scuttle the boat along with her cargo on some remote part of the African coast, take to the liferafts and hope to be rescued before we succumb to exposure. But even if we were successful there's still the crew to be considered. A skilled interrogator might not find everyone unwilling to talk.'

'Impossible!' stormed Wohldorf.

Rink smiled tolerantly. 'Then we can always put our trust in the Portuguese. As far as I'm aware the Higher Authority always had a measure of influence among certain members of her government.'

For the first time Wohldorf did not voice instant disapproval; the suggestion demanded to be given the fullest consideration.

Kernbach eyed Rink shrewdly. He knew Rink better than anyone, and suspected he was keeping something back from them, that he had yet another alternative in mind, one far removed from the others already mentioned. 'If you'll excuse my frankness, sir,' he quietly put forward, 'I really don't find myself in favour with anything we've so far discussed.'

Rink glanced around the waiting faces. 'Then what if we were to consider the possibility of helping ourselves to fuel?'

The faces instantly registered wonder and astonishment. Even Kernbach was unprepared for such a wild suggestion. He said cautiously, 'You mean attack the fuelling station on Sao Vicente – Porto Grande?'

A mysterious smile passed across Rink's bearded face. 'Not quite, no.'

Wohldorf's patience was at breaking point. 'Then *what*?' he demanded.

'We might stop a tanker.'

Wohldorf looked at Rink strangely. 'Are you serious?'

'I've never been more serious,' Rink stated with equanimity.

Wohldorf was unconvinced. 'And how would we know the vessel carried the type of fuel we require?'

Rink answered candidly, 'We wouldn't – but if she were also a *motor* vessel then her own fuel would certainly be of a similar grade to ours, irrespective of what she might be carrying in the way of cargo.'

Ingersoll's face split into a gap-toothed grin. 'That's true!'

'I'd go along with that,' stated Kernbach.

Wohldorf was afraid to allow his hopes to soar. 'But can it be done?' he questioned hesitantly.

Rink shrugged. 'I don't see why not. She wouldn't be the first vessel we stopped in our time.'

'But what about afterwards, sir?' It was Erlanger. 'Her crew?'

'Naturally the crew, like the vessel, would have to remain unharmed,' Rink stated categorically. 'I've already given considerable thought to the question. And make no mistake, with the surrender of the Fatherland we'd be embarking on a venture which would certainly constitute an act of piracy in a Court of Law, and if we were unfortunate enough to be apprehended, then I've no desire to add murder to such a charge.

Therefore the solution would appear to be that we put her crew under lock and disable her wireless in order to get clear of the area before word breaks about what happened.'

Wohldorf now felt himself influenced by the enthusiasm of the others. 'How are we going to set about this?'

Rink edged his cap back off his brow. 'Our best chance would lie in stopping a tanker bound west, or south-west for Latin America, and follow her out for a day or two. Then she'd either have to make port with news of what happened, or else meet with some other vessel and use her wireless before the authorities could be notified. Either way it would give us plenty of time to get clear of the area, and the South Atlantic's an extremely large piece of ocean in which to hunt down a single U-boat. Remember the *Admiral Scheer*?'

'I say we give it a try,' Kernbach enthused. 'We've nothing to lose.'

Wohldorf was impressed by the silence of general agreement. 'When do you propose to launch this venture?' he asked Rink.

'It depends on Kernbach and Ingersoll here. Our diesels will have to be at peak performance. Once refuelled we must clear the area at maximum speed in order to make good our escape.'

'You can confidently leave it to us,' stated Kernbach.

'I have another suggestion, sir,' Ingersoll put in. 'It might also be possible to repair those ruptured storage tanks.'

'True,' Kernbach agreed. 'We were going to suggest this earlier today after we carried out an inspection of these tanks, then decided against doing so on account of the fact that it would have impaired our state of readiness if we'd been forced to put to sea in a hurry.'

Rink was doubtful, hesitant. 'Can such repairs be accomplished?'

Ingersoll said, 'We have the necessary equipment required to carry out the work in question, sir.'

'How long would it take?'

'Thirty-six hours at the outside,' said Kernbach. 'Perhaps less. It would mean working around the clock.'

'The diesels would be stripped down during that time anyhow, sir,' stressed Ingersoll.

Rink found it a difficult decision to make. With *U501* unable to put to sea if an emergency arose, they were utterly helpless.

Yet they had taken more than one chance already and Fate had smiled on them benevolently. 'Then thirty-six hours,' he stated. 'We must be ready to give chase to our tanker whenever the opportunity presents itself.'

Coxswain Lamm ventured a question for the first time. He said, 'What about the crew, sir? They're going to be curious about what's going on when we begin work.'

'I propose to talk to the crew later,' said Rink. 'But for the time being they must be kept fully occupied. There's to be no time for thinking. Do anything to keep them busy and their minds occupied. And see to it the lookouts up on the knoll keep a log of every vessel passing these islands so that I can form an idea of the type and volume of traffic in the area. Any questions?'

The men glanced about them at each other but remained silent.

'Then stand down,' said Rink.

After an early breakfast work began on the task of overhauling the diesels and repairing the ruptured storage tanks amid much speculation and discussion among the crew. First the after liferaft was launched, then by flooding and blowing the ballast tanks, Kernbach and Ingersoll laid *U501* over to port, cushioning her against the volcanic jetty with fenders and scrub, exposing her hull starboard side. By mid-morning all available hands were scattered along the hull and in the liferaft, hard at work in the company of machinists and technicians.

Apart from a brief halt to eat a cold meal on shore at midday, work was uninterrupted until shortly before 16.00 when a startled cry of, '*Achtung! Aircraft approaching from due South!*' echoed down through the gully from the eastern cliff. The men working on the upperdeck scattered instantly, several of them racing across the gully to throw themselves in under the camouflaged shelters, others scrambling into the scrub-camouflaged liferaft or crowding aft along the inclined hull to gather under the overhang of the *wintergarten*.

Crouching on the bridge, Rink and Erlanger peered out through the scrub which festooned the jumping-wires and standards while the muffled sound of aircraft motors rapidly increased in volume, until suddenly the reverberating roar was overhead and the squat belly of a Sunderland flying-boat of

British Coastal Command lumbered over to vanish to northward.

With its disappearance, Erlanger turned anxiously to Rink. 'Do you suppose they could have picked up our attempt to contact Schemmel yesterday with their Direction Finding equipment at Freetown, sir?'

Rink glanced around the inlet which was to all outward appearances totally deserted. 'It's impossible to say. That may have been just an aircraft on routine patrol.'

'But if they found us here, sir?'

Rink lifted his shoulders in a philosophic shrug. 'I doubt if they could do much more than inform the Portuguese government, or its agent in Praia. However, my main concern right now is to see work completed on the diesels and storage tanks. Everything else we will deal with when it happens.'

When the Sunderland failed to show any further interest in the island, the men returned to work, and only with the approach of dusk did the machinists and technicians put away their oxyacetylene torches which had begun to send a flickering glare over the rocky walls of the inlet, something which would have meant certain betrayal of their presence to a passing aircraft.

At that time Rink sent for Coxswain Lamm. 'The men will have to remain on shore tonight. With the boat listed over like she is at present, no one can be expected to try and sleep on board.'

Supper that evening was also cold, then everyone, except the men still working on the diesels in the engineroom and those on lookout duty, huddled themselves in blankets and settled down under a star-scattered sky with a heavy dew falling on the camouflaged shelters.

Later that evening Rink was in the control-room discussing the progress of the work in hand when Berger appeared in the opening of the for'ard watertight bulkhead. 'May I speak with you, Herr Kommandant?'

One glance at Berger's face was sufficient to betray the fact that he was the bearer of still more grave news. In the gangway outside the W/T office he extended a slip of signal paper. 'This is a copy of a news bulletin which we picked up a few minutes ago, sir.'

Rink took it from him and read: TODAY AT 02.40 CENTRAL EUROPEAN TIME GENERALOBERST ALFRED JODL, OFFICIAL

REPRESENTATIVE OF GROSSADMIRAL KARL DONITZ, WHO ON THE DEATH OF THE FÜHRER ADOLF HITLER AT 15.30 APRIL 30, WAS APPOINTED HIS SUCCESSOR, SIGNED A DOCUMENT EXACTING TERMS OF UNCONDITIONAL SURRENDER ON ALL FRONTS ON HIS BEHALF IN THE PRESENCE OF THE ALLIED SUPREME COMMANDER, GENERAL OF THE ARMY DWIGHT D. EISENHOWER IN THE ECOLE PROFESSIONNELLE ET TECHNIQUE DE GARCONS IN PARIS. ALL HOSTILITIES WILL OFFICIALLY CEASE AT 00.01 HOURS MAY 9.

Rink felt numb, drained of all emotion, convinced they were now in possession of irrefutable evidence that the last tragic blow had fallen; Hitler really *was* dead and the Fatherland had finally succumbed to the combined Powers of East and West. He raised veiled eyes to Berger's shocked face. 'Where did you get this?'

In an emotion-filled voice, Berger weakly replied, 'French-Moroccan Radio, sir.'

'Then I see no need to remind you that not one word of this is to be leaked to the crew.'

'Of course, sir.'

'Do you have anything else for me to see?'

Berger produced the signal log. 'The ether was jammed solid with traffic of every description till shortly before 19.00 hours, sir. Then for no apparent reason there has been almost complete silence since.'

Rink flipped through the pages. The signals related to the surrender of various U-boats and instructions concerning the course they were to set for Allied ports. 'Put this away in the confidential cabinet,' he instructed Berger as he tucked the copy of the French-Moroccan bulletin into a pocket of his battle blouse.

The rest of the night Rink spent pacing restlessly back and forth on the ledge of rock to which *U501* was moored, burdened by a strange mixture of emotion. Privately he felt a vast sense of relief with the knowledge that the war was at an end, that at least some would be spared the final holocaust of death and destruction. He had lost a great deal of which he held precious to himself, countless friends and comrades, then, thinking of others, he saw himself as being fortunate in the respect that the war had not claimed his own parents, both of whom had died prior to 1938.

Eventually his troubled gaze fell on the sleeping men in the shelters under the dark shadow of the slope nearby, and he wondered at the thoughts which passed through their minds while they slept fitfully under the stars. Undoubtedly they were concerned with home, with families and relatives, some long since lost forever, others perhaps never to be seen or heard from again. And in the days ahead there was little doubt that the great plains of the Fatherland in east and west would become littered with the anonymous graves of the thousands still fleeing. But he was determined that at least his own crew would survive, that they would be saved even if only from the ignominy of defeat.

All through the night he remained alone in silent contemplation, until he finally saw the first shafts of dawn streak the eastern sky, when he summoned Wohldorf, his officers, and Warrant Officers to the control-room while the crew woke to eat a cold breakfast on shore. When everyone was assembled he passed the copy of the French-Moroccan Radio bulletin amongst them.

Only Wohldorf was prepared to express comment on it. Without marked conviction, he retorted, 'Are we to believe this?'

'I think we can accept it as being relatively close to the truth,' Rink quietly countered. 'But what interests me most regarding its contents is the fact that it states hostilities are to *officially* cease at 00.01 hours May 9th. In which case I see it as imperative that we move quickly to take our tanker if we're to remain within that same deadline, although if we should be unlucky enough to be caught such a minor technical detail is unlikely to aid our defence if it were to come to a War Crimes trial. However, it would appear that the area isn't entirely devoid of opportunities. Petty Officer Hoven spent yesterday up on the knoll and his log indicates that nine vessels in all passed in close proximity to our hiding-place, *three* of them motor-tankers, one American and two British, two of them outward bound from Porto Grande on a westerly course.'

The significance of Rink's statement was not lost on the gathering of men around him, and was greeted with murmurs of enthusiasm and approval. 'You can rely on us to give you every effort, sir,' Kernbach pledged on their behalf.

But, despite the ensuing activity on board *U501*, the day still contrived to move at a sullen crawl for Rink. By midday the increasing number of spare hands had retreated out of the glare of the sun to the shelters where they sat around gossiping, playing cards, or just plainly brooding. Rink did not like it. There were too many restless faces in evidence, glum faces, faces that were obviously concerned with problems of personal conflict. Then Kernbach appeared on shore, his body basted with sweat, and with a triumphant grin exclaimed, 'That's it! Diesels and storage tanks ready for trials. All that remains now is to right the boat and redistribute the fuel. Then we should soon know if all our work and effort has been in vain or not. Personally I'm extremely optimistic.'

Rink felt a burden lifted from his shoulders. 'Then let's hope we don't meet with further disappointment, Otto.' Next he turned to look for Lamm, saw him, and beckoned him across. 'Get the boat righted, Cox'n. The Chief here will take charge. Afterwards you'll find several crates of beer stacked beneath my bunk. Break them open and see to it that every man gets a bottle. The same with cigarettes. And give the non-smokers an issue of chocolate. Kolb has the key for the for'ard store locker. Later work-parties will be formed to replenish the water tanks. I want the boat ready for sea at a moment's notice.'

Thirty minutes later, with the boat safely righted and the various issues made, most previously glum faces had found flashing grins with which to look out on the world, and the improvement in morale was even more dramatic when the first swallow of beer had gone down and cigarettes were lighted.

'*Achtung*!' The sudden cry from above echoed through the inlet, brought all activity and conversation to an abrupt halt. '*Patrol boat headed this way!*'

Beer and cigarettes were instantly forgotten, and Rink started along the gully at a run, calling to Kordt, 'Break out the machine-pistols and ready the 20 mm armament!' Then scrambling up the steep incline of the cliff to eastward he flung himself down beside PO Seaman Weber. The young blond Dortmunder passed his binoculars and gestured to eastward. 'There it is, Herr Kommandant!'

Rink brought the converted fishing schooner into sharp focus. Painted light grey, she was of no more than twenty tons, holding placidly to a course which kept her close to the shore. Several figures were gathered around the wheelhouse, the predominant colour of their clothing khaki, red and gold caps glinting in the hard sunlight. 'Could be a routine patrol. With that machinegun in her bows unmanned it's unlikely they're looking for anything special,' He passed Weber back the binoculars. 'Stay here and leave this to us below.'

When Rink reached the inlet he found the crew gathered in apprehensive groups alongside the boat. 'As Petty Officer Weber reported, there's a patrol boat headed this way. I counted about ten, twelve men on deck. She's probably out of Sao Felipe or Praia. Unfortunately they can't miss us if they decided to pay the inlet a visit. Berger, man the *wintergarten* with the AA gunners. But don't start anything unless I give you the signal. Erlanger, take Kordt and four men and cover the eastern side of the entrance. The other four men with machine-pistols come with me. Cox'n, get everyone else on board out of sight.'

Both parties of armed men were lying concealed among the rocks either side of the entrance when the patrol boat rounded the base of the cliff to eastward, the rhythmic knocking of her small diesel engine heralding her approach. Breathlessly the men lay listening, ready to open fire at the command, Wohldorf and Schramm, Lugers in hand, ensconced among rocks to Rink's left. Then the sound of the diesel fell away abruptly, and Rink cautiously raised his head and peered seaward. The boat was lying about two hundred metres from the entrance while a discussion appeared to be taking place between two figures in the wheelhouse and the men gathered on deck, evidently some form of argument on the merits of whether or not they should inspect the inlet. For several minutes the sound of animated voices carried indistinctly across the intervening expanse of water, then the men on deck having apparently enforced their view on the others, the two men in the wheelhouse stepped back from the window and with a tiny clatter the diesel found its former rhythm and the boat continued on its way with the strains of an accordian drifting back across the water as the men resumed their light-hearted patrol.

Rink breathed relief and lowered himself back down among the rocks. 'They decided at the last moment not to pay us a visit after all,' he explained generally.

Fifteen minutes later, with the men still waiting anxiously around, Signalman Hagen appeared on the rim of the cliff to westward. 'All clear!' he called down through cupped hands. 'They're still headed north!'

With the report Rink at once stood the men down and started back towards the jetty where they were met by the remainder of the crew.

Kernbach said, 'What happened out there?'

'They changed their minds and moved on,' explained Rink. 'But more important, how are those tanks holding up?'

Kernbach said with a grin, 'As good as the day they were fabricated. We can now move out of here at the drop of the proverbial hat.'

Immensely relieved with the news, Rink looked around the gathered officers. 'Then I think it's time I explained the situation to the men.'

Wohldorf harboured doubt. He said uneasily, 'Do you consider that a wise decision at this stage?'

'Wise or not, we must have the full cooperation of every single man if we hope to achieve success.' Rink turned to find Lamm. 'Cox'n, see to it all hands are present and accounted for apart from lookouts. I propose to make a general statement to them in a few minutes.'

By the time Rink climbed to the bridge in company with Wohldorf the officers and men had formed into three presentable ranks.

'All hands present and accounted for apart from lookouts, sir,' Erlanger reported to the bridge.

Rink had decided that what he had to say could only be said with uncompromising frankness. And whatever the outcome, discipline had to be maintained with a firm hand. Even so, he expected there to be grievances and differences of opinion. When it was disclosed that the Fatherland had accepted terms for unconditional surrender there was certain to be at least several men in favour of complying with the general directive, while others might elect to make an immediate return home. Now it was up to him to convince them that it was in their best interests to continue their voyage to the Argentine. And so in clear, even tones which carried through the gully, he began, 'Men, it is my sad duty to inform you that we are in receipt of news which indicates that the Fatherland has signed terms with the Allied Powers for unconditional surrender on all fronts. All hostilities will officially cease at 00.01 hours May 9th. Further, I fear it must also be accepted that the Führer is dead.' A gasp of shock and disbelief swept through the assembled ranks. 'This news has forced me to devote the most careful consideration to the hazardous position in which we presently find ourselves. As you are all aware, Oberleutnant Bestelmeyer has been sunk, and unfortunately, I must also inform you that Kapitanleutnant Schemmel, Kommandant of the U-tanker with which we were to have rendezvoued at the secondary refuelling position west of Santo Antao, has chosen to surrender to the Allies. As a result of his action we are therefore left without means of receiving sufficient fuel to enable us to continue towards our destination. In these circumstances the alternatives with which we are left are pitifully few. The first is to comply with the general directive made by Headquarters to all U-boats and report our position before we set course for the nearest Allied port in order to surrender. In our particular case that port would be the British Naval Base at Freetown.

'Yes, I know there are those among us with wives, families, and relatives whom they hold dear, and who may wish to comply with that directive, but the quandary with which we are faced here is when we consider the sort of reception we are likely to receive once we give ourselves up. With this in mind I must remind you not to overlook the fact that we are *not* engaged in an ordinary war cruise, but charged with the delivery of Shipment No. 11372 to the Argentine, and the possible outcome when this fact became known to Allied interrogators, I leave to your imagination.

'However, I personally see nothing to be gained in surrendering, and even if we were to do so, when we might see our loved ones is anyone's guess. Instead I urge you to give serious thought to the possibility of continuing our voyage to the Argentine.'

In the stunned silence which met Rink's announcement, men cast disconcerted glances at each other before a muttered conversation broke among comrades.

'Permission to speak, sir?' Silence again descended with Control-room PO Morgen's interruption.

Rink looked down at him. 'Yes, Morgen?'

'How can we possibly reach the Argentine without sufficient fuel, sir?' Morgen had given voice to the question uppermost in everyone's mind.

Rink in turn answered unhesitatingly, 'Because it's my intention to stop a tanker on the high seas.' A collective exclamation of astonishment and disbelief met his announcement. 'Yes, it may sound a wild and irresponsible idea but as long as we choose the right vessel as our victim I envisage little difficulty in obtaining fuel. However, if we were to stand any chance of success it would require the wholehearted cooperation of every man among us. I tell you that now.'

'But how would we know the right vessel to stop, sir?' This time it was Able Seaman Hessler who spoke out of disconcertment.

'Because our choice of vessel would be a *motor-tanker*. In which case her own diesel fuel would almost certainly be of a similar grade to ours, irrespective of what she might be carrying in the way of cargo.'

After a period of indecision several heads indicated agreement, and Rink saw that enthusiasm for the idea had gained foothold.

'Even so, sir,' Torpedoman 1st Class Wassermann put in, 'What would happen to us if we were caught?'

Rink answered frankly, 'The South Atlantic is a vast expanse of ocean, Wassermann. But, yes, we would have committed a crime which would undoubtedly constitute an act of piracy in Court of Law, and if we *were* unfortunate enough to be caught, then the least sentence we could expect to receive would be a lengthy term of imprisonment.'

'What would become of the tanker and her crew, sir?' asked ERA Dornberger.

'Both would remain *unharmed*,' stressed Rink. 'Only her wireless would be rendered useless.' He paused to glance through the assembled ranks and noted growing enthusiasm. 'Men,' he said earnestly. 'Most of us have known each other for a considerable time, and in that time I hope you have found you can respect my thoughts and actions, that your interests are constantly in my mind. Therefore I ask you to listen to me when I say I was officially informed that a warm welcome awaits us in the Argentine, despite the fact that there technically exists a state of hostility between herself and the Third Reich. And for those of us whose thoughts are at home I must explain that at present we possess barely sufficient fuel to cover six hundred miles, so we must therefore discount any possibility of returning to the Fatherland. That leaves us with just one other alternative, and I already mentioned the dangers concerning surrender.'

The faces on shore were stamped with varying degrees of thoughtfulness, enthusiasm, indecision, and eagerness.

Wohldorf stepped to Rink's shoulder. 'May I address the men?'

Rink looked at him, hesitating. He had no idea what Wohldorf had in mind to say, and he was wary of allowing him to say anything at all. Yet he was curious to learn if Wohldorf might possess more detailed information regarding the reception awaiting them in the Argentine than he himself possessed. 'Very well. But be careful not to damp the fuse.'

Wohldorf looked down at the men and braced himself stiffly. 'Soldiers,' he began authoritatively. 'Before any decision is taken concerning our future I wish to say that, having listened to Kapitanleutnant Rink, I'm convinced that you would be foolish to turn your backs on this opportunity to retain your freedom. Again, like Kapitanleutnant Rink, before I left Berlin it was impressed on me that in the Argentine, irrespective of the fact that a state of war exists between our countries, we not only have many highly placed and influential sympathisers committed to take every care of us on arrival, but an elaborate Party Organisation dedicated to doing everything within its power to ensure our rehabilitation, and for those of you with families and relatives it may even be arranged one day for them to join you in your new lives. That is all I have to say.'

Rink was both impressed and relieved by the favourable reaction to Wohldorf's address, even though it was evident that his knowledge of the reception they were likely to receive on arrival in the Argentine was meagre, little more than his own. 'Any further questions?'

Faces lifted to the bridge but on this occasion there were no questioning voices raised.

Erlanger glanced along the ranks. 'No questions, sir.'

'Then stand the men down,' Rink directed. 'Cox'n and Chief Gunner's Mate to the bridge.'

Lamm and Kordt stepped on board and swung up the ladder to the *wintergarten*.

'Lock away all but one of those machine-pistols,' Rink informed them, 'and arrange for an armed guard to be mounted on the bridge tonight. Also see to it that the lookouts presently on watch are informed about what has just taken place.' He paused to glance at his wrist watch. 'Give the men an hour among themselves, then begin replenishing the water tanks.'

Wohldorf had listened to Rink's instructions with a marked

degree of cynicism. 'Do you really believe such a precaution necessary? Surely you noted that the general reaction among the men was a favourable one.'

Rink sent a glance at the men on shore where they stood in small groups engaged in animated discussion. 'Yes, I noted the general reaction – but let me put it this way – I don't expect everyone to be of the same frame of mind.'

Wohldorf's brow darkened. 'But what could anyone do?'

'I don't pretend to know that,' answered Rink. 'Perhaps someone may decide to attempt to disable the boat. That's one of the reasons why everyone will sleep on shore tonight, and every night till we sail.'

After supper Rink went to his quarters, collected his sheepskin coat and binoculars, and returned to the bridge where he found Kordt waiting with ERA Steiner.

'Steiner here will stand first watch on the bridge, sir,' the CGM reported. 'And Leading Machinist Guntel will relieve him at midnight.'

'Then listen, Steiner. You're not to allow anyone on board the boat during the hours of darkness – no one. Do I make myself clear?'

Steiner answered emphatically, 'Yes, Herr Kommandant!'

Rink directed his attention at Kordt. 'Make certain Guntel also understands those instructions.' In company with the CGM he walked aft to the *wintergarten*. 'The only personnel on board at the moment are Leutnant Berger, Bergold, and Vogel in the W/T office, and the Chief and Second Engineer who are preparing to run a charge into the batteries. They're the only ones allowed to come and go as they wish. Now I'm going up to the lookout post on the knoll along with the Quartermaster and Signalman Meyer. I want to take a look for myself at every vessel passing here during the night.' Dismissing the CGM, Rink swung down the *wintergarten* ladder to meet Erlanger and Meyer on shore, and together they started up the far side of the gully towards the knoll in the gathering dusk.

Meanwhile, lying on the shingle beach where it shelved steeply to meet the clear waters of the inlet, Wassermann watched the three men disappear over the rim of the cliff, momentarily silhouetted against the darkening skyline, then turned back to Vollmer and Elser where they had lain sprawled beside him since the men had been stood down after replenishing the water tanks. 'I don't care for any of this,' he determined bitterly. 'It won't be anywhere near as easy as it sounds. And if we get caught . . .'

'Yes,' Vollmer acquiesced. 'That also worries me.'

'But what did he mean by a lengthy term of imprisonment?' Elser wanted to know. 'Two years? Five years?'

'He said the *least* we could expect was a lengthy term of imprisonment,' Wassermann emphasised with a scowl.

Vollmer and Elser searched Wassermann's bleak face. 'And what does *that* mean?' Elser's dry whisper did not conceal his fear and apprehension.

'You mean they might *shoot* us?' Vollmer's face was a pale, waxen shadow in the growing darkness.

Wassermann sneered, 'The English don't shoot criminals – they *hang* them.'

Elser felt his heart contract. 'Well they aren't going to hang *me?* Not if I can help it!'

Wassermann cast a glance around the gully, then leaned closer. 'Listen,' he said. 'That first night I was on cliff lookout I climbed this hill behind us here and that island they call Fogo isn't really so far away. You can see the lights of Sao Felipe even without binoculars. With a boat we could reach it without any difficulty, in a few hours. A kid could do it.'

Vollmer's long morose face remained expressionless, while Elser showed outright alarm. 'You can't mean that!'

Wassermann retorted, 'Of course I mean it!'

Thinking clearly, Vollmer said in a composed voice, 'All right, even if you do mean it, where are you going to find a boat?'

Wassermann curled a supercilious lip. 'What do you think that is lying astern covered in scrub?'

Vollmer and Elser sent a glance at the camouflaged liferaft lying secured astern on the starboard side. Vollmer's face expressed doubt. 'But what good would it do us even if we reached Fogo?'

'We wouldn't end our days swinging at the end of a rope – that's what good it would do us', Wassermann impressed. 'Besides, why should we risk being hanged now the war's over? I doubt if the Portuguese would even bother to have us interned now. All we'd be doing is giving ourselves up, asking for asylum.'

It sounded a logical argument to Vollmer. His brow furrowed with the effort of concentrated thought. Always a careful, cautionary man, he was apprehensive of making hasty decisions. 'Yes, what you say is probably true,' he conceded. 'And why *should* we risk our necks any longer?'

Elser was hesitant, wary. 'But what if we're caught before we get clear?'

Wassermann stated confidently, 'I can handle this. Leave me to take the risks. Just be ready to do what I tell you.'

Elser looked at Vollmer for aid in his decision. 'What do you say, Franz?'

At that moment Vollmer's thoughts were with his wife and son. With a sense of remoteness, he said, 'But how would we ever get home?'

'The Portuguese won't imprison us,' answered Wassermann. 'What harm have we ever done them? We're certain to be repatriated, like Distressed Seamen in peacetime. We will be back home in Munchen before we know it,' he confidently predicted, anxious to impress his argument now he sensed victory. 'As for you, Elser, you'd be better out of it anyway, like me. Those two SS men aren't going to forget that we were involved with Bartz, and you know what happened to *him*. We're marked men, Elser. You know it.'

Elser shuddered, wishing fervently that he had never opened his mouth about the contents of the packing case. 'What about Zeller? He's in this too. Are we going to leave him behind?'

'Zeller can fend for himself,' Wassermann retorted. 'If those two SS men had it in mind to harm him he'd have gone the same way as Bartz did that night.' Then awaiting Vollmer's decision, he said anxiously, 'Well, Franz?'

For Vollmer, the deciding factor was the prospect of seeing his wife again, and the son whom he had never seen except in the snapshot which he carried in the pocket of his battle blouse. He nodded. 'All right.'

Wassermann grinned his relief. 'You won't regret it, Franz.'

'Me too,' Elser decided. 'I can't be any worse off.'

'Good!' Wassermann exclaimed jubilantly. 'Now listen. This is what we do . . .'

At 23.50 Wassermann took over the Middle Watch on the cliff to eastward, the sky a high transparent vault littered with stars, the air chill, damp with dew. Snuggling deeper into his watchcoat he put the binoculars on the inlet and made a careful study of the scene. All appeared quiet, the sleeping figures huddled in blankets beneath the camouflaged shelters. Finally he turned his attention to *U501* where a dark shadow moving slowly back and forth in the fore part of the bridge, betrayed Guntel's presence. Dropping the binoculars down, he peered at his wrist watch: 00.25.

Nerves taunt, the chill forgotten, he climbed to his feet and started cautiously down into the gully. It took him nine minutes to cover the slope, and in the gully he crouched to regain his breath and quiet his nerves. When he reached the beach opposite the bows he stopped to peer about him, then started along the ledge of rock that was the jetty. When close to the tower someone in one of the shelters close by groaned aloud in his sleep, and he froze, waited until the man again settled down, then called in a hoarse whisper to the bridge, '*Guntel*?'

A more assertive voice answered from overhead, 'Who is it?'

'Me, Wassermann.'

'What do you want?'

'Another blanket.'

Guntel hesitated. 'All right. Come on up.'

Wassermann sent another cautious glance at the shore before he stepped on board and swung up the ladder to the *wintergarten*.

Guntel regarded him with suspicion. 'I thought you were on lookout?'

'So I was,' Wassermann affirmed in a plaintive tone. 'Only I didn't feel so good after supper. The Cox'n had Bittrich relieve me. Now I can't settle down to sleep. It's cold out there.'

Guntel said defensively, 'You know I'm not supposed to allow anyone on board. You had better stay here and let me get that blanket.'

Wassermann said indifferently, 'Suit yourself.'

Guntel leaned the Schmeisser against the bridge casing and started to climb into the tower. Waiting his chance, Wassermann stepped quickly forward and grabbed the machine-pistol to swing it in a vicious arc, slammed it against the side of Guntel's skull, and saw him crumple with a gasp and drop into the tower with a sickening thud when he struck the deck-plates.

Wassermann held his breath, listening, heard only the pounding of his own heart, then scrambled aft to the *wintergarten* and swung below to the after catwalk where he saw the dim shadows of Vollmer and Elser huddled on the jetty. He hissed impatiently, 'Come on – and watch where you put your feet!'

Hurriedly they cast off the liferaft's mooring line and slipped soundlessly into the water off the saddle tanks. With only their heads above the surface, hands grasping the side of the liferaft, they kicked out cautiously and started towards the entrance in a quiet swirl of water. When clear of the entrance they quickly hauled themselves inboard, tossed the scrub out, and grabbed the paddles. And keeping close to the shore, they started eastward, paddles dipping into the water with frantic energy.

Fifty minutes later they cleared the eastern extremity of the island and saw the dark mass of Pico do Cano jutting into the sky further to eastward. For the first time they allowed themselves to rest, dragged air down into their aching lungs, and stared back along the shore.

Elser said fearfully, 'Do you suppose they've discovered what's happened yet?'

Wassermenn retorted with garrulous contempt, 'What the hell does it matter? They won't come after us.'

Vollmer said apprehensively, 'What did you do to silence Guntel?'

Wassermann grunted, 'I slammed the bastard on the head with his Schmeisser!'

Vollmer was shocked. 'I hope you didn't kill him.'

Wassermann spat across the side in contempt. 'You worry too much.'

In the same fearful voice as before, Elser said, 'What makes you think they *won't* come after us?'

Wassermann was overflowing with confidence. 'Well, not after it gets light they won't. It would be too risky, and they aren't going to risk *everything* on account of *three* men.' Then he laughed aloud, startlingly. 'I wish I could see their faces when they discover that little memento I left behind for them to remember me by.'

Vollmer's gaze narrowed suspiciously. 'What do you mean?'

Wassermann turned his attention towards the distant lights of Sao Felipe. 'Nothing. Forget it. Now let's get moving.'

Three-quarters of an hour later, Vollmer, every muscle in his back and arms aching, blistered hands sticking to the paddle, glanced back towards Brava. What he saw caused him to sit upright in alarm. 'Look!' he called to the others. 'Something's wrong!'

Wassermann and Elser rested on their paddles to catch at their breath in short deep gasps. Wassermann armed the sweat from his eyes. 'What is it?'

Vollmer gestured towards the dark shadow that was the island of Brava, and said in consternation, 'We're off course – we're losing way!'

Wassermann and Elser directed their attention from Brava to the jutting mass of Pico do Cano. 'He's right!' Elser's voice was sharp-edged with panic. 'We're moving southward!'

Although they had put considerable distance between themselves and Brava they appeared to be no nearer the sprinkle of lights that was Sao Felipe than when they had cleared the eastern extremity of Brava.

Wassermann hefted his paddle determinedly in both hands. 'It must be the current,' he gritted between his teeth. 'Come on – dig deep!' And he commenced to dig his paddle into the water with prodigious sweeps while, chased by their own fears, Vollmer and Elser hurriedly followed his example.

But before another thirty minutes elapsed Elser collapsed against the side of the liferaft exhausted. Eyes filled with despair he gasped, 'It's no use – we aren't getting any nearer!'

'He's right,' said Vollmer between sobbing breaths. 'We're drifting further and further to south-eastward.'

Wassermann cursed violently and glanced along the horizon, eyes blurring, breath wheezing. Although they were about equal distance between the two islands, Brava now showed to north-westward, and Fogo to north-eastward. It was plain to see that they had dropped a considerable distance away to south-eastward since they had last stopped, swept by the current towards the distant coast of French West Africa.

'What are we going to do?' whined Elser, close to tears.

Wassermann sat in dark silence, jaw and neck muscles corded with determination. Physically he was stronger than both Vollmer and Elser, but even his own shoulders, back, and belly muscles were gripped by spasmodic flutters of protest. He believed that now their only chance was to try it over the side. He said fiercely, 'With the three of us on the life-lines on one side we should be able to make better headway if we kick out strongly enough. Besides, someone's bound to see us from Sao Felipe when it begins to get light.'

Neither Vollmer nor Elser were in any condition to protest, and in numb desperation they followed Wassermann into the water to grasp the life-line shoulder to shoulder. Wassermann glanced at their despairing faces. 'Ready?'

Heads held clear of the surface, eyes fixed on the distant lights of Sao Felipe, they renewed their fight against the current.

Over the next forty minutes their movements gradually became more and more feeble as their determination ebbed, until they reached the stage where they were forced to give up hope of making any marked headway. In a haze of exhaustion, limbs seized with cramp, Elser clung desperately to the life-line, afraid of drifting away. 'It's no use!' he whined. 'I can't move my legs!'

Gasping for breath, Vollmer hauled himself painfully inboard and grabbed Elser's wrists. Wassermann trod water mechanically while he watched Elser follow Vollmer in across the side of the liferaft and, forced to accept that they were faced with an impossible task, he hoisted himself inboard over the sprawled bodies of his comrades. Falling forward, he was vaguely conscious that dawn had filled the sky in the east with a soft rosy light and that the towering mass of Pico do Cano now lay almost due North, more distant than ever, its slopes misted by the morning haze. And then like Vollmer and Elser, he lapsed into an uncaring stupor, only dimly aware of the warming heat of the sun on his back and shoulders.

The night passed uneventfully for Rink, Erlanger and Meyer in the lookout post high above the island. Not a solitary vessel of any description had been sighted on any point of the compass during the hours of darkness, and the sun was beginning to strike glittering bands of dazzling light from the ocean when a feather of smoke cast a dirty blemish against the sky beyond Sao Vicente. Shortly afterwards the vessel responsible thrust her bow out seaward. High, angular, black, there was no mistaking the fact that she was an antiquated freighter.

Erlanger promptly gave vent to his disgust. '*Verdammt!* What in hell's become of all those tankers?'

'*Herr Kommandant?*'

The three men turned in surprise at the sound of Kordt's urgent shout, and looked down to see Wohldorf, Kordt and Zeller, Meyer's relief, labouring hurriedly up the steep incline below the knoll. Then Wohldorf stopped, looked up at the faces above him, and cried out breathlessly, 'Vollmer, Wassermann and Elser have gone! They took the liferaft!'

In sudden vision Rink saw disaster poised to descend on them. 'When did it happen?' he hurled down.

Wohldorf struggled over the lip of the knoll and tumbled into the lookout post, striving to regain his breath. 'Probably somewhere around one o'clock. But Guntel isn't certain about the exact time. Kernbach found him unconscious in the tower when he came ashore shortly before first light after he and Ingersoll began to run a charge into the batteries. We immediately roused the Cox'n and made a roll-call. At first we thought that only Vollmer and Elser were missing, but when Hessler went to relieve Wassermann on lookout he wasn't anywhere to be found.'

'You can see the liferaft from the eastern cliff, sir,' Kordt interposed. 'Away to south-eastward.'

Rink at once started up the rugged slope of the island behind them, Wohldorf accompanying him, then dropped down and crawled on to the skyline to focus his binoculars. He found the liferaft immediately, a tiny speck set against the shimmering expanse of blue ocean. 'They obviously started out for Fogo, for Sao Felipe, and were caught up by the current. Once they get further to southward there's every likelihood that the Equatorial Current will then sweep them in towards the Sierra Leone Basin.'

An expression of incredulity spread itself across Wohldorf's face. 'You mean you aren't going after them?'

'No,' said Rink. 'It would demand too great a risk.'

'But if *we* can see them from here,' Wohldorf argued, 'then there must be every chance that they can *also* be seen from Fogo, from Sao Felipe.'

'True,' Rink agreed. 'But I can only just make them out from here, and with that heat haze from southward closing down over the ocean we aren't going to be able to see them for much longer.'

Out of frustration Wohldorf snapped, 'But they ought to be shot!'

A thin smile lit Rink's face. 'From up *here*?' he said.

Wohldorf snorted angrily, but relinquished his argument.

Rink still had the binoculars focused on the distant liferaft. 'All three men are from Munchen – comrades. I ought to have given thought to that fact before. They must have bolstered each other's confidence to the point of foolhardiness.'

They waited watching, and soon afterwards all trace of the liferaft vanished in the haze through which the sun now shone as a ball of pale, fuzzy light. Rink was troubled; he knew that with their desertion the three men had put the safety of *U501* and her crew in extreme jeopardy. All it required was for them to be picked up by a passing vessel and a full-scale search would almost certainly be launched even if the men did not volunteer any information on how three healthy U-mariners came to be bobbing around the South Atlantic in a liferaft. Therefore it was now imperative that *U501* should disappear quickly, that they accept whatever opportunity might present itself.

Finally he climbed to his feet and started back towards the lookout post. 'Was Guntel badly hurt?'

'Not really, although he took a severe knock on the head.'

'Remain here with Zeller for the time being,' Rink instructed Erlanger. 'And keep your eyes open. If you sight a tanker, even a motor vessel of any description, start back down to the inlet without delay. We now have to take our chance with whatever comes our way. If those three men are picked up in the next few hours and taken to Praia or Porto Grande we're going to have big trouble on our hands. So if you hear two shots don't waste time getting back.'

*

By 05.50 *U501* was cleared ready for sea, her crew back on board, lookouts on the cliffs doubled. Yet nothing occurred to give concern, and the morning dragged itself slowly into afternoon, the desertion of Vollmer, Wassermann and Elser the main topic of conversation, each and every man on board alive to the possibility of their discovery should the trio be rescued by a passing vessel. Then at 14.40 an excited shout sent Rink and Wohldorf hurrying to the bridge.

Coxswain Lamm flung out an arm to where PO Seaman Hoven stood silhouetted on the cliff to westward. 'Hoven just reported that the Quartermaster and Zeller are on their way down from the knoll in a hurry, sir.'

'Then alert the Chief Engineer and tell him to join us on the cliff with Hoven. This could be what we're waiting for.'

Rink, Wohldorf, Kernbach, and the two lookouts were waiting impatiently on the western cliff when Erlanger and Zeller arrived. 'She's a motor-tanker, sir!' the Quartermaster reported breathlessly. 'British and around 3,500 Gross Register Tons. But she's *southbound*,' he warned.

Forty minutes elapsed before the tanker eventually hove herself into view, well to seaward. Rink screwed her into focus. A motorship, her lines were evidence that she had been built at some time in the past two years; a well-cared for vessel, although badly in need of a fresh coat of paint. But more to his satisfaction, she was loaded well down to her Plimsoll line, her speed in the region of ten knots. When she drew closer on her southbound course he saw that she flew the Red Ensign. He passed the binoculars to Kernbach. 'Give me your opinion, Otto.'

Kernbach made a detailed study of the vessel in silence, then said, 'Yes, I'd be inclined to take a chance with her. Not too large either.'

Rink put the vessel back into focus. 'It's a pity she's southbound but it can't be helped. My only fear is she might be headed for Freetown, and that would be a little *too* close for comfort.'

Erlanger asked with boyish enthusiasm, 'Are we going to take her, sir?'

'I originally intended to follow our victim out for a day or two, but time is now against it,' answered Rink. 'Instead we will take her whenever it gets dark. That ought to allow us sufficient time to refuel within the official deadline for the cessation of all hostilities, although that's unlikely to contribute to our defence if anything goes wrong. But our first task is to organise a competent boarding-party, and we don't have many spare hands.'

As Wohldorf viewed the tanker through Hoven's binoculars he experienced an overwhelming sense of relief and elation. Although it was in a way a grudging admission, he had to concede that it was entirely due to Rink's determination and ingenuity that all their difficulties were now on the verge of being resolved. Yet he harboured serious reservations concerning certain points of Rink's plan to deal with the tanker and her crew, was convinced that it lacked the necessary element of ruthlessness to absolutely ensure their own safety. And with that particular fear in mind, he said, 'Schramm and I will be quite prepared to accompany the boarding-party if required.'

Rink accepted the offer at face value. 'Very well. But Berger will have to take charge as I can't risk anything happening to Erlanger here if there should be trouble. Apart from myself he's the only remaining officer on board with any real experience of navigation.' He directed his attention to Kernbach. 'What plans do you have for the refuelling-party?'

'Ingersoll and Dornberger will have to take charge of everything on board the tanker, while Steiner and myself will see to everything at our own end. Also you can draw on one or two of my machinists for your boarding-party if needed. I can spare a few hands.'

'Then we will have to board her in two parties,' stated Rink. 'I don't want too many people milling around at one time and getting in each other's way. We can't afford casualties. Therefore Berger will lead the first party and take command of the vessel. The refuelling-party and lookouts will board her later. I want at least four reliable lookouts stationed on her bridge and in her rigging. The last thing we want is for another vessel to blunder down on us while engaged in refuelling. But there must be no trouble, certainly no shooting. I must impress that on Berger at all cost.'

Rink gave the order to strip *U501* of her camouflage at 16.00. The berthing-party went about their task with gusto, heaving the scrub which festooned the jumping-wires and *wintergarten* over the side until a cry of surprise went up from the for'ard catwalk, when several hands had began to strip the tower and its casing.

'Seems one of our departed friends left us something to remember him by, sir,' CGM Kordt reported to the bridge.

Curious, Rink leaned across the wind-deflector and saw the replica of the Party's swastika medallion, the Golden Pheasant, painted in bright yellow on the fore part of the tower casing where normally the Flotilla insignia would have been situated. There was no doubt about the culprit; Wassermann was the only amateur artist on board, and had previously been responsible for the maintenance of the Flotilla insignia on board *U207*. 'It's too late to do anything about it now,' he informed Kordt. 'Carry on and get the rest of that scrub across the side.'

U501 slipped her lines at 16.10 and moved slowly out astern from the inlet on electric drive. Once clear of the shore Rink brought her around on to a course due South, and submerged.

The distant mass of Pico do Cano had lost itself in the gathering dusk when he brought the boat back to periscope depth, satisfied himself sky and ocean were deserted, then surfaced with the bridge watch and AA gunners crowding out on to the bridge behind him.

'Both three times full ahead!'

The diesels hacked, coughed, and broke into a full-throated roar, exhaust fumes clouding the still air astern. *U501* swiftly gathered way, the quiet ocean hissing back along the casing to boil up white astern, raising a cool breeze to fan the faces of the men on deck. Twenty-two minutes later they sighted the faint shadow of the tanker where she lay hull down on the horizon directly ahead, her running-lights coming on without warning, startling the watch so that for the first time they were struck by the fact that the war was really over, that the enemy were no longer forced to skulk around the ocean with their ships blacked-out, not daring to show the hint of a light which a few days earlier would have proved the harbinger of their destruction.

'Both emergency ahead!'

U501 shuddered through the quiet ocean as the revolutions were hurriedly applied, spray showering the for'ard catwalk with jewelled light.

Rink held to the tanker's track, closing on her from directly astern in order to offer any vigilant lookout only the smallest silhouette possible, tension and excitement mounting among the crew while the distance between the two vessels steadily diminished.

'Chief Engineer to the bridge.'

Kernbach was on the bridge at once, peering anxiously southward.

Rink said, 'Is your party ready?'

'Ready and eager,' Kernbach affirmed. 'When do you expect to close her?'

'Ten minutes ought to do it.'

Kernbach nodded, his gaze fixed on the tanker out ahead.

'And remember,' Rink impressed. 'Tell Ingersoll not to waste time.'

'He knows,' said Kernbach, and prepared to climb back into the hatch. '*Glueck auf!*'

Rink made another all round sweep with the binoculars. The mill-pond smooth ocean reflected every detail of the cloudless sky overhead, made it impossible to decide just where the two met.

Meanwhile *U501* continued to steadily overhaul her unwitting prey, the radar obviously unmanned, or else *U501*'s tower undetectable in the turbulence of the track astern, although Rink reasoned the degree of alertness had probably decreased with the knowledge that the official deadline for the cessation of hostilities was only a few hours away. He put the binoculars on the tanker yet again, *U501*'s bows driving through the flat water, a fine spray falling back across the bridge superstructure and *wintergarten*. Now he could distinguish her name and port of registry: *Cassiopeia – Milford Haven*. '88 mm gun crew on Battle Stations. Boarding-party standby.'

In reply CGM Kordt and the 88 mm gun crew piled out through the hatch, rushed aft to the *wintergarten*, and swung below to the catwalk.

Rink next sought out Meyer. 'Ready with your signal-lamp.'

'Cleared away and ready to open fire, sir,' Kordt reported from the for'ard catwalk.

Rink called down to him sharply, 'Remember what I told you – don't hit him. And if he uses wireless take the aerials.'

The distance between the two vessels appeared suddenly to have diminished dramatically. Yet *U501* apparently remained undetected by the tanker's watch and lookouts. Now the time had arrived for Rink to activate his next manoeuvre, to sweep *U501* out from astern to a parallel course on the tanker's starboard side. 'Right rudder – steady!' *U501* seemed suddenly to lose way, to allow the tanker to speed on ahead while she drew out from astern. The distance widened – five – six – seven hundred metres. 'Steer 175 degrees.' And now they were back on parallel course with their prey, seven hundred metres distant, steadily overhauling her again. A black silhouette mounted with glaring lights in her midship and stern superstructure, her wash foamed beneath her counter to leave a phosphorescent light to play through the depths astern.

Rink held her in steady focus. They were drawing up fast on her again, drawing level on her starboard beam. 'Half ahead both,' Rink ordered in clipped tones. 'Standby W/T office to intercept. Prepare for gun action.'

As *U501*'s speed fell away abruptly, Rink's binoculars swept the tanker's decks while she drove serenely on, not a solitary crewman to be seen anywhere. He turned to Meyer. 'Make: STOP – MAINTAIN RADIO SILENCE OR WE OPEN FIRE.'

Meyer sighted the signal-lamp on the lighted wing of the tanker's midship superstructure and deliberately triggered out the message.

The result was absolutely no reaction at all from the tanker.

'Repeat that,' Rink ordered with a frown. 'They must have cracked a bottle in celebration of victory.'

Again the message winked out across the intervening expanse of mill-pond water, and incredibly, the result was as previous.

Rink growled impatiently, 'What the hell are they doing across there?' Then to the for'ard catwalk, he shouted, 'Give him one across the bows!'

Kordt laid the cannon and took aim. '*Fire!*'

Following the flash and *crack* on the for'ard catwalk, the smell of cordite and hot metal lashed back across the bridge.

All eyes watched the column of water geyser up out of the ocean ahead of the tanker's bows, so close that it subsided back across her forepeak.

'*Donnerwetter* – if they didn't see *that* – then she must be the *Flying Dutchman* in disguise!' PO Seaman Hoven swore in awe.

Suddenly Rink saw several figures crowd themselves to the lighted windows of the tanker's midship superstructure. 'Repeat your message,' he instructed Meyer.

Meyer quickly sighted the signal-lamp, but before he had completed the message the tanker increased speed perceptibly, and in the W/T office Chief Telegraphist Bergold jammed down his key on the urgent crackle of morse which suddenly filled his earphones. 'Ship using wireless!'

'Take the aerials!' Rink shouted to Kordt and his gun crew on the for'ard catwalk, then flung across his shoulder, 'Give him a burst!' to the AA gunners on the *wintergarten*.

Kordt took delicate aim while the two twin 20 mm cannon on the *wintergarten* opened fire to send a burst of tracer shell across the tanker's for'ard well, the lighted trails of metal flaming between the for'ard mast and the midship superstructure. Then Kordt ripped at the firing lanyard and before the vicious *crack* cleared his ears he saw the bright flash above the tanker's bridge followed by a tangle of aerials and stays collapsing across the superstructure.

'Wireless cease sending!' was Bergold's immediate cry from below.

On the for'ard catwalk Kordt was sighting the cannon for another possible shot when the tanker began to lose way.

'*Halt Batterie!*' shouted Rink. 'Stop both!'

Meanwhile a signal-lamp began to wink out a message from the starboard wing of the tanker's bridge.

'She's asking: WHAT SHIP?' Meyer reported.

'Ignore her,' directed Rink. 'Make: STANDBY TO RECEIVE BOARDING-PARTY.' And in the same breath called below, 'Boarding-party on deck at the double!'

Leutnant Berger was quickly followed out on to the bridge by Wohldorf and Schramm, and five other ratings, all armed with Schmeissers except for Berger and Wohldorf.

Rink watched them hurriedly break out the liferaft from its stowage in the for'ard casing, launch it across the side, then pile into it. When it cast off and started towards the now stationary tanker, he turned, warning the bridge watch and AA gunners, 'Keep a sharp watch on sea and sky!'

'There's been no acknowledgement to the signal I jammed, sir,' Bergold reported from the W/T office. 'I'm maintaining watch on the 600 metre wavelength.'

The boarding-party headed the liferaft towards the ladder which they saw thrown across the tanker's side for'ard of the midship superstructure. The instant they bumped against the steel wall Berger grabbed the ladder and swung upward, Walther drawn, Wohldorf at his back.

Two frightened Lascar seamen and a stocky, tattooed Englishman dressed in a white singlet and blue dungaree trousers were stationed at the head of the ladder when Berger clambered across the bulwarks into the pool of light thrown down from the lighted windows of the bridge. The Englishman's eyes opened wide at the sight of Berger's cap and the drawn Walther, and he raised a stupefied face to the figures crowding the windows of the bridge overhead. '*Christ!*' he announced in a loud Welsh accent. '*They're Jerries – they're bloody Jerries!*'

Berger brandished the Walther at him. 'Your Kapitan! Where's your Kapitan?'

The man came swiftly to life as the remainder of the boarding-party clattered across the bulwarks, seabooted feet thudding on the iron deck. 'There – up there on the bridge.'

Berger snapped out, 'You – Weber, cover the for'ard well and forepeak! You – Rothfels, take the after well and fantail!' Then with Wohldorf and Schramm in attendance he followed the boatswain aft into the starboard midship companionway, followed him in through an open doorway, then started up a carpeted stairway which gave entrance to the rear of the bridge. Berger then bundled the man aside and levelled his Walther to cover the disconcerted figures awaiting their arrival. There were nine men present, six Englishmen and three Lascars, three of the former dressed in pyjamas. None of them yet appeared to be prepared to believe their eyes. Berger searched the bewildered faces. 'Which of you is the Kapitan?'

One of the Englishmen, a burly, dark-complexioned man somewhere in his early fifties, stepped forward. 'I'm the Captain,' he stated with cold deliberation. 'Captain Noel Thomas.' His angry and indignant gaze moved from Berger to Wohldorf, fastened on the black and silver cap with its glittering Death's Head insignia. Then he returned his attention to Berger. 'Would you mind explaining just what you think you're doing by boarding my ship in this manner?'

Berger snapped. 'Let me see your ship's papers!'

Captain Thomas stood his ground stubbornly. 'But the war's over, man! Don't you know that?'

Wohldorf's eyes hardened. 'You have sixty seconds to produce those papers or I shoot you where you stand!' he stated in a voice cold with menace.

Captain Thomas dropped his gaze to the Luger in Wohldorf's hand, but made no attempt to comply with the order.

'Maybe you had better do as he says, Captain,' one of the figures in pyjamas, a short, balding man with a pipe still clamped between his teeth, prompted.

Berger made a gesture with his Walther. 'If I were you, Herr Kapitan, I'd seriously consider listening to your comrade's advice, because it isn't our intention to stand around here all evening engaged in frivolous discussion.'

Captain Thomas still hesitated.

In a voice charged with venom, Wohldorf snapped out, '*Move!*'

Captain Thomas eyed him with contempt, then turned and walked unhurriedly to the chart-room in the after end of the bridge. Berger followed, saw him open the door of a safe, extract some papers, and drop them contemptuously on the chart-table. Berger reached for them and rifled through them until he found one which detailed the cargo. His face at once brightened. 'We're in luck!' he exclaimed to Wohldorf, and started out on to the starboard wing of the bridge. At an open window he cupped his hands to his mouth. 'Eight hundred and fifty-six tons of first grade diesel fuel in tanks Five and Six for-'ard!' he called across to the low silhouette which now lay less than a hundred and fifty metres off the *Cassiopeia*'s starboard beam, the Golden Pheasant on her tower gleaming dully, like beaten gold.

'Then standby to receive us alongside!' Rink's voice drifted back in reply.

Berger returned his attention to Captain Thomas. 'How many crew do you have on board, Kapitan?'

Captain Thomas answered reluctantly, 'Thirty-eight. Officers and bo'sun are British, the remainder Lascars. The officers are all present on the bridge here except for the Chief Engineer who's below on watch.'

Berger said curtly, 'Then you have two minutes to muster everyone on the for'ard well, and that includes the duty watch. After roll-call the most experienced members of your crew will then make ready for refuelling starboard side for'ard.'

Captain Thomas set his jaw pugnaciously. 'This is outrageous!' he stormed. 'The war's over – finished!'

A humourless smile ghosted across Wohldorf's face. He said, 'Tell us again and we may *just* believe you, Kapitan.'

Captain Thomas seemed about to argue, glanced at Schramm where he stood covering them with a Schmeisser, then turned to the men gathered around him with a resigned shrug, and said, 'I suppose all we can do at this stage is to go along with them. I see no necessity for anyone to get hurt. The Royal Navy will take care of this.'

Rink brought *U501* alongside the *Cassiopeia*'s gently lifting hull starboard side on electric drive. 'Standby with fenders. Secure and stow the liferaft.'

Overhead a crowd of dark faces with fear in their eyes were lining the tanker's bulwarks, each of them ready with manilla fenders and mooring wires.

'Stop both. Slow astern.' The vessels gently rubbed hulls with a creak of straining fenders, Rink's orders echoing across from *U501*'s bridge. Mooring wires were next to drop down out of the overhead glare of light, and under Kordt's supervision were secured fore and aft while the secondary boarding-party hastily followed Ingersoll and Dornberger in across the tanker's bulwarks. Meanwhile on the after catwalk Kernbach and his party were piling their refuelling tackle out through the after hatch to arrange it on the upperdeck in readiness.

Berger appeared on the tanker's well above *U501*'s bridge. 'She's bound for the British Admiralty Bases at Ascension and St Helena with an assorted cargo, sir,' he reported to Rink. 'There's plenty of first-grade diesel fuel in tanks Five and Six, and she's also equipped with rubber fuelling hoses.'

'Very well, Berger. But first douse those running-lights and put all spare hands under lock and key.'

When Berger turned away, Ingersoll was next to appear in the well, a wide grin lighting his face. 'I don't see any problems,' he called below to Kernbach. 'It's all prime stuff, and they have a hundred and sixty drums of lubricating oil on board.'

'Then give me ten,' Kernbach instructed.

The rubber fuelling hoses were next to be swung out across the tanker's side and were grabbed on board *U501* by Kernbach and his men. Then the tanker's running-lights were suddenly extinguished, and moments later the other lights began to go out in swift succession. Meanwhile on her after well-deck Wohldorf and PO Seaman Rothfels were herding a batch of eleven Lascar seamen and firemen aft to the storeroom beneath the fantail, where Rothfels thrust the men roughly into the darkness of the confined space, slammed the steel door shut, secured the clips, and rammed home the exterior bolts, grinning with relish at the muffled protests from within. 'They won't break out of there in a hurry, Herr Hauptsturmführer,' he confidently opined.

When they returned to the for'ard well-deck they found that pumping had commenced and that Ingersoll had gone below with the tanker's Chief Engineer, leaving Dornberger in charge on deck. 'Where's Leutnant Berger?' demanded Wohldorf.

'I think he and your aide have the Kapitan and his officers under guard in the lower saloon, Herr Hauptsturmführer.'

Wohldorf and Rothfels found the lower saloon situated opposite the bottom of the main bridge stairway. Berger, Walther in hand, was stationed just inside the door with

Captain Thomas and his officers arranged along one side of the heavy dining-table. 'Where's Schramm?'

Berger motioned towards the bridge stairway. 'He went to attend to the wireless in the W/T office on the bridge, sir'.

'And the other crewmen you sent for'ard with Weber?'

'They put them in a paint locker in the forepeak tunnel out of harm's way.'

'Don't think you'll get away with this!' Captain Thomas stated furiously, half rising from the table, his face dark with rage and frustration. 'The Royal Navy will be after you by morning!'

Wohldorf's face twisted into a supercilious smile. 'Is that what *you* think?'

'That's what I *know*!' Captain Thomas corrected as Schramm entered the saloon to toss a fire-axe contemptuously into a corner.

'That took care of your precious wireless,' he sneered in Captain Thomas's direction.

'We don't require a wireless to take care of *you*,' Captain Thomas argued. 'All I need do is turn my ship around for Porto Grande or Praia.'

Wohldorf's gaze narrowed sharply, and he exchanged a fleeting glance with Schramm and Berger. Suddenly Berger snapped to attention and Wohldorf turned to see Rink enter the saloon.

'Is everything under control? No trouble?'

'No, no trouble, Herr Kommandant,' answered Berger, levelling his Walther at Captain Thomas and his officers. 'On your feet!' he rapped out.

The men got up reluctantly from the table, their attention focused on Rink, faces sullen and resentful.

Rink casually regarded each of them in turn. 'Which of you is the Kapitan?'

Captain Thomas spoke out belligerently, 'I am – why?'

Rink addressed him politely. 'Then I apologise for having to stop you in this manner, Herr Kapitan. But I'm afraid the fortunes of war demand it. However, you have my word that no harm will come to any member of your crew so long as they obey the instructions of my officers and men. It's my intention merely to take on board a small quantity of diesel fuel and several drums of lubricating oil, nothing more.'

'You won't get far,' Captain Thomas predicted. 'I promise to see to it personally.'

Rink answered with continuing politeness, 'That's as it may be, Herr Kapitan.' Then he turned to Berger. 'What did you do with the remainder of the crew?'

'Most of them are imprisoned in the forepeak paint locker, sir. A further nine are in a cordage locker port side amidships.'

'We locked the others into a storeroom below the fantail, Herr Kommandant,' explained Rothfels.

'Then I assume everyone has been accounted for?'

'The only absentees are the Chief Engineer and two firemen who are below with Oberleutnant Ingersoll and Leading Machinist Guntel, sir.'

Rink's gaze swept the saloon with its black-out curtains drawn across the scuttles as he walked to a door at the after end, pulled it open, and found himself in the main pantry. There were no scuttles, just ventilation trunking, and the door was of solid teak. He returned to where Berger was standing guard over Captain Thomas and his officers. 'Lock them in the pantry aft. And see no harm comes to anyone.'

After Rink departed, Berger ushered Captain Thomas and his officers into the pantry and locked the door. At the same time Wohldorf gestured at the heavy dining-table. 'Barricade the door with that table and anything else you can find,' he instructed Schramm and Rothfels.

'But they're going to find it difficult enough to break out of there as it is,' Berger protested.

Wohldorf said coldly, 'But not difficult *enough*. Go find Guntel,' he instructed Rothfels. 'Bring him here.'

Berger voiced his puzzlement. 'What do you intend to do?'

Wohldorf smiled mysteriously. 'Assure ourselves of survival.'

Berger suddenly sensed the implication behind Wohldorf's statement. An expression of disbelief spread across his face. 'You can't mean you intend to sink the ship!'

His voice edged with ice, Wohldorf said, 'I'm afraid our friend Kapitan Thomas is too determined and stubborn for his own good.'

'But he must still turn his ship around for the Cabo Verdes before he can give any details of what happened,' Berger argued. 'And even so it will take time before anyone can break free.'

Wohldorf's anger flared. 'Don't argue with me! When we reach the Argentine I promise you'll find the situation vastly different to what it presently is on board *U501*. And don't forget you were personally responsible for almost causing the loss of *U501* and her cargo already. Or has it conveniently slipped from your mind?'

Berger subsided into a troubled silence, saw himself trapped, a victim of his earlier indiscretions, and he despised himself for his weakness.

Minutes later Rothfels returned with Guntel whose head was swathed in a white bandage as a result of the attack made on him earlier by Wassermann. Wohldorf measured him with a shrewd gaze. 'I believe there's a means of sinking a vessel by flooding her – is this so, Guntel?'

The bluntness of the question took Guntel aback. He hesitated, sent a disquieted glance at Berger.

Wohldorf snapped impatiently, 'Well, Guntel?'

Guntel stiffened, answered promptly, 'Yes, Herr Hauptsturmführer. One can open the sea-cocks. When I was with Oberleutnant Krausnick we once sank a tramp steamer which wasn't worth a torpedo by opening the sea-cocks. We captured her off Charleston. She sank in thirty-five minutes.'

'So?' Wohldorf mused, and glanced at Rothfels where he stood beside Schramm, his face cast in stone. 'What do you think, Rothfels, eh?'

'I don't think anything, Herr Hauptsturmführer!' Rothfels rapped out unhesitatingly. 'I do what I'm ordered to do.'

Wohldorf smiled. 'A wise man, Rothfels. A wise man. And *you*, Berger?'

Berger saw he was in the minority, swallowed uncomfortably, but remained silent.

'Now we're getting somewhere,' announced Wohldorf. 'Tell me more about these sea-cocks, Guntel. Where are they situated?'

'There are several in the engineroom, Herr Hauptsturmführer.'

'In that case make certain you're last to leave the engine-room when refuelling has been completed, then open them. But see to it she doesn't go down too quickly. I don't want her to founder while we still have her in view.'

*

The time was 23.40 when Kernbach reported to Rink on the bridge. 'Finished – tanks full to the brim – next stop the Argentine.' Then to Dornberger on the *Cassiopeia*'s for'ard well-deck, he called up, 'Stop pumping. Standby to clear hoses.'

Dornberger raised a hand in acknowledgement as Wohldorf appeared at his side.

'Start to get the men back on board,' Rink called to him. Then to Kordt on the for'ard catwalk, he called out, 'Secure for sea. Standby wires and fenders.'

At 23.50 Rink was waiting impatiently to cast off.

'Diesel loading hatch secure, sir,' ERA Steiner reported.

'Upperdeck secure for sea, sir,' Kordt was next to report.

Rink saw the first members of the secondary boarding-party start down the ladder to the catwalk while the sound of the *Cassiopeia*'s auxiliary machinery died to silence within her hull. Then Ingersoll and Dornberger clambered across the bulwarks. 'Where are the others?' Rink wanted to know.

Ingersoll said, 'I think they're back aft somewhere, sir. Do you want me to chase them on?'

'No, get on board.'

Erlanger looked anxiously at his wrist watch. 'Time's getting on, sir.'

Suddenly Rothfels and Guntel swung across the bulwarks on to the ladder, Wohldorf, Schramm, and Berger in rear.

'What kept you so long?' Rink demanded when they streamed through the horseshoe.

Wohldorf said indifferently, 'We had to take care of the Chief Engineer and two firemen, and they weren't very co-operative about it.'

Rink switched his attention to the catwalks. 'Let go fore and aft. Standby main engines.'

On the catwalks the berthing-party hurriedly dumped the mooring wires across the side and stood ready with fenders. 'All clear fore and aft, sir,' Kordt reported.

Rink cast a glance about him while the vessels drifted slowly apart. 'Clutches in. Small ahead port.'

The diesels broke a cloud of exhaust fumes above the after casing and *U501* eased away from the *Cassiopeia*'s side to leave wires and hoses dangling against her dark hull and passed out beyond her bows.

'Secure upperdecks. All hands below. Stand fast bridge watch and AA gunners. Stop port. Both emergency ahead.

Steer due South. Let's see how those diesels can perform, Chief.'

The tempo of the diesels increased sharply while the hands hurried below, and *U501* leapt ahead, the clear mill-pond ocean hissing and foaming along the hull, bubbling through the gratings.

Thirty minutes later Rink put his binoculars on the *Cassiopeia* where she lay astern, a dark, silent shadow, starlight glinting on her bridge windows. Then he summoned Erlanger to take over the watch and hurried below to the control-room where he went directly to the chart-table.

He had already reasoned that once word of the incident with the *Cassiopeia* was passed to the authorities it would almost certainly be surmised on the part of the British Admiralty that a renegade U-boat loose in the South Atlantic after refuelling at gun-point would have only one destination in mind – the shores of Latin America. And if Vollmer, Wassermann, and Elser were rescued and betrayed *U501*'s destination under interrogation, then the resultant sea and air search would undoubtedly be concentrated on, or in the vicinity of, the recognised shipping lanes between the islands of Cabo Verde and the Argentine, which would make any attempt to reach such points of landfall along the Latin American coast as Pernambuco, Bahia, or Rio de Janeiro, an extremely hazardous venture. Instead he had earlier decided to continue due South towards the equator and the Intertropical Convergence Zone, passing through The Doldrums and Horse Latitudes, then turn on to a south-westerly course and thereby keep well to mid-ocean in the hope that he would only have to concern himself with meeting day to day traffic when they crossed the North American-Cape Town, and Latin America-Cape Town shipping lanes. Although it was a more circuitous route than that which was originally ordered, it was infinitely safer than to make an attempt to reach the coast of Latin America by direct route.

Next he went for'ard to the W/T office where both Bergold and Vogel were on watch. 'Keep a sharp watch on the 600 metre international wavelength,' he instructed. 'That will be where hell will break loose when that tanker puts back to Porto Grande or Praia.'

But, strangely, with midnight all reports from the W/T officer were negative, and throughout the night *U501* continued on her way unmolested through a limitless expanse of ocean, diesels hammering out their relentless cacophony, driving her ever nearer the equator, fans drawing a draught of cool air down into the hull where the temperature had climbed to a stupefying 122-F.

By noon next day Rink had resigned himself to accept the fact that they were unlikely to hear anything further about the *Cassiopeia*. The most likely explanation, he believed, was that whatever port she had made for would long since have been reached and her story told, and that for reasons known only to themselves, the British Admiralty had decided to keep all details of *U501*'s act of piracy secret, and had quietly mounted their sea and air search along the direct routes to Latin America. He was certain within his own mind there could not be any other explanation. And that night while he renewed acquaintance with the familiar constellations of the Southern Hemisphere which he had known so well in former years, he felt himself convinced of the ultimate success of their voyage.

BOOK FOUR

Twilight of the Gods

THE crew of *U501* had sighted only one vessel, a shabby Spanish freighter, her flag of neutrality still displayed on her scarred hull amidships. They had met with her one evening in the late dusk, plodding across their bows, all lights ablaze, headed north-west, probably out from Cape Town and bound either for Rio de Janeiro or Santos.

Then on the morning of June 17, thirty-nine days after their encounter with the *Cassiopeia*, the duty bridge watch saw their first cumuliform clouds of any dimension since leaving the African coast behind, clouds painted delicate shades of rose and amber, clouds which were piled high and which appeared to extend a welcome to the continent of Latin America.

An electrically charged air of excitement ran through the boat; the end of the voyage was in sight and the long days of monotony were suddenly forgotten. The men crowded the *wintergarten* and catwalks, eager for a first glimpse of the New World which held so much promise for them, where life was to begin anew, where dark memories of war and defeat, parted families and friends, would fade against its carefree background. It was now a dream on the verge of reality, and the men feasted hungry eyes on every detail of the new morning, the sun to eastward, the pale azure sky, the pastel-tinted mass of cloud, and the emerald green ocean which washed southward under a freshening breeze.

Rink glanced at the bearded faces crowded around him in the horseshoe, Kernbach, Erlanger, Berger, Wohldorf, Schramm, and Kordt, each of them with his gaze fixed intently on the western horizon, each of them engrossed in his own thoughts.

Unable to contain his excitement, Wohldorf said, 'How soon do you expect to sight land?'

'If the morning fix can be relied on, then we ought to be within sight of Punta Mogotes some time around noon.'

'Then we're here – really *here*!' Wohldorf enthused.

Rink searched the crowded faces on the *wintergarten*, saw Bergold, and instructed him to man the radio which he had ordered shut down on the evening of the third day after the incident with the *Cassiopeia*, in a bid to keep the crew from brooding over the constant stream of bulletins, announcements, and proclamations which had filled the ether when the Allies began to wallow in the after-effects of victory. Instead he had decided it was better to remain ignorant of events, and consequently *U501* had become a world on its own, plowing through the vast wastes of the South Atlantic, its existence unknown to anyone outside the hull. At first the men had found it a difficult decision to accept, but as the days had lengthened into weeks, their minds had gradually turned from the past to the future and all it appeared to hold for them.

Over breakfast Rink re-acquainted himself with the procedure for communicating word of their arrival to their anonymous hosts waiting on shore. The instructions were simple. They were to transmit the cryptic signal: ERWACHE – ERWACHE – ERWACHE every fifteen minutes on a given frequency when within fifty miles of Punta Mogotes, a signal which it was hoped would be heard by a clandestine radio station somewhere in the vicinity of General Alvarado. Yet Rink was not wholly certain about what they might expect in the way of a reception. After the incident with the *Cassiopeia* he had decided not to transmit the codeword WESTWARD to signify that *U501* had successfully refuelled and was proceeding on her voyage in the event that it would serve to betray their position, and as a result it was possible that they had been given up for lost.

Bergold and Vogel were at the radio when Rink called at the W/T office, eager to renew contact with the outside world. After issuing them with the necessary instructions for the attempt to make contact with the shore, Rink made his way up to the bridge and found the upperdeck a hive of activity, with men airing their Number One blues while others were bathing from buckets thrown over the side. Also outside ERA Hossbach had set up a barber shop on the *wintergarten* and a line of men were waiting impatiently for the scissors and mirror. Rink offered no comment, although he regarded the shore preparations as being somewhat premature. Even if contact was successfully made with shore he doubted if they would be extended an invitation to enter the harbour at Mar del Plata with the crew lining the catwalks and the War Flag fluttering in the breeze. But in order that he should not be the odd man out he retrieved his own uniform blues from his locker, put them to air on the *wintergarten* and went below to bathe on the after catwalk. Later, when he had shaved and had his hair cut by Hossbach he dressed in his uniform and pulled on a pair of leather seaboots.

The time was 10.18 when Leutnant Berger reported to the bridge. 'Signal, sir. Just this moment received.'

Rink took it from him and read: DELAYED GLAD TIDINGS. RENDEZVOUS WITH SANTA ELVIRA 100 MILES DUE SOUTH PUNTA MOGOTES 18.00 HOURS – MATZHOLD.

He found Wohldorf and Schramm in the wardroom, immaculate in dress uniform, and handed the former the signal. 'We just made contact with the shore. It would appear they intend to effect the transfer of cargo at sea. We're to meet with a vessel named the *Santa Elvira* 100 miles due South of Punta Mogotes, at approximately the same distance south-east of Necochea. My guess is she's probably been lying in Necochea harbour for some time ready to put to sea on our arrival.'

Wohldorf found it impossible to contain his excitement. 'Excellent news!' he jubilantly exclaimed. 'I must confess there were times when I thought I'd never see this moment. How about you?'

Rink's thoughts were elsewhere. 'My concern now is centred on what's to become of my command and her crew.'

'Ach, no doubt the future of both has already been decided.'

From Wohldorf's flippant reply it was obvious to Rink that he no longer cared about either of them, and when he returned to the bridge it was to hear the first sighting of a vessel in the process of being reported. Once again they were in dangerous waters, among the shipping lanes which terminated at such ports as Uruguay's Montevideo, and the Argentine's La Plata, Buenos Aires, and Rosario. It was not the time to cast discretion to the winds. He bent his head to the voice-tube. 'Left rudder. Come to course 190 degrees. Clear the upperdeck of all spare hands.'

U501 swung around on to her new course to southward while the spare hands on deck reluctantly made their way below with a last lingering look at the western horizon.

By noon the breeze had freshened considerably to set up a choppy sea which broke across the catwalks, and by mid-afternoon a haze had formed to eastward and a ghostly sun assumed an ugly opalescent light.

'Fine,' Rink remarked to Erlanger in a caustic voice. 'We come all this way and now the weather deteriorates.'

*

It was 17.42 when Leutnant Berger sighted a vessel making a course of south-south-east towards them. Rink immediately joined him on the bridge and all eyes watched in anticipation as she approached, *U501* rolling in the stiff seas. A motorship of around 2,000 GRT, she was of sleek new design, bridge and superstructure situated aft, painted brilliant white, her funnel a contrasting light blue, the hull dove grey. Driving resolutely to south-eastward on an interceptory course, her bows sent curtains of spray back across her forepeak and well-deck.

When at a distance of nine hundred metres, a signal-lamp winked out from the port wing of her bridge. It read simply: SANTA ELVIRA.

'Small ahead both,' ordered Rink. While *U501* lost headway, the bridge watch waited for the vessel to cross their bows, several figures on her bridge waving enthusiastically. 'Half ahead both.'

The diesels hammered and Rink swung *U501* around the *Santa Elvira*'s stern, the port of registery on her counter reading *Comodoro Rivadavia*, in order to pull in under her lee side sixty metres distant, where at once the War Flag broke from her jackstaff and the emotive strains of *Deutschland uber Alles* boomed out from her upperdeck broadcast system, and in that moment of drama every man snapped to attention.

'Permission to break out the War Flag, sir?'

Rink glanced to see Signalman Meyer stationed beside the jackstaff, and signified approval; and, with a snap of the halyards, Meyer sent *U501*'s War Flag streaming into the breeze in reply.

When the music ceased one of the figures on the *Santa Elvira*'s bridge raised a loud hailer to his mouth. 'Congratulations, Herr Kommandant,' the voice echoed metallically. 'Glad to see you finally made it. We had actually given you up for lost.'

'We had our troubles,' Rink called back in reply.

The metallic voice answered in sympathy, 'So we imagine.

Sorry about the weather. However, the met report indicates that this breeze should blow itself out during the night. Can you keep us company till morning?'

Rink waved acknowledgement, and saw the *Santa Elvira* turn on to a course of west-south-west at slow speed.

With the onset of darkness Rink dropped *U501* further astern to take up station off the freighter's starboard quarter as they stood into the waters of Bahia Blanca, watching her lights pitch in the choppy seas.

Supper that evening was ignored by most of the hands who were impatient and restless now that the voyage was at an end. And for'ard in their own quarters, Wohldorf and Schramm held themselves apart as if, now that their journey was drawing to a close, they were preparing to return to a way of life and matter of interests far removed from that of their late comrades.

*

At around 02.00 on the morning of June 18, the wind dropped and the short, foam-streaked seas began to subside, and then only occasionally did spray drench the watch on the bridge of *U501*, their gaze scarcely leaving the *Santa Elvira*'s lights.

Daylight brought an overcast sky and a choppy green sea which ran in towards the stretch of shoreline between Punta Rasa and Bahia Blanca. Then at 06.20 the *Santa Elvira* eased speed and *U501* drew slowly abeam on her starboard side to see the three figures of the previous evening re-appear on her bridge.

On board *U501* Rink pushed into the starboard sector of the horseshoe in anticipation of receiving orders, and reduced speed to that of the freighter.

'I'm afraid there will have to be an alteration to our plans, Herr Kommandant,' the man with the hailer explained. 'Our original plan was to effect the transfer of your cargo further south in the Golfo de San Matias, but according to the latest met report there promises to be another sharp deterioration in the weather soon. Therefore we now propose to effect the transfer without further delay. I'm sorry.'

'Then it will require the use of every fender you possess,' Rink informed him. 'And if you stand your port side to seaward I will attempt to come alongside in your lee.'

By way of reply the *Santa Elvira* immediately began to turn to port, to leave *U501* wallowing astern.

Rink called below, 'Berthing-party on deck. Standby port side.'

The berthing-party were ready lining the catwalks when Rink saw the *Santa Elvira* lose way and her crew begin to drop fenders across her starboard wall. 'Stop engines. Clutches out. Switches on. Group down. Small ahead both.'

Now on electric drive, *U501* moved cautiously up along the dove grey hull starboard side until level with the well-deck, the hulls of both vessels rising and falling ten metres apart. 'Stop both!' shouted Rink, and watched heaving lines snake down from above before the mooring wires were quickly hauled on board to be secured under the watchful eye of the CGM. Then with All Secure, the *Santa Elvira*'s electric winches took the strain and drew *U501* gently in under her lee side, fenders effectively cushioning the jolt when the hulls impacted.

On the *Santa Elvira*'s bridge tense faces had watched every move. 'Is everything well with you, Herr Kommandant?' the man with the hailer wanted to know.

Rink watched the rise and fall of the cushioned hulls. Conditions for effecting a transfer of cargo were far from ideal but with the *Santa Elvira*'s hull acting as a breakwater the independent movement of the vessels was not sufficient to endanger their safety, although the creaking and groaning of fenders sounded ominous. 'I think we can go ahead and risk it.'

'You don't mind if I take my leave of you now?'

Rink turned to see Wohldorf standing on the bridge behind him, brief-case in hand, muffled in his elegant greatcoat, the War Flag streaming in the breeze from the jackstaff above him on the *wintergarten*. 'As you wish.'

'Then please see to it that my personal luggage is first to be transferred. Schramm will remain with you till that's been accomplished.'

Erlanger watched Wohldorf turn aft to the *wintergarten*, climb below to the after catwalk, then start up the ladder which dangled against the *Santa Elvira*'s hull. 'The SS don't believe in wasting time, do they, sir?'

Rink shrugged indifference, watching the *Santa Elvira*'s derricks swing out overhead. 'Break open the fore and after hatches,' he called below to Kordt on the for'ard catwalk.

From the bridge hatchway Coxswain Lamm said, 'Leutnant Berger reports that he's ready to commence with off-loading, sir.'

'Then inform him to carry on.'

Wohldorf and Schramm's personal luggage, including the two oblong metal boxes, was first out through the for'ard hatchway accompanied by Schramm, who watched Berger and Kordt supervise its loading into a cargo net. Then the first two cases from the after torpedo-room were manhandled out on to the catwalk as the whirr of machinery overhead preceded the first load being lifted inboard from the for'ard catwalk.

Shortly after Schramm had transferred to the *Santa Elvira*, a voice called down, 'Care to crack open that celebration bottle now, Herr Kapitanleutnant?'

Rink found a dark, handsome face smiling down from the bulwarks above, one of the men whom he had previously seen on the bridge. He hesitated, glanced to seaward.

'I assure you that it's quite safe, Herr Kapitanleutnant,' the man confidently announced. 'We're well off the beaten track out here and we have plenty of lookouts stationed to warn us against surprise.'

Rink motioned to Erlanger. 'Take charge till I get back. And keep those cases moving. Begin on those canisters located in the outside torpedo stowage immediately we rid ourselves of the cases.'

The man was waiting for Rink when he climbed in across the *Santa Elvira*'s bulwarks. Snapping stiffly erect, he clicked his heels and flung up his right arm. '*Heil Hitler!*' Then with a smile, offered the same hand and said, 'Welcome on board, Herr Kapitanleutnant. You can't imagine how much pleasure this moment gives me. My name's Heinrich von Geyr, representative of Dr Alfred Matzhold, official agent of Reichsleiter Martin Bormann. May I extend my sincere congratulations on your belated but safe arrival. Actually we had prepared ourselves for the worst. Now if you would care to accompany me.'

Von Geyr led the way aft, climbed to the accommodation deck, and ushered Rink through an inboard companionway to a stateroom below the bridge. After the austere conditions on board *U501* Rink was ill-prepared for the luxury of the *Santa Elvira*. Pannelled with rich mahogany and black leather, the deck lushly carpeted, it belonged to another world along with the concealed lighting and the aroma of cigar smoke.

A punctilious man, von Geyr again stood stiffly to attention, and in a sombre voice announced, 'Gentlemen. Kapitanleutnant Wolfgang Rink.'

Rink saw that apart from Wohldorf and Schramm, there were two other men present, the two men whom he had previously seen on the *Santa Elvira*'s bridge along with von Geyr.

Von Geyr indicated the slightly smaller figure in a tan lounge suit. 'Herr Dassel. Carl Heinrich Dassel. Senior representative of your host Dr Alfred Matzhold.'

A sour-faced and pedantic-looking man, Dassel acknowledged the introduction with an almost imperceptible, but condescending movement of his bald head. 'Delighted, Herr Kapitanleutnant,' he said formally.

'And our Kapitan for the trip,' von Geyr continued in formal explanation. 'Herr Soltmann. Hans-Bernd Soltmann. Formerly of the *Admiral Graf Spee*,' he added with a secretive smirk.

A tall burly man with close-cropped iron-grey hair and a severe manner, Soltmann slicked his heels and stiffly inclined his head. 'Pleased to finally have you with us, Herr Kapitanleutnant.'

Rink studied the ex-Kriegsmarine officer with interest. 'Thank you, Herr Soltmann.'

Von Geyr offered a humidor of cigars while Soltmann cracked open a bottle of champagne at the table and filled six glasses, passed them around, then proposed his own toast. 'To your safe arrival, Herr Kapitanleutnant. The Third Reich salutes you. *Heil Hitler!*'

The gathering drank in sombre and respectful silence.

Then while von Geyr replenished the glasses and offered his gold cigarette lighter, Dassel said, 'We were extremely concerned for you, Herr Kapitanleutnant. We were quite certain you'd met with misfortune. First we heard from home about the unfortunate incident with Norwegian partisans in Hardangerfjord, then later we were informed that U-Bestelmeyer had failed to answer his call-sign and in the circumstances had to be presumed lost. Frankly we didn't know what to think when it was learned that Schemmel had surrendered to the Allies, and from there on the situation became totally confused, so much so that it was generally feared you had also been lost.' Dassel paused to sip at his champagne, then with calculated off-handedness said, 'However, Hauptsturmführer Wohldorf has been recounting some of your adventures to us. And may I say that stopping the British tanker *Cassiopeia* as you did might be considered a stroke of genius. If it's of interest to you, she earned herself the unenviable distinction of being the first peacetime loss of a British ship at sea.'

Rink was disconcerted by Dassel's statement. With a frown darkening his brow, he said, 'I'm afraid you have me at a disadvantage, Herr Dassel.'

'Indeed?' There was a patronising, amused tone in Dassel's voice.

Rink was instantly suspicious of the entire gathering, instinctively sensed that they shared a joke among themselves and that he was the only person in ignorance of it. And busy with his thoughts, he sent a searching glance at Wohldorf who in turn regarded him with the incurious stare of a disinterested stranger.

Dassel thrust a newspaper across the table. 'I wondered about the article at the time, had some sixth sense about it. That was the reason why I retained the newspaper. I think the front page will interest you.'

Rink reached for the newspaper from the table. It was the *Buenos Aires Herald* and carried the date May 14, 1945. In English it read:

SOUTH ATLANTIC CLAIMS FIRST PEACETIME VICTIM

It was established yesterday that the wreckage first observed by an aircraft of British Coastal Command on the morning of May 12, 55 miles south of the Cape Verde Islands has been identified as belonging to the British motor-tanker CASSIOPEIA *registered at Milford Haven. Bound for St Helena and Ascension Island with a cargo of fuel oils, it is believed that she sank a few hours after leaving the fuelling station at Porto Grande on the island of St Vincent. Owing to the fact that no distress signal was reported, it is assumed by the British Admiralty that she was the victim of a drifting mine, although there was no report of an explosion or fire in the area in which she was lost. The* CASSIOPEIA *is believed to have carried a crew of thirty-eight. A concentrated search of the area had revealed no traces of survivors.*

Rink felt the blood drain from his face, felt himself go cold with rage long before he concluded reading the article. Suddenly he knew the reason behind Wohldorf's delay in leaving the *Cassiopeia* after they had refueled, suddenly realised why there had been no hue and cry about the incident, why there had been no large scale sea and air search mounted in an attempt to hunt them down. And experiencing immense difficulty in restraining his anger, he looked up at Wohldorf where he stood with Schramm on the far side of the stateroom. Wohldorf in turn met his gaze with silent defiance, as if assured of Dassel's approval and support. But while Soltmann offered no comment, von Geyr sensed the awkwardness of the moment, and said hurriedly, 'Is it all really so important?'

Dassel ignored him, and instead addressed himself to Rink. 'Ach, what are a few Britishers more or less? No one will ever guess at the truth, nor even suspect it. Hauptsturmführer Wohldorf merely sought to make certain of survival, like I myself would have done. Your conscience is clear, Herr Kapitanleutnant. Forget about it, as everyone else will.'

Embarrassed by the strained atmosphere which enshrouded the scene, von Geyr sought to change the subject, and said with the polished formality of a diplomat while he sipped at his champagne delicately, 'You know, of course, Herr Kapitanleutnant, that the Führer is dead – died on the barricades fighting to his last breath?'

Rink answered without enthusiasm, 'We heard word to that effect, yes. Although the situation regarding any news we received was somewhat confusing.'

Von Geyr proclaimed in a stoic voice, 'Nonetheless it's a tragedy from which we shall recover. Like Barbarossa – the Reich will rise again from the ashes of yesterday.'

Rink murmured, 'Of course.' And found that the atmosphere had turned even more oppressive with von Geyr's impassioned display of patriotism.

In turn von Geyr saw that his patriotic intrusion did not have the desired result. With an embarrassed cough, he drained his glass and set it on the table. 'Well now, Herr Kapitanleutnant,' he declared in more congenial tones. 'No doubt you're anxious to learn what's to become of *U501* and her crew.' Sweeping a chart around on the table, he placed a manicured finger on the Golfo de San Matias, to the north of the Peninsula Valdes. 'Orders are you scuttle your boat here.

We propose to accompany you south immediately the transfer of cargo has been completed. After your charges are set you and your crew will then join us. Arrangements have been made for us to dock at Avellaneda tomorrow morning during darkness. From there you'll be taken to an *estancia* near Olavarria where senior members of our Organisation will be waiting to extend their congratulations to you on behalf of the New Reich.'

The New Reich; Rink listened to von Geyr in amazement.

'I assume the charges necessary for the destruction of *U501* will be in place ready for detonation by the time we arrive in the Golfo de San Matias, Herr Kapitanleutnant?' von Geyr was saying. 'We have no wish to waste precious time.'

'Naturally,' said Rink.

Von Geyr said, 'Then do you have any questions, Herr Kapitanleutnant?'

Rink returned his attention to the chart. 'Wouldn't it have been easier for all concerned to have effected the transfer of cargo in the Golfo de San Matias as originally planned rather than out here?'

Von Geyr looked to Dassel for aid in answering the question.

Dassel said easily, 'I already explained the situation, Herr Kapitanleutnant. According to the Ministerio de Marina's latest meteorological report another sharp deterioration is expected in the weather soon and this influenced the decision of myself and my associates here to make the transfer at the earliest possible moment rather than proceed south to the Golfo de San Matias, primarily for the reason that we have no wish to be forced through adverse weather conditions to have both vessels loitering indefinitely in the vicinity in which *U501* is to be scuttled. That's a risk we don't wish to take. No, it's simply a question of time and opportunity, Herr Kapitanleutnant.'

Rink could find no argument with Dassel's explanation, yet for some unaccountable reason he felt disquieted.

'Now I assume that you wish to return to *U501* in order to inform your officers and crew of our arrangements, Herr Kapitanleutnant,' said von Geyr.

Before Rink turned to follow von Geyr, he flung a challenging glance in direction of Wohldorf and Schramm, but found that neither of them offered the merest flicker of recognition, while Dassel and Soltmann pointedly devoted themselves to lighting fresh cigars. Evidently everyone was eager to have the meeting concluded.

On the way for'ard he made a guarded appraisal of the crew working on deck. Most of them were obviously Latins except for two or three Europeans who might have been German. Yet strangely, they all seemed to studiously avoid acknowledging his presence.

When they reached the ladder von Geyr again snapped to attention, clicked his heels and extended his right arm. 'Long live the Fatherland. *Heil Hitler!*'

Rink in reply touched a hand to his cap in military salute. And dispirited both with his hosts and their reception, he climbed out on to the ladder and dropped down on to *U501*'s after catwalk. When he arrived on the bridge he received a progress report from Erlanger, tossed the stub of his cigar across the side, then climbed into the tower.

Kernbach and Ingersoll were below in the control-room. 'How was the champagne?' Kernbach inquired with bright enthusiasm, then hesitated when he saw the serious cast of Rink's face. 'Something must be wrong,' he accused.

'Perhaps. I don't know,' Rink replied falteringly. 'But there's something about the demeanour of those people that disturbs me.' Then he went on to explain about Dassel, his associates, Soltmann and von Geyr, and the absent Dr Matzhold.

'Who's this Dr Matzhold?' questioned Kernbach.

'According to von Geyr he's the Reichsleiter's official agent.'

'So?' said Kernbach. 'And did you hear any news of the Reichsleiter?'

'There was no reference made to him.'

'Perhaps he went the same way as the Führer.'

'I very much doubt it,' said Rink with a wan smile. 'Certainly not intentionally, not after he arranged for a cargo such as ours to be shipped halfway around the world. A man with such foresight and ability doesn't make mistakes where his own well-being is concerned.'

Kernbach mused thoughtfully, 'Then perhaps he's already here.'

'That may well be so,' Rink conceded. 'But at this moment there are problems which are of more concern to me than the Reichsleiter's whereabouts.'

Ingersoll broke in impatiently, 'What about us, sir?'

Rink said, 'We're to head south for the Golfo de San Matias

when the transfer of cargo is completed. There the boat is to be scuttled. The *Santa Elvira* will then put us ashore at Avellaneda tomorrow morning. From there we're apparently to be taken to a place called Olavarria to meet the senior members of what I assume to be the local Party Organisation – presumably our senior host Dr Matzhold and his associates.'

Kernbach commented with heavy sarcasm, 'What do you know – now we really are travelling in style.'

Rink was silent, wrapt in uneasy thought.

Kernbach's gaze narrowed. 'There's something more, isn't there?'

Rink said quietly, 'The *Cassiopeia* went down with all hands.'

Both engineers were stunned by the disclosure.

'I read a brief account of her loss in an Argentine newspaper dated May 14th,' Rink explained. 'Apparently the British Admiralty attribute her loss to a drifting mine. There were no survivors.'

Ingersoll exclaimed in solemn reflection, 'Ach, so that was why there was never any fuss raised.'

Kernbach was instinctively suspicious. 'That seems one hell of a coincidence, don't you think?'

'It *wasn't* a coincidence,' stated Rink, his face set in a grim scowl. 'And it's a matter which I intend to take up with Berger the moment we clear the *Santa Elvira*. Along with Wohldorf and Schramm, he, Rothfels and Guntel were last to leave the *Cassiopeia*. My guess is they opened the sea-cocks before they left.'

The two engineers stared back at him, incredulous.

Rink said, 'I wondered why Berger became increasingly withdrawn and morose. I was inclined to attribute it to the incident with the Liberator when he panicked, but now I believe that his knowledge of what happened that night on board the *Cassiopeia* had been weighing on his conscience. However, Wohldorf was the brain behind her sinking. Dassel admitted as much.'

At that juncture Coxswain Lamm put his head through the circular opening in the for'ard watertight bulkhead. 'Excuse me, Herr Kommandant. The last canisters are now being removed from the outside torpedo stowage.'

'You had better standby main engines,' Rink told Kernbach and Ingersoll as he climbed into the tower. Two minutes after he arrived on the bridge the last grey metal canisters were being winched inboard across the *Santa Elvira*'s bulwarks.

Shortly afterwards Soltmann leaned from a window in the starboard wing of the *Santa Elvira*'s bridge. 'All accounted for and ready to let go whenever you are, Herr Kommandant.'

Rink looked below to where Berger and Kordt were waiting on the for'ard catwalk. 'Standby to let go fore and aft. Ring on main motors.'

From overhead came the whirr and clatter of machinery and suddenly the mooring wires fell slack.

Rink glanced the length of the upperdeck. 'Let go fore and aft.'

Below on the catwalks the berthing-party dumped the wires over the side and saw them winched inboard across the *Santa Elvira*'s bulwarks.

'All clear fore and aft, sir,' Kordt reported to the bridge, while around him a jubilant cheer went up from the crowded catwalks when the hulls began to edge apart.

With Rink in the horseshoe and Erlanger stationed on the *wintergarten*, both men watched intently while the hulls began to drift apart, rising and falling in the swirl of green water. 'Secure upperdeck. Small ahead both.'

Astern the diesels coughed into a rhythmic roar.

With his attention still focused on the widening expanse of water between the two hulls, Rink did not see the three concentrated charges of grenades lobbed out from behind the *Santa Elvira*'s bulwarks to drop in a lazy arc towards the crowded catwalks. Nor did he see the tarpaulins stripped from the twin 20 mm cannon on her forepeak and from the multiple Bofor gun on the fantail. The first he knew that anything was wrong was when he was dealt a tremendous blow in the back and enveloped in a vivid flash of orange flame, the blast of the explosion flinging him violently against the casing in the forepart of the bridge. Stunned, the breath driven from him, he lay sprawled on the duckboards, his mind only vaguely registering the other shuddering explosions and the bewildered and panic-stricken screams which followed on them. He shook his head in an effort to clear his senses and attempted to claw himself upright only to fall back to the duckboards amid the deafening hammer of guns firing at point-blank range, drowning the sound of the diesels. Then he became aware of a high-pitched scream of agony which seemed to trail on forever, and he twisted his head around to see Erlanger lying beside the periscope standards, his boyish face contorted with shock and pain, threshing about in a widening pool of blood, his left arm blown off at the shoulder. And further aft, sprawled in a crumpled heap of twisted limbs, he saw the blast-mutilated bodies of PO Seaman Hoven, Signalmen Meyer and Hagen, and one of the AA gunners. As for the other three gunners, who seconds earlier had been standing on the *wintergarten* beside Erlanger idly watching the two vessels drift apart, there was no sign.

Then summoning all his strength, he hauled himself slowly upright, the air thick with the stench of burnt cordite, mutilated flesh, and scorched paintwork. Below him the for'ard catwalk was a scene of carnage, with bodies strewn everywhere while a hail of cannon shell scythed along the length of the upperdeck and churned the surrounding water into a white curtain. The few men still on their feet were running desperately for cover on the starboard side of the tower, some to be cut down screaming and disappear outboard across the casing. It was the sheer calculated cold-blooded butchery of defenceless men caught packed together on the upperdeck in party mood and gunned down like unsuspecting bystanders on a crowded pavement.

In the control-room Kernbach and Ingersoll had been slammed to the deck-plates by the combined blast of the three exploding charges, the one on the bridge having occurred a split-second before the other two in the region of the open fore and after hatches, and now Ingersoll scrambled to his feet, conscious of the sound of shooting and the screams of the dying on the upperdeck, and out of instinct threw the engineroom telegraph over to Full Ahead. When nothing happened and the diesels failed to answer, Kernbach pushed past him and started aft, trampling over the torn and blood-stained bodies in the devastated central gangway beneath the open after hatch, vaguely aware that among them lay Kolb and Leading Machinist Guntel. Then a bewildered Dornberger came out of the engineroom and ran straight into him. The young ERA gaped uncomprehendingly at the carnage strewn around him, and said inanely, 'What is it, Chief? What's happening?'

Kernbach did not bother to attempt to answer him, merely yelled at him, '*Give me full ahead!*' Then he returned for'ard to scramble into the tower, thrust aside the sprawled body of Coxswain Lamm, and slid into the helmsman's seat to give the boat full right rudder, the fact having registered automatically with him that by doing so he was pulling *U501* away from the *Santa Elvira*'s hull, and like the few men below deck, all was ignorance and confusion to him regarding what was happening above.

On the bridge Rink had recovered from the initial shock of the attack to realise that it had obviously been cold-bloodedly intended all along to send *U501* and her entire crew to the bottom in order to secure their lasting silence after they had served their purpose. Evidently the mouths of so many men represented too great a risk to take with the blanket of secrecy which surrounded Shipment No. 11372 and its delivery. He also realised that if the other two concentrated charges of grenades had found their intended targets like the one which had dropped cleanly through the after hatch to explode within the hull, then *U501*'s pressure hull would have been ripped apart and she would have sank like a stone. Instead someone had delayed the order to lob the charges for too long, and two of them had missed the open bridge hatch and for'ard hatch, one to explode on the after end of the horseshoe, the other to explode on the for'ard catwalk.

In the grip of overwhelming anger, he stumbled aft to the *wintergarten*, blood streaming down his face from a scalp lacerated by shrapnel splinters, aware that the men still crowding up through the for'ard and after hatches in bewilderment and panic were being shot down before they reached the catwalks, and he swung the port twin 20 mm cannon around to sweep the *Santa Elvira*'s decks with a thunderous burst of fire, spent brass hulls showering the gratings beneath his feet.

Meanwhile in the tower Kernbach was still ignorant of the situation on deck except for the fact that someone on the *wintergarten* was at last returning the fire which had punched gaping holes in the tower casing around him. Then the startled face of Control-room PO Morgen appeared at his side. '*Here – take the helm!*' he ordered, and clambered up the ladder to the bridge where he stumbled across the sprawled bodies of Erlanger, Hoven, Meyer, Hagen, and one of the AA gunners. Blood was spattered everywhere and the reek of the explosion which had shattered the after end of the horseshoe hung about it in an acrid cloud. Then his gaze fell on Rink who, covered with blood, pushed aside the port twin 20 mm cannon and started towards the front of the bridge only for his left leg to collapse beneath him.

Kernbach reached out to help him to his feet. 'What happened?' he shouted into the bloodied face above the noise and confusion.

Rink straightened up and drew a sleeve across his face to wipe the blood from his eyes. 'They tried to sink us as we pulled away!'

Kernbach was incredulous. 'The bastards! The murdering bastards!' Then: 'And you – are you badly hurt?'

'Never mind me – just tell me the situation below.'

'I'm not sure, apart from the fact that there's been an explosion just inside the after hatch and that we're taking water somewhere. Lamm's among the dead and Morgen has the helm. Also the telegraph isn't working. I had to go aft and have Dornberger give me Full Ahead.'

Rink steadied himself against the bridge casing. 'Then get someone in the after hatch to relay engine orders. Hurry!'

As Kernbach disappeared back into the tower, Rink again turned his attention to the upperdeck. Bodies still littered the catwalks, although many had been washed clear by the seas breaking across the casing. Ironically, he saw that among the bodies still lying on the for'ard catwalk below the tower were those of Berger and Rothfels. Yet *U501* herself had suffered serious damage, her bridge and tower riddled by shells, while the piercing shriek of high-pressure air was a certain indication that the ballast tanks were badly punctured. Then he saw Kordt who was covered with blood from shrapnel wounds sustained when the concentrated charge of grenades aimed for the open for'ard hatch had missed to explode on the crowded catwalk. Holding himself steady with the aid of the jumping-wire, the CGM was yelling at the hands who had taken shelter on the starboard side of the tower.

With *U501* still turning to starboard, Rink again wiped blood from his face and looked aft to see the *Santa Elvira* on the port quarter. Had *U501* not been so severely damaged, and had there been sufficient torpedo mixers to muster on Battle Stations, then at such range a single torpedo would have blown her apart. 'Midships!' he called into the tower with ice-cold deliberation, then aft he saw Dornberger thrust his white face cautiously out through the after hatch. 'Slow ahead, Dornberger!'

Dornberger promptly withdrew his head and *U501*'s speed fell away.

On the for'ard catwalk Kordt looked expectantly to the bridge, the hands who earlier had been sheltering on the starboard side of the tower gathered around him, clearly awaiting order to man the 88 mm cannon.

Rink gritted his teeth against the searing pain which burned up through his left leg, then yelled, 'All right, Kordt! Prepare to open fire whenever I put us about!'

The order galvanised Kordt and his men into action and they swarmed around the mounting as Rink turned to the bridge hatch. 'Hard left rudder, Morgen.'

U501's bow swung around to port until she had doubled back on to her previous course, and at Slow Ahead she headed towards the *Santa Elvira*.

Rink had already decided on the course of action to adopt, one which would allow Kordt and his gunners a clear, close-range opportunity to pound their target at will. He called calmly down into the tower, 'Midships. Right rudder. Steady at that.'

U501 slowly angled out on an opposing course, headed back towards the still stationary *Santa Elvira*, committed to a run which would take her down along the freighter's starboard side. And now, unable to bring her Bofor gun to bear owing to the acute angle of *U501*'s approach, only the twin 20 mm cannon on her forepeak renewed fire.

Then a sudden thud and jolt passed through *U501* and cordite fumes gusted back across the bridge as Kordt sent the first round of high-explosive on its way. Rink instantly saw a direct hit register on the *Santa Elvira*'s deck below the drop from the forepeak, then watched the foremast fold crazily on itself amid the orange flash and cloud of smoke.

As yet apparently undecided about what course of action to pursue, the *Santa Elvira* continued to remain stationary, then prompted by the accuracy of Kordt's shooting, the water boiled around her counter and she swung her bows towards *U501* in order to present as small a target as possible while she gathered speed for an attempt to ram.

Then Kordt's third round found its mark high on the starboard bow, and when the smoke and debris cleared, the twin 20 mm cannon was silent.

Rink cupped his hands to his mouth. 'Go for the bridge!' he directed.

*

On the *Santa Elvira*'s bridge Wohldorf was standing beside Soltmann and Dassel when he was suddenly hurtled back off his feet in the exploding flash of orange flame which seared the air with its blast. When he next sat up, dazed and shaken, it was to see that the choking cloud of black smoke had begun to clear, exposing a jagged hole in the superstructure on the port side face of the bridge. Then he saw several shattered bodies scattered around him, one of them Dassel's, his bloodstained clothing on fire. Next von Geyr appeared from the starboard wing, crawling to where Soltmann was hauling himself upright with the aid of the unattended wheel, and Wohldorf started to rise to his feet only to be knocked back to the deck when another shell slammed into the superstructure. Winded and concussed by the crashing explosion and displacement of air, he was vaguely aware that flames were beginning to lick up through the dirty smoke, and through it he saw Soltmann and von Geyr groping their way towards the stairway at the rear of the bridge which led below to the main stateroom on the accommodation deck. Out of fear and panic he struggled to his feet and blundered after them, pursued by thick clouds of black smoke being funnelled down the stairway from the bridge above by the draught.

He was still descending the stairway when the blast of the next explosion lifted him bodily across the debris-littered stateroom. This time he picked himself up off the carpeted deck immediately, only to come to an abrupt halt when he caught sight of the blackened and scorched figure of Schramm appear like an apparition through the smoke on the stairway above. With slow, deliberate movements Schramm made his descent, both hands clasped to his abdomen, eyes wide and staring, face slack, mouth open. Suddenly, as though the physical effort of the descent demanded too much of him, he stopped and sat down heavily on the bottom step. Air wheezed in his throat and he relaxed wearily back against the balusters, intestines bulging in a tangled coil from between his blood-stained fingers, his gaze fixed in a mute, pleading stare on Wohldorf and von Geyr. Then he looked down at himself, lifted his hands from his abdomen, saw a jerky stream of blood pulse out from around the tangled coil of intestines, and slowly raised that same terrible gaze to Wohldorf again. 'Shoot me – shoot me,' he pleaded in a vexatious whisper, 'Please, shoot me.'

Von Geyr swiftly turned his head away, shocked by the reality of unaccountably finding himself face to face with violent death, then flung himself panic-stricken across the stateroom to claw his way out into the inboard companionway, where he turned aft in the direction in which he had seen Soltmann disappear seconds earlier.

In order to counteract the *Santa Elvira*'s attempt to ram them, Rink had turned *U501* sharply to port, then had turned again to put the freighter broadside on to starboard when she lost her manoeuvrability and began to steer an erratic course, swinging away to port, to north-eastward. Now at a range of less than four hundred metres, Kordt found it impossible to miss hitting his target, and he laid the 88 mm cannon low to send shell after shell into the exposed hull at the waterline so that with each explosion plates buckled and flew out in all directions.

Meanwhile on the bridge Rink saw that *U501* was beginning to settle alarmingly by the stern, so badly that Dornberger was forced to surrender his position in the after hatchway when water began pouring in around him.

In the control-room the deck-plates were awash and Kernbach, in a desperate attempt to lift the boat, ordered all the valves to be opened, then rushed aft with Ingersoll when they heard Dornberger's shouted pleas for help in an effort to shut the after hatch. There, in the cramped space of the central gangway, drenched and pummelled by the torrent of water gushing in on them, the three men struggled in vain to secure the hatch. Finally Ingersoll turned on his comrades yelling, 'It's no good! That explosion knocked it out of all shape! It will never close now!'

Dornberger shouted wildly, 'She's going, Chief!'

Kernbach countered angrily, 'Like hell she is! Not before she takes those murdering bastards along with her!'

Ingersoll said, 'Who's back there in the engineroom?'

'Only Steiner,' answered Dornberger.

'Then get him out of there. Get him for'ard.'

Dornberger tripped and fell across Guntel's body where it floated among the debris in the flooded gangway as Ingersoll followed Kernbach back to the control-room, regained his feet and struggled aft, wrenched open the door to the engineroom and saw Steiner pushing for'ard knee-deep through the black oily water lapping around the diesels. 'Come on! There isn't anything more we can do here! Leave them running and let's get for'ard! She can go at any time!'

Soltmann had found shelter on the fantail beside the Bofor gun abaft the accommodation deck where he cursed Dassel violently for his hesitancy in issuing the order to drop the concentrated charges of grenades on *U501*. Obviously afraid lest the *Santa Elvira* should sustain damage to her own hull in the resultant explosions, Dassel had delayed his order to the men crouching behind the starboard bulwarks with the charges until the two vessels had drifted too far apart to ensure accuracy when they aimed for the open hatches. Although Dassel had since paid for his hesitancy with his life back on the bridge when it had taken the first direct hit, the *Santa Elvira* had as a result sustained serious damage in the ensuing engagement, although Soltmann was not certain about where exactly she was taking the shells because of the smoke drifting back from the blazing bridge superstructure.

In desperation he turned on the two Latin seamen who were struggling with the wheel on the after auxiliary steering position. 'Get her around to port!' he screamed at them. 'You hear, Gutierrez? *To port*! I must get the Bofors gun to bear!'

Although numb with fear, Ramon Gutierrez and fellow seaman Munuel Cuartero automatically leant all their strength to the wheel in an effort to wrench it around.

Ignoring the flying shrapnel and debris, Soltmann leaned out across the fantail to peer into the smoke drifting back from the bridge in order to catch a glimpse of the U-boat, and suddenly through the smoke he saw the flame belch in the muzzle of her 88 mm cannon when she drew abeam of the *Santa Elvira*'s stern. 'Standby, Runzheimer! Full depression starboard!' he shouted at the blond layer of the waiting Bofors gun crew.

When *U501* pulled out astern of the *Santa Elvira* a hail of Bofor shells swept her upperdeck and bridge superstructure, and with only Hessler still at his side, Kordt carefully laid the cannon on the fantail above him, heedless to the shells exploding around him, and ripped at the firing lanyard. In the vivid flash of light which followed the explosion, debris flew through the air and a body cart-wheeled out across the *Santa Elvira*'s stern into the ocean while *U501* slewed to starboard and her diesels spluttered into silence.

On *U501*'s bridge Rink saw that the seas now washing cleanly across the catwalks had taken the remaining bodies with them, to leave only Kordt and Able Seaman Hessler alone at the cannon. 'Clear lower deck!' he yelled urgently into the tower. 'Break out the for'ard liferaft!'

The first men out through the bridge hatch were Control-room PO Morgen and two members of the control-room crew, followed by Vogel and Bergold.

Rink thrust past them and clambered below where he found Kernbach, Ingersoll, Dornberger, and Steiner all struggling waist-deep in black oily water, the deck slanted to port and down by the stern. 'Everyone on deck! She's going fast – move yourselves!'

Suddenly the angle of the deck increased sharply and water roared in through the bridge hatch as Dornberger and Steiner pushed upward through the deluge.

Rink immediately grabbed at Kernbach and Ingersoll and started for'ard. 'This way – the for'ard hatch!'

They found Ordinary Seaman Zeller among the tangle of bodies swilling around in the water for'ard, blood streaming from his nose, mouth, and ears. Rink grabbed him and hoisted him out through the hatch to Kernbach and Ingersoll when they reached the catwalk, then scrambled up to join them.

The acrid black smoke and intense heat in the *Santa Elvira*'s main stateroom finally drove Wohldorf to seek shelter elsewhere. Without another glance at Schramm where he still lay on the stairway with both hands clasped to his abdomen and a strange, high-pitched keening wail issuing from his bloodied mouth, he blundered through the smoke towards the doorway through which Soltmann and von Geyr had earlier disappeared. Outside he was immediately confronted by smoke and flames which made access to the for'ard part of the accommodation deck impossible, and forced him aft along the inboard companionway where, before he had taken more than a few steps, he fell across von Geyr's body. Frantically pulling himself to his feet, he rushed aft until he came up against the screen door to the fantail which he found jammed fast on its clips as a result of the explosion which had destroyed the Bofor gun. In blind panic he beat against it with both fists, received no response, and retraced his steps to the stateroom where he remembered the scuttles on the port side that had faced directly out on to the ocean, started through the smoke towards them, stumbled against some article of overturned furniture, and went down.

He was on hands and knees groping for his bearings when a deathly tremor passed through the deck beneath him, followed closely by a low rumbling detonation somewhere deep within the *Santa Elvira*'s bowels.

On *U501*'s for'ard catwalk Rink, Kernbach, and Ingersoll heard the ominous low rumble and turned their attention towards the *Santa Elvira* where she lay some four hundred metres off the starboard beam, then through the drifting pall of smoke they saw her plates buckle outward in the vicinity of her engineroom to reveal a dull red glow, and in the next instant she disintegrated in a blinding pillar of flame which fountained skyward to turn the base of the overcast blood-red.

Rink dropped to the catwalk to shield Zeller's body while white-hot debris rained down into the ocean all around, spitting and sizzling in the water, and when the three men again lifted their heads all that remained of the *Santa Elvira* was a dirty brown haze and a mass of broken water. Then without warning the catwalk suddenly rose upward and pitched them into the ocean. Rink and Kernbach surfaced together, saw Zeller nearby, and together they grasped him and struck out away from the boat. Once clear they turned to look back and saw that the long flight of the *Golden Pheasant* had drawn to a close. With her scarred bows slanted high into the air, the War Flag streaming from her jackstaff, she began to slip slowly back stern-first beneath the surface.

The two men stared at each other, afflicted by an overwhelming sense of loss and grief, yet offered each other no words until Rink looked away to see the empty liferaft bobbing on the waves some way distant. 'Over here,' he told Kernbach. 'This way.'

They reached the liferaft as a rain-squall broke to turn the ocean a dark funereal grey, blotting out all visibility, and together they hoisted Zeller in across the side, the rain drumming on the fabric, then climbed in after him. When he regained his breath Kernbach said, 'What happened to the others? Ingersoll was with us when we went into the water. I saw him.'

Rink peered into the gloomy curtain of rain which fell hissing on the dark ocean, and cupped his hands to his mouth. 'Is anyone out there? Can you hear me? Ingersoll – Kordt – Hessler – Steiner – Dornberger.'

Together the two men listened intently but failed to hear a single voice raised in answer.

Then as the choppy waves clipped across the side of the liferaft, Rink saw that Zeller was staring wide-eyed into the rain. 'How is he?'

Kernbach leaned his head against Zeller's chest, listened for a moment, then sat slowly upright. He shook his head. 'He's gone.' Then passing his hand across Zeller's eyes, he noted Rink's blood-drenched left leg. 'Don't you think you had better take a look at that leg?'

Rink pulled the cuff of his trousers from his leather seaboot and saw that his calf had been sliced through by a shrapnel splinter in the explosion which had ripped through the after end of the horseshoe.

'Here, let me.' Kernbach wrenched a sleeve from his overalls and bound it around the wound, rain streaming down his face. Then peering into the murk, he said, 'Have you any idea where we are?'

Rink gestured to westward. 'These are the waters of Bahia Blanca. The Bahia Anegada shoreline lies somewhere to westward there.' Then he fell silent, overwhelmed with the knowledge that they had been exploited and betrayed by their fellow countrymen in the name of patriotism, ruthlessly bombed and gunned down, murdered. And suddenly all that remained of a long and hazardous voyage which was to have ended in glory and acclaim, was a bitter, tragic memory.

Then a corpse floated past nearby, face-downward in the water, arms flung outward; and from out of the murk seemed to reach the haunting and poignant strains of The Song of the Dead Soldiers – *Ich hatt einen Kameraden.*

And then only the rain beat down.

EPILOGUE

Dr Alfred Matzhold completed his inquiries in Buenos Aires during the afternoon of February 17, 1955, when he returned from General Madariaga to make a phone call to Peru, and another to Ezeiza Airport.

On the morning of February 18, he arrived by Peruvian Airlines at Callao Airport, Lima, and left fifty minutes later on a flight of Nacional Airlines for Arequipa in southern Peru.

When he arrived at Arequipa he was met by two of Martin Bormann's Spanish bodyguards, Jose Tuero and Louis Parada, ushered to a waiting Mercedes, and driven to the Villa Blanco in the Rio Chili valley. After a hot bath and change of clothes, a manservant led him to the library where a table was laid with a cold luncheon. Bormann entered the room shortly afterwards and the two men shook hands warmly. More than three months had passed since Dr Matzhold had seen the former Reichsleiter and he was impressed by his apparent well-being. 'You look exceptionally well,' was his sincere comment.

Bormann answered wryly, 'As the saying has it – a change is sometimes regarded as being as good as a rest – and presently I'm enjoying both.' He indicated the two places at the table, and sat down in one of the chairs. In general conversation, he remarked, 'So how is everything in Buenos Aires?'

Dr Matzhold settled himself at the table. 'I'm afraid the Peron regime is slipping fast. I can't see how he can possibly save himself. The secrets are now there for everyone to see. Rumour has it that he's even in process of being excommunicated by the Vatican. Also, support for the Generals Lonardi and Aramburu is on the upsurge, frighteningly so. There are few of our people who haven't left for more favourable climes. Muller left for Caracas last week, and Glucks arrived in Santiago yesterday morning. I received a call from him late yesterday afternoon to assure me of his safe arrival.'

Bormann grunted and declared bitterly, 'It will be anything but easy under Lonardi and Aramburu – and one can soon begin to get weary with moving around interminably.'

'Naturally,' Dr Matzhold agreed, and inquisitive about Bormann's recent visit to Friedrich Schwend at Callejon de Huaylas, he said, 'As a matter of personal interest, how was Freddy when you saw him?'

Bormann answered perfunctorily, 'Comfortable, safe, and not without sufficient funds. One requires nothing more to assure survival.'

At that juncture they were interrupted by the manservant who entered with the soup – chupe de camerones – made from potatoes, milk, shrimp, hot chili peppers and eggs.

Bormann watched Dr Matzhold sip at his soup tentatively. Without bothering to conceal his impatience and curiosity in the presence of the manservant, he said, 'I take it that your visit relates to a matter of considerable importance.'

Dr Matzhold hesitated, placed his spoon in his plate, waited for the manservant to withdraw, then lowered his voice to a confidential tone. 'Indeed, yes,' he answered affirmatively. 'Brunner was right – Wohldorf *is* buried on the shore south of San Martes. There can be no mistake about it whatever. I had everything checked out most diligently – *everything* – just as you directed.'

Bormann thrust his plate aside. 'Go on,' he said.

'Although the officer at the Ministerio de Marina in Bahia Blanca who was concerned with the business at that time is now retired and lives in Corrientes, his file on the bodies found around San Martes is still on record. No one appears to know what became of the identity discs and the scraps of letters and documents handed over by Father Barea, but the file lists full particulars of the names of those bodies positively identified.' Dr Matzhold extracted a slip of paper from his pocket-book and passed it across the table. 'This is a copy of the number taken from the file where it relates to Wohldorf. I was in touch with Kramer in Magdeburg immediately it came into my possession. Three hours later he was back to me confirming it as being Wohldorf's official SS serial number. I can also state emphatically that Gutierrez and Cuartero, two of the names which appear on the graves in the cemetery at San Martes, sailed as members of the *Santa Elvira*'s crew the day she left Necochea to rendezvous with *U501*. I thought the name

Gutierrez had a familiar ring when you questioned me on the subject, and a check of old financial records put the matter beyond doubt. Heinrich von Geyr used both men frequently. Indeed, Cuartero's widow is presently living out at Florencio Varela. But that isn't everything.' Dr Matzhold was finding it increasingly difficult to contain his impatience and excitement, while he continued to unfold one revelation after another to a Bormann whose receptiveness was unmistakable. 'I also discovered that two other bodies were washed up on the shore near Belgrano and identified by much the same means as those at San Martes. The names are Ingersoll and Runzheimer. Official Ministerio de Marina records state that the former was found on August 9th, the other on September 3rd of the same year, 1945.'

Bormann lifted a restraining hand. 'You were able to confirm these men as being from the crew of *U501*?'

Dr Matzhold shook his head. 'No, but I knew Runzheimer personally. I first met him in February 1940. Like Soltmann, he was a former crew member of the *Admiral Graf Spee*, a Petty Officer who was wounded in action with the cruisers *Ajax*, *Achilles*, and *Exeter*. Having lost a foot during the battle, he was landed at Montevideo with the rest of the wounded and subsequently interned. Then in February he escaped to the Argentine in order to rejoin the remainder of the ship's company. I actually arranged for him to continue medical treatment at the time. And also like Soltmann, he later went to work for me, along with several of his comrades. In fact, the gun crews who sailed with the *Santa Elvira* to meet with *U501* were composed entirely of ex-seamen from the *Graf Spee*. Runzheimer was a member of the Bofor gun crew, and as both the Bofor gun and the 20 mm cannon were stowed below decks when they sailed, they were also required to position both weapons on their improvised mountings on the upperdeck during the run south to rendezvous with *U501*.'

'And this Ingersoll?' Bormann questioned.

Dr Matzhold shrugged. 'I don't know, although I suspect he was a member of *U501*'s crew. And as a matter of interest, he was identified from a name stamped on a garment of clothing, no more. But of course, it's impossible to confirm whether or not he *was* a member of *U501*'s crew, as there was never any record of her complement made available to me.'

Bormann's face had darkened. Not having acquired an

official record of *U501*'s complement before she left the Mecklenburg Compound had since proved to be a gross oversight which he had found reason to regret ever since. 'You were in touch with Penns and Pfaff? Didn't any of those names mean anything to them?'

'Yes, I contacted them in Valdiva two days ago, but as they've always stated, the only names which mean anything to them are Rink and his Executive Officer, von Heydekampf. Although they agreed that the numbers relating to Dornberger and Rothfels on the Ministerio de Marina file are unmistakably those of men serving with the Kriegsmarine, it's impossible to go beyond that. But then we've been over all this on countless previous occasions and nothing new has ever emerged. Even inquiries among ex-U-mariners back home only revealed the names of three officers known to have sailed with Rink on board *U207* – Kernbach, Erlanger, and Bergold. And discreet inquiries over the years have confirmed that the families of von Heydekampf and Bergold have never at any time found reason to doubt the official statement issued by the Naval High Command that both men were considered to have perished with *U501* when she became overdue on voyage from the Mecklenburg Compound to Kristiansand. As for official records of *U207*'s original complement, then they were either lost or destroyed like so many others after the Fatherland's capitulation.'

Bormann studied Dr Matzhold in silence for a lengthy moment. Finally he said, 'One point which puzzles me – why was there never any official statement released by the Ministerio de Marina concerning the finding of these bodies at the time in question? Also, why did they never consider any connection between those bodies found around San Martes and those two you now say were found at Belgrano? Such information would have been of inestimable value to us at the time.'

Dr Matzhold said easily, 'I don't think it's as strange as it sounds. Two other vessels were lost around the same time as the *Santa Elvira* disappeared. Ministerio de Marina records list them as being the Norwegian tanker *Patria* which left Bahia Blanca on June 18th in ballast for Punta Arenas, and the Dutch freighter *Neermoor* which left Necochea for Cape Town on June 19th. Neither of these vessels was ever seen or heard from again, and meteorological records from that time corroborate what we already know, that a period of unprecedented bad weather had a number of vessels in serious difficulty between June 18th and 23rd. This is almost certainly the reason why they were in confusion about the bodies reported to them later. Without a detailed list of their crews they could only have assumed, and quite naturally so in my opinion, that they came from one or the other of these vessels. Besides, bodies were being washed up on beaches all around the world in those days. There was nothing unusual about it. But they most certainly never had any reason to connect them with the *Santa Elvira*. She was cleared by their own officials in Necochea when she sailed on June 18th as being bound for Santos. And whatever scraps of letters or documents that led to the identification of Gutierrez and Cuartero, they could *not* possibly have disclosed much in the way of personal information other than their names, or else their families would have been notified. No, they were nothing more than mere names, with nothing to connect them either with Buenos Aires or the *Santa Elvira*. Had such been the case it would have been mentioned at some point of the Inquiry into the loss of the *Santa Elvira*, and I attended that Inquiry which was heard at Comodoro Rivadavia in October of the same year. The official finding was that she was taken by an act of God and presumed to have foundered with all hands somewhere on voyage between Necochea and Santos. The underwriters accepted the findings without demur, a decision which speaks for itself.'

Bormann failed to find argument with Dr Matzhold's explanations, yet he was consumed by mounting frustration. 'Even allowing so, none of this leads us any nearer to learning what became of the *Santa Elvira* and *U501*.'

Dr Matzhold remained unflustered. 'Perhaps not, but one fact now established beyond question is that Wohldorf perished along with Gutierrez, Cuartero, and Runzheimer, three men known to have sailed with the *Santa Elvira*, and Wohldorf arrived here on board *U501*. More important, do you remember Dr Roberto Lenz, the hydrographer? I talked several times of him in the past.'

Bormann gave an impatient thrust of his jaw. 'I recall the name, yes.'

Dr Matzhold sat forward in eagerness, shoulders haunched over the table. 'Lenz is now retired and lives in General Madariaga. Being naturally curious about why those bodies should more or less be found along the same stretch of coastline between San Martes and Belgrano, I decided to consult him on the matter, and from his knowledge of the waters of Bahia Blanca, together with a study of Ministerio de Marina meteorological records of the period between June 18th and 23rd, 1945, he offered the opinion in accordance with the then existing winds and tides, and the area where the bodies were eventually washed ashore, that it indicated their vessel having most probably foundered somewhere to westward, somewhere between Punta Rasa and San Martes itself, and not too far from shore.'

Bormann took his time to consider the implications and questions which Dr Matzhold's information now raised. He said with emphasis, 'Is Lenz *certain* about this?'

Dr Matzhold answered, 'He's a very careful man, and not without distinction in his own field.'

Bormann nodded, and said reflectively. 'Then what if we were to carry out a discreet survey of the area in question? Could such an operation be undertaken without arousing suspicion and conjecture?'

Dr Matzhold was hesitant to answer, reluctant to become involved in argument and speculation.

Bormann said abruptly, 'Well?'

Dr Matzhold sighed, and said reluctantly, 'With all due respect, I'd personally be tempted to allow everything to remain as it is for the present. Times are extremely difficult. If we should arouse suspicion even by pursuing our inquiries, never mind launching an attempt to mount a survey, and word of our activities reached Buenos Aires, be it to the ears of Peron, or Lonardi and Aramburu, then they most certainly wouldn't rest till they exhausted every effort and means to learn the reason behind our interests. No, I beg you, let everything remain as it is for the time being. Why take unnecessary risks if one day we should find our goal within easy access?'

Bormann's pulse quickened and a surge of anger swept over him. He slammed a fist down on the table violently. 'Have you so easily forgotten the contents of the Wohldorf Shipment?' he stormed.

Dr Matzhold dropped his gaze down, slighted by the inference. Then in a chastised voice, he murmured, 'How could I ever forget something like that? As you well know, Carl Heinrich Dassel wasn't only my deputy – but also my son-in-law.'

Bormann slowly regained his calm, rose from the table and made his way out onto the patio where, hands clasped behind his back, he lifted his brooding gaze out across the Rio Chili valley to the snow-capped peaks of the Andes.

Dr Matzhold quietly joined him to await his decision, and for a long time both men stood wrapt in their own thoughts, until Bormann, worn by inner conflict and loath to regard the contents of Shipment No. 11372 to be lost beyond recovery for all time, finally announced in an emotionless voice, 'Then let it be as you suggest. But at the first time that an opportunity should present itself in the future . . .'

*

That same afternoon, some two thousand six hundred and fifty miles away in the Caribbean, on the yachting resort of Marina Cay in the Virgin Islands, two men made their way across the waterfront from a ship chandler's store near the junction of B street. One of the men, slim and blond, walked with a discernible limp of the left leg, while his short and stocky companion possessed the broken features of a pugilist. On reaching the jetty they boarded the sixty-foot cabin cruiser *Alcantara II* which they had chartered to a party of four American tourists, and minutes later were headed out on a south-easterly course towards Fallen Jerusalem and the turquoise waters of Anegada Passage in search of blue marlin. And as they passed into the distance, the sign above the small wooden jetty which they left behind read: WILLIAM ROHMER & OLAF KERMACH – SHIP CHANDLERS, DIESEL ENGINEERS – BOAT HIRERS.

*

On December 22, 1959, a party of Liberian soldiers, out searching for a government light aircraft reported to have been forced down in the area south-west of Tobakoni Point, came across the rotted fabric of a liferaft washed high among the sand-dunes. In it, partially buried in sand, reposed three sun-bleached skeletons, their limbs outstretched in an attitude of supplication: PO Electrician Franz Vollmer, Leading Machinist Reinhard Elser and Torpedoman 1st Class Horst Wassermann, who fourteen years earlier not wishing to risk being hanged by an International Military Tribunal on a charge of War Crimes committed on the High Seas, had instead found a last resting-place on a barren stretch of Liberia's Grain Coast.

*

As for the former Reichsleiter of the Third Reich and his agent Dr Alfred Matzhold, who died in Buenos Aires aged sixty-two and was buried in the German Cemetery on April 14th, 1961, it is not known if they ever arranged for a survey to be carried out in the more accessible waters of Bahia Blanca, but while on vacation in the region of Bahia Anegada during February 1969, the Madero family from Las Flores uncovered a sprinkling of coins on the vast shore, among them several Dutch florins and gold marks. In their innocence, it probably never occurred to Porfinio and Liliana Madero that their previous owners might have burned twenty-five years earlier in the ovens of Dachau, Auschwitz, and Buchenwald.

THE END

THE MEMORY OF EVA RYKER *By* Donald A. Stanwood

April 14, 1912 ... the Titanic sinks after it strikes an iceberg. Among the survivors are young honeymoon couple, Jason and Lisa Eddington ...

November 1941 ... the Kleins a middle-aged couple holidaying in Hawaii, are brutally murdered in one of the most sensational unsolved crimes of the decade ...

September 1962 ... as a multi-million dollar salvage operation explores the wreck of the Titanic, an elderly couple scheme to lay their hands on a fabulous treasure they know will be found in the rusting hulk ...

Three unrelated stories ? Or one sinister tale of greed and treachery that spans more than fifty years ?

One woman – Eva Ryker – has the answer. The only witness to events so horrifying, so painful that she has spent a lifetime erasing them from her memory. One man – Norman Hall is determined she will remember. Who'll stop at nothing to uncover the monstrously evil plot that has already taken seven lives and threatens to claim yet more.

0 552 10999 1 **£1.00**

THE DAY OF THE JACKAL
by Frederick Forsyth

'As a political thriller it is virtually in a class by itself; subtle, fast moving, superbly written, unputdownable, easily beating Ian Fleming on his own ground. The entire French background is convincing, and beautifully atmospheric – down to the last whiff of Gauloise.'—*Sunday Times*

'A compelling, utterly enthralling first novel ... some of the tensest thriller writing I can remember reading.' —*Sunday Express*
'The tension, excitement and pace are brilliantly maintained to the last page.'—*Sunday Mirror*

'THE DAY OF THE JACKAL works beautifully ... I was held spellbound ... riveted to this chilling, superbly researched story. A remarkable ring of authority ... a superb piece of mystery.' —*Guardian*

'Electrifyingly exciting ... within or without the pages of fiction there can rarely have been such a meticulously efficient, cold-blooded human killer. Mr. Forsyth is clever very clever and immensely entertaining.'—*Daily Telegraph*

0 552 09121 9—**£1.00**

THE ODESSA FILE
by Frederick Forsyth, *author of The Day of the Jackal*

The life-and-death hunt for a notorious Nazi criminal unfolds against a background of international espionage and clandestine arms deals, involving rockets designed in Germany, built in Egypt, and equipped with warheads of nuclear waste and bubonic plague. Who is behind it all? Odessa. Who or what is Odessa? You'll find out in *The Odessa File* . . .

'In the hands of Frederick Forsyth the documentary thriller achieves its most sophisticated form – Mr. Forsyth has produced both a brilliant entertainment and a disquieting book'
—*The Guardian*

0 552 0943 6—£1.00

THE DOGS OF WAR
by Frederick Forsyth

Sir James Manson – smooth, ruthless City tycoon – discovered the existence of a ten-billion-dollar mountain of platinum in the remote African republic of Zangaro. With a hired army of trained mercenaries, Manson planned to topple the government of Zangaro and replace its dictator with a puppet president. But news of the platinum had leaked to Russia – and suddenly Manson found he no longer made the rules in a power-game where the stakes had become terrifyingly high . . .

0 552 10050 1—£1.00

TOUCH THE LION'S PAW

by Derek Lambert

A COOL £14,000,000!

It would be the biggest diamond robbery ever. A king's ransom in uncut gemstones. It would take a year to plan. The action would range from Antwerp to New York, by way of London, Florida and Spain. The underworld's best brains would be involved. Security was said to be impenetrable but to Johnny Rhodes, mastermind of the operation, NOTHING was impossible...

By the author of 'The Yermakov Transfer'.

0 552 10345 4—75p

THE GREAT LAND

by Derek Lambert

Larson ... ex GI, in love with the beauty and wildness of Alaska, fighting the rape of the great land by the developers, the hunters, the oil-men...

Browning ... hard, ruthless, the oil-fever burning in his veins, ready to tear the land apart for the black treasure at its heart ...

Two men ... each hating all the other stood for, yet their destinies were inextricably linked. And in the end came the ultimate test, that could have only one victor – the great dog-sled race from Anchorage to Nome, right across the frozen waste of Alaska.

Woven against the great panorama of the snowlands is the breathtaking, epic tale of the men who lusted for untold wealth, pitted against those who struggled for survival itself: the story of black gold, the discovery of Alaskan oil...

0 552 10795 6—95p

THE YANGTZE RUN *By* Patrick O'Hara

May 1949. In Shanghai the rich and influential of Old China wait anxiously for an opportunity to escape Mao's advancing Communist forces . . .

To Shanghai comes Henry Wan who has stolen two tons of gold bullion from his bank and wants it retrieved from its hiding place up the Yangtze River. With him are his wife and bodyguard, whose plans for the gold differ greatly from his own. Unknown to them all, others have discovered the gold's existence, and will stop at nothing to secure it . . .

But only one man – 'Mad' Harry Lord, owner of the powerful motor launch JACARANDA – has the cunning and the sheer nerve to snatch the bullion from under the noses of both Communist and Nationalist forces – by way of the notorious 'Yangtze Run! . . .

Climaxing in a desperate chase down the Yangtze Kiang to the sea, THE YANGTZE RUN is a taut and exciting adventure in the tradition of Alistair MacLean and Desmond Bagley.

0 552 10730 1 **85p**